Dear Target Guest,

What a thrill to have *The Late, Lamented Molly Marx* chosen as a Target Club Pick. I was an early Target devotee, starting when I was a kid in the sixties. Whenever our family traveled to Minneapolis from my childhood home in Fargo, North Dakota, we made an enthusiastic pilgrimage to the very first Target; my mom became so impressed by the store that she (very wisely) bought stock. It was a happy day indeed for me when Target expanded to the East Coast, where I now live. I cannot pass a store without loading up on darling clothes for my nieces and nephews, lingerie, state-of-the-art kitchenware, every beauty product known to man, and—of course—books.

I'm quite sure that Molly Marx, the heroine of my novel, would have been a Target shopper too, since she appreciates a good value, hails from the Chicago suburbs, and, when she was alive, worked as a stylist for magazines. One of the most wonderful pieces of feedback I've gotten from readers is that women see themselves in Molly—and even though they immediately discover that she is no longer alive, this does not diminish the connection.

As an author, I am delighted that readers find this book to be funny. That they also find it moving is even sweeter. Molly Marx is a young wife and mother who lost her life under mysterious circumstances. We meet Molly at her funeral, which she discovers she has the ability to watch. Throughout the story, as she looks down from a location I call the Duration, Molly observes her loved ones in their private moments—her daughter, her fierce but devoted sister, her parents, her cunning mother-in-law, her best friend, her husband, and another man in her life to whom she is drawn.

Many book clubs have started reading *The Late, Lamented Molly Marx,* leading to intriguing discussions about the afterlife, adultery, and at what point a woman ends a marriage. Hard questions all, but ones that make for stimulating conversation. A reader I was recently introduced to shared that not a day goes by when she doesn't think about the message of *The Late, Lamented Molly Marx*—that each decision we make has a lasting impact.

Especially if you are a mother, a wife, or a sister, I hope this book touches your heart and that you will pass it on to other women dear to you.

Sincerely yours,

*Sally Koslow*

Praise for

# The Late, Lamented Molly Marx

"[Molly Marx] looks down from 'the Duration' . . . with a decidedly other-world perspective, but with her sense of humor still alive and kicking. . . . With a cast of characters purposefully and hilariously stereotyped, a touch of irony and some down-to-earth philosophy, Koslow's novel thoroughly entertains."  *—Jewish Book World*

"Funny, poignant."  *—Life & Style Weekly*

"By the time we meet Molly Divine Marx in the opening pages of *The Late, Lamented Molly Marx,* she is dead. But that by no means detracts from the many charms of Sally Koslow's wonderful new novel. . . . Filled with remarkable clarity about how to embrace life while you can."  *—BookPage*

"Dive into one of the season's standout cliff-hangers: *The Late, Lamented Molly Marx.* . . . When Marx observes her intimates— and the investigation into her death—from the hereafter, she's both tickled and ticked off by what she learns. You will be, too."  *—Self*

"For a weekend away . . . [an] unexpectedly spunky book about life after death."  *—Redbook*

"Will keep you hooked to the end."  *—Real Simple*

"[A] comic romp through the afterlife." —*More*

"Koslow's story of 'a life examined' in the hereafter makes readers truly care about her protagonist, foibles and all." —*Booklist*

"Charming . . . [Koslow] knows her way around expertly tuned phrasing, and Molly is a delightful gem of a heroine. Equal parts self-deprecating, wry and sassy, Molly is honest about her faults and equally forgiving of the others' as she reviews her life with a hearty does of honesty and humor. . . . The narrative's . . . hilarity and heartbreak will win readers over." —*Publishers Weekly*

"Reading Sally Koslow's latest novel is like being at a cocktail party with the sharpest guest in the room. With her laserlike—and very funny—observations of human foibles, her wit and insight, Koslow has created a character with both heart and brains. You will love every minute you spend with her!" —EMILY LISTFIELD, author of *Best Intentions*

"Heaven only knows how Sally Koslow pulled off this novel with such precision and wit, and a narrative that drives you to the very last sentence. A story of love, friendship and family told from both sides of the grave, *The Late, Lamented Molly Marx* is a treasure no matter how you look at it." —BETSY CARTER, author of *Swim to Me*

"Molly Marx speaks from the grave with a voice that is fresh, funny and warm. In examining Molly's late, lamented life, Sally Koslow delivers a story about marriage, motherhood, and friendship that anyone who has ever been a spouse, a parent, or a friend will recognize. And who knew hanging out with the dead could be such a delight!"
—MEG WAITE CLAYTON, author of *The Wednesday Sisters*

# The Late, Lamented Molly Marx

### A NOVEL

## Sally Koslow

BALLANTINE BOOKS TRADE PAPERBACKS / NEW YORK

2010 Ballantine Books Trade Paperback Edition

Published in the United States by Ballantine Books, an imprint of
The Random House Publishing Group, a division of
Random House, Inc., New York.

BALLANTINE and colophon are registered trademarks of Random House, Inc.

RANDOM HOUSE READER'S CIRCLE & Design is a registered trademark of
Random House, Inc.

Originally published in hardcover in the United States by Ballantine Books,
an imprint of The Random House Publishing Group,
a division of Random House, Inc., in 2009.

This book contains an excerpt from the forthcoming hardcover edition of
*With Friends Like These* by Sally Koslow. This excerpt has been set for this edition only
and may not reflect the final content of the forthcoming edition.

ISBN 978-0-345-52514-7

Printed in the United States of America

www.randomhousereaderscircle.com

2 4 6 8 9 7 5 3 1

Book design by Susan Turner

*To Rob, Jed, and Rory*

*The true mystery of the world is the visible,
not the invisible.*

—OSCAR WILDE

The Late, Lamented Molly Marx

# One

# KILL ME NOW

*W*hen I imagined my funeral, this wasn't what I had in mind. First of all, I hoped I would be old, a stately ninetysomething who'd earned the right to be called elegant; a woman with an intimate circle of loved ones fanned out in front of her, their tender sorrow connecting them like lace.

I definitely hoped to be in a far more beautiful place—a stone chapel by the sea, perhaps, with pounding purple-gray waves drowning out mourners' sobs. For no apparent reason—I'm not even Scottish—there would be wailing bagpipes, men in Campbell tartan, and charmingly reserved grandchildren, or even great-grandchildren, coaxed into reciting their own sweet poetry. I don't know where the children's red curls come from, since my hair is chemically enhanced blond and straight as a ruler. The bereaved—incredibly, those weepy old souls are my own kids—dab away tears with linen handkerchiefs, though on every other occasion they have used only tissues. The service takes place shortly before sunset in air fragrant with lilacs. Spring. At least where I grew up, in the Chicago suburbs, that's what lilacs signify: the end of a long winter, life beginning anew.

I didn't expect to be here, in a cavernous, dimly lit Manhattan synagogue. I didn't expect to be surrounded by at least four hundred people, a good three hundred of whom I don't recall talking to even once. Most of all, I didn't expect to be young. Well, maybe some people don't think thirty-five is young, but I do. It's far too young to die, because while my story isn't quite at the beginning, it isn't at the end, either. Except that it is.

*She's dead,* all those bodies in the pews must be thinking. *Depressing.* On that last count, they would be wrong. In fact, if the congregation knew my whole story—and I hope they will, eventually, because I need people on my side, not on his, and especially not on *hers*—it would be clear that I, Molly Divine Marx, have not lost my joie de vivre. On that point, I speak the truth.

"She would be here if she could," he says. "She would be here if she could." That's Rabbi Strauss Sherman, pontificating over to my right. I wish he were the twinkly junior rabbi whose adult ed classes I kept telling myself I should take, not that I am—*was*—keen on the music of Jews in Uganda. But the speaker is the senior rabbi, the one who says everything twice, like an echo, though it stopped short of being profound the first time. I suppose I should get off on the fact that he's the big-shot rabbi invited to homes of people who contribute gigabucks and, thus, rate succulent, white-meat honors on holidays. I wonder if Barry, my husband, made sure Rabbi S.S. spoke today just to stick it to me, since whenever he gave a sermon I'd squirm and mutter, "Kill me now." I'd hate to think God decided on payback.

I realize I am not being kind about either Rabbi S.S. or the heartsick husband. Barry's sizable schnozz is chapped from crying, and I caught more than a few people noticing as he discreetly swiped his nose on the sleeve of his black suit, soft worsted in a fine cut. *Armani?* they're wondering. Not a chance. It is a close facsimile purchased at an outlet center near Milan, but if they took it for Armani, Barry would be glad. That was the general idea.

Perhaps some women in the pews wonder what I'm dressed in. The casket is closed—talk about a bad hair day—but I am being buried in a red dress. Okay, it's more of a burgundy, but one thing that's putting a smile on my face (only metaphorically, unfortunately) is that for all eternity I will get to wear this dress, which cost way too much, even 40 percent off at Barneys, where I rarely shop because it's generally a rip-off. I'm sure if it had been up to my mother-in-law, the enchanting Kitty Katz, today I would have been stuffed into a button-down shirt and pleated pants that made me look like a sumo wrestler, but my sister, Lucy, intervened. Lucy and I have had our moments, but she would understand how psyched I was to be wearing the dress to a Valentine's party this coming Saturday.

Wherever it is I'm off to, I hope they notice the shoes—black satin, terrifyingly high slingbacks, with excellent toe cleavage. I only wore them once, those shoes, and that night Barry and I barely left the dance floor. When we shimmied and whirled, it was almost like sex: we became the couple people thought we were. The Dr. and Mrs. Marx I, at least, wanted us to be. I loved watching Barry move his runner's body in that subtle but provocative way of his, and how he nestled his hand on the small of my back, then cupped my butt for the whole world to see. It's a pity we couldn't have merengued through life as if it were one endless Fred and Ginger movie.

Will there be dancing where I'm headed? I digress. I do that. Drove Barry nuts.

"Our dear Molly Marx, she would be here if she could," Rabbi S.S. is saying. That makes three. "The circumstances of her death may be mysterious, but it is not for us to judge. It is not for us to judge."

As soon as someone tells you not to judge, you do. Everyone in this chilly sanctuary is judging—both Barry and me. I can hear it all, what's in people's heads as well as on their lips.

"Foul play."

"Killed herself."

"Jealous boyfriend."

"*She* had a boyfriend? That mouse?"

"You have it all wrong. *He* had a girlfriend."

"If it's suicide, then why the ginormous funeral?"

I hear a smug tone. "For Jews, with a suicide it's the burial place that gets questioned, not the funeral."

"He won't be single for six months."

"Especially with the little girl."

Yes, there is a child. Annabel Divine Marx, almost four, black velvet dress, patent leather Mary Janes. My Annie-belle is clutching Alfred the bunny, and the look on her face could make Hitler weep. Right now, I will not allow myself the luxury of thinking about my baby, who wonders where her mommy is and when this nasty dream will end. If I could be alive for five more minutes, they would be spent memorizing Annabel's heartbeat and synchronizing it with my own, tracing the bones in her birdlike shoulders, stroking the creamy softness of her skin. *I will always be Annabel's mother.* My mantra.

People can call me anything, but in the mommy department, there was never a moment when I wasn't trying to do the right thing. I attempted to live for my child—not through her, for her. I tried. I really did. I never would have abandoned Annabel. Nothing ever mattered more to me than my unconditional love for her, a long, unbroken line that continues even now. The best compliment I ever got was from Barry when he said simply, a few weeks after Annabel was born, "Molly, you get motherhood. You really do."

"Our dear Molly, our lovely Molly," the rabbi is saying. "She was so many things. To our grieving Barry—a trustee of this very institution— she was a beloved wife of almost seven years, a woman with her whole life ahead of her. To Annabel, she was Mommy, tender, devoted. To her parents, Claire and Daniel Divine, she was a cherished daughter, and to Lucy Divine, she was an adored twin sister, absolutely adored. To her colleagues, she was a . . ." Rabbi S.S. refers to his notes. "A decorating editor at a magazine."

Wrong. I stopped being a decorating editor when Annabel was born. Lately, I was a freelance stylist—the person who brings in the tall white orchids and fluffs a room so when it's photographed for a magazine it shames most of the readers, since there's no way their homes are ever going to look like that. Then they blink and smugly wonder if people actually live in that picture with not one family snapshot in a teddy bear frame sold at a Hallmark store. Who actually buys white couches and scratchy sisal rugs? How do you clean them? They turn the page.

I wasn't brokering peace in the Middle East, or even teaching nursery school like my twin sister. But I loved my work, and in my sliver of a world, I was a giant. What I could do with a mantel was almost art. People must have hated inviting me to their homes, for fear that I'd re-arrange their bookshelves and suggest that they sell half of their tchotchkes on eBay.

"Molly was a loyal friend, an accomplished biker, a graduate of Northwestern University with a major in art history."

Is the rabbi going to recite my entire résumé? Disclose that I was rejected from Brown and never made it off the Wesleyan wait-list? Share that I took a junior semester in Florence and skipped every class—did I even buy textbooks?—while Emilio fra Diavolo taught me Italian of the nonverbal variety? Mention the two jobs from which I was fired and the fourteen-month gap between them? Point out that Barry and I were seeing a marriage counselor?

There's Dr. Stafford right there. Goodness, she looks quite moved. I always imagined that when Barry and I were carrying on at her sessions she was thinking, *How did I get stuck with these two completely shallow, nonintrospective, loser brats? Oh, I have three private school tuitions to pay. That's why.* But I see tears and I can tell they are real.

The Lord giveth and the Lord taketh away, and when he takes away big-time, I have discovered he compensates you with a finely tuned bullshit detector. It is a minor consolation, but I think I am going to like it.

"And now we will hear from Molly's husband," the rabbi says. "Barry. Dr. Barry Marx."

Barry kisses Annabel on the head and untangles his hand from hers. She takes a look at Kitty—who forbids the word *grandma*—and considers whether to move closer to her. "Kitty smells funny," she used to say. "It's just her cigarettes, honey," I would respond. "Don't smoke when you grow up or you'll smell funny, too." I hope Annabel remembers that. If she becomes a nose-ringed, tattooed fourteen-year-old hanging out in the East Village with a cigarette dangling from her lips . . . there won't be a damn thing I can do about it.

Kitty is wearing a severe black suit—either Gucci or Valentino. She'd be horrified to know I can't tell or appreciate the difference, though I admit it looks stunningly appropriate. The tailoring shows off her yoga-buffed sixty-four-year-old body, which, in clothes, we both privately acknowledge looks a good bit better than mine. Today she seems to have hijacked the first floor of Tiffany's. With Kitty, more is more. She is wearing diamond studs the size of knuckles, a sapphire-and-emerald brooch dribbling over her breast like Niagara Falls with a bracelet to match, and a black lizard handbag that, no doubt, contains her smokes.

I hope Annabel eventually inherits some of Kitty's baubles. I'm not saying Kitty's glad I'm dead, but at least she has a good excuse now for not willing me any jewelry.

When Barry arrives at the front of the synagogue and bounds up the six steps, he clears his throat and takes some notes from his jacket. He tears them in half with a flourish. I knew he would do that! We saw the same stunt at my aunt Julie's funeral last year. Does he think my family won't notice he stole it? Ah, but he doesn't really care about them, does he? And what makes it worse is that except for the Divines, everyone in the congregation is buying into his heart-wrenching grief. From every corner, I hear sniffles and snorts and see tiny tributaries of tears.

"I fell in love with Molly when I was a senior at college," he begins.

I was a sophomore. He was the pre-med guy who finally had room in his schedule for a class on twentieth-century art and took a seat next to me in a darkened auditorium. Barry wanted to become a collector, he said, and I remember thinking the remark pretentious; no one I knew aspired to own anything more than an Alex Katz dog litho or a student's work snagged at a silent auction on open-studio night. But Barry dreamed on a grand scale. When five years later I found out that he'd become a plastic surgery resident at Mount Sinai in Manhattan, I wasn't surprised. If ever a doctor were born to woo women into rhinoplasty, it was Barry Marx, who managed to incorporate his own nose into his well-delivered pitch.

At least forty of his patients must be here today. All those weepers with the delicate, symmetrical noses aren't my mommy-buddies, magazine pals, book club friends, or cycling partners. Do Barry's patients have a phone tree, like the one at Annabel's school in case of inclement weather? Did someone start making calls at 5:30 A.M.? "Sorry to wake you, but I thought you'd want to know Barry Marx is single. The funeral's at ten. Pass it on."

"There are four things you should know about my wife, Molly," Barry begins. "First, she had the most musical laugh in the whole world. Many of you know that laugh. I married her for that laugh. I cannot believe I will never hear it again."

So far, okay. To be fair, there was a lot of laughing, and no one thinks Barry married me for my breasts, which most wives of plastic surgeons would have had enlarged from nectarines to melons.

"Second, Molly was the most brutally honest person I know. You couldn't get much past her. She was honest about her shortcomings—"

He's going to discuss my *shortcomings*?

"—and mine."

Would that include flirting with more than half of my friends?

"Third, I have never known anyone who loved life more than Molly. She should have lived to be a hundred."

No argument there.

"And one more thing . . ." Barry falters. "One more thing . . ." He bows his head slightly. I don't need a bullshit detector to realize he must truly be bereft, because his yarmulke drops, which allows the whole congregation to see his baby bald spot. Barry doesn't rush to return the yarmulke to his head. Rabbi Sherman comes over and cradles him with his arm. Barry walks to the casket, kisses his fingers—on one he's wearing his wedding band, which he usually keeps in a drawer—and presses them to the mahogany. Then he returns to his seat and pulls Annabel onto his lap.

I guess I'll never learn what the other thing is.

"Molly's closest friend, Sabrina Lawson, wishes to speak now," the rabbi says. "Sabrina Lawson."

I am glad Brie has volunteered for this eulogy, because I can safely say that Brie, who has recently decided she is a lesbian, is one friend who hasn't succumbed to Barry's charms. She definitely wasn't gay when we were roommates, but last year she met Isadora, the gorgeous Chilean architect who wound up moving into the loft she designed for Brie. Isadora tenderly kisses Brie on the lips before Brie walks to the front.

I have always been proud to be Brie's friend. We were quite a pair. She is almost six feet tall—a model before she became a lawyer—and I topped out at five-three. Today her glossy brown hair is braided down her back and she is wearing a flawless charcoal trouser suit over a crisp white blouse. Everything about Brie is hard edges except her heart.

Brie takes no small measure of pride in being the first of our friends to try girl-on-girl sex. I'm glad she's found Isadora, but I wouldn't bet my life, if I still had one, that Brie won't switch back to Team Hetero. I can't believe that anyone who liked men as much as Brie did will give them up. In a voice that sounds ready to break, she begins.

> *There's something quieter than sleep*
> *Within this inner room!*
> *It wears a sprig upon its breast—*
> *And will not tell its name.*
>
> *Some touch it, and some kiss it—*
> *Some chafe its idle hand—*
> *It has a simple gravity*
> *I do not understand!*

My poetry appreciation stalled at e. e. cummings, but Brie kept Emily Dickinson by her bed. When she gets to the last stanza, she sobs and bites her lips.

> *While simple-hearted neighbors*
> *Chat of the "Early dead"—*
> *We—prone to periphrasis,*
> *Remark that Birds have fled!*

After a moment, Brie goes on. "Molly sometimes forgot to eat, yet she had more energy than anyone I know. She was always begging me to go on long bike rides. Just last Saturday, she picked me up with Annabel in her bike seat and insisted we pedal over the Brooklyn Bridge to go to this diner. . . ." Another memory is of us getting lost on a mountain trail in Aspen. I wonder if people aren't now thinking of me as an extremely dumb jock.

"We have one last speaker," Rabbi S.S. says. "Representing the Divine family . . . Lucy?"

No one ever took the two of us for sisters. We were fraternal twins, though I wondered why there wasn't a more apt term. At our bat mitzvah, Lucy towered over me by eight inches and outweighed me by forty pounds. Everyone clucked about how awful it must be that I hadn't gone through puberty yet, when Lucy had bazooms. But I know she hated looking at me in my mini, and I just thought she was fat. Envy spiced our relationship like a red hot chili pepper, and most of it came from Luce. I got married, while every relationship she's had has ended—often with a guy moving to another continent with no forwarding address. I had a child. She wants one, desperately. People misunderstand Lucy. She wasn't an easy sister, but I adored her.

"When Molly and I were five," she says, "she convinced me that broccoli was an animal, and that my real name was Moosey. We were Molly and Moosey."

Her timing is good. The congregation laughs. I am sorry I saddled her with that name, which stuck until she left for college—*she* got into Brown—and probably cost my parents twenty thousand dollars in therapy bills. Lucy rambles and shares too many anecdotes from seventh grade. Mourners check BlackBerrys. "I will tell you one thing," she concludes. "We will find out who did this to my sister, Molly. If you are out there, the Divine family will hunt you down." My sister sounds as if she is giving a speech on the eve of a doomed election.

People snap back to attention. The rabbi does not like Lucy's tone any more than the buzz of conversation that has trashed the decorum of his service. He rushes over to Lucy, who shoots him the fierce look that scared away her last five boyfriends. She stares down Barry. He won't meet her eye.

"Interment will be private," the rabbi says quickly, "but shiva will begin tonight at the Marx home." He announces our address and then, suddenly, a stranger with an unmistakable Barry-crafted nose breaks out in song. Accompanied by the synagogue's turbo organ, her volume crescendos. "I could fly higher than an eagle," she sings, knowing that the Upper West Side is the closest she will get to Broadway, "for you are the wind beneath my wings."

I am mortified. Thank God I am in a box. Every one of my true friends—there have got be at least sixty in the room—as well as my parents, sister, and aunts and uncles are embarrassed by this ignominious display. Is this song Barry's idea of a joke? Or Kitty's?

Kill me. Kill me now.

# Two

# JUST. LIKE. THAT.

I don't know if I am dead or alive. I remember little. The spires of Riverside Church. Pain everywhere. A long, bottomless blackness.

This wasn't the way I'd planned it. My bike? Where did it go?

I hear the river, steady, like a pulse. Instinctively, I count the waves, which match my weakly pounding heart. One, two, three . . . forty-eight, forty-nine . . . one hundred one, one hundred two.

Cold.

Cold.

Cold.

Snow falls. Flakes cover my face.

So.

Damn.

Cold.

I am still wearing one biking glove, shredded and streaked with blood, which exposes my frostbitten fingers.

Never.

Been.

This.

Cold.

Nev—

With the wisp of a shallow exhale, I am gone. A leaf blowing away, an ash falling off a cigarette, a dewdrop evaporating on a flower petal.

Just.

Like.

That.

No.

Big.

Deal.

I have watched too many bad movies. There is no traveling down a tunnel with an eerie white light, harps and—on the other side—clouds like Provence crème. I have crossed over, but there is just darkness and the *whoosh-whoosh-whoosh* of traffic on the Henry Hudson Parkway.

Dawn arrives. Not ten feet from where I lie, under the tangle of bushes between the rock-bordered Hudson and the bike path, I begin to hear runners. This time of year, at this hour, they pass infrequently and keep their gazes straight ahead, because this is not Central Park, a social watering hole. The path is lonely and narrow. "Only an idiot would jog here," Barry said once to a friend who boasted about the purity of running by the river. "I don't know why you ride your bike there, either," he added, turning to me.

It was one of my favorite short trips, up to the George Washington Bridge, where a little red lighthouse still keeps guard on a tiny spit of land in its vast shadow—for me, a small, private holy place. I loved reading the little red lighthouse book to Annabel, just as I loved when my mother had read it to Lucy and me.

The runners continue, and then I hear her voice. "Oh my God," she says, barely audible, and then she yells the same words. Her footsteps grow closer. Above my legs stands a woman in tight black running pants and a loose parka. She removes an iPod earbud. "Are you alive?" she shouts to me. "Are you alive?" She tries, unsuccessfully, to push away brambles that cover the upper half of my body as she bleats those words again and again.

Her voice is trapped in her throat, as if she were screaming in a dream. She takes out a cell phone, pulls off her gloves, and punches in 911.

"I'm in Riverside Park," she says between heaving breaths. "There's a woman here—and I'm not sure if she's . . . alive."

I learn that my angel's name is actually Angela, a grad student in philosophy at Columbia. I am sorry because I know that for the rest of her life she will carry the hideous image of how I looked in death.

When the police and paramedics arrive, they determine that I have been dead for several hours. There is no record, they say later, that I was reported missing.

## Three

# A GATED COMMUNITY

I admit it. I am being buried in New Jersey, land of big-box discount stores, earsplitting accents, and oil refineries. The *garden* state? C'mon.

My parents wanted me flown back to Chicago to rest happily ever after next to Nana Phyllis and Papa Louie. Kitty was fine with the idea of shipping me off like a camp trunk. At the end of the day, so to speak, she probably wants a berth by her only son—the next best thing to a double bed. But Barry vetoed Chicago. "Molly's a Marx," he declared. "She belongs in the family plot."

There was, however, a glitch: only one more Marx could squeeze into the real estate in Beth David Cemetery, within earshot of the Belmont Park racetrack, where Barry's father and grandparents were laid to rest. So, faster than he chose his last laptop, Barry bought into a truly gated community, my new home away from home, Serenity Haven. I will, forever, be only six exits away from Ikea. A shame I don't need any furniture, because I have plenty of time to decipher the directions.

Outside the synagogue, a cold rain starts to fall. Most of the mourners scatter back into their lives: jobs, lunch dates, toddlers to collect after nursery school. Three limousines gridlock in front of the building's entrance. Barry, Annabel, and Kitty pile into one. My parents and Lucy fill the next. Second-tier Marxes and Divines crowd the third. Isadora and Brie streak away in a blur of British racing green Jaguar, while at least twenty less-distinguished cars packed with friends, neighbors, cousins, and colleagues follow the hearse.

Though it is only eleven-thirty, headlights glow through the drizzle. I feel like a drum majorette from the Chippewa Valley High School marching band, which we watched at the Thanksgiving Day parade a little over two months ago surrounded by a large, loud group in our own living room, with its Central Park West view. On account of Barry's vodka-heavy Bloody Marys—not, I suspect, Big Bird—few guests ever refused our annual invitation.

A familiar khaki-colored Jeep joins the halting procession of cars but abruptly exits the Henry Hudson Parkway at 125th Street. Did the driver simply lose his nerve or did he suddenly get the yen to shop at Fairway? If that's the case, I hope he's buying the makings for a nourishing soup thick with root vegetables. I believe he's in need of comfort.

It might have seemed odd if Luke had stuck with the entourage, odd to everyone but me. I would have liked him there, with his black overcoat flapping against his long legs, the pale blue cashmere scarf I gave him for his birthday tied around his neck, mirroring the color of his eyes and still smelling faintly of my perfume. Would he have cried? Cursed in silence? Introduced himself to my parents? Barry? Pulled Annabel to his chest and wept? How would he have explained himself? Too many questions.

Perhaps it's just as well he's not here, because we have arrived at the cemetery. The graveside service is abbreviated yet unbearable. Annabel hides her face against Barry's hip. My parents—suddenly looking ten years older than the sixty-two they turned last year—lean on each other and Lucy like fragile plants whose roots have grown together for support. The gravediggers struggle as they center my casket. I am having trouble centering as well. I focus on the grimy granite bench nearby and wonder if Barry and Annabel will ever return to sit on it and talk to me. Or will Barry come alone? Will he apologize—or find a reason to complain?

There are prayers in both Hebrew and English. Then I hear it, the thud. Like a bomb, a shovelful of dirt wallops the top of the casket. Barry, the envy of every thirty-eight-year-old at the gym, pitches the earth with athletic zeal. My parents go next. At intervals of about a half minute, I feel tremors. Lucy brings Annabel to the grave and, with my daughter's tiny, purple-mittened hands atop hers, which are bare and raw, they sprinkle a handful of gravelly Jersey mud that lands above my left shoulder, the one that didn't break. Brie and Isadora approach the casket and hold each other around their narrow waists as they do the same. Kitty stands back, her head tilted down. At the end of the line, some of the others walk tentatively to the casket and dump in a shovelful. Unfamiliar with my religion's ritual, they look shocked when, as if on cue, every member of the tribe suddenly chokes up ten seconds into the Kaddish, the prayer for the dead. *Yeetgadal v'yeetkadash sh'mey rabbah* . . . The foreign yet familiar words of finality pierce my flesh. This spiritual punctuation is for me, Molly Divine Marx.

*Aleynu v'al kohl yisrael v'eemru.* The Kaddish is over. *Amein.* Barry bellies back up to the grave and with the help of the Serenity Haven hunks blankets my casket with dirt until it is fully covered. Never again will I complain about lack of privacy.

"I'm starving," I hear someone say. In the English translation, I believe this is the last line of the Kaddish.

"There'll be a spread at Molly and Barry's." A voice repeats our address.

"From Zabar's?"

"Barney Greengrass."

"Even better. See you there?"

The mourners disperse, leaving me behind. I wonder how many will do a little shopping on Route 4 on their way back to Manhattan.

## Four

# SWIMMING WITH THE NOVA

*B*arry and I moved into our apartment four years ago, when I was seven months pregnant with Annabel. Until then, we rented the dollhouse-sized one-bedroom on Jane Street that I'd found the year before we got engaged. In the back of a brownstone, the apartment overlooked the owner's garden, and from our kitchen you could see a crab apple tree blooming in May and in the winter squirrels gathering black walnuts. Usually I was behind schedule—organization never being my strong suit—but once in a while, before I left for work, I made time for a scone with bitter orange marmalade washed down with Earl Grey and let myself imagine I lived in London.

I would have been content to stay in this cozy nook and keep our baby in a cradle next to the bed. But Kitty insisted that it would be "disadvantageous" for Barry's practice if potential patients thought we couldn't afford a larger place. Word would get around—plastic surgery candidates research. Neither Barry nor I was drawn to the suburbs, and bigger apartments were hard to come by in the Village. Despite the fact that few of my magazine friends lived above Fourteenth Street, Kitty— who was lending us two-thirds of the down payment—declared SoHo and Tribeca to be Sodom and Gomorrah, the East Village Siberia, and the complete borough of Brooklyn junkie heaven, even though real estate prices were through the roof. Which is how we landed uptown. Barry wanted the East Side, to be near girls' schools, he said, though I suspected his mother on Park and Seventy-sixth was the real draw. Rather irritably, I told him I'd never be old enough for that neighborhood, although I loved gawking at Madison Avenue's windows as much as the next woman. If we were to live uptown, I saw myself on Riverside Drive, which to me is—next to the Village—as British as Manhattan comes.

We settled on Central Park West, an East Side–style street that leapfrogged west of the park, in the kind of building where on Wednesday every owner receives the *New York Review of Books.* I tried to talk Barry into letting me create a neo-Victorian fantasy. I fell in love with a paint shade called Grape Thistle, wallpaper that mimicked damask, and a stuffed peacock perched inside an iron aviary six feet tall. In our classic six—two big bedrooms with a Lilliputian room off the kitchen where Delfina, our nanny, slept—I wanted worn, Turkish rugs, leather-bound Jane Austens, and tattered footstools. Maybe an English spaniel I'd name Camilla. I longed to walk through my front door and shake off the twenty-first century. I shared my vision with Barry.

"Where will I put a plasma TV?" he asked. "Molly, are you nuts? I'll never be old enough for an apartment that looks like what you're describing. I can practically feel my asthma kicking in from the dust." With a look you'd offer a closely related lunatic, he pulled me toward him. "Must be the pregnancy hormones. It's okay, honey."

I pushed him away and ran out of the room, slamming a door behind me, my fantasy shattered like bone china hurled down a staircase. I could be dramatic.

Again, we negotiated, which in decorating is no different than it is in anything else—nobody gets what he or she wants. Our capacious kitchen looks as if it belongs in New Canaan, Connecticut, with glass-fronted, white-lacquered, nickel-latched cabinets, the home for an undistinguished collection of blue-and-white transferware bowls and platters. The countertops are creamy marble, which immediately became stained by red wine. To Kitty's horror, I painted the old wood floor shiny cobalt, like the ocean in *The Little Mermaid.* When she saw it she said, "Why don't you work with my decorator?" using a tone that demonstrated, for her, considerable restraint. "My treat, darling," she added, which translated to "No taste, moron."

"Because I'm a decorating editor, Kitty," I reminded her. This never impressed my mother-in-law.

Except for Barry's dumbbells, which I invariably tripped over on the way to the bathroom at night, I rather like our bedroom; it has a spindly-legged secretary desk and no fewer than five different muted flowered prints, all from vintage fabric I found while on a photo shoot in a Portobello Road shop. Annabel's bedroom is baby-chick yellow, with a green velvet upholstered rocking chair in the corner next to a bookshelf whose marquee items include *Eloise,* my mother's copy of *The Secret Garden,* and every other book a small girl might have read before *Dora the Explorer.* But the rest of the place is spare and bare. Modern or soulless, take your pick.

Barry got his monster television, which rules the room where I would have liked a mellow, scratched dining table with leaves meant for many large dinner parties. Instead, the table, which seats only six, is glass and steel, and in front of the TV is a pair of recliners. The leather couches are butch enough for a buckaroo. I will say I love the fact that a few moody black-and-white photographs hang on the walls and there are several examples of art pottery, although I can't tell Weller from Roseville to save my life, an expression I just realized I'd best retire.

I'm being snide about the apartment, which is a lot more luxurious than most city dwellers'. I wish I could say I wasn't occasionally petty, but if I can't be honest now, then when? I had flaws. I liked to gossip. I didn't always rejoice at others' successes. I occasionally forgot birthdays and relied too much on takeout food. I IM'd at Mommy and Me classes. I never voted in primaries and ate dark chocolate every day far in excess of the 6.3 grams that might have lowered my blood pressure. I don't even know how much 6.3 grams are. And I should have lost five pounds. Okay, eight. I let the *New York Times* accumulate unread, especially the Science section, and I never opened Circuits, not once. I failed to polish my shoes, which I allowed to run down at the heels. I didn't wash my hairbrushes and sometimes went to bed without removing my makeup. E-mail chain letters terminated on my watch, and

I never looked at friends' Internet photo galleries. I subscribed to two cheesy celebrity magazines. Unless my parents were visiting, on Friday nights I preferred to go to the movies and gorge on a tub of popcorn for dinner instead of making a proper Shabbat meal with a roast chicken and challah. I could never complete a crossword puzzle (not even the easy one on Monday), play Internet Scrabble, or understand football. My abs were going to hell because I did crunches only sporadically. I hated opera and spin classes. In whodunit movies, I could never follow the plot, even when someone explained it to me afterward as if I were in third grade.

I could have been a better wife. The problems in our marriage were as much my fault as Barry's. To piss him off, I have been known to force myself not to laugh at his jokes, which were frequently the pee-in-your-pants kind our friends quoted for years. I used too much witless detail when I told him a story. I only gave my husband a blow job every few months.

I could go on recounting my negatives, and probably will. One thing I did right, though, was to hire Delfina Adams and pay her a living wage.

Today Delfina has recruited her friend Narcissa and a few other stray Jamaican dynamos and the apartment looks as buffed as it ever has. Dull black synthetic fabric, supplied by a funeral home, drapes the enormous mirror in the foyer, and around the living room, following Jewish custom, squat cardboard boxes—where the immediate family will sit—have popped up like online ads.

On the piano, next to a bouquet of lush white roses—which Delfina must have bought, because Jews aren't big on flowers during mourning—at least ten framed photos have been gathered and stand in a conga line that represents the life of Molly Marx: Lucy and me as newborns; me dressed as Malibu Barbie for Halloween; my high school graduation picture, proving definitively that short brown Audrey Hepburn hair is not my look; Brie and me burdened with backpacks during our postcollege Roman holiday; my wedding portrait in the strapless gown now carefully preserved for Annabel; big fat me, hugely pregnant; beach-bunny me, and damn, I didn't look as bad in my bikini as I thought, which makes me wish I'd had dessert every night, as kitchen magnets suggest.

"She was cute," a brunette in skintight black suede pants observes, "in a midwestern way." Who is this stranger who feels comfortable enough to critique my appearance on the first afternoon of a weeklong shiva? She must be a friend of the funeral's soloist because together they march over to Barry and give lingering hugs.

"I am so sorry for your loss, Dr. Marx," Black Pants says as she leaves her hand on Barry's arm. "I'm Jennifer, Adrienne's sister. I wanted to pay my respects."

To his credit, Barry doesn't extend the conversation, although—I can't be positive—he may have rested his hand on Adrienne's perky behind for one short beat, which is one beat too long. I do notice that he is wearing a small black ribbon with a tear in it on his lapel. If he were really traditional, he would have cut his funeral suit, which would have been a shame. It was expensive, even if it's faux.

"What a waste," I hear Lucy say. I'm not sure if she is referring to my life, my death, or the food. I think it is the last of these, since the delicacies Kitty has ordered, augmented by the crowd's offerings, cover every inch of the dining table: a sea of Nova Scotia smoked salmon and sable sprinkled with capers, pickled herring, sturgeon, whitefish salad, cream cheese with and without pale shoots of green chives, bialys, bagels, and babka, both chocolate and cinnamon. Much babka. All washed down with cup after cup of high-octane coffee. Kitty must have rented dishes for the occasion, because my Tiffany china— service for ten, a blue and white chickadee pattern—is nowhere in sight. Shiny silver bowls heaped with cashews, chocolate truffles, and other delicacies line the side tables. Kitty obviously made sure that Delfina and her crew got out the polish. I was lax in that department. Flaw number fifty-one.

By four o'clock, the crowd swells to more than a hundred. Guests leave their coats downstairs on a rack off the lobby. At our front door Delfina's sister, in a dignified black dress instead of her usual sequined jeans, gracefully accepts bakery boxes tied with red string. End to end, there is enough rugelach to pave a road to Scarsdale. Inside the kitchen, platters of sandwiches and mountains of fruit—fresh and dried—artfully arranged under colored plastic wrap arrive by messenger at the apartment's back service entrance. Manhattan Fruitier should write me a thank-you note, although I'm not sure why people think the bereaved have a sudden yen for unripe papayas. I predict that my practical mother and sister will eventually check out whether City Harvest accepts donations.

"Molly would have loved this party," Brie says as she divides a white-chocolate-covered pretzel and feeds half to Isadora. Indeed, a party is what it seems to have become. Guests drift away by five-thirty but come back in triple the force by eight, when Rabbi S.S. holds a short service.

After the prayers, Annabel's meltdown begins. My parents put her to bed, Alfred the bunny at her side and her thumb in her mouth, although she hasn't sucked it for over a year. Her serious blue eyes close in less than a minute.

My spirit settles in beside her, arms around my tiny, motherless child. I try with all my strange might to will her to dream of us together, so she can feel how much I love her. I conjure up her third birthday, where every guest brought her favorite doll and we had a real tea party. "Mommy, can we do this every year?" Annabel had asked. "Of course, Annie-belle. It'll be our tradition." I had already started planning her fourth-birthday party, for which I'd wanted to order a real tea set. The catalog sits by my bed, with a stickie on page thirty-two. Now what? Will Barry take her to McDonald's instead, hire a juggler, and give her a video game?

I want that tea party dream as much for me as for Annabel, but she is too tired to dream. She sighs deeply and curls into a fetal position, a tiny comma whose blond curls barely peek above the soft white blanket. I breathe in Annabel's powdery innocence and count her sweet breaths, wishing my chest could move along with hers. And then I force myself to return to the living room, vibrating with nearly 150 visitors. Which is why, at first, I don't see him. Luke arrives with Simon, his business partner, and brings paperwhites in a white china pot. I am sure anyone who notices Luke and Simon assumes they are a couple: matching handsome men wearing kindness and Italian loafers of fine, thin leather.

Simon walks toward people he knows. Luke searches the room.

"You must be Mrs. Katz," he says, approaching my mother-in-law, who appears surprised and flattered by the attention of this black-haired stranger.

"And you would be . . . ?"

"Luke Delaney," he says. "A friend of Molly's." No reaction from Kitty. "From work."

"Luc?" she says. "Like Jean-Luc Godard?"

I hear him think, *Cool Hand Luke,* what I called him. "Like Luke Skywalker."

The reference is lost on Kitty. "Where did you say you and Molly worked?" she asks.

A small smile begins to light up Luke's face, crinkling his eyes. "I'm a photographer," he says. "We met on a shoot in London."

Kitty says nothing.

"Molly was very talented," he adds.

"I see," Kitty says. "Do you know my son?"

"No," Luke says. "But of course Molly talked about him all the time." Guilty as charged.

Kitty looks around the room. Luke thinks she is trying to find Barry, but I know she is simply pretending to do that because she has no interest in Luke, which is fine, because Luke does not want to meet Barry. Not tonight, of all nights. Kitty excuses herself. Luke walks over to the photograph display.

The picture he stares at is of me cuddling Annabel when she is a month old. I hear him think, *You're beautiful, both of you,* even though I am without makeup and my hair can benefit from not just a cut but a shampoo. When he senses no one is looking, he touches my lips gently, as if he can feel them. He moves his finger back and forth.

I swear that I can feel the warmth of his fingertips.

# Five

# I, GOOGLER

*I* keep thinking there's something I could have done."

"You weren't even in this hemisphere," Brie's lover, Isadora, murmurs. She tenderly kneads almond oil into Brie's long back, starting at her square, slim shoulders and ending where smooth olive skin meets the top of her heart-shaped tush. I look away, and not just because I always thought Brie's butt was better than mine, which was shaped like a bustle no matter how skinny I got, or because girl sex has never been my thing. To exercise my gift now feels like a grievous violation of intent. I'm sure my ability wasn't given to me so I could visually Google a friend.

"But there had to be a clue," Brie says as she sits up on the tautly made white bed. Her dark brown hair, unfurled from its braid, spreads across a crisply starched pillow sham. The design of the loft shows well-muscled discipline. Every surface is black or white-white, the floors are a deep walnut, and each piece of metal—down to the hinges— is matte stainless steel that shows not one fingerprint. Books and magazines sit in neat piles, as if the owners go on a daily rampage with a T square. The furniture is the direct offspring of esteemed midcentury designers—Knoll and Saarinen and names lost on me. It's so pure here

I always wanted to show up wearing rock-and-roll drag, carrying carnations dyed electric blue.

To live as Isadora thought they should, Brie jettisoned three-fourths of her possessions. It may still be unknown to Isadora that the stuff wasn't sold on Craigslist, as Brie led her to believe, but landed in a Bronx mini-storage bin. At least Brie listened to me on that one. I'll bet right now she wishes she were wrapped in an old granny quilt, rocking in the rickety blue chair we scored at a barn sale in Bucks County.

"A clue?" Isadora says. "Like a mysterious phone call?"

Color rises in Brie's face.

"Kidding," Isadora says in her seductive Spanish purr.

"I was hoping," Brie says, "a postcard, at least, with a word on it."

"Well, the New York mail may be bad, *mi amor*," Isadora says, "but it's been over a week." She reaches for Brie's hands, but Brie slips on her robe—whipped-cream white, matching Isadora's—walks to the window, and stares toward the street below. "I'm sorry," Brie's lover says. "I know you're hurting. I wish there was something I could do."

Isadora leaves the room—she realizes nothing she can do or say right now will be a comfort or received well. Brie continues to look into the beating rain. "I can feel you, Molly," she whispers. "I know you're here, close by. I can't explain it. I swear I can smell your perfume." Every duty-free shop called my name; I'd worn Eternity each day of my life for the last five years. Half a bottle of the eau du toilette spray still sits on my bathroom counter.

"Yes, I'm here," I say. "I'm here. Turn around." Brie was as true a friend as any woman could want. There was nothing syrupy about her, yet she always let me know she wanted only good things on my behalf. Brie brought out my best self. In her presence, even if it were only over the phone, I wanted to rise to the occasion and try to be more—funnier, happier, sharper. I wish she knew I was with her now. "I'm here," I say.

Brie looks out the window, seeing nothing. "Molly, send me a sign," she says.

*Six*

# THE DURATION

*I*'m Bob," he says as he shakes my hand. "I've been assigned to be your guide."

"Are you an angel?" Have I read one too many of the *Guideposts* Delfina has left behind?

He is well pressed, dark-haired, square-jawed, as snappy as the young priest the Vatican puts on television. "Are *you*?" Bob asks seriously.

Am I?

Bob clears his throat and laughs. "Yes, Molly, that was humor. We try not to use loaded words like *angel*. A little woo-woo for us. Think of me as a personal trainer, a seeing-eye dog, a big brother."

"I never had a brother."

"We know," Bob answers. "That's one reason I was assigned to your case. I'd have introduced myself sooner, but you seem to be figuring out the rules on your own."

Is this a compliment?

"Yes," Bob says. "You can take it as a compliment."

"Thank you," I say.

"Frankly, over the last few days, I've been dealing with my needier cases. You know the type. Can't tell an insight from an isosceles triangle."

I try to remember what one of those looked like, or if I ever knew.

"Molly, don't worry," Bob says. "Taxes? Spreadsheets? Unless you do logarithms to amuse yourself, math is entirely optional here."

Perhaps I will like wherever it is I am.

Bob takes out a clipboard. "We should, however, review some basics. Let's start with just now, when you were hoping to reach Brie in her bedroom."

"Yes?"

"Everyone tries that at least once." He tsks. "You remember that phrase your mother always used, 'Like talking to a wall'?"

My mom said that to Lucy and me at least four hundred times. "Bedtime, girls." We'd tune her out, glued to *Love Boat*. "Molly! Lucy!" No answer. "Like talking to a wall," she'd mutter.

I get it.

"I knew you would," Bob says, and winks. "You'll only upset yourself trying to communicate that way." He refers to his notes, then sinks into a loveseat upholstered in suede as soft as kitten fur and pats the spot next to him. I sit.

I've never believed in heaven. For that matter, I have also never believed in hell. Most Jews are like that, planning vacations to Patagonia and Prague, but never making long-term celestial plans. But if I *had* imagined heaven, I'd have pictured it like an enormous Guggenheim Museum, with stairs that circle up and up and up into the wild blue yonder. Wherever it is that I've landed now, however, looks and feels more like an upscale fitness resort. It could be any day of the year in San Diego—neither warm nor cold. We are in a sunny solarium. Leaded glass windows overlook a lush green park webbed with cobblestone paths where people of all ages are walking briskly as if they have places to go.

"Now, some of our newcomers," Bob says, "get a little overwhelmed by the ability they discover they have to, hmm, flit about."

"Like yesterday?" One minute I was in Annabel's room, and the next I was staring down at Barry. This was before I moved on to Brie and Isadora's. I was like the cursor on my computer before I learned how to control the mouse.

"Exactly," Bob says. "You were the proverbial cheap suit."

"Could you use a different metaphor, please? How about wallpaper?"

"Fine. Now, Molly, did you ever practice yoga?"

"Occasionally. Badly."

"Ah," he says. "Then what I would encourage is for you to simply count up to your age—thirty-five, right?—before you allow yourself to relocate. That's the term we prefer, *relocate*. This will help you reserve your powers for where they're needed most."

"But how will I know where they are 'needed' at all?" I sound shrill, but Bob is kind enough not to roll his eyes.

"You will know," he says, articulating each word slowly, clearly, and—I have to admit—as if he has a warm, beating heart. "For example, you have no need to know whether or not the president and First Lady have intercourse, so stop thinking how 'interesting' it would be to see if they share a bedroom and, if so, what they do there."

Damn.

"This leads me to another point. You have discovered that you now possess the ability to hear what people think."

"Incredible."

"You must promise to listen to only one person at a time. If you abuse this privilege, it will end. Do you hear me? Kaput, over. This will mean that while you are monitoring one person, you will miss the thoughts of another, but so be it. Those, dear Molly, are the rules. I cannot emphasize this too strongly. Do you know the term *cacophony*?" Bob asks.

I nod.

"Exercise your eavesdropping talent selectively, or you will feel as if you're living through a Stones concert in the Times Square subway station during rush hour."

"Bob, you look grave," I say. He is a Ken doll that has just lost his job.

"Good one, Molly," he says, chuckling. "I will like working with you. But let's stay on point. If you don't choose to listen to just one voice or inner thought at a time, I warn you, you will suddenly become . . ." He pauses for emphasis. "Stone deaf."

Got it.

"Now, to the power that you ever so delicately referred to as a bullshit detector."

Am I blushing?

He waves his hand. "As good a name as any. I'll let you in on a little secret. You always had that ability. You just never bothered to activate it. Not many people who have that gift do."

I try to take it in, but I am distracted by how earnest Bob is. I picture him in a short-sleeved plaid shirt, shopping at Sears, going to the barber for his biweekly trim, never forgetting to floss or remember his grandmother's birthday. I wonder if he showed a calf at the Iowa State Fair.

"Not a calf," he says. "A blue-ribbon sow, as gorgeous as Miss Piggy. And not Iowa. Northern California." He smiles. "And no, I did not eat a deep-fried Twinkie at the fair, but yes, I was an Eagle Scout, played football and French horn, and graduated from med school. Pediatric resident. Engaged. I had a pretty sweet life until the accident. Drunk driver with a big pot belly filled with beer. Splat. Hit and run."

I don't know what to say.

"There's nothing *to* say," Bob says, and looks at me so kindly his eyes are like sunlamps. "Except that, of course, you can ask me anything you wish, either now or later. Anything, do you hear? In the Duration, I'm your Sherpa, remember?"

But it's all too much. I feel as if I'm at a job interview where I've been quizzed for two hours and now can't manufacture one intelligent question in response. "These powers I have, Bob," I say finally. "How long will they last?"

There isn't a harp in sight, but someone has cued Elvis, who's singing, "I can't help falling in love with you." The taste of raspberries is on my lips. In the distance, a Milky Way of dewy white roses catches the morning light and, faintly, their fragrance wafts our way. It is a fragrance far more pleasing to my nose than Eternity.

"Molly, that I can't tell you, because I don't know. None of us knows. But you are lucky—for most people, these powers are over before they even get here. For a few, of course, they last forever." Bob

touches my arm. "I believe," he says, "and this is purely private specu-
lation, that our powers last only as long as they need to last. I am not a
religious man, though neither am I a cynic."

I blink.

Bob is gone. Nearby, a plump robin lands on a branch. I could
swear I see it wink.

## Seven

# A FOOTNOTE IN BRIDAL HISTORY

*B*arry and I were married in my parents' backyard beneath a canopy of willow branches twinkling with—may the God of Abraham, Isaac, and Jacob forgive me—tiny white Christmas lights. Rain misted us halfway through the seven benedictions, so by the time I heard "makest the bridegroom to rejoice in his bride," I was fully engrossed in whether my hair would frizz and thought only for an instant about Barry.

Several months before the wedding, at a restaurant in the Village where Barry and I went for my birthday lunch—I was turning twenty-seven—I found a Burberry box on my chair. Attached to an umbrella inside was a poem Barry had written about protecting me from life's storms. There was also a hunky emerald-cut diamond ring.

I stared at it as if it might explode. We hadn't even talked about living together. I was hoping Barry might be extravagant, and had visions of an Art Deco bracelet or a pair of expensive gold hoop earrings I'd been stalking at Saks. Instead, after only six months of dating, he was asking me to marry him.

"Molly Divine, you are the woman for me," he said. "I knew that the moment I met you."

After Barry and I had briefly dated in college, I'd had three serious relationships: Trevor, who dumped me for Sarah; Jeff, whom I dumped when I began falling asleep during sex; and Christian, whom I broke up with not because he was Christian but because if your idea of hors d'oeuvres is deviled eggs made with Miracle Whip, you can't grow old beside me.

I considered Barry's good qualities. There was his playful manner with friends' small children, and his ability to navigate life without maps—the man was a living, breathing GPS who from memory or by scent, for all I know, could retrace his steps five years later to a remote address he'd visited once, while I have the uncanny ability to consistently turn left for every right. I considered the breadth of his shoulders, the taper of his waist, the length and steadiness of his immaculate surgeon's fingers. I noted the fact that he seemed to know exactly the life he wanted, whereas I couldn't tell you if I'd rather eat a Cobb salad or tuna for lunch.

I liked that he liked me. Wanted me. Loved me, apparently.

I decided on the spot that twenty-seven was the perfect age at which to get engaged: you're young enough not to be too cynical or wrinkled for a long white dress, and old enough—presumably—to know what you're getting into. You also have a fair shot at conceiving before life becomes hot-and-cold running infertility specialists.

The day he popped the question, Barry Marx had all the right words. "I will marry my soul to yours," he said. I cried, spilling tears on the tablecloth. I actually thanked him for proposing.

He must have assumed I'd say yes, because from the restaurant we drove immediately to his mother's apartment, where at least a dozen relatives and family intimates had gathered to toast our future happiness. "To Dr. and Mrs. Marx," Kitty said, raising a glass of Veuve Clicquot. Until that point, it never occurred to me that I'd ever not be Divine. My name was as good as it gets, even if I had to share it with an obese drag queen. But Barry echoed Kitty with "To Mrs. Marx," and I was smothered by well-wishers. Only late that evening, when Barry dropped me at home on Jane Street, did I call my parents.

"Larry who?" my father asked.

"Barry," I said. "Barry Marx. The doctor."

"The plastic surgeon?" my mother asked.

"He prefers *cosmetic.*"

The silence between New York and Chicago stood between us like ice. "Are you sure, sweetie?" my mom continued. "You just ended things with Christopher."

"Christian," I said. "And it's been nine months." Our breakup had been a load off for my mother, who offered me a subscription to J-Date within hours of hearing the news. "Marriage is hard enough without Jesus coming between you," she'd said.

"When will we meet this Barry?" my parents asked more or less in unison; then and there I saw myself as an ungrateful brat because I'd impulsively agreed to marry a man my parents had never laid eyes on. My mother and father, I always felt, had been nothing less than perfect— two people I genuinely respected, who were generous and just interfering enough for me to know they cared.

"We'll work it out," I said quietly.

"Has Lucy met him?" my father asked. If Lucy approved of Barry, it would be good enough for him. Divine family lore classified my father and Lucy as the sensible ones, while I was considered to be a good-hearted and dizzy blonde like my mother.

"Not yet," I said. This wasn't going the way I'd hoped. I wanted my parents to be bouncing with happiness, not shooting questions as if our conversation were a press conference. "Aren't you pleased?" I finally asked. If I whined, I note in my defense that it was late and my face hurt from smiling.

"Molly darling, if you want to marry this man, he must be extremely special," my mother said. Not only was she always a steel beam of support, she knows when to end a conversation. "But don't rush. Have a long engagement."

The next day, Barry and I set a date for only four months later and I kicked into action. Calligraphy or my mother's distinctive penmanship? DJ or band? Cornish hens or Chilean sea bass? Tent or no tent? Peonies or hydrangeas? Noon or twilight? Vintage Bentley or a Cadillac in Mary Kay pink? Hair up or hanging loose? No detail was too small to be deconstructed as if it were a line from the Talmud.

Except for the Bentley and band, Barry didn't voice strong opinions. "You're only going to do this once, Molly—I'll go with whatever you want," he said, and made me feel as loved as I ever had by a man.

"I never took you for a psycho bride," Brie said as we gown-shopped in New York three months before the wedding.

Brie was right. I fulfilled every cliché, obsessing over decisions as if the lives of babies depended on them. A pink wedding? Too cupcake. Yellow? Unflattering on 80 percent of skin types, claims *Allure*. Blue would do, but "nothing too Cozumel," I lectured as I whipped out a paint chip to show the wedding coordinator, whom I'd forced my parents to hire at considerable expense. "It's got to be barely blue, like a duck's egg." Terms like "too matchy-matchy" infected my vocabulary. I am sure people were mocking me, but ensconced as I was in my bride bubble, how could I hear or see?

When it came to the gown, however, Brie talked me down to earth. After I considered no fewer than five hundred possibilities culled from every bridal magazine—even *Las Vegas Wedding*—and we had the ooh-la-la shopping experience, tea and all, I spent one-fifth the cost of a Vera Wang when Brie dragged me to a garment-center hole in the wall. "I'm the last person in the world to ever say no to designer clothes," she said, standing tall and tailored as I tried on fourteen gowns in thirty minutes. "But don't throw money at a dress. You could look good in a dry cleaner's bag, and honestly, strapless is strapless."

In the world of fashion, I'm a foot soldier, not a commanding officer, and so I did whatever Brie suggested. She guided me to a slim column of satin with just a spritz of blue-gray crystals. "To pick up the blue of your eyes," she said, but I suspect she was thinking a sheath made me look thinner. We sewed a pirated Carolina Herrera label into the lining and Kitty not only never knew of the counterfeit, she bragged about the gown to her friends at the engagement party she threw a month later. This is when my parents met Barry. Between his surgery schedule and my bridal dementia, we'd never made it to Chicago.

At the party, held at the country club Kitty made her second home even as a widow, Barry danced with my mother and Lucy and invited my dad to play golf. I assumed the evening had gone splendidly. "So?" I said in my parents' rented car on our drive back to the city, the first moment when we were alone together. "What do you think?"

"He's handsome, Molly," my mother said. "His nose isn't as big as you said. It fits his face."

"Uh-huh," I said, waiting for more.

"Great food tonight, but the mom's a piece of work," my father said. He hates when a woman other than my mother tries to make him samba.

"Yeah, well, what about Barry?"

He paused. "If you love him, we'll love him," he said finally.

"Great dancer," my mother added. I could tell she was stretching.

I turned to my sister.

"He complimented my tits," Lucy said.

"He did not," I shrieked, while I heard my mother sigh. Lucy is the most cleavage-focused woman I've ever met. She thinks every man is staring at her boobs, trying to decide if they're real. They are.

"Did."

"Did not."

"You two . . . ," my mother said.

"Molly, give me three reasons why you want to marry this guy, and that headlight of a ring doesn't count," Lucy said.

I stared at Lucy. I couldn't say "You're just jealous," not so much because the remark crossed a line I didn't want to pass, but because some unplumbed nook of my psyche considered that she might be on to something. I looked out the window, but there were no answers in the passing cars.

"He'll make a good father," I offered.

"That's crucial," my mother quickly responded. She didn't ask me how I could tell, and I wouldn't have been able to explain. Just intuition.

"He worries about me," I said. "I like a man who doesn't want me riding the subway alone past ten." As if I couldn't make that decision for myself.

*He may love me more than I love him* was something I didn't think I should list. I still thought it was wildly desirable for that to be the working dynamic in a successful relationship, and in our case, the only reason I believed it to be true was that he'd asked me to marry him with record-shattering speed. *Because I'm attracted to him?* I can tell my mother anything, but talking about sex with my dad? Nope. *I trust Barry?* I wasn't sure I did.

"Lame," Lucy snickered.

"Do you want me to screw up by marrying Barry?" I asked her.

"You hardly know the guy." I noticed that this failed to answer my question.

"My fiancé has a name—Barry—and we've been spending every minute together," I said, though it was a lie. His work always seemed to get in the way. "Mom and Dad had an even shorter engagement." After knowing each other for two months, they eloped.

"Point taken," Lucy said.

The four of us remained mute for the rest of the ride.

August arrived. The day of the wedding, Lucy showed more décolletage than a random Hollywood starlet. It was a small price to pay to have her drop the subject of my making a mistake. "You can still get out of it," she'd said sotto voce at my bridal shower the month before, which she threw at a Chicago lingerie shop that specializes in X-rated undies with toys to match. I got enough thongs to outfit a brothel and the thirty-one guests each received a vibrator disguised as a lipstick.

Three weeks later, I was a comely footnote in bridal history, not a radiant headline. Wearing my hair up was definitely the wrong move—I looked like a hostess at Howard Johnson's—but it wasn't that or the fact that Rabbi S.S. had double-booked and had to send his twitchy sidekick. When I looked at my pictures later, I saw a frightened bride.

I walked down the aisle on my father's arm. Under the chuppa, six feet away from me, a stranger was waiting. It took a moment to realize he was Barry Marx, who in ten minutes would become my husband. Forever. I broke a sweat and, worrying that perspiration stains would show, stumbled on the white carpet that had been unfurled down the middle of our lawn, dividing the Divines from the Marxes. My dad, pale as milk, steadied my arm. We exchanged a glance and in his face I saw the fear I felt.

I don't remember the vows. I don't remember anything about the actual ceremony except Barry's lengthy, theatrical tongue kiss. What was the romantic ballad I had obsessed over that accompanied our first walk as husband and wife? My ears echoed with silence.

But then the reception began—loud, long, throbbing. In summer, the Chicago twilight comes late, and at ten, along with a fistful of stars, lights hidden in the oak trees lit up like pavé diamonds. On account of the heat, everyone drank not just the pomegranate martinis circulated after the ceremony but cases and cases of crisply cold pinot grigio and, later, Champagne.

There's nothing I find less appealing than a drunken woman, but I definitely had a buzz on. Loose-limbed and smoking, Lucy and I did our Molly and Moosey number, alone in a circle of clapping girlfriends, a performance saved from lewdness only because it was performed in bridal frou-frou. Soon Brie, my other Northwestern friends, and the New York crowd joined in, watched on the sidelines by Isadora, too soignée for such a display.

"This must be what happy feels like," I said to Brie as we twirled in the middle of the dance floor, our booties bouncing to the beat.

When the band took a break, I went in the back door and upstairs to powder myself with scented talc and keep the dainty bride thing going. As I walked out of my bathroom door, I heard Barry's laugh. He owns the kind of guffaw that makes people turn around in movie theaters; aspiring stand-up comics should pay to have that appreciative noise in their audience. The sound stopped abruptly, but it had come from downstairs, and I moved toward it.

I got to the foyer as Barry walked out of the guest bathroom and continued in the other direction, toward the hallway that led outside. I was ready to call his name when the door opened again. One of his guests from New York—Remy, Romy, Ronnie?—exited the bathroom and sashayed in the other direction. Which made us collide.

"Molly," she said, nonplussed. Her Toffee Frost lipstick was smeared, her long red hair disheveled. I couldn't tell if the hairdo was intentional or if a neo-beehive had collapsed due to avid fondling. "Beautiful wedding!" she gushed, and flew away, innocent as a butterfly.

I staggered outside, searching for the nearest chair.

"I've been looking all over for you," Barry said, running toward me. "C'mon, sweetheart—the cake."

"I need a moment," I said, but a waiter was rolling in three towering layers of chocolate pastry, heavy on the whipped cream, studded with enormous strawberries, topped with blazing sparklers. Barry and I completed our drill—his hand on top of mine, the new gold band gleaming against his tan—as the knife sliced through the layers and the shock sliced through my heart. We smiled for the camera.

"Is Mrs. Marx ready for her life to begin?" Barry whispered as he drew me toward him. His breath was minty, his smile confident, his teeth unnaturally white.

*Mrs. Marx has another idea about where to stick this knife,* I thought as he kissed me and the photographer snapped.

*Eight*

# OLD SOULS

*I*f anyone imagines that during shiva a moratorium is declared on discussing the widower's social life, they would be dead wrong.

"Whenever you're ready, let me know, because my wife's sister—you remember Stacey?"

"Stacey with the chest?" Barry asks.

"Precisely. Stacey and her husband? *Finito.*"

I overhear at least six proposed hook-ups, including one from our accountant, who wants Barry to meet his daughter. She's a senior at Stanford but, he promises, "an old soul."

"I thought you could use some dinner," a divorced mom from Annabel's school class says as she presents an armful of vegetarian lasagna. "For you and Andrea."

I hear Barry think, *Not my type,* as he sizes up her double-wide hips, but the only words out of his mouth are "Thanks. Annabel and I appreciate it." He hands off the Pyrex to Delfina, who crams it into the freezer next to a pot roast, turkey chili, and a tragic casserole of Velveeta and canned pinto beans that's made from a recipe I passed by last month on the AOL home page.

"Should have gone for the bigger Sub-Zero," he says to Delfina as he returns to the living room.

"A lot of things you shoulda done," she says to herself after he leaves the room.

While many Reform Jews do a token shiva for a day or two, my family goes the whole nine yards: seven days, with time off for good behavior on the Sabbath, when Barry shows up at temple, both Friday night and Saturday morning. Throughout the week, I carefully monitor my husband. Has Model Mourner researched funeral customs? Although he dresses carefully, in a black cashmere turtleneck and gray flannel pants, he doesn't shave, which leaves him looking just this side of seedy. On at least a dozen occasions he gets teary when someone mentions my name.

It took me two days to notice, however, that Dr. Barry Marx has varied his meticulous routine. Before dinner, were it not for shiva, he'd have gone for his usual after-work run followed by a shower that would last five to fifteen minutes, depending on whether or not he jerks off. After dinner, he'd log time at his laptop to look at e-mail (he has three accounts: barrymmd@aol.com and bmarx8@earthlink.net, plus the one he doesn't know I know about, bigbare@hotmail.com). He'd then check out the *Wall Street Journal*'s take on medical developments, followed by a spot of porn while he'd blare the TV—always a marital sore point. Because of shiva, he's taken a break from these pursuits, but the rest of his evening remains intact. At eleven-ten, Barry does two hundred sit-ups and fifty push-ups, kisses Annabel's forehead, and spends eight minutes on WaterPik maneuvers. Letterman's opening monologue follows, then exactly one chapter of a book—mystery, history, or athlete's biography—before his midnight curfew.

But he's added an intriguing detail. Barry has taken to wearing his wedding ring, which every night he now deposits in the Cartier box in which it arrived, the one he keeps in his second-from-the-top drawer. The box is in pristine condition, since the ring has seen little action. This never bothered me—my father doesn't wear a wedding band and plenty of cheaters I know do. Nonetheless, the ring—engraved with our wedding date and the word *forever*—has started appearing on his finger.

Tonight he looks at the shiny band as if he'd never seen it before, turning it over in his hand as the phone rings.

"Hideous," he says after picking it up. "I'll be glad when this ordeal is over."

The slightly nasal voice on the other end is the same person who has called around eleven every night for the last week.

"Thank God it's the last day," Barry says.

I study Barry's face. His eyes look puffy, and I see wrinkles, newly engraved.

"How do I feel? Like dog shit."

This does not make me unhappy.

"I think she's doing okay, but it's hard to tell—she's been practically mute."

Wrong. Annabel's been quite a little chatterbox when Barry's not around, especially when she's alone.

"Everyone's all over her—Delfina, my mother-in-law, and that loudmouth Lucy. Oh, and Molly's friends. "

Who've come, one by one and in small groups, every night of shiva.

"Yeah, especially the lipstick lesbians."

My gang has really been here.

"Tomorrow? Impossible. I'm back in surgery."

That poor nose.

"No, my feelings haven't changed."

Does he care about this woman? I can't tell. After the wedding, I never could tell if he cared about me.

"I'm hanging up now."

The voice sounds even more nasal.

"Have a little decency," he says.

He looks at the clock.

"I mean it. I'm beat. Another time, Stephanie."

*Stephanie.*

Barry crawls into bed. He avoids my side as if rolling there would mean that he, too, will land in a grave, and falls asleep in less than two minutes.

———

It's true that he has surgery in the morning, but not until ten. A detective named Hicks arrives at seven forty-five. He is African American, no older than his early thirties, one earring, a discreet gold stud. I can't resist watching him, a man who is far more handsome than he guesses.

"Mr. Marx," he begins, taking inventory of our living room.

"It's Dr.," Barry answers reflexively. *Putz,* he thinks, *why did I say that?*

"Excuse me," Hicks says. "*Dr.* Marx. I'm sorry for your loss and intruding at this time, sir, but as I told you on the phone, this is standard. Just a few questions."

"I'm all yours," Barry says.

*We'll see about that,* I hear Hicks think. "The evening that Mrs. Marx went out biking—the night before she was found dead, that is. Where were you?"

Barry answers immediately. "I was running. In Central Park. Training for the marathon."

"Same here," Hicks offers, in a friendlier tone than I would have predicted.

"Well, then you know how much time you have to put in," Barry says. "At least an old guy like me does." He laughs as he attempts to grease his way with charm. He guesses that he isn't actually too many years older than Hicks, but the detective isn't going to reward him with personal workout details.

"Did anyone see you that night?"

Barry takes a minute to answer, but he has already decided what to say. "The doorman."

Alphonso, our evening doorman, can't remember if you had a colony of bats delivered twenty minutes ago, and he loves Barry, who gives him a few Yankee tickets every season.

"And where did you run in the park?" Hicks says.

"Entered across the street, ran south, up to the north end of the park, then back out on Eighty-first," Barry says. "The usual loop."

"How long did it take you?"

Barry shifts in his chair and twists the wedding band. "That run usually takes me about forty-five minutes."

Barry looks as if he is waiting to be congratulated on his seven-minute miles, but instead Hicks asks, "Did anyone see you running?"

*What the fuck,* Barry thinks. "Sure, a lot of people, I guess, but we don't all stop and introduce ourselves." *It's not speed-dating, for Christ's sake,* he thinks.

"Was there anyone you can think of who would have wanted to harm your wife?" Hicks asks.

After a long, considered pause Barry says, "Everyone loved Molly. She wasn't a threat to anyone." Not exactly the highest praise, but I imagine he thinks he is complimenting me to, well, the heavens.

"Was Mrs. Marx upset about anything?"

*Besides me?* Barry says to himself. "Nothing out of the ordinary. She led a very fortunate life." Cushy. Pampered. Privileged. True, true, true.

This is really his point, and Hicks gets it.

"So I appreciate your visit, Detective, and I hope"—*and expect,* he thinks—"that all the muscle of the New York Police Department will get behind finding the fucking monster who did this to my wife."

*Whoa,* Detective Hicks thinks, *this hothead's getting way ahead of himself, considering that his wife's death might be a simple, stupid accident or even a suicide.* "That's all for now—we'll be in touch, Dr. Marx," he says, and gets up from the chair. "Sorry to intrude." He shakes Barry's hand and gives him his card. I notice his hands, large, strong, as meticulously groomed as my husband's.

"No problem," Barry says, slipping the card in his pocket. After the detective leaves, Barry sighs. It sounds like the wheeze of an elderly man. In two minutes he, too, is out the door. It's raining, but he forgets his umbrella.

I check on Annabel. She's been playing rabbi all week long, sitting shiva with her American Girl dolls. I am the pretty blonde, Elizabeth, who serves tea and is presumed to have good penmanship. I, Elizabeth, have been spending the week asleep. I keep wondering if Annabel will let me wake up.

"I miss you, Mommy," she says. "I love you." She tenderly tucks her tattered blankie around Elizabeth. Around me. "Are you warm enough, Mommy?" In her pink flannel nightie and bare feet she pads across the room to the toy baskets and, one by one, dumps them on the floor until she finds a minuscule plastic plate with a tiny brown muffin attached.

She places it next to Elizabeth. "You must be hungry, Mommy," she says. "Got to eat." I recognize the musical tone as my own.

On the dot of eight-fifteen, Delfina quietly raps on the door as she opens it, singing, "Good morning, sunshine." She takes in the mess—toys and books everywhere—and the dolls tidily lined up for prayers.

"You've been busy, haven't you, miss?" she says, love in her voice. "Don't worry—I'll watch over your friends here, but we gotta get dressed—time to go back to school."

Annabel doesn't budge.

"What do you want to wear?" Delfina asks. "Pick anything."

My daughter rummages through her drawer and finds the velour sweats that almost match mine, last Mother's Day's gift from Kitty. I wore my set only once, because they made me feel as if I should be heading out for the early-bird special in Boca. Annabel hasn't worn hers since last summer. Her skinny arms and legs stick out by inches.

"Perfect," Delfina says. "Now hop to it, miss. Waffles!"

After Delfina leaves the room, Annabel takes one last long look at Elizabeth. "You take a long sleep now," she says.

## Nine

# MISSIONARY'S DOWNFALL

From where I lie now, it's easy to ask myself why I didn't confront Barry at our wedding when I saw that witch wiggle her tush out of my parents' powder room. But what was I supposed to do, yell "rewind" with 250 wedding guests panting for cake? As they say in life, timing is everything. In death, not so much.

Hawaii won the honeymoon sweepstakes, and the morning after our wedding, Barry and I flew west. For the first day, I wanted to strangle him with an orchid lei, but my fury started to mute as I soaked in a hot tub and sipped innumerable pineapple cocktails—not that I could tell a Missionary's Downfall from a Tropical Itch. When we weren't getting hammered we were having sex, on the bed, in the hammock, and on the fine white sand, this way, that way, and yes, once *that* way. By the end of the trip, I'd convinced myself that maybe I'd imagined the debacle of the powder room. I returned to New York with a grass skirt, five new pounds, and a urinary tract infection. In the honeymoon afterglow, I made a secret vow to become a forgive-and-forget kinda wife worthy of a Country Music Award and my husband's everlasting affection.

Three weeks after the wedding, I had lunch with Brie, who hadn't yet started law school and was still the centerpiece of faraway photo shoots—she'd just returned from Kenya—although at almost twenty-eight she'd stopped getting top American bookings. Her last job had been for the second-best women's weekly in Johannesburg.

When she asked me about married life I reported that I'd been dragging myself out of bed every day to kiss Barry goodbye before he left for the hospital. "I'm buying fresh flowers twice a week, and every night I play a bunch of jazz CDs recommended by that guy we like at Tower Records, the one with the dreads."

I didn't tell Brie the half of it, and I don't mean that I also played Lyle Lovett and Michael Bublé. Every day, I made mental notes on wry observations and worthy conversational themes, often stolen from the blogosphere, which, along with three proper courses, I'd serve at dinner to stimulate—make that simulate—amusing repartee. I ordered napkins embossed with "Barry and Molly" and took Barry's shirts to the dry cleaner for laundering. How could I have known he preferred them on hangers, rather than three to a box like a weekly birthday present?

Brie stopped flipping through pictures she'd taken on a safari tacked onto her shoot. "Excuse me," she said, "but have you seen my friend Molly?"

"Your point being?"

"You shouldn't be sweating it like this." Brie leaned forward and nailed me with her eyes, smoky as graphite but not as soft. My bridal sell-by date, which had veiled me from criticism, had apparently expired. It was the first time since I got married that anyone—even Lucy—was talking turkey to me. "You're borderline pathetic," she added, in case I hadn't gotten the message.

I turned my wineglass in a circle on the bare wood table. My wedding band caught the light, its channel-set diamonds marching in a circle promising eternity.

"I hear you," I said.

"I'm not sure you do," she said, putting her hand on mine to stop the twisting. "Look at me."

Reluctantly, I did.

"If anyone belongs on a pedestal, it's you, Molly. Not him. Ever since you met Barry Marx you're acting all 'I'm the bottom, you're the top.' " For extra emphasis, she sang the Cole Porter song.

"Okay, that's enough," I whispered. Brie's singing had captured the attention of two women at the next table. Her vocal stylings leave something to be desired. "Thanks for the big vote of confidence, but I want to make my marriage work."

"Yeah?" she said. "And this is it?"

"Nobody teaches you how to be married," I said, in what even I recognized as a tone better left to a motivational speaker. "I can't very well imitate my parents—they've set the bar so high it's a damn curse." Perhaps I used a different adjective. Anyway, it's not like Dan and Claire Divine coo to the point where you gag, but they still crack each other up, and sometimes I catch my dad staring at my mom—even when she's come in from tennis, sweat dripping down her back and curling the hair around her delicately lined face—with a look that says, *How did a dumb putz like me ever win Mega Millions?* For her part, Mom respects the power of lingerie. I always assumed I could tell a lot about my parents' private life by her boudoir wardrobe, which is heavy on silk charmeuse in styles skimpy enough to show off her cellulite-free legs, each wisp of a gown coordinated with robes—sheer cottons, embroidered kimonos, and velvets in Elizabethan hues. Lucy calls her the Geisha.

"Besides," I added, "you don't even know Barry all that well. I think you're being a little arrogant."

"You're right, Molly," Brie said, leaning back in her chair. "I'm single. What do I know?" Her words were apologetic; her voice was not. "It's just that I don't want you to forget you."

"I love that you worry about me," I said after about a minute. "I worry about you, too. Mostly that you'll elope." Brie was then five boyfriends away from declaring herself a daughter of Sappho. "I'm selfish. I'm afraid I'll lose you to someone who'll make you live without blow-dryers and Crest Whitestrips on the dark side of the moon."

Brie laughed, a deep, throaty gurgle I wish I could hear this very minute. "Tell me again about the photographer you met," I said. She described her latest conquest, Luke whatever, in head-to-toe detail. Black hair, blue eyes, long legs.

My mind was stuck in the Molly-forgetting-Molly groove. Still, I must have subliminally absorbed something, because a year later, when I met Luke Delaney, wires connected deep in my brain, and I approached this particular man with my version of candor. To begin with, I made a point of looking him in the eye, something Barry repeatedly told me I neglected to do, a deficiency among many that, in the second year of our marriage, he was only too happy to draw to my attention so that I could become a more perfect person and mate.

I was at Kennedy Airport when I met Luke. "Excuse me, but aren't you Molly, Brie's friend?" a black-haired man asked right after I was told my flight to London had been overbooked and I'd need to take the next plane out hours later.

"Yes, I'm Molly," I said. "Molly Marx." I tried to smile but, aggravated as I was about the delay, the best I could do was not frown.

"Luke Delaney," he said. He shook my hand and smiled for both of us. "I got bumped, too."

"Are you as pissed as I am?" I asked. "If there hadn't been so much traffic on the LIE . . ."

"You at least have an excuse," Luke said. "Got a late start. No one to blame but myself." As he spoke, I noticed his eyes were the exact shade I'd wanted for my wedding, blue as a sunny sky over Nantucket. I shifted from his eyes to his mouth. His lips were full, his nose rather long, and his bottom teeth endearingly crooked.

It was going to be a slog waiting for the next flight. Barry'd made no particular fuss about my going away for a week on a business trip, my first since our wedding. In fact, this morning he seemed determined to pick a fight, castigating me for forgetting to take care of paying the cable bill before my departure. He made most of the money, but writing checks was my domain.

My smile arrived.

"What do you say I buy us both a drink?" he asked. "Once we're in London, we'll be working such ridiculous hours I'll be too damn exhausted to hit a pub."

"*We?*"

He grabbed my tote—which overflowed with files, a liter bottle of water, and a pashmina big enough to upholster a couch—and guided me toward the first-class lounge. "Samuel Wong cancelled this morning. I got booked at noon." That explained why the name Luke Delaney hadn't shown up on my memos.

The lounge was crowded, but photographers have eagle eyes—he spotted two armchairs on the far side of the room. "Grab 'em," he said, "and I'll get us something. You drink . . . ?"

"Thanks. Pinot noir."

As I reached the empty chairs a mom with a toddler catapulted into them. I walked back to Luke, who was balancing wineglasses on a tray along with nuts and a weapon-sized Toblerone bar.

"We lost our spot to a mommy," I said.

"But here's another." He charmed a love seat into vacancy.

After fifteen minutes of unremarkable chat, he asked, "Can I make a confession?"

*He's still in love with Brie,* I thought. He wouldn't be the first man my best friend had turned into mush after she'd moved on. Knowing he was most likely under her spell made me relax. Or maybe it was the wine, which I'd already finished. "Confess away," I said.

"I'm scared shitless about this shoot."

"Really?" I asked, genuinely surprised. "Why?" To me the assignment was routine. In those days, I ran a magazine's decorating department staffed by four slaves who bushwhacked ahead of me to set up. The magazine was photographing Mayfair district houses, each chicer than the next. It was the kind of job I could do in my sleep, assuming the owners didn't freak about the photographer's aides-de-camp dropping cigarette ashes on Mummy's threadbare rugs. Oh, there'd be dogs to corral—the Brits always had dogs. But as long as I kept them happy with biscuits and picked up the nightly bar tab for the owners and our gang, I expected peace in the kingdom. We'd already made reservations at numerous restaurants deemed "bloody brilliant" by *Time Out London.*

"I'm a fashion guy," Luke said. "But I don't think I can stand one more model tantrum. From now on I want to be all about inanimate objects."

"I don't blame you. Anything I can do—" I started to say, but the loudspeaker interrupted to announce that our flight would be delayed—by how long the plummy voice didn't say.

After Luke returned to gather a second round of drinks, I reported in to Barry, as a wife is supposed to do, even when she's begun to realize she's in a continual state of low-grade anger iced with disappointment. I doubted he'd be home, but I planned to leave a message.

He answered on the first ring. "Really, Molly?" Barry said, and seemed to listen attentively to my tale of transportation inconvenience. "How about I pick you up and take you to dinner?"

Suddenly Barry was acting like an ideal husband while I was guzzling wine with a guy who was looking better by the sip, someone I'd be working with across an ocean for six days. Into what alternate reality had the airport limo deposited me? "You would do that?" I asked, incredulous.

"Why not?" he said. "I'll hop in the car—get there in, say, forty minutes? Tomorrow's my day off. I can afford to get to bed late."

I felt like a horse's ass. Who was this spouse so concerned for my well-being? I wondered as Luke returned with more wine. "Barry, I love you for offering, but they aren't saying when my plane will leave. You could drive all the way out here and I'd take off before you even parked."

He waited a few seconds before responding. "Got it," he said.

"It just seems better this way," I said. That sounded feeble. "But it would have been . . . fun." Feebler still.

"Well, good luck," he said. "Love you."

"Love you, too." I said it loudly, as much to remind myself I was married as to alert Luke in case he'd missed my rings.

Eventually, the two of us boarded and were seated side by side. I debated whether to proceed with dabbing Neosporin in my ears and above my lip, my preferred retaliation against the germ warfare that is airplane air.

The Neosporin stayed in the bag. Luke and I continued to chat, and somewhere above Greenland I discovered that he, too, was a twin, an identical twin. His brother, Micah, taught English at Dartmouth.

"Maybe we should fix up your brother with my sister," I said.

"I think not," he said. "My brother's married. But why not me? That is," he added, "if your sister's anything like you." The fourth glass of wine—or maybe it was the fifth—had erased the shy guy I thought I'd met earlier in the evening.

It's not as if the Virgin Mary appeared in my window to announce that this companion would ever be anyone important in my life, but at that moment I realized that even though I didn't know what to do with Luke, I didn't want to regift him, to my sister or to anyone else.

"Why not, indeed?" I said. "I'll get on it as soon as I'm back."

My first lie.

Luke was dovetailing far too perfectly with my doubts. I needed to shut down, despite the fact that I would have happily jabbered all the way to England. "Better get some sleep," I said. "Supposed to meet my staff tomorrow at eleven to go over two hundred shoot details."

"I'm a babbling idiot," he said. "Sorry." Still, he pulled out an eye mask and put it on. "Do I look like Zorro or just a pathetic perv?" he asked, turning toward me and speaking in a low Jeremy Irons growl. "Are you scared?"

In my wine-addled haze, he looked cuter than a panda with an extra helping of testosterone. "Terrified," I admitted as I burrowed beneath my pashmina tent.

When I woke at dawn, I discovered Luke's legs under the shawl, his feet—in red socks—touching mine. I faked sleep until the flight attendant rocked my shoulder to make sure I was alive.

Those were the days.

# Ten

# DOO-DAH, DOO-DAH

My mother, my father, and Lucy are gathered around the pine farm table in the kitchen, sipping their second cups of black coffee. Light snow stencils the patio and yard, and whatever sun shines over Illinois cowers under menacing clouds.

Since my death, no one in the family has slept past dawn, even after Ambien—which, unfortunately, Costco does not sell over the counter in jars the size of buckets. Lucy took the commuter train north last night and slept in our childhood bedroom—a circa 1985 homage, lilac for me, aqua for her, Madonna posters, now faded, for both of us. She's made this trip for the last two weekends and believes she's here to console my parents, but it's more the other way around. Lucy is alone; my parents have each other. They speak their grief wordlessly—in the car, while my mother massages my father's neck; as he brings the morning newspaper to their bed; when they spoon through cold, fitful nights.

"Don't pick the crumbs off the crumb cake," my mother says.

"Don't treat me like I'm ten."

"Don't start, you two."

*Don't, don't, don't, you two, you two.* The Divine family anthem. *Doo-dah, doo-dah.*

"So, should I call Barry?" Lucy asks. She asked the same question last night at dinner. "I want to know if anything's happened with the case that he hasn't told us."

"No, honey," my mother says. "Dad should do it." I hear her worry that if Lucy asks, Barry will get his back up. Lucy can turn a chat about seasoning hamburger patties into a military engagement.

"It's too early to call New York," my dad says, eyes on the sports pages. He dreads speaking to Barry. *Putz,* he's thinking. My father, I have learned, is not quite the gentleman he presents to the world, but he tries hard to see Barry's side. "Poor guy may be full of himself, but he's still just lost his wife and has to raise a daughter alone," he says to the women in his family, though I suspect it's to convince himself to treat Barry with decency.

The Divines are determined to have Annabel visit for Passover. For the last three years, Barry, Annabel, and I spent Thanksgiving with Kitty and Passover with my parents, so my parents and Lucy feel they own that holiday. Since shiva ended, they call Annabel every night on the dot of seven, but the conversations are as unsatisfying as tickling an insect bite.

"Annabel would be up now," my mother points out. "She'd be watching cartoons."

"But Barry might have gone back to sleep," my father counters. "It's Saturday. Give the guy a break."

"A break?" Lucy shrieks. "What about my sister?"

My mother groans. "We can live without the melodrama, Lucy," she says, looking down at her newspaper and pretending to read. Fatigue mutes her voice. "Dan, call at eight our time."

With deep affection, he salutes her. "Yes, Sarge," he booms.

My family returns to their breakfast, but after a minute Lucy pours her coffee down the drain. "I'm going for a run," she announces, and bolts upstairs. From her small duffel, she plucks out sneakers and several layers of winter-ready sports clothes. While I left behind a wardrobe of girly gear—lace, chiffon, clingy cashmere, low-rise thongs, numerous garments constructed of fabrics better suited to gift wrap, and an unworn pink wool jacket trimmed in lace—Lucy believes in fibers built to withstand a trek from Kathmandu to Everest. If our father were president, her Secret Service code name would be Patagonia.

Lucy pulls her curly hair, the color of dark maple syrup, into a ponytail that bobs beneath a snug knit cap. Its string ties dangle over her ears like the *payes* on a Hasidic rabbi. In a flash of black and purple, without saying goodbye, she's out the door.

Lucy's completed several marathons, which is probably why my equally competitive husband has started training for one. Barry doesn't especially like to run, but what he likes less is my sister outdoing him, and Luce loves to run—in any weather, at any time of day, her gait long and lithe. At a distance, under her gear, a casual observer wouldn't know if she is male or female but would admire her grace.

Sadly, the effect ends as soon as she stops, not so much because her walk is a sturdy clomp but because Lucy is the only person I know for whom exercise becomes foreplay to aggression. After a workout, when most people seem ready to nap, Lucy appears ripe for a fight. The more she runs, the less mellow she becomes.

*At least we can dismiss suicide,* she thinks. *No one would ever think my sister would or could kill herself.* As she hits her stride, she synchronizes every thought with a footfall. *Loved her Annie-bell too much.* She repeats my daughter's nickname in exactly the too-sweet voice I said it in. *A lot to live for.* She starts up a hill. *But Barry could have driven her to it.* She pushes harder. *He'd drive me nuts—he could make any woman ride her bike into the water.* She turns. *Or off a cliff.* She reaches the top. *All marriages are like that.* Picks up the pace. *Men . . . morons.* She's going strong. *Douche bags. Cretins. Fuckers.*

Wind whistles through bare trees as Lucy runs six miles, her mind circling in and out of possibilities. She whips past the diner where our parents treated us to blueberry pancakes every week after Sunday school. Two former high school friends wave—they're continuing the Country Kitchen tradition with their own kids. Lucy looks through them.

"We sent a hundred-dollar fruit basket," one of the young matrons says. "She could at least stop to say hello."

"Run your butt off, Moosey," the other one hisses softly. "If her sister hadn't just died, I'd shout it," she says to her friend.

Lucy is in her own head and wouldn't have heard. *Pills, maybe.* She starts to pant a bit as she begins her last mile. *Or carbon monoxide.* She catches her breath on the home stretch. *But not this way.*

Lucy charges back into the kitchen.

"Where were you?" my mother asks. "You were gone almost an hour."

My sister ignores her as she unlaces her shoes and strips, layer by sweaty layer.

"You'll never guess who called," my father says.

*Molly?* Lucy thinks.

"Barry's mom," my mother says. "Inviting us all to New York for the seder."

Lucy skewers our mother with a stare. "You declined, obviously."

"I thanked her. Said we'd let her know."

"Mom," Lucy snaps. When her face contorts like a gargoyle's, my sister must give her tiny students nightmares. "Why are you such a sucker? It's manipulation. Can't you see that? If Annabel doesn't visit now, a precedent will be set and—"

"Lucy, apologize," my father interrupts, wishing he could be playing poker or listening to his vinyl LPs—Odetta, Buddy Holly, early Bob Dylan—or getting a massage at his golf club, and curses the fact that it's closed through March. He'd like to be anywhere but here, with the difficult daughter, the daughter who rips and rumbles through life, no matter how much she means well, which she usually does.

"Dan, calm down," my mother says. "Lucy has a point. But Kitty claims the trip would upset Annabel. She thinks it's too soon for her to travel, that it will disrupt her schedule. I want what's best for our granddaughter."

"Barry!" Lucy bleats my husband's name as if it's profanity. She's down to her silk long johns and the sports bra that compresses her DDs. My dad looks the other way. "What a wuss. Has his mommy call."

Lucy can't get a rise out of my parents, who've seen it all before. My mother walks to her only living daughter and begins to stroke her matted hair. Lucy shakes off her hand. "I'm calling him myself," she says.

*Eleven*

# REARVIEW MIRROR

In London, I loved that Luke was far more attentive than your usual photographer. He wasn't afraid to ask my opinion, courtship more subtle and effective than roses or the occasional deep, meaningful gaze. "How do you want the shot set up?" "Here or there?" "Think we got it, or do we shoot another roll?" As he picked my brain he would casually touch my arm, the electric whisper of flesh brushing flesh ending almost before it began. He had to notice that I never pulled away.

True to his word, Luke wasn't a partier. Every night he bowed out early. Whether he took dinner in his room or got together with friends—or a woman—he'd never say, and only on the last night did Luke join our posse. "To Molly!" he toasted as the evening began. "Who allowed me to pass through this firing squad barely bruised."

"To Luke," I said, raising my wineglass across the table and admiring his appeal, which was soft enough around the edges for me to believe that he was deep and sensitive. "And beautiful results."

They were. The next week, when my magazine's editor scrutinized our pictures, her praise was like a bath full of bubbles. "I don't know why this Luke Delaney's been wasting his time shooting fashion," she declared. "Put him under contract before someone else does."

By the end of the month she'd signed him. From then on, Luke and I weren't just thrown together on shoots—we began speaking almost every day when we didn't have an actual meeting. There was always a detail over which to obsess: South Beach or Belize? The fussy food stylist or the lazy one who plied us with charm and homemade pumpkin muffins? Brocade love seat or creamy Italian chaise?

This happened just as Brie abandoned modeling—and me, temporarily—for Columbia Law School. While she chewed through contracts and torts, our daily calls dwindled and Luke began standing in as my best friend. At least that's what I told myself. He gave excellent text message and the two of us could soon be mistaken for juniors exchanging gossip in trigonometry class.

Through my rearview mirror, I see that as far as my marriage went, Barry and I were as close to bliss as we were ever going to come—if only I'd recognized it. He didn't worship me, but then again, I didn't see myself as worthy of adoration. He didn't seek my opinions, and that offered a certain relief, since on many topics I'm not sure I would have been confident enough to voice any. He continued to point out flaws I never knew I had—my legs could have been longer from the knee to the ankle or my answers to people's questions shorter. I usually could see his point. Barry and I settled into a routine that may have been a few hallelujahs short of ecstasy but riffed on movies, Sunday night Chinese at Kitty's, and four-course dinners in the company of couples just like us, who owned ten place settings of barely used bone china and dreams to match. Only now do I realize that Barry and I spent virtually no time alone, face-to-face. Not counting bed.

I didn't think of myself as unhappy. I thought of myself as adjusting, and on that I scored an A for effort. If Barry called to say that something had come up, that he'd need to miss dinner, for instance, I wouldn't settle in with a soup bowl full of Raisinets and a large box of tissues. Instead, I'd read an intelligent novel while I ate lean grilled protein, a leafy green vegetable, and a complex carbohydrate. My life felt balanced and whole.

Then Luke got a girlfriend. She wasn't just any girlfriend. Luke started seeing Treena, my assistant, a recent present the publisher wouldn't let me exchange because she was his stepdaughter.

Treena was as fuckable as she was tall, with a jingly laugh you could hear down the hall. She had the kind of innate confidence that beauty breeds and money shines. Her wardrobe, which bore no relationship to her salary, was so ahead of the curve that the week after she broke out something new, which was often, all the other assistants copied her, generally with profoundly painful results. A rumor floated that Treena had a boyfriend, a hedge fund manager. This explains why I paid no heed to the giggly chitchat on her end of the phone whenever Luke called my office.

One night Barry and I were having dinner in the Village with another doctor and his doctor wife. It was a Friday in late June, when outdoor tables fill up first and New Yorkers try to pretend they aren't living in the middle of a malodorous communal steam bath. After dinner, the four of us strolled by Da Silvano, and there was Luke, wound around Treena like a bandage.

"Molly!" Treena called, putting down her glass of prosecco so she could wave an artfully sculpted arm. On her wrist, at least twenty skinny Indian bracelets jangled and didn't even look cheap. "Barry! Hello!" She may as well have been a hunter with a duck call and Barry a brain-damaged mallard. He walked straight toward her, while I lagged behind. Luke froze, or maybe he was simply comatose on account of being skunk drunk. I'll never know, since my first impulse was to feel silly, as if everyone at a party had allowed me to walk around with a price tag hanging off my shirt.

"C'mon—have a drink!" Treena trilled. Luke didn't say a word. I could see that Barry was ready to accept, although there was obviously no room for all of us around their table for two, under which I noticed Luke and Treena's knees touching. But fortunately, our dinner companions had a babysitter at home who was charging more per hour than a plumber, and they weren't eager to drag out the evening. After an exchange of glances with them—not me—Barry shrugged and said, "Another time." There was then so much cheek kissing you'd have thought someone had won a Grammy.

After the goodnights, Barry and I walked to our car. "You never mentioned that your photographer buddy had hooked up with your assistant," he said as we were driving home. His tone drifted in my direction with an edge of condescension overshadowed by curiosity.

"News to me," I admitted. I tried to sound neutral, not furious, which I was slowly realizing I was.

"Lucky schmuck," he said. "Could have sworn he was a *fagele,* though—what do you suppose she sees in him?"

While I tried to parse which part of Barry's question was most offensive, I was asking it in reverse. I didn't have to think hard. Treenas rule the earth.

In the middle of the night I woke from a dream, my teeth clenched so hard my jaw ached. I reached for Barry, and we made love with uncharacteristic roughness and abandon. I stared into his eyes. The face I was seeing was Luke's.

"More, Molly, more!" Barry grunted with each thrust. "Yes, yes!"

*No!* I was thinking as I arched my back and rotated my hips. *No!*

The next morning Barry brought me breakfast in bed—iced coffee and a chocolate croissant on our wedding china, its blue border perfectly matching a hyacinth in a bud vase.

I didn't respond to Luke's calls, text messages, or IMs on Monday, Tuesday, or Wednesday. But on Thursday we had a meeting, where I acted so excruciatingly polite you'd have thought I was having tea with the First Lady. Afterward, Luke pointed this out. "Do you want to talk?" he asked.

"What's there to say? You're going out with my pea-brained assistant and, speaking of peas, didn't have the balls to tell me." I'd like to admit I only thought the second half of the speech, but I actually did say it.

"It just happened," he said.

"Da Silvano takes planning," I said. "Reservations are involved."

"She asked me."

"You didn't say no," I pointed out.

"I'm not sure why we are having this conversation."

*Because I want you all to myself, although I am married and you and I are just friends.* Because. Because. Because. Luke had given me an opening, but this was not a door I was ready to walk through. The only thing I was sure about was my own discomfort.

"No good reason, Luke," I said, and forced a laugh, trying to pretend that I had recovered my sense of humor. "I'm being a possessive bitch. But I wish you'd told me you were seeing Treena. Not that you don't have every right to. But she is my own damn assistant."

"Thank you, Molly Marx, for giving my social life your seal of approval." He spoke this with a particularly corrosive brand of sarcasm.

"Luke, that's enough," I said. "Let's agree I was a baby. A self-centered idiot. I'm sorry."

"Unless you have something else in mind." The expression on his face read, *I double-dog-dare you.*

"Such as?"

"The thing about you, Molly, is that you don't know what you want or who you want it with." He shrugged and walked away. Two days later, he sent a friendly enough text message, as if everything were back to normal. I knew, of course, it wasn't. Everything had changed.

*Twelve*

# KISS, KISS

"There's Snuffleupagus, Mommy." Whenever we passed the sprawling granite outcropping crouched over Central Park, Annabel pointed it out. But today, as she holds Delfina's strong, slim hand, the beast who rules my daughter's imagination doesn't get as much as a glance. She soldiers ahead, silent and grim.

Delfina and Annabel enter the elevator at our synagogue, and the nursery school director swoops down to four-year-old level. "We're so happy to have you back, Annabel," she says. "We've missed you."

Though Annabel used to greet this woman with a giddy grin, she bites her lip and says nothing. When she and Delfina reach the threshold of the classroom on the sixth floor, Annabel turns to Delfina. "Do I have to?" she asks.

"Your friends want to play with you," Delfina says. "And school's your job. We all have our jobs."

Annabel's face carries the worry of an old crone. I wait for tears.

"Your dolls?" Delfina asks. "You're thinking about your dolls?"

Annabel nods.

Delfina bends to whisper. "Can you keep a secret? If you go to school, when I pick you up we'll eat with your friend Ella. It was going to be a surprise."

Annabel allows a small smile to creep across her face and turns to search the classroom. She catches the eye of her best friend, who's already in the playhouse. Ella sees Annabel and runs across the room on her chunky legs. "Annabel!" she shouts. "I'm making pizza. C'mon." Ella towers over my daughter and, in the tradition of anatomy as destiny, considers herself older, wiser, and now responsible for looking after her friend whose mommy died by the river like a character in a goose-pimply Grimm's fairy tale, the ones she won't let her dad read to her anymore.

"See you later, alligator," Delfina says to Annabel, and bends to give her a hug.

"After a while, crocodile," Annabel says. One of her purple mittens is missing, but she hangs her red jacket with the furry trim in her cubby, which features a family picture—Barry, me, Annabel as a toothless baby. Every move is fluid and concise. I hope Barry remembers that I had planned to enroll her in ballet. I am positive she is on the Clara track for *The Nutcracker.*

"I'll be the mommy," Ella says, "and you'll be the girl." They play until the teacher asks all eighteen students to gather in their morning circle. Annabel walks with the rest to the center of the classroom.

"Good morning, class," the teacher says.

"Good morning, Miss Rose," the children sing out.

"Let's talk about what we did this weekend," she says. "Did anything interesting happen to anyone?" A girl raises her hand. "Emily?"

"I saw *Shrek,*" she says.

"Me too," a few others yell.

"Class, we wait until we're called on, remember?" A boy waves his hand as if he's conducting an orchestra; with his wild curls he looks like a vest-pocket-size Simon Rattle. Miss Rose points in his direction.

"My gerbil died," he says.

"Last month we had to put our dog to sleep," another boy says. "He had bad cancer inside him."

I beam down on Annabel, trying to absorb her pain. But Annabel does . . . nothing. She looks at the window and fixates on dust floating in the brilliant morning sun. A few children turn in her direction, but soon Miss Rose calls on Ella. "My babysitter, Narcissa, let me stay up until eleven o'clock," she says.

In the hallway, there's a racket. A mother and child are late for school. "Kiss, kiss, Jordan," the woman says to her son. He is a thin child with sad, deep-set blue eyes and wiry red hair cropped short. He pecks her cheek. The mother is a heavily highlighted brunette whose distinguishing characteristics are very large teeth, very long nails, and very high heels. "Kiss Mommy goodbye." I listen closely. I know that nasal voice.

Stephanie.

I take another lingering peek at Annabel, and while I long to stay and watch her, I cannot resist getting a closer look at this woman who each evening is verbally tucking my husband into bed. I look closely to see if Stephanie was among the unknown bereaved rubbing away their mascara streaks at my funeral, but she looks only vaguely familiar, one of many faces I may have seen milling around the school, waiting to collect a child. Her son enters his classroom and she returns to the elevator.

Downstairs, Stephanie meets another woman, one who has apparently seen *Vertigo* one too many times. The companion has pulled her hair, bleached to platinum, into a French twist, and her sharply tailored gray wool gabardine skirt and jacket recall 1958. She is fiercely attractive, with porcelain skin and carefully reddened lips. Although the weather is brisk, the pair leave their coats open as they walk down the tree-lined street. The height of their heels doesn't prevent them from quickly reaching a coffee shop four blocks away. As they settle into a table near the window, the light betrays Kim Novak. I can see that she is older than I'd estimated, probably early forties. Maybe ten years beyond Stephanie.

"Aren't guys lucky?" Stephanie says. "They can be in the world's worst marriages, but when they lose their wives, the universe genuflects at their doorstep."

"At least you are," the companion says. "What's going on? Did he actually say his marriage sucked?"

Stephanie pauses, sits back in her chair, and looks her friend straight in the eye. "Not exactly, but how good could it have been if he's showing this much interest?" she says, and smiles as she stirs sweetener into her paper cup.

Is this the circulating myth, that Molly Marx's marriage was as dead as she is now?

"He's been showing interest for some time now, actually," Stephanie adds.

I feel as if I've turned into Lucy; I'd like to tear out this Stephanie's eyeballs after I pull off each long eyelash one by one, pee in her vente latte, rage like Tinker Bell on crystal meth. What marriage is a perfectly made bed, never creased or spotted, without its secrets and disappointments? Like a criminal defense lawyer, I long to defend my relationship with Barry, flawed as it may have been, despite what he might have let dribble out in a chance occurrence with a woman, this woman, any woman.

The blonde puts down her coffee, leaving a kiss of MAC Russian Red on its rim. "Steph, you think you might be getting a little ahead of yourself?" she asks. "And why this guy? He's not the only single man in New York, and you're not exactly staying home every night plucking your eyebrows."

"Some women ask why. I ask, why the fuck not?" She shrugs and sips her latte. Her teeth are as white as its foam.

"Has he even asked you out?"

My bullshit meter is going off so loudly I'm surprised they can't hear it.

"He's saying he wants to wait a few weeks, even a few months," Stephanie says. " 'What will people think?' You know me—Ms. Patience." She pauses, examines her nails, and looks up. "I give it two weeks."

"I've been single for three years and had one boyfriend who was sixty-two and dumped me for a salesgirl from Circuit City," the blonde says with what I am fairly sure is affection. "You're single for a year and have—I can't count that high." This surprises me. The blonde wins the beauty bake-off, but I was always an innocent, thinking that perfection had anything to do with lust or, for that matter, love. "You should be teaching a course at the Learning Annex." She looks at her watch, an Ebel I used to covet because four dozen diamonds don't stop it from masquerading as sporty. "Keep me in the loop on this."

"See you at the gym," Stephanie says as her friend collects her shopping bags and walks out the door. "Kiss, kiss."

Stephanie opens her *Times.* She scans the Thursday Styles section, turns to the movie listings, then reaches for her phone and speed-dials Barry's cell phone.

"I know you're probably in surgery," she says, leaving a message. "But I just wanted to tell you I'm thinking about you." She lowers her voice. "All the time. I'm ready whenever you are."

Wolves, I recall, are highly social animals.

*Thirteen*

# PLAYDATE IN PARADISE

W hat kind of old lady goes to bed at seven-thirty?" Luke said, standing in the door of my room.

"The kind who's exhausted." *The kind who's trying to behave.*

"Want to join me?" He had changed into flip-flops, linen pants, and a faded Hawaiian shirt. I was always a sucker for a shirt that says aloha.

It was two months past Treena, who'd become engaged to her Wall Street wizard. Luke and I were on location, this time in a warm, sunny place. On the plane, we chatted like two bubbles at bridge, and I was cheerful as a baboon—until we landed. That's when I discovered that the eight enormous suitcases of borrowed objets d'art I'd schlepped from New York—in case I needed to pull an alabaster statue or two out of my ass to accessorize the house we were photographing—were missing. The bags would be arriving on the same once-daily flight the next afternoon, or so Air Banana promised.

Always one to career toward a worst-case scenario, I was convinced the bags had been delivered to the Bermuda Triangle. Even if they did show up, we'd be getting a late start the next day. Suddenly, I was so tired I couldn't remember my phone number. Luke had to help complete the claim form. I thanked him, but sulked as we drove to the resort where we'd be staying for the next five days, and as soon as we checked in, I escaped to my room. After a call home and a long shower, I emerged smelling like a smoothie—the management had cornered the market on papaya-infused products—but in a vastly improved state. I was looking forward to room service and an early night. That's when I heard a knock on the wall. *Bump-bump-de-bump-bump. Bump. Bump.*

I knocked back, but this time the return knock was at my door. Through the chain lock, I could see Luke wearing a smirk as silly as a party hat.

"Sorry, Molly Marx is closed for the night," I said.

"I know you're young, but you're not eight," he said. "C'mon."

"Nope, I have a rule against drinking anything that pink," I said, pointing to the half-empty glass in his hand.

"House specialty," he said. "A lot more potent than it looks."

Was it bitchy of me to abandon Luke? The rest of our team had arrived the day before yesterday, and they'd left us a note saying they were off to the other end of the island for roast suckling pig. Luke and I were on our own for the evening, and I'd left him stranded. I stood there, barefoot, trying to decide what to do, when he decided for me.

"I love a woman in pajamas," he said, eyeing me up and down.

I was wearing chaste white cotton PJs—it was my mother's tradition to give Lucy and me a matched set every year for our birthday. The cuffs were embroidered with purple pansies. My hair was wet. I laughed and blushed.

"And I love a woman who blushes."

I didn't say what I was thinking: *You've had a few of those drinks already, haven't you, Luke?* But he looked lonely. Or maybe that was my justification machine talking. "Meet you in the bar in fifteen minutes" slipped out instead.

I towel-dried my hair, put on a minute's worth of makeup, and changed into a white eyelet sundress. My vestal virgin image intact, I walked to the resort's outdoor bar. Next to Luke, a drink the color of a lawn flamingo was waiting, its umbrella angled as if it were an index finger pointing at me. *Get with the program, Molly,* it seemed to say.

"Isn't this better than hibernation?" Luke said as I hopped up onto a tall bamboo stool next to him.

"It depends on whether or not this drink comes with food," I said.

Luke got the attention of our server, and a bowl of chilled jumbo shrimp arrived along with a tangy sauce and a basket of crisp fried plantain chips. We nibbled and drank while the sun faded into the horizon over the quietly lapping sea. Steel band music played in the background, its rhythm easing us into the evening. Soon enough, we could count stars in the navy blue sky, and at the outdoor restaurant next to the bar every table glowed with a fat candle. I had one of those moments when I thought I should pay the magazine for allowing me to be their decorating editor. Tonight was a playdate in paradise.

The maître d' led us to a table close to the sand. As I began sipping Champagne—compliments of the house, as thanks for renting six rooms in what was the shoulder of the off-season—I realized I hadn't been this relaxed in weeks. No, longer, much longer.

Luke and I reviewed minutiae, making plans for far more setups than we'd ever be able to squeeze into one day. "This is all assuming the bags show," I said.

"Why do you worry so much?" he asked. In case I missed the point, in his best West Indian accent, he sang "Don't Worry, Be Happy."

"Worrying is my job," I said.

"You do it well," he said. "The job. Not just the first-class fussing."

"As do you." We clinked our crystal flutes.

Luke and I had quickly become, everyone in the industry agreed, a formidable team. He was hot fudge to my vanilla ice cream, and together we became better than each of us alone. We'd already had an offer from another magazine to buy us out of our contracts at the end of the year.

Since we'd been collaborating I'd become more excited about my work than ever. People who haven't tried to explode their creativity might not understand the high that comes through stretching your imagination, but all of this was very important to me. Where a few months earlier I'd basically checked out, now I woke in the middle of the night to scribble and sketch ideas I dreamt. Half of them weren't bad. After a bike ride, when my mind inevitably wandered, I'd usually get on the phone to tell Luke I knew *exactly* what we needed for the next job, right down to the vintage gilt napkin rings, the color of the parrot tulips, and the number of almond-stuffed olives in a bowl.

As we were finishing our dinner—pompano for both of us—and sharing coconut sorbet in a frosty aqua dish, the music gave way to a singer performing the kind of tunes my parents play in the car. What the soloist lacked in talent, he made up in enthusiasm. "Dis next song is for de lovers," he said, his gold tooth flashing. Luke and I, who'd finished our Champagne, wore the kind of dopey smiles common to people who flunk Breathalyzer tests.

"Do you wanna dance under de moonlight?" the singer crooned. His rendition crossed the Beach Boys with John Lennon, but the slow calypso beat was all his own. "Hug and kiss all through de night, now. Oh baby, do ya wanna dance?" As he repeated choruses of "wanna wanna wanna" he boogied over to us and motioned for Luke and me to get up on the tiny, empty dance floor. Luke stood.

I hesitated. I didn't trust myself in Luke's embrace. But his look beguiled. I got up to join him, stumbling in my most stratospheric sandals. He grabbed me and held me close. I could feel his heart beating, and within a few minutes, I realized our hearts were beating together. He felt pleasantly warm and smelled of citrusy aftershave, his own sweet sweat, and papaya body scrub. As I swayed in his arms—I was more than a little dizzy—I nestled my head in his neck and tried to name the other fragrance I was picking up. What was that bottom note? I knew that smell, that perfect smell. As the song ended, I figured it out. Desire.

"Do you wanna?" he whispered.

I did.

"I know I do," he continued. The three-piece orchestra had struck up a quicker beat, but we were still moving in slow motion. I, for one, didn't want anything about that night to move fast.

He locked his fingers in mine and rubbed them gently. The gesture was both tender and erotic. "I'm waiting for an answer," he whispered.

"I'm too tired."

My second lie.

"Then just come to my room and sleep."

"Sleep?"

"I'd like to know how that would feel." I'm not sure if Luke spoke those words or if I just thought them, if he was reading my mind or if I was reading his.

Conventional wisdom suggests that infidelity is about punishing the husband or the wife. I beg to differ, and always did, starting that night. It's too late now to sort this out with Dr. Stafford, my marriage counselor. More's the pity, since last month our health insurance certified Barry and me for ten more sessions. In our therapy, which we went to for several months, I always claimed that I never got involved with another man to get back at him. Well, it's past my dying day, and that's my story and I'm sticking with it. Luke was never, ever the not-Barry. He was always Luke, with his own magnetic field. I can't explain why I was drawn to Luke Delaney. Why does someone love the color orange or a Mozart sonata? I just was.

People who contemplate an affair imagine or pretend that they are on their own little islands, encapsulated in a romantic snow globe, safe from reality. The fact was, Luke and I had indeed landed in Margaritaville. We were literally on an island, fifteen hundred miles away from home, good common sense, and, on that evening, sobriety.

Did Barry have not-Mollys? It's my guess that throughout our engagement and marriage he felt intercourse was compulsory with at least a half dozen women who weren't me. I never tried to prove this in a court of law—only once did I snoop through receipts—yet at some level I always knew he was a cheater and I looked away from it. But this wasn't what was on my mind that night. At the moment when Luke took my hand to walk me to his room, I was thinking only about Luke. Well, condoms and Luke. Carefree I am not.

At his door, he fumbled with his keys. The maid had turned down the quilt, set the rattan ceiling fan to a lazy whirl, and put two chocolates on the pillow. He unwrapped one chocolate and put it in my mouth. I did the same for him. The evening was cool now—it was past midnight—and he lit a candle. The flame danced in the room like a trailer for a romantic French movie.

I kicked off my sandals as he slipped off his shirt and pants. He had a long torso and, even though he was thin, small love handles that only seemed to make him more real and, thus, more appealing. As I closed my eyes, the patch of dark hair on his chest made me think once again of the Bermuda Triangle. Was I getting lost or being found?

*Fourteen*

# MAYBE, BABY

"Molly, I've been thinking it over," Barry said. We'd decided to start with cocktails at the Four Seasons and follow with dinner at Tao. "But first . . ." He signaled for a server. "Two martinis, please," he said. "Grey Goose."

For a woman whose idea of drinking used to center on scouting wine stores for the most ironically labeled under-$15 pinot grigio, I was relieved that courage was on its way in a stemmed glass. Had Barry actually picked that night to say he didn't think things were working out? It was, after all, our first anniversary.

On a scale of 1 to 10, I gave our wedded life a 5. Straight down the middle, Jack and Jill Doe average. I'd recently read on a tarot card website that only 8 percent of married couples believe their partner is a true soul mate. I'm no math whiz, as my SATs verified, but factoring in today's divorce rates, this means that it's the rare bride who connects with a groom who instinctively puts his hand *there* and stars in the X-rated fantasies that top her playlist.

Barry and I seemed on par with every other married couple we knew. In our three sessions of required premarital counseling, the rabbi singled out sex and money as the sinkholes that swallow most relationships. As far as I could see, we had no terminal problem with either. In fact, since we didn't go in for smarmy public displays of affection, I thought we could definitely expect a longer shelf life than the husband and wife with whom we socialized who practically copulated on the table every time they invited us to dinner. In their shiny condo with its gleaming bamboo floor, I always suspected we'd been summoned to bear witness to their libido as much as to the panoramic city view from the floor-to-ceiling windows on the thirty-third floor.

While I busily categorized myself as garden-variety married, someone might wonder if I conveniently overlooked what had happened with Luke six weeks earlier. Not exactly. After that business trip, I shelved my memory of *l'affaire Luc* in the contemporary women's fiction aisle of my brain. Our fling, I told myself, was meaningless and it was over. I told no one, not even Brie.

Maybe I was wise beyond my years and understood that every union is like a mixed-breed puppy adopted from a shelter: you have no idea how it will turn out until it grows up. That night, in a hotel lounge, Barry was looking as if he had a lot of sleek Labrador retriever in him, with maybe some Tibetan terrier and giant schnauzer. No pit bull in sight. He was wearing all black—well-tailored jacket, fine cotton shirt, lizard belt, jeans—and, fortunately, the effect was more European art snob than Johnny Cash. His nose kept him from being pretty-boy handsome, but with his wavy black hair and dark brown eyes fringed by lashes that rightly should have belonged to me, the overall effect of Dr. Barry Marx was striking. His bravado finished the package.

"To us," he said, raising his glass.

"Us," I echoed as we clinked. "You and me."

"First, I want you to have this," he said, handing me a Bergdorf's bag, always a promising receptacle, especially if small. I carefully opened the box, where a velvet pouch revealed a sterling silver cuff incandescent with quartz stones big as pistachios. Had I been auditioning for the part of goomar, the bracelet would have been a fine accessory. My first thought, however, was that Kitty had selected it.

"Wow," was all I could say. "This is really unexpected." I'd been hoping for a gift, of course, and had done my best to hint about a two-foot shell-encrusted obelisk I'd been ogling in a dusty Village antique shop. But what I imagined would add considerable panache to our coffee table, perhaps Barry saw as competitively phallic. I admired the bracelet, tried to glisten with appreciation, and castigated myself for being ungrateful. Chances were Barry was going to hate the blue enameled cuff links I'd bought for him. Now that I thought about it, I wasn't even sure he liked French-cuffed shirts.

"You deserve it, baby," he said, slipping the present on my wrist. Was he trying to see his reflection in its luster? "And speaking of babies," he added, "it's time, Molly."

In a screenplay, the look on Barry's face would read "long, meaningful gaze." For me, it'd be "sheer, frozen panic."

Some couples chew over the baby question endlessly before they even get engaged. These must be the same people who organize their shoes in transparent boxes, rush their annotated tax prep to an accountant by January 31, and get around to ordering their wedding album. There are also men and women who understand exactly where they stand on parenthood, even if they've only discussed it with their shrinks, as well as husbands and wives who haven't figured out the answer but welcome bright-eyed, bushy-tailed dialogue on the subject. Barry and I fit into none of these categories.

"I'm not sure I feel adult enough to be anyone's mother," I admitted.

"Oh, c'mon," he said. "You'll be a great mommy." His tone was jocular.

In our family, it was Lucy who'd majored in kids—bossing younger children in the neighborhood, working every summer as a camp counselor, teaching nursery school. She loved every child, and they returned the affection.

"Whenever anyone asked me to babysit, I always pleaded term paper," I said. "I'm not maternal."

Barry let loose such a loud, incredulous "Ha!" that people at the next table turned to see if someone required the Heimlich maneuver. "Molly, listen. It's an open secret that most parents only appreciate their own flesh and blood and think other people's kids are sniveling rugrats."

"That's a penetrating observation, Barry," I said, fairly sure he might be right. But what if I didn't like my own child? What if my child didn't like me?

The previous year, I'd volunteered as a reading tutor. My first-grade charge insisted on *Hairy Scary Spiders*. I can still hear his creepy falsetto lip-synching: "My net catches an insect. I kill it with a simple bite. I crash and grind the insect's body with my steel jaws and pulverize it into juice. Dinner is served." An innocent bug in a tarantula's net. I was feeling that way at the moment.

"But I don't know how to be a mom." What if I couldn't understand or slept through my baby's ear-piercing patois? Got revolted by spit-up? I especially didn't want to think about the effect of forty-five extra pounds on my stomach, which wasn't concave even now, or how a nine-pound infant was going to pop out of my nether regions. "May I have another martini, please?" I asked the server.

"Molly, you're being ridiculous—do you think my mother knew how to be a mother?" The answer to that question did not bolster Barry's argument. He gamely switched tactics. "You'll be like your mother," he said.

"I could never be as good a mother as my mother," I snapped back. Who could? Claire Divine is warm and patient. I am the definition of impatience, and although I could be kind enough to deserving parties, Barry liked to point out that people often took me for aloof. When I suggested that these hypersensitive types were sadly unable to discern shyness in a grown woman, I saw his skepticism.

As I finished my second drink, overcome by insecurities I never knew I had, I began to feel claustrophobic, despite the bar's towering ceiling. I was pleased when Barry called for the tab and we moved on. As we entered Tao, a sixteen-foot-tall Buddha gazed down on us. I implored him to tell me what to do, but all Buddha-boy seemed to say was, *Order the Peking duck for two*. We did, and switched to our usual dinner talk, Barry's tales from the operating room, which kept us going through a calorie blitz called a Zen Parfait. I passed on the giant fortune cookie. What fortune had in store for me I would gladly wait to discover.

"How about a Chai Kiss?" Barry said, looking at the menu of after-dinner drinks.

"How about home to Jane Street?" I said. In the taxi, I closed my eyes and leaned against Barry's well-muscled body. With the help of a good romp in bed, perhaps I could talk my husband into postponing baby making for a few years—maybe a decade—and during that time grow up and figure out what I wanted.

At our apartment, still blurry from all I'd had to drink, I slipped into a blue silk teddy. Barry pulled me toward him tightly. He was in the locked and loaded position. "Happy anniversary, sweetheart," he whispered hotly into my ear. "Molly Divine Marx, you will be a wonderful mother."

I looked at him, sleepily and skeptically.

"I don't know very much," he said, "but I know that."

There was something about the way he said those words that felt utterly tender and authentic. I deeply wanted to believe him, to live up to them, to feel sure about this step that for most women isn't even a choice. "Really?" I asked, a prayer as much as a question. In that moment, I felt that marrying Barry Marx was the smartest and best move I had ever made.

As he blew out the candle I kept by the bed, and the scent of lily of the valley filled our small room, he said, "Let's make a baby, baby."

Months later, we did.

## Fifteen

# PIECE OF WORK

Detective Hicks stretches his long legs and scans the room. Sitting on a black leather Eames chair, he might be taken for another sleek minimalist object in Brie and Isadora's loft. "Ms. Lawson, was that reading of yours at Mrs. Marx's funeral by Elizabeth Barrett Browning?" he asks, as if he honestly cares about Victorian poetry.

"Emily Dickinson," Brie says. She's wearing her Jessica Rabbit–goes-to-court suit, bought to scare the nuts off opposing counsel. It has a tight jacket, strategically unbuttoned to show a peek of cleavage. The pencil skirt, which hugs her butt, ends just below her knees. Her hair is pulled back into a severe chignon. Isadora sits beside her on the couch, a wrinkle that I've never noticed etching a delicate valley between her slightly hooded hazel eyes.

"I knew it was one of those depressed women," the detective says, helping himself to chocolate biscotti that Isadora has set out on a square white china plate. "Now, I gather from Mrs. Marx's funeral that you two were close," he says. "Can you tell me a little about the . . . relationship?" The question is directed to Brie, but he glances toward Isadora as he drops a crumb, which disappears into the thick charcoal rug. Isadora's wrinkle deepens as she sees the biscotti bit vanish, but Brie looks straight at Hicks.

"Molly and I were randomly assigned as freshman roommates," she says. "It was one of those fortunate matches. We hit it off and became inseparable. The next year we got an apartment together and kept it until we graduated."

"Can you elaborate?" Hicks' eyes wear an amused expression, in which Brie is reading a taunting, sub rosa suggestion. Which is his intention, to tick her off. *Don't fall for it.* I beam this message with the futile hope that Brie can hear it.

"We did what college friends do," she says. "Study, shop, party."

In reverse order, as I recall.

"Anything else?" he asks.

"Sure," Brie says, "eat pizza, gain ten pounds, diet, meet guys, root for the home team, take vacations in skimpy bikinis, and try not to think about what we'd do when we grew up. Should I go on?" As she reels off this list, the speed of her speech picks up, as does the pitch of her voice. I am surprised that Brie is allowing frustration to show. Don't they teach keeping cool in law school?

"Ms. Vega, would you mind if I had a few moments alone with Ms. Lawson, please?" asks Hicks. Isadora stands and smooths away nonexistent creases on her sleeveless black dress, in which she manages to appear as dignified as a head of state despite the fact that it clings to her tiny waist and curvy hips. Isadora possesses the kind of beauty that generally requires a passport. We were the same height, but she looks a head taller than I ever felt. On the middle finger of her right hand, a ring featuring a large, lemony stone—I have no idea if it's a rare diamond or a hunk of glass—reflects the afternoon light.

"As you wish," she says, and walks into the bedroom and closes the door. Hicks and I both know that through the wall Isadora can hear much of what's said.

"So, Ms. Lawson, what's that phrase people use nowadays? Friends with benefits? Did that apply to you and Mrs. Marx?" I'm getting the feeling that he is going out of his way to offend.

Brie scowls ever so slightly. "No, Molly and I were always friends," she says. "No 'benefits.' " She signals quotation marks with her fingers, her manicure a flawless taupe.

Hicks says . . . nothing.

"In those days I had boyfriends," she adds, although he hasn't asked.

"Thank you for the clarification, Ms. Lawson," he says. "Now, let's see. How would you describe the state of Mrs. Marx's marriage?"

Brie shifts from left to right and back again. "You never really know what's going on in another relationship."

It sounds reasonable to me, but all Hicks says is, "Ms. Lawson, the question, please?"

"They weren't exactly one of those couples with a joint mission statement tucked away in a drawer, but in their own way Barry and Molly were devoted and well matched. He was very caught up with work, has a difficult mother, and could be a flirt, but I always thought Molly took it all in stride. He's a loving, doting daddy, and I know that meant a lot to her. She and Annabel were his home port. His heart. She knew that."

*Tell me something I don't know,* Hicks thinks. *Did Barry kill his wife? Was she cheating on him? Was he cheating on her and did he want Molly out of the picture? Did this lawyer lady do it, or maybe the jealous señorita in the next room?*

"Barry criticized Molly, but I always read it as affectionate teasing, and assumed Molly did, too," Brie added. "He'd never hurt Molly, if that's what you're wondering."

"Because he loved her?" Hicks asks.

"Well, that," Brie says, "yes, of course—that's a given—and . . ." Brie hesitates.

"Go on," Hicks say.

"Because I imagine that any kind of brutality would effectively terminate his career." She makes an odd noise. It's her nervous laugh, a dry, low gurgle.

"How so?"

"Detective, women are pretty damn scared to go under the knife—can you imagine using a cosmetic surgeon rumored to be a butcher?" *A goddamn butcher* is what Brie thinks.

"Interesting," Hicks says. He gets up from the Eames chair and moves to the far end of the low burnt orange sofa across from its twin, where Brie is sitting. From this spot, the view of her legs is even better.

"And Mrs. Marx—did she love her husband?" he says, picking up a book, a biography of Maxwell Perkins, which he absentmindedly pages through and puts down while he waits for Brie's answer. "Didn't that guy always wear a hat to work? Maybe I should start that."

"Without a doubt, yes," Brie shoots back, and I'm not sure if she means the hat or is answering Hicks' question. "Barry could get to her, but he was also her flotation device." *Where in the hell did I come up with that term?* Brie is asking herself. And why is she so sure about this? I wonder.

"Her what?" the detective asks. Now he's interested.

"I always thought Molly pretended her marriage was worse than it was. Some sort of self-deprecating shtick."

But Brie has it wrong. I think she wanted my marriage to be better than I presented it. Brie was the kind of friend sure enough about herself that she didn't need my happiness to be less so she could convince herself that hers was more.

"Can you elaborate?" Hicks asks.

*I wish I could,* Brie thinks. *I wish I had evidence.* "Just a sense I had."

Did Brie take me for a big, empty complainer?

"Tell us about the last time you saw Mrs. Marx," Hicks says.

"It was a bike ride. Remember when we had that string of sixty-degree days in February?"

Global warming. I wonder if I'll be around to see how that plays out.

Hicks removes a black leather notebook from his jacket pocket and scribbles in it. "You mention that the husband's family was . . . what was your word, 'difficult'?"

"Molly got along with them fine," she says, although she knows that Kitty only tolerated me, sometimes politely. "The same with her parents and sister."

"The sister," Hicks says. "What's up with her?"

"Excuse me?" Brie asks.

"At the service . . . you don't think she was a little intense?"

"It was her twin sister's funeral," Brie says, icy. "How was she supposed to act?"

"Okay," he says. "Sorry if I'm outta line. But what about the sisters? Were they close?"

"Do you have a brother or sister, Detective?" Brie asks. "You know how it goes. Sometimes you love them, and sometimes you wish your mother had drowned them at birth." As soon as the words fly out of her mouth, Brie regrets them. "The thing with Molly and Lucy is they knew how to press each other's buttons, but they were very tight." *They loved each other,* Brie thinks. *Lucy worshipped Molly. Molly was in awe of Lucy.*

"Were you and Lucy tight, too?" he asks.

Brie pauses. She always found Lucy smug and provincial, probably because she knew Lucy found her smug and pretentious. "Mutually respectful," she says.

Hicks chuckles ever so slightly.

Isadora walks out of the bedroom carrying a large handbag. I can't take my eyes off it—black leather embossed with swirling flowers, possibly even a canary. She walks to Brie, puts her arm around her shoulder, and grazes her lips with a kiss.

Hicks seems to be enjoying the show. He grins. "Well, we'll be winding things up soon here, Ms. Lawson," he says. "Just a few more questions. Where were you the night that your friend died?"

Brie squeezes her eyes shut, trying to stop the onset of tears. "I was working," she said. "In Brazil."

*When I was bowling in the Bronx,* Hicks thinks. "Anything else you'd like to tell me?"

Brie looks pale and tired. A lock of dark hair falls out of her chignon, and she brushes it away from her face. "Nothing I can think of."

"Okay, then," Hicks says. "Just one more thing. Do you know a Luke?" He pulls out the notebook again. "Luke Delaney?"

"Luke Delaney," she says. "Yes—yes, I do. We met years ago, when I was a model."

*A model,* Hicks thinks, not surprised. "And what was Mr. Delaney's relationship to Mrs. Marx?" he asks.

"Work associates. He's a photographer."

"That's all you want to tell me?" he asks.

Brie finds her courtroom game face. "That's all I know."

Hicks gets up and shakes Brie's hand. I am fairly certain he holds her palm for a moment longer than necessary, but I can't be held accountable for my observations, because the mention of Luke, whom I have refused to think about, has my mind in orbit.

"If there's anything else that you remember, here's my card," the detective says. He's switched his tone to neutral pointing toward cordial, presses the card into Brie's hand, and walks out the door. His rear view is possibly his best angle.

After he leaves, she steps to a desk and puts the card in the skinny, empty drawer on the right. *Hiawatha Hicks,* it reads. She says the name out loud. "Hiawatha?" The laugh that fills the loft is the laugh I remember, and from where I am, we laugh together.

*Sixteen*

# BAD BANANA

*B*arry?" Lucy said. "I hope I didn't wake you." The truth is that Lucy wishes she could haunt his dreams as a blood-sucking, scythe-wielding vampire. Furthermore, it's Sunday morning, and if he's not up now, at nine o'clock, my sister will surely mark it in the ledger she keeps of Dr. Barry Marx's scurviest sins.

"Who's calling, please?" Barry says. He sounds winded, which doesn't surprise me, because although it's raining heavily, he has just come in from a run. Standing in a baseball cap and poncho, he drips water on our kitchen floor. Barry knows the caller is Lucy: our voices were the only thing about us that was virtually identical, and I doubt he thinks I've rung him up from the grave to tell him he forgot to buy the right kind of milk (organic, 2 percent)—something he's done.

"Your favorite sister-in-law," Lucy announces.

Barry takes a moment to think, *Big-tit bitch.* "Good morning, Lucy," he says. "To what do I owe the pleasure?" He sounds even, pleasant, as behooves a well-paid surgeon. Shortly after we were married, he worked for a few months with a speech consultant in order to soften the New York in his vowels. My idea.

*You don't like me and I don't like you—let's not pretend,* Lucy thinks. "I want to make arrangements for Passover," she spits out. "I'll fly into New York, pick up Annabel, and bring her to Chicago for the beginning of her vacation. I'm off myself, so it's easy for me to swing, and I can spend the whole week with her."

"Continue."

"My parents will fly her back," Lucy says, encouraged. "We have a lot of plans—the Field Museum, American Girl Place, the two seders, of course. And matzo brei on the first morning of Passover—Divine tradition."

"Uh-huh."

"Do I take that as a yes?" She is working to keep the exchange breezy but on a pad of paper is drawing circles, heavy and black with her worry.

"Lucy, it's not going to happen," Barry says. "Your dad mentioned something about this, but Annabel's therapist thinks it's too much for her to travel so soon."

Lucy says, "Annabel's therapist?" at the same time as I think it. She has a pediatrician and a dentist. Since when does my daughter have a therapist?

"I've had several consultations with a highly credentialed colleague who specializes in childhood grief," Barry says.

"Oh, really?" Lucy says. "Who might that be?"

"Joseph," Barry says.

"Joseph who?" Lucy asks. She is sitting in front of the computer that my parents keep on the kitchen counter and has already called up Google.

"Joseph is the last name."

"What's his first name?" Lucy asks briskly.

"Why is this important?"

"I asked you a fair question."

"Okay," he says. "Stephanie."

Unfortunately, Lucy can't hear me snort.

"Well, the Divine family has consulted a therapist as well," Lucy lies. "And our highly credentialed expert from the University of Chicago who specializes in early-childhood trauma says that to deprive Annabel of contact with her maternal family right now will be . . ." Lucy takes a second to think. "Would have long-term, reverberating negative consequences."

"Reverberating, huh?" Barry says. "So, Luce, should we have our therapists meet in Central Park for a duel? Plenty of room to reverberate there."

Annabel walks into the kitchen in her nightgown. Her toenails sparkle, the handiwork of Delfina, who left for church this morning as soon as Barry walked through the door after his run. He's been paying her extra to sleep in the apartment every night.

My daughter puts her half-empty bowl of Cheerios in the sink and wanders over to her father. "Daddy?" she says. "Daddy?" The word flutters from her mouth. "I can't find my Dora DVD. *Fairy Tale Adventure.* I need it. Where is it?"

Barry would have a better chance of finding God. "Lucy," he says, "Annabel's here. Gotta go."

"Is that Aunt Moosey?" Annabel asks. When she smiles, her dimple shows. "Can I talk to her?"

"Barry, put Annabel on," Lucy says. The breezy tone has blown away; she's defaulted to shrill with a 70 percent chance of shit storm. The circles she's doodling have grown as thick as snakes and fill a page of legal pad.

"Not a good time," Barry says. "Annabel and I are heading out in five minutes." His eyes settle on a wall calendar decorated with a lioness and her cubs. "We're going to the zoo."

"I didn't know we were going to the zoo." Annabel examines the rain pounding the windows in almost horizontal freefall. Even a three-year-old can look dubious. "And I want to talk to Aunt Moosey."

"Just put her on for a minute," Lucy says. Google has coughed up a few Stephanie Josephs—two attorneys, a hipper-than-thou teenage blogger, and an Atlanta podiatrist.

"Hang on," he tells her. "There's a call." Barry puts Lucy on hold. "Are your ears burning?" Barry asks.

"Not my ears," Stephanie says. She sounds sultrier on a rumpled Sunday morning than I ever did on my most torrid Saturday night.

"You're a therapist, right?" he asks.

"Was," she says. "Two careers ago. Social worker at a geriatric center. Dentures, Depends—not my thing," she laughs. "May I ask where this conversation is going?"

"Not important," he says. "You were saying?"

"I took one look at this storm and had a vision for this afternoon," she says. "Jordan and Annabel could watch cartoons, and we could do . . . whatever."

"Whatever, huh?" he says, talking quietly. "I lettered in whatever in college. How did you know?"

Annabel tugs his hand. "The zoo, Daddy?" she says. "When are we going?"

"Honey, can't you see it's raining?" he says. "And that I'm on the phone?"

"I want to talk to Aunt Moosey! I want to find Dora!" Her face is getting red.

My eyes dart back and forth between Chicago and New York. Left on hold, Lucy sticks out her lower lip and glowers.

My father walks into the kitchen just as she slams down the phone. "Take it easy, partner," he says. "What's wrong?"

Lucy runs upstairs and when she gets to the hallway outside our former bedroom door shouts, "That sleazoid thinks he can have things any way he fucking wants. Well, he better think again." My father stares at his grown daughter with the look men get when they're stuck in an estrogen choke hold.

"Boyfriend trouble again, sweetie?" he shouts back.

My sister slams the bedroom door.

In my New York kitchen, Barry is savoring every detail of the description Stephanie offers up of the afternoon's prix fixe. "Think about it, Dr. Marx," she says, her mind bouncing between the equal appeals of Barry's big dick and big bucks. "Raindrops on the windowpanes, jazz or opera—your pick—and a side trip to the bedroom for as long as you want. Should I go on?"

"Oh yeah, baby—do," Barry says while he idly plays with the curls on Annabel's head. She tugs on his sleeve. He bends over to give her a kiss.

"Daddy," she says loudly, "the zoo! When are we going? And you need to find my Dora DVD, 'member?"

"You're not seriously thinking of going to the zoo, are you?" Stephanie asks.

"*Fairy Tale Adventure*'s my best favorite." Annabel is hanging on Barry's leg. "I want to watch it before we go."

"No, not now," Barry says.

"Are you talking to me, Bear?" Stephanie says. Kitty calls Barry "Bear." Which is why I never did.

"Daddy! I want to see the part where the mean witch puts Boots to sleep."

"Bear, you there?"

Annabel begins to stamp her feet. "Stephanie, actually, maybe this isn't a good time," Barry says. "Call you later?"

She laughs. "Certainly. Promise?"

"Promise," he says as he clicks off, measured seduction replaced by exasperation.

"Dora needs to turn into a True Princess to wake Boots up," Annabel says, dissolving into tears. "He *has* to wake up. He's Dora's best friend. He has to."

"What happened to her friend, honey?" He pulls our daughter onto his lap.

"Daddy—you know!" she wails. "He ate a bad banana. Very, very bad." As a new torrent of tears bursts, Annabel's nose drips on her nightgown, a ribbon of mucus catching on one ear of Alfred the bunny. "We're not going to the zoo, are we?"

"No, kitten, I don't think that's such a great idea," Barry says, trying unsuccessfully to use his nylon poncho to wipe her nose. "Not today."

"You lied!" Annabel says. "You always lie!" As she flies out the door, letting it slam behind her, I am seeing Lucy, circa four years old: my sister a powerhouse, especially next to me, as passive as a sugar cookie. I watch helplessly, in awe of Annabel's will. How will Barry ever manage her alone?

"God damn it, Molly—what the fuck do I do now?" Barry says, clenching his fists. He puts his head down on the kitchen table and softly bangs his forehead several times. I see tears, though whether they are from grief or frustration I cannot say. "Molly, you weren't supposed to die. You weren't supposed to die."

I forgot that someone could yell and cry simultaneously.

I hurt for my Annie-belle, who has lost her mommy. I hurt for my sister, Lucy, for how hard it must be to be her. I hurt for my parents, who have been forced to surrender half their heart. I hurt for all of them and I hurt for me, because I miss every one of these tortured people whom I love and whom I've left behind, broken and bleeding. I hurt for how much I miss my life. I would gladly go to the zoo in the rain and muck; I would stand in shit and sleep in wet straw and smell terrible smells, just to be alive for another day.

But what surprises me most is that I am feeling something new. The emotion is a foreign spice whose name I don't even know and that I can't decide if I like. I am feeling something for Barry.

I am so fixated, I barely notice Bob standing beside me. "Sometimes," he says, "it's best not to watch. Or listen." But I wave him away. I can't stop doing either.

# Seventeen

# LEMON TART

B eets?" Barry said. "Again?"

When I was pregnant, I had a fetish for beets, which until then I'd bought only in cans and only on sale. Barry started calling me "the Beet Queen," which I took as a compliment, not so much because a novel by that name was one of my favorites, but because fresh beets suddenly struck me as the ultimate root vegetable, food my Middle European great-grandmother must have grown and cooked. I felt as if all the beets I was consuming were allowing me to reconnect with my ancestors. This, I guess, is what pregnancy does to some women.

"I found a new way to make them," I assured Barry as I tied a starched white chef's apron around my eight-and-a-half-months-pregnant girth. "From Nigella." If I had had a girl crush, it would have been on a woman like Nigella Lawson, who, even though her last name is Brie's, reminds me of Lucy, if my sister had a cultivated BBC accent instead of a Chicago honk. Freud would have a chuckle with that one, so forget the crush. But I'd made Nigella's beet, dill, and mustard seed salad at least eight times.

Barry grabbed three big red onions and started juggling, which along with performing surgery and manual foreplay starred in his skill set. After a two-minute routine, he parked the onions on the counter, came up behind me, and gave me a long hug, pressing his warm palms on the spot where our baby had, for the moment, stopped doing flip turns. His erection pressed against my behind.

"You're in a good mood," I said, not that such a mood was unusual lately. We were getting along exceedingly well. Throughout my pregnancy, Barry's disposition had rarely dipped below good and occasionally spiked off the charts, and his sex drive seemed to increase as gestation progressed.

"I'm enjoying this new domestic you," he said, scanning the recipe in the opened cookbook. As he started to chop fresh mint, I breathed in the picnicky fragrance and had a sudden yen for a tall glass of lemonade. Had it not been past eight on a Saturday night, I might have begged Barry to run out and buy enough lemons to fill a jug with a homemade brew, but I was hungry. The table was set with rustic pottery, chunky amber goblets just right for his wine and my water, and beeswax candles, waiting to be lit. I still had to finish our pasta, a simple recipe heavily reliant on pecorino Romano.

As peak experiences go, there are some women who find pregnancy overrated. Seeing your butt, once hard and high, swell into a beach ball you know will deflate and sink; finding your nose spread across your face; watching tributaries fan out from bulging varicose veins—I was determined not to notice such things happening to me. I was too distracted by the good stuff, like my brand-new, God-given cleavage, which I showcased at all hours in deep V-neck clothes so clingy they literally stretched the boundaries of good taste and should have been labeled Slut Mommy.

During the winter, as my bump grew, it felt cozy and efficient to be a baby-making machine. I was awed by the knowledge of cells multiplying inside of me like disciplined Marines, and I indulged in cup after cup of steaming cocoa, ignoring the verboten caffeine, reminding myself I required the calcium. Every weekend, I settled on the couch wrapped in cuddly cashmere with grilled cheese sandwiches, spending long afternoons watching Turner Classic Movies and memorizing name books.

Barry wanted a boy. He was sure it was a boy. Kitty analyzed my body—the baby bulge staying relatively narrow—and declared that yes, it would definitely be another Marx heir, since I looked like she did while pregnant with Barry. I interpreted this to mean that I was one of those rare attractive pregnant ladies, since when Kitty favorably compares your appearance to hers it is the highest form of flattery.

Barry insisted on a strapping name, a manly name, a name like a power drill. He tossed off my suggestions—Dylan, Devin, Jesse, Sebastian, Nicholas, Eliah, Raphael, Oliver, Graham, Kieran—like small, twee doilies in favor of Hank, Jake, Cal, Kurt, Max, Nat, Bart, Tom, Abe, and Zack, stopping just short of Thor. I let him know I thought his choices were the kind of names wit-challenged pet owners bestow on Chihuahuas. We ultimately agreed on Alexander William, but when I suggested that Master Marx could be Sasha for short, Barry made a unilateral decision: if the baby was a boy, we would go with William Alexander. Given the remote possibility that we would produce a girl, Barry, marinating in his testosterone, graciously said I could pick whatever name I wanted for this unlikely female offspring.

*William Alexander.* It was a solid, multitasking name. William Alexander Marx, spelling bee king, bar mitzvah boy, Phi Beta Kappa, juris doctor, and Supreme Court justice. Will Marx, captain of the squash team, not a pimple in sight. Wild Willy Marx, starting pitcher for the Yankees. Billy Marx, renegade indie film director, winner of the Palme d'Or at Cannes. William A. Marx, Ph.D., curer of AIDS or cancer, possibly both. President William Alexander Marx, the first Jew in the White House.

I sometimes let my mind wander to William Alexander's future sibling: Daniel James.

They'd be the Marx brothers, just as wicked, only gorgeous. But living with a sextet of balls—what would that be like? How do you change a boy's diaper without getting a squirt of pee in the eye? Would a small male and I have anything to chat about? What if he was one of those perpetually moving children who start downing Ritalin before solid food? For a number of weeks I felt uniquely unqualified to be the mother of even one son. I warmed to the idea of having a boy, though, when I considered that he might be as attentive to me as Barry is to Kitty, calling at least once a day.

I never focused much on the reality of there being an actual person inside my body, and I learned to keep visions at bay of future projectile vomiting. I was shocked when people expected to hear me opine on points I'd never considered, like whether I'd let the baby watch the Wiggles, a quartet whose popularity I learned rivaled that of the Beatles, despite the fact—or maybe because of the fact—that they perform "Hava Nagila" in Bavarian folk costume.

I wasn't in a hurry for my pregnancy to end. It was a contentment zone I'd never before imagined or visited. Tonight I sang "I'm a Woman" as I finished cooking our meal—"W-O-M-A-N"—putting the pasta in a big white bowl, snowing the top with even more cheese. I could picture the calcium going straight to my baby's tiny, precious bones, making them hard as diamonds.

Sure, there had been morning sickness, when I'd catapulted from cabs to lose my breakfast in the gutter while enduring withering stares from fellow New Yorkers. Nighttime leg cramps woke me, and my shrieks scared the bejesus out of Barry, although, as a doctor, he was able to massage away the cramps, for which I was grateful. Nor was I immune to belching, backaches, or cravings for mashed potatoes laden with the caramelized goop that KFC calls gravy. Twice I dreamt that my baby was Satan's child, with translucent skin and beady, marble eyes. I also grew sensitive to odors. Barry's oral hygiene could win a national competition, yet his night breath made me gag. But it was all part of the grand pregnancy experience, along with learning to smile benevolently when strangers patted my stomach and asked me if I knew the sex of the baby.

I did not. Pregnancy's mystery was much of its power.

That Saturday, Barry and I lingered over dinner. The beet salad was tangy; the whole-wheat baguette, crusty; the pasta, sensuous; and the candlelight, flattering.

"Dessert?" I asked Barry. "I bought that lemon tart you like."

"Just a sliver," he said. "You're going to drop thirty pounds, bingo, but mine will still be here." He'd gained a pound for each of my ten, but hearing him, you'd think he was now classified as morbidly obese.

I carried the dishes into the kitchen and loaded the dishwasher before I cut the tart, which I'd transferred to my favorite cake stand, heavy turquoise glass with swirls shaped like sperm. If New Year's Eve were a plate, it would look like this. I was wiping the big wooden salad bowl when I heard Barry answer his cell phone.

It wasn't unusual for him to be phoned at all hours, especially on Saturday, since Friday is popular for surgery. Every patient thinks she'll be the lucky ducky who won't bruise like an overmatched prize-fighter. Such a woman is deluded enough to imagine that if she grabs a Friday slot, she'll be back at work on Monday, her colleagues none the wiser, despite heavy spackling and the fact that Barry has reengineered her nose inside and out.

"Not now," he said to the caller.

My husband wasn't speaking in his soothing, practiced Barry Marx, M.D., demeanor. I wouldn't even have noticed the conversation if he didn't seem perturbed. "I will call you tomorrow," he said, clipping each word. *"Promise."*

It was the whisper of "promise" that gave him away.

The cake knife in my hand hovered above the plate as my insides twirled. I'd convinced myself that Barry had become Old Faithful. Just the day before, when Brie and I were layette-shopping, I'd said, "I think my leopard has changed his spots. I practically want to remind him he's still married to me, Molly Never-Gets-It-Quite-Right."

"Are you suggesting this change includes fidelity?" Brie had asked, putting down a sweet green jammie as soon as she saw the whopping price tag for what amounted to less fabric than a dish towel. Brie forced me, as she so often did, to visit a dark street in the fluorescently lit megalopolis of Denial. I turned over the question in my mind.

"I think I do," I'd said, twice. The second time was out loud.

"Not a moment too soon," she'd said, giving my hand a firm squeeze.

I'd always kept Brie informed of what I suspected were Barry's dalliances. I was long on intuition and short on hard evidence, but every six months or so I'd get a psychic whiff of adultery and report in. Brie would then declare that my suspicions qualified only as paranoia and that if I was going to be this pathetically insecure, I would doom my marriage all by myself. Once she'd ruled, it allowed me to relax and concentrate on my congenial, manageable life: work, home, family, friendships and, lately, Baby Marx.

I had been going through a cycle—every three to six months—when I ruminated, complained, and ultimately put my worries to rest. Never once did I confront Barry. But that night's "promise" ricocheted off the kitchen walls, and as Barry walked in, carrying the empty bottle of pinot noir, my face must have registered panic.

"Molly, what's wrong?" he said. "Are you feeling something?" His voice sounded no less solicitous than it had three minutes before.

"Oh yeah, I'm feeling something," I said. Fury. Malice. The desire to shoot a gun.

"Tell me what's wrong," he said.

"What's *wrong*?" I repeated. "Doctor, why don't *you* tell *me*?"

"Excuse me?" His facial expression withered into resentment and distrust.

"Who is she?" I snarled. "Or should I say, who is she this time?"

"You really know how to turns things foul, don't you? I have no idea what you're talking about, except you've spoiled a perfectly pleasant evening."

"*I've* spoiled things?" I snorted. Barry can handle me when I'm cranky, petulant, sad, or worried. What he can't take is when I show some grit. Like at that moment. So I kept going. From somewhere, I was feeling an energy surge so powerful you'd think I was getting it through an IV drip. "You have a rap sheet four years long," I said, my voice rising. "How many other women have there been, Barry?" I pronounced his name as if it were a fatal virus carried by fruit bats. "All you doctors think you're God!"

"Go ahead, Molly, slam the whole profession," he said with equal contempt. "For this whole pregnancy I've put up with your mood swings, your anxieties, your goddamn beet addiction. I've come to almost every doctor appointment—"

"Was this all a terrible hardship? Did it take you away from your 'special friends'?" Despite the knife in my hand, I made that asinine gesture that suggests quotation marks, while he was sticking with the best-defense-is-a-good-offense strategy. At least he was being offensive.

"Do you think you've been easy to live with?" he said. "Or that you look so cute? And how about your complete lack of interest in sex?" His voice kept getting louder and his face closer. With the third question, spittle landed on my cheek.

That's when I put down the cake knife, hauled off, and threw the plate. I loved that plate, a wedding gift from my aunt Vicki.

"Shit, you're dangerous!" he said as he ducked. "Get a grip!"

"I don't want to get a grip, you jackass," I said. "I want a normal marriage. I want respect. I want—"

"If you act like this, I guess it's just your plight to have no respect."

"So now I have a *plight*?" I said, parking my hands on my massive belly. I suddenly understood what evolutionary biologists don't: why a female praying mantis tears off the male's head when he approaches her from behind, flapping his wings and strutting in hopes of having doggie-style sex. Obviously, she has just heard Mr. Mantis call his girlfriend. "Barry, last I noticed, we are having a baby. If you—when you—cheated on me before, which I'm fairly sure you have, I was willing to write it off as your version of immaturity. But the rules have changed. If you cheat on me now, I swear to God, you will wake up one morning"—I eyed the knife—"and your penis will be gone." Sweat was dripping off my face. "Do not," I shouted, breathing hard, "underestimate me."

"Holy crap," he shouted back. "You make me *want* to cheat on you. And I can think of a few of your friends who'd be more than willing."

Barry turned his back, which was just as well. At the moment the sight of his contorted, purple face, handsome as it might be in repose, repulsed me. "I've got to get out of here before I do something I regret."

"You don't regret what you've already done?" I bellowed as he left the room. "You don't regret anything?" But he didn't answer. Then, like an exclamation point, our front door slammed.

I stood in the kitchen, surrounded by shattered glass, a fitting tribute to our marriage. As I waddled to the closet to find a broom and dust pan, I caught my reflection in the cabinet glass; it took a second to register that this mess was me. My shoes trampled the yellowish ooze that once was a tart. I carefully swept up the larger pieces of broken glass, dumped them in the trash, and filled a pail with soapy water to wash lemon debris off every surface, including my face. What a waste of a luscious tart. What a waste, period.

It took me a full ten minutes until I began to cry, but when I did, the tears came like grenades. I began heaving so intensely I abandoned my cleaning, stumbled into the bedroom, hoisted my heavy body onto the bed, and pulled the comforter up to my neck. I grabbed a pillow and sobbed until I slipped into a dreamless sleep of uncertainty, anguish, and unadulterated exhaustion.

Around three in the morning I woke, my head throbbing. I instinctively felt for Barry in total darkness, but his side of the bed was empty. As I came to, the full force of our battle repeated itself like a badly written, atonal soundtrack for a movie called *Oh, Shit*. I walked into the bathroom and tried to remember what kind of pain meds my obstetrician allowed me to take. Not aspirin, she'd warned. Only Tylenol. My face was swollen and my hair was like burnt grass. I ran warm water in the tub and dumped in the first bath product I found, an unfortunate potion that smelled more like turbo-strength disinfectant than the spruce for which it was named.

I soaked until every bubble popped and the water grew cold. Shivering, I turned on the shower and quickly washed my hair, then wrapped myself in a none-too-clean towel and got out the blow-dryer. My arm felt too weary to lift it. I aborted the mission and began walking back to the bedroom to find a pair of granny underpants and my faded flower-sprigged flannel nightgown, wondering if Lucy still owned its voluminous red twin.

Dribbles of water followed me as I padded across the room. I made nothing of it. But when I bent down to open a drawer, a persistent trickle leaked on the taupe carpeting. Stupidly trying to deny the source of this pink fluid, I stumbled to the bed, laid the towel on the comforter, and crawled on top of it, hoping what was now a small gush would end.

I closed my eyes and dozed. When I woke, the clock on the nightstand read 4:48 and the towel was soaked. I remained inert. At 5:10, I felt a dull pulse inside both thighs, as if I were getting my period. Nothing operatic. But a half hour later, the pain returned with twice the force.

If I lay very still, would the pain and pressure stop? Whose idea of a bad joke was this? *Not now,* I thought. *Not fucking now.*

A more reasonable part of me laughed aloud and began to hear my mom's voice. *Get yourself together, Molly, my darling,* she trilled. *This is a wonderful day. You are going to be a mother. Find Barry and start timing the contractions. Yes, that's what they are, silly goose. Don't you remember what they taught you?*

I called Barry's cell phone. It wasn't turned on. I left a message. "Call me." To make sure he didn't interpret the words as a preamble to an apology, I repeated the demand. "Call me immediately, you douche bag."

I considered the suitcase I was supposed to have packed. Typically, I'd not gotten around to it. With surprising calm, I threw some random clothes into a large tote. Later on, I wondered what had made me think that in the hospital I'd need lacy camisoles and matching thongs. White silk, yet.

I kept looking at the clock. Each minute ticked by slowly. Maybe nothing was really happening. I was overdramatizing, as Barry often accused me of doing. Now I was sorry I'd called him.

But then another pain came, burning like a torch. Twenty minutes had passed. I found Dr. Kim's number and left a message with her answering service. Five minutes later my doctor returned the call.

"I think my water broke," I said.

"I'll meet you at the hospital, Molly," she answered, upbeat.

I wanted to be strong. Again, I dialed Barry's number. His cell phone was still off. "I'm going to the hospital," I said, trying not to sound electric with emotion. "Nice if you could join me," I added—a phrase impossible to say without sarcasm.

What, I thought, would Lucy do if she were having a baby? Squat on the floor, punch someone's lights out if they suggested medication, drop a ten-pound infant, and run a half marathon? I had a sudden need to talk to my titanium sister. She answered on the fourth ring. "Molly, do you have any idea what time it is here?" she croaked. In Chicago it would be 5:35 A.M., and she is not one of those people who rise and shine.

"Sorry," I said. "But I think I'm having the baby."

"This is not entirely unexpected." There was a long pause. "And?"

"And I'm all alone," I snorted as I wiped my tears on my sleeve. "Don't ask. What should I do?"

"Man, what did I smoke last night? Please tell me I'm dreaming."

"Honest to God, Luce, I'm having contractions. The doctor wants me to go to the hospital." I started to whimper. "Barry is MIA. It wasn't supposed to happen this way."

"Listen to me, and don't be a twit," she said, now firmly in control. "Get in a taxi. Go to Mt. Sinai. That is, unless you want your doorman to deliver that baby."

"Okay," I said. "You're right." My sister, the good teacher, had spoken. "Okay."

"God damn it, I wish I could be there," she barked. "Where's that scumbag husband of yours? No, don't answer. I don't want to know. Call Brie. Have her meet you."

"Call Brie," I repeated mechanically.

"Have her call me!" Lucy shouted as I clicked off.

I took a deep breath. "Good morning," I said to Brie. I sounded almost sane until a contraction tightened around my stomach like a steel band. "Could you meet me at the hospital?" I whispered.

"What's going on?" she answered, wide awake, no doubt having already devoured the *Wall Street Journal* and her usual orange before she set out for a six o'clock training session.

"Nothing, probably," I said. I hoped it was nothing. But "nothing" was hurting at regular intervals, poking deep, as if someone were trying to locate each of my internal organs and rip them out one by one with a garden hoe. "Barry has an emergency," I lied, "and I just need you to hold my hand, okay? I'm thinking it's a false alarm."

"Got it," Brie said. "See you at Sinai."

I mustered the wherewithal to limp out the door and hail a taxi. Which wasn't hard. The sight of a whale-woman flailing her arms on a street corner at dawn tends to get a driver's attention. And evidently I wasn't the first frightened, frantic pregnant patient the hospital crew had seen stagger in solo. Within minutes, I was certified by insurance, wearing a gown, and declared to be six centimeters dilated. By the time Brie arrived I was surrounded by nurse-angels and hooked up to every kind of beeping *Star Wars* machine. Between contractions, I mentally redecorated the birthing room: sky blue paint and orchids. I refused to let myself think about Barry.

I thought it would make me feel better to have Brie at my side, but every time I felt a contraction, her jaw clenched as if she were having a wisdom tooth extracted without anesthetic. She'd yammer away, shouting, "Oh! Does it hurt? Does it hurt a lot? Christ, that was a big one. Whew, it's over now. We can relax." Which meant she could relax. But she didn't. Brie was hopeless; I could see that by the time I gave birth, she'd need a visit to a sanitarium.

One hour passed. Two. And then I lost count. The pain kept coming, as if the Weather Channel were replaying hurricane footage. I didn't think about Barry. What would he have done, anyway? Make me feel it was my fault that the baby was showing up three weeks early, upsetting his surgery schedule?

I tried to let myself feel proud. *Molly Marx, superwimp, a woman who wouldn't be able to dispose of a mousetrap, is having a baby.* Part of me seemed to hover on the ceiling, watching myself groan and grunt and look hideous but mighty all at once. I was a stick of dynamite ready to blow.

When the contractions were down to five minutes apart, I turned to Brie and said, "You don't have to stay."

"I won't leave you," she answered, mopping my forehead with a cool, damp towel.

An epidural was the next order of business. "It's going to get bloody."

"I can handle it."

"Any word from Barry?"

"I didn't try to call him again," she said, and I'll never know if that was true. "What happened between you two?"

I waved away the thought of him. "Not important," I said, which was true, because I suddenly thought my uterus was going to fall on the floor, to be followed by an elephant calf wandering out to nurse at my breast.

"Okay, liftoff," said the deliriously gleeful nurse. I wanted to slap her. With amazing speed, I was greeted by Dr. Kim, who emerged from the haze wearing a smile and a shmatte over her silky black hair. She is one of the few women I know who looks good in aquarium-green drawstring pants and Crocs.

"Are you ready to have a baby, Molly girl?" she said.

"Hell, no," I yelled.

"I beg to differ," she said. "You! Are! Ready! When I tell you to push, push."

What did she mean, push? A wallop of drugs had kicked in, and I wouldn't have been able to feel an apartment building fall on my head.

"Okay, now, push," she said.

"We have to push," Brie said, in case I hadn't heard. Brie was standing now, wearing a gown over her gym clothes. The glimpse of face behind her mask looked deathly pale. All I could hear were a sorority of women yelling "Push" and "Good girl" and "Wow" and "Great" and finally "Here it comes—here it comes—here it comes." Were we all having a group orgasm?

I felt a creature slither out of me. Then there were cheers, as if the Giants had hammered the Patriots in the Super Bowl. I felt carbonated with joy. Had my feet not been in stirrups, I might have jitterbugged.

I had made and delivered a *baby*. Me, me, me. I could split an atom, box with a bear, dog-paddle to Hawaii.

I closed my eyes and talked to God. *Let this child be healthy. Let him have all the appropriate body parts. Let him be wise and strong and good. Let him not have Barry's nose.* For minutes on end, I believe, I held my breath in suspense.

When I opened my eyes, my little boy was clean and resting on my chest. William Alexander was screaming. He had the most exquisite, pinched face, bigger than a grapefruit, and a few random hairs flattened into a comb-over. "We're a team now, kiddo," I whispered into his miniature ear. "I'm your mommy and I love you. I will always, always, always love and protect you."

I examined my child carefully. He had wrinkly pink skin, ten fingers, and ten toes. He didn't, however, have a penis. My first thought was that the baby was deformed. Then I realized that I, Molly Divine Marx, had produced a female child. A very small me.

"She's unbelievably gorgeous, Molly." Brie looked at me, crying. "She's one of us. I love you both."

I was the mother of a daughter. A girl! I hoped she would love me half as much as I loved my own mother. My second thought was that Barry would be disappointed. My third thought: what he felt didn't matter.

Soon enough, the baby was whisked away, Brie went home to change, and I was wheeled to a room I had to share with a loud, big woman surrounded by her loud, big family who set the air-conditioning so high I thought I was in a meat locker. After I did some heartfelt begging, a nurse finally appeared with an extra cotton blanket, thin as a sheet. I was doing my best to calm my chattering teeth when Barry walked into the room, carrying an enormous vase of pink peonies and a large white teddy bear.

I tried to read his expression, searching for regret. But Barry acted if it were normal to have missed the birth of his five-and-a-half-pound daughter and to find his wife marooned in a maternity wing. He tried, at least, to win me over with a compliment.

"I saw her," he said. "She's the prettiest one in the nursery."

I hadn't comparison-shopped, but I said, "I'm sure you're right."

"I'm proud of you."

I glared. He stared. I glared some more.

"And I'm sorry, very sorry."

What the apology covered wasn't clear. Barry was too proud to elaborate and I was too exhausted to ask. For better or worse, wherever it would take us, we were parents now, together. We called an unspoken cease-fire blessed by the birth of our child, who was—thank God—healthy, a Perdue Oven Stuffer trussed in a pink cap and gown. I cradled her silently, with Barry perched tentatively on the edge of the narrow bed.

"Do you want to hold her?" I asked after a few soundless minutes. He looked terrified.

"Try it," I said, as if I were coaxing him into sampling gruel. He took his daughter in his arms and started to sing "Born in the U.S.A."

"Be careful," I said as I shut my eyes. "Your tears are falling on her nightie."

I hadn't intended to sleep. When I woke, it was evening and no fewer than eleven supersized versions of my roommate overflowed into my space, sounding joyful in a guttural language. Barry was not in sight.

"Excuse me, but my daughter-in-law needs her rest," I heard Kitty say. "I believe the rule is no more than two visitors at a time." She was using her freezer-burn voice, which could have run Microsoft, and the sound of it caused most of the large merrymakers to scatter. My mother-in-law—dressed impeccably in a fitted gray jacket, black turtleneck, and trim black pants and looking about as much like a grandma as I did the winner of an MTV music video award—grimaced as she brushed away one of the other patient's neon-orange helium balloons, which had invaded Marx turf. "Mazel tov, darling," she said. "How do you feel?"

"Like I ran the marathon in high heels three sizes too small," I said.

"She looks like Barry did as a baby," Kitty said. I took that to mean she was adorable. Was I supposed to thank her for complimenting my child? I'd been a mother for just hours and already was confused, so I said nothing.

Kitty gazed at her rings. Recently colored honey-blond hair framed her determined face. "I want to ask you a small favor." She sucked in a breath and lifted her face to look at me, pushing her mouth into an expression almost like a smile. "I'd like you to name the baby for my mother."

I nodded. "I see," I said. "You want me to name my little girl Gertrude?"

"It tears me apart that she doesn't have a namesake." In case I didn't get the point, Kitty took out a monogrammed handkerchief and dabbed her eyes. I looked carefully. No tears.

I thought of Granny Gert, four foot ten and two hundred pounds. To her credit, she was said to be an ace canasta player, and based on the stockpile of paper bags found after her death, she'd been a recycler far ahead of her time.

"Gertie Marx," Kitty said hopefully. "Those old-fashioned names are chic again."

Sophia, Sadie, Emma, or Isabella, certainly. Violet, Helen, Hazel, or Lily, of course. Fritzi, maybe. Not Gertrude. Not if I had anything to say about it, which I did.

Kitty took my measure. "Gertrude as a middle name? Or maybe just a G-name? Grace? Gabriella? Greer?"

I thought about it for a second. No, less. Like a butterfly, a different name flew into my brain.

I buzzed for the nurse. "Could you bring me my daughter, please?" I asked.

Ten minutes later, as my infant snoozed in my arms, Barry returned, armed with turkey sandwiches, chocolate cupcakes, Champagne, and plastic cups. I sat up as straight as my bloated, beleaguered body allowed.

"You all need to be formally introduced," I said to my husband and Kitty with a tingle of devilish pride. "Meet Annabel. Annabel Divine Marx."

*Eighteen*

# THE FAMILY DIVINE

"inden," Detective Hicks tells the taxi driver. "Highland Park."

Hicks is riding through Chicago's northern suburbs, a green belt of wealth that grows more impressive by the mile. He cranes his head to see the flat, gray splendor that is Lake Michigan. *The shining Big-Sea-Water . . . level spread the lake before him . . .*

In my parents' neighborhood, many of the houses have been bought by young couples who've knocked them down to build at oblique angles and accommodate three-car garages and five-thousand-square-foot turreted, gabled, centrally air-conditioned homes with gyms, disco-balled entertainment centers, and ADD-inducing playrooms. Chez Divine, however, is the beta version and looks more or less as it did in 1928, when a one-car garage wasn't a quality-of-life-compromising issue. The twenties were when my grandparents were born, and should I come across them in the Duration, I plan to ask them a thing or two. Did Grandma Phyllis fret about her cellulite? Did Papa Lou consider work/life balance?

My childhood home is neither Snow White adorable nor men's club macho. It's homey, with gray shingles, glossy black shutters, and—in the summer—blue clematis that climbs a filigreed trellis. A flagstone walk leads to the door, now all but obscured by an evergreen in need of serious pruning. My parents don't decorate this towering fir for Christmas, which makes Mrs. Swenson next door gnash her teeth.

*Just take it slow,* Hicks says to himself as he steps out of the car and asks the driver to return in three hours. Mine is the first case he's handled solo. He is nervous but reminds himself, as he digs through my history, that he can simply pretend he is a biographer. It is a little known fact that Detective H. Hicks has an undergraduate degree in English literature from one of the windy upstate branches of SUNY.

I admire Hicks not only for his professional joie de vivre but also because he is one of those lean men who wear clothes well. An unbuttoned, bronze Harris tweed overcoat hangs handsomely from his broad shoulders along with a cashmere scarf in a spicy brown. He carefully walks around spots of brackish ice that refuse to melt in the March gloom and gives my parents' door knocker two confident hits.

> *With a look of joy and triumph,*
> *With a look of exultation,*
> *As of one who in a vision*
> *Sees what is to be, but is not,*
> *Stood and waited Hiawatha.*

Detective Hicks of Manhattan's Twentieth Precinct is twenty minutes late, but now that he's here, my mother is more atwitter than before he arrived. A grin paralyzes her face as if she were a stroke victim, and her eagerness is like a cocker spaniel's.

On a usual Sunday afternoon, I'd expect to see my mother in the kitchen making soup, wearing Levi's, an ancient red turtleneck, and worn velvet slippers, her streaky blond hair twisted up in a clip, but today her hair is freshly blow-dried and she's in a midcalf charcoal wool skirt over flat boots polished to a military gloss. Instead of her usual dangling earrings from a random craft show, she is wearing pearl studs. Her geranium-hued sweater set is so mom-correct I wonder if she speed-ordered it from the Lands' End catalog when this appointment was scheduled four days ago. I hope she's tucked the tags inside and will return it tomorrow.

"Detective Hicks," she says. "Welcome to Chicago."

"Thank you," he answers, carefully wiping his shoes on the door-mat. "Sorry—my driver couldn't find his way out of an empty parking lot." He sounds harsh, which is not his intent. "But at least I got to see more than I expected. You have a beautiful city."

*Could this be any more uncomfortable?* both of them are thinking. My father appears only slightly more relaxed. "Take your coat?" he offers after he shakes Hicks' hand—cool, firm grip meets cool, firm grip—and repeats to himself, *Keep it together, keep it together.*

"Glad you didn't run into that blizzard coming our way," he says out loud. The knowing nose predicts snow before nightfall—special delivery from Canada—and the air feels slightly damp.

For my dad's sixtieth birthday, Lucy, Barry, and I gave him a colossal television set—Barry's idea—which dominates one wall in the den, where my father generally parks himself. He's Chicago bred, suckled on team spirit—da Bulls, da Bears, and of course da Cubs—and only last year quit playing sixteen-inch softball, the indigenous sport of his youth. But this afternoon French doors close off his darkened sanctuary, and my parents guide Hicks through the neglected living room, where a fire has been kindled and lamps softly glow.

"Lucy called," my father reports. "The roads are icing up—she's gotta take it slow. She said to eat without her."

*From its bosom leaped the sturgeon . . .*

For this occasion, my mother has bought out Once upon a Bagel, and not just the sturgeon but the whitefish, the pickled herring, the nova, the works. It's shiva all over again, minus cardboard boxes on which the immediate family shift their butt cheeks, avoiding another cookie for fear that the precarious seating will collapse. In the absence of a pamphlet to guide a mother on how to entertain an officer of the law investigating the mysterious death of her daughter, Claire Divine is making it up as she goes along. She considers hospitality an art form. A New York detective is visiting—on a Sunday, not Saturday, since she and my father are in the traditional, yearlong mourning for a child, and Saturday is their Sabbath, which includes going to the synagogue. Hence, my mother has produced Sunday brunch, in the tradition of our tribe.

"Your daughter Molly—did you have any reason to think she was unhappy?" Hicks begins gently after he offers condolences and they take their seats.

My parents look at each other to determine who should answer. "From what we could tell, she was over the moon," my mother says. "A child, a marriage, a lovely home, even a part-time job—she had it all." She's already cracking. "What kind of monster would take this away?"

"Can you think of anyone who might have meant Molly harm?" Hicks asks.

"What are you talking about—reckless endangerment?" My father, whose favorite author is Elmore Leonard, jumps in. "Of course not. People adored our daughter."

"So you think that if this was . . . a crime . . . the perpetrator was a stranger?"

"To begin with, of course it was a crime," my father says, careful to not add *fucking*. "As to who did it, there are so many goddamn nut jobs out there, I wouldn't know where to look first."

"So you're thinking it wasn't anyone Molly knew."

"I'm not sure about anything," my father says. "Because people, you know, well, they have their secrets."

My mother glances at him as if to say, *What people would that be?*

"Are you thinking of anyone in particular?" Hicks asks. The detective and I both wait for him to expand on the thought, but my father only shakes his head. So Hicks moves on to "How would you describe your daughter?"

I wouldn't be surprised if a string quartet popped out of the den and played a requiem commissioned by my parents. "Adored; many, many friends; a good wife; a great mother," my father says.

*Let's canonize her,* Hicks thinks. *What about the woman's faults? How do I ask about those?* "Anything else you can tell me to round out the picture?"

My dad stares blankly out the window at snow powdering the edge of the lawn. "Molly could be impulsive, a little scatterbrained, and unsure of herself, especially with her husband's family." His answers sound as if he is responding in a job interview when you're asked to produce faults and you fish for assets disguised as flaws.

"What did you think of your son-in-law?"

*Not as worshipful of Molly as he should have been,* my mother thinks. *Spoiled egomaniac* rattles around my father's brain. *Way too attached to that haughty mother of his.* But what they offer, in unison, is "We loved him," and they immediately know from Hicks' face that he isn't buying it.

"Okay, the guy could be a hothead—he wasn't the husband I thought my daughter deserved—but he's not a killer," my father says. "That's preposterous."

"No one said he's a killer."

"Well, Detective, if you're wondering, I'm not thinking it," my father says. "Last time I looked, being selfish isn't against the law." His voice rises. "Doesn't even make you a sociopath." It's only taken my father five minutes to lose it. "So, for Christ's sake, let's not mince words and waste our goddamn time. Who do you think did it?"

"Mr. and Mrs. Divine," Hicks says evenly, glancing first at my father and then at my mother, "we're looking . . . everywhere, and at everything." He feels flop sweat gather in his armpits, and is glad he's wearing a sport coat. "And on that score, what about Molly's . . . mental health?"

I can't imagine that my parents have ever once considered any aspect of my health that wasn't physical. I got braces and every appropriate inoculation, took jars of vitamins, and left for college with birth control and a fact sheet about chlamydia. My mother and father are born midwesterners whose set point is caution and optimism, one foot solidly planted in each camp. If anything, they've always thought that Lucy was their *meshuggener,* their nut job, not me.

"Excellent," my father guesses. "Molly's 'mental health' "—he drags out the words—"was exemplary."

"Molly would never hurt herself," my mother adds, picking the world's most obtuse euphemism, "if that's what you're getting at. Never. Obviously, someone meant ill to my daughter, but if you think she brought it on—blaming the victim? Outrageous." As she tenses, I notice that her carefully applied foundation has settled into delicate vertical lines around her lips. I long to reach out and pat it back in place. "Maybe our daughter was simply in the wrong place at the wrong time, that's what I think. I always told her she shouldn't be riding that bike alone. . . ."

She did. I never listened, just as I ignored her when she'd told me to major in education, stay in Chicago, join Hadassah, wear pastels, and not rush to marry Barry.

My mother stares into the middle distance. I can see that she pictures me as I looked at twelve—scrawny, all legs and arms—and wants to reach out and hold that child and breathe in the scent of her newly washed hair and well-scrubbed skin.

"Claire, honey, what is it?" my father says to her, and covers her hand with his large paw. She only shakes her head, dabs away a tear, and takes a deep breath.

"Detective, I can't go on just now," she says. "Please, let's have lunch." *I'd rather they were talking about my death,* she thinks. *Why couldn't it have been me?*

The conversation dwindles away as the three begin to politely peck at their bagels and all four kinds of fish, picking up speed as the meal progresses. They are ready for apple cake—baked by my mother, to mitigate the excess ethnicity—when Lucy blasts through the front door. She hangs her bulky white fox-trimmed parka in the front hall closet, kicks off her Uggs, and walks in green stocking feet to join them, while she shouts, "Hi, everyone—I'm here." She kisses each parent hello. "I'm Lucy," she says, extending her hand to Hicks and meeting his eye. Her hands are a miniature version of my father's, broad and capable.

"Hiawatha Hicks."

*He's got to be kidding,* Lucy thinks. She almost succeeds in keeping a straight face as she wonders if he has a sister, Minnehaha. Ha, ha, ha. "Sorry . . . traffic," she says, failing to recover self-control before both of my parents show a pulse of embarrassment. "What did I miss?" Before Hicks can answer, she loads up a bagel, including a substantial slice of Bermuda onion, which the others have politely avoided along with difficult questions.

The detective is young and good-looking, Lucy notes, and no gumshoe. He's wearing decent leather oxfords that have escaped slush stains. She registers that his skin is a rich milk chocolate and his hair short and recently barbered. She can't pin him down as either Puerto Rican or African American. A more exotic cocktail, she decides.

"So, your name—someone liked nineteenth-century American poetry, huh?" As Lucy rips into the bagel, she catches our mother's eye and shoots a look that says, *What's with the food? This guy probably wants sausage and eggs.*

"Fortunately, Mr. Longfellow's not around to ask for a licensing fee," Hicks answers. Nobody laughs, so he moves on to the shock-and-pity approach. "The truth is I never got to ask about the whole name saga. I was eight when my mother was killed in a car accident. I was raised by my grandmother."

My parents and Lucy are too blue-state to ask about a father. None of them is as riveted by Hicks' sad story as they might usually be, because there's something bigger and grimmer that's crept into the room: death. Hicks' declaration has lifted the black veil, and my mother sucks in her breath so fast she almost pants. Now they can get started. "Shall we have coffee in front of the fireplace?" she suggests.

"Great," my father announces, although the question has been pitched to Hicks. They decamp to the living room, which is overrun by family pictures: twin girls with hair in pigtails, cut short, and grown long; graduation pictures, pre- and post-orthodontia; camp snapshots; bat mitzvah portraits; my parents' vacation photos, my mother's right arm always strategically placed around my father's waist to obscure his love handles. There are at least ten photos of Annabel, including the most recent in a silver frame. My daughter wears one of my old smocked Florence Eiseman dresses. The dress is blue, the Molly color; Lucy always wore red.

My parents huddle, holding hands. Facing them, Hicks and Lucy square off like prizefighters.

The room, paneled in cherry, radiates warmth, and Hicks admires it. "Mr. Divine," he says, "please tell me where you were when you got the news."

"Already at work," he says. "I get there early. Claire—my wife, that is—called that morning the minute she heard from Barry." He squeezes my mother's hand.

"I could hardly make out a word he said," my mother adds. After decades of marriage, they are vinaigrette, no longer simply oil and vinegar, and don't even notice that they finish each other's sentences.

"Claire knew from Barry's voice that it was bad," he says.

"Annabel, I thought—something had happened to our baby girl." My mother's eyes flood, and my father pulls her to his barrel chest. I, too, wish I could feel the familiar comfort of his slightly sweaty protection.

"So I came home, to be with Claire," he says. His voice started off big but has already shrunk. "We got to New York by eight."

"By then we knew the worst," my mother says. "For a few hours, Barry let us think there was hope, but he called us right before we boarded to tell us the real story." She remembers how she spent the flight, staring blindly at the unresponsive heavens, which quickly faded to black. Was I floating in the cosmos like an errant balloon, an unmoored soul? It was a bad dream then, and far worse now—for all of us.

Hicks patiently listens while my parents account in excruciating, small-print detail the most unimaginable day of their life, when, defying every law of nature, their daughter had died, possibly by someone's hand. That the hand might be her own they cannot imagine. Did a stranger lure a foolish me to a remote spot by the river? Was I meeting someone I knew and thought I could trust? Did I simply lose control of my bike? Was I so momentarily insane that I deliberately rode toward the water, perhaps to try to drown? (This last theory is tossed out by Lucy.) They talk until it seems they must be spent, but suddenly the timbre of my father's voice downshifts and darkens, a thundercloud ready to burst.

"What I need to know, Detective," he says, his face dangerously red, "is that you're going to catch the goddamn sonofabitch who did this."

Lucy winces, but he goes on.

"There's a murderer out there," my dad yells. "My daughter's dead. Gone. Our granddaughter's lost her mother. Our lives are shot to hell. Nothing in this family will ever be the same. There's a fucking monster somewhere, and you, my friend, have got to find him. Am I making myself clear? Do I have your word that my daughter Molly's death won't be just another crappy little unsolved case that gets a week's cursory attention before it's shelved for something bigger and flashier?"

Hicks listens. He does not respond. *This guy isn't done yet,* Hicks knows.

"Are you going to turn yourself inside out to find the scum bucket who did this?" With each short blast, my father's voice gets louder, as if someone's pressing the volume button on the remote. He doesn't feel better for having made his point.

"I hear you, Mr. Divine," Hicks says, awed by this father's pain. *I want to find the killer,* he says to himself. *If there was one.* "Sir, you have my word." And then he turns to Lucy.

She looks nothing like the pictures of Molly. Bigger, taller, tougher. Her mouth is wide, and the lips are sensual and full—fuller than most white women's—and red-stained, as if she's just sucked on hard candy. Probably prefers Chapstick to lipstick. Bitten nails. Starter crow's feet, not unappealing. Wild hair—the kind that defeats a comb, two shades richer and darker than cider. She's a woman who will improve with age, he predicts, as long as gravity is kind to those breasts, too motherly for his taste.

"Lucy, where were you that day?" he asks.

My sister feels he says this with menace, but she tries not to let her hostility crash in a heap at his feet. "Out of town," she answers. Neutral voice, not giving anything away. Hicks' face suggests that she continue, and Lucy does. "It was Presidents' Day weekend. I wanted to snowboard, and some of the other teachers were going to Wisconsin. I started driving there, but then I got Mom's call, so I reversed directions and came home. I flew to New York the next day—first plane out."

*A no-alibi alibi,* Hicks thinks.

I have a sudden urge to flee this overheated room and zoom in on Annabel with my afterlife babycam. When I checked on her earlier this morning, she was sniffling. Has Barry tutored her in nose blowing? Encouraged her to drink tea with honey? I used to be able to coax Annabel into taking a few swallows, especially if I used one of my grandmother's flowered teacups and set the tiny table with the blue faux Wedgwood doll dishes. But no, I feel this is where I need to be, planted like the evergreen sentinel out front.

"Mr. Hicks," Lucy says in her voice of natural authority, assuming you are four. "Where are you, for real, with Molly's case? Do you have any suspects?"

Lucy is someone who wants what she wants and doesn't give up, Hicks thinks; a woman for whom a defect can become a strength, and strength a defect. "It's a bit premature for suspects," he says. "That's why I'd be interested in hearing from you on that score."

"The obvious," she says. "The husband, for starters—"

"Lucy!" my mother trumpets, as if her daughter had announced that their guest has farted. "You are talking about our son-in-law."

"Mrs. Divine," Hicks says calmly, "Lucy's right." His brown eyes pin my sister. "What do you know?"

I hear inhales and exhales, and Hicks thinks that she knows nothing but can't get past hating that poor schmuck Barry. She probably would have hated any man her sister married.

"It troubles my parents, Detective," she says finally, "but it was a marriage . . . with problems." My father looks out the window. Sugary snowflakes are continuing to fall.

"Big enough problems for it to get this ugly?" Hicks says. *Ugly?* Talk about understatement. "This violent?"

"Maybe," Lucy says. "My sister put up with a lot of"—she looks at our parents and amends her language—"garbage." Still, our parents glare at her. "But it's not for me to say," she says, sinking into the corner of the couch to make the retreat complete. They are back to silence souring the air.

"What I want to tell all of you," Hicks says, "is that in cases like this, don't expect a red carpet to unroll and lead us back to the cause of death." While he elaborates, his eyes catch a photo of three generations of Divines—aunts, uncles, cousins, us—taken at my grandparents' fiftieth-anniversary party. Lucy and I are fourteen. Everyone is smiling into the camera except my sister, who looks accusingly at me. I had never noticed this before—I'd always been focused on myself, horrified by my dotted dress from the girls' department, while Lucy got to wear a black sheath in a woman's size. Now I'm wondering what I might have said or done to piss her off.

"Detective Hicks," Lucy says as he winds down, "want to take a drive? Check out the 'hood?"

My parents wince at her attempt at humor.

"I wouldn't be putting you out?" he answers, writing off her comment as nervousness, glad to spend time with her.

"C'mon, let's go," she says, dangling car keys and offering the smile she reserves for auto mechanics and her best students.

Hicks postpones his driver's arrival by ninety minutes. Lucy begins the Molly Divine Memorial Tour, swinging past Ravinia, the site of my first make-out session, followed by the homes of three former boyfriends and finally Highland Park High School. Her voiceover proclaims that I was an A-minus student who was in charge of prom decorations and insisted on an unfortunate *Blue Lagoon* theme. In my defense, I was hoping to capture the azure of a Bahamian sea, but under lights the color of turquoise eye shadow, everyone simply looked late-stage tubercular. As both Hicks and I are beginning to worry that the point of this meandering drive is for Lucy to render me solid-gold average, she says, in a voice as rehearsed as a novice trial lawyer's, "I keep wondering if Barry had a girlfriend who . . ."

"Who what?" he says.

"It's a feeling I have, that someone meant Molly harm," she says. "Maybe that person was Barry, or someone Barry knew." She slows the car and parks on a side street. Night has almost cloaked the town in blackness, and through barren trees snow steadily falls. "My parents would freak if they heard this—they thought Molly was an angel even before she died. Not that I'm judging, but my sister may have had another man in her life." *Besides that schmuck husband,* she thinks. "Maybe you can find him."

In the dusk, her face looks hard. "This guy, did you meet him?"

"Never," she says. "I only heard about someone once, and it was before Annabel was even born. Could have been a big nothing, over years ago. Or maybe she made it up, to make me feel like less of a loser, you know, like shaving your head because your sister's going through chemo." Lucy laughs nervously and alone. "I feel disloyal even mentioning this, like I'm besmirching my dead sister's reputation."

Hicks is all ears.

"She and I weren't the type to write little poems about our every feeling, you know. Like I have to tell you that we are—were—very different."

"Keep going."

"My point is, I can't say I'd have blamed her if she played around."

"Uh-huh," Hicks urges—too obviously, it seems to me. As if Lucy needs encouragement.

"She was too damn trusting. If you ask me, to a fault." *Which no one would accuse me of,* Lucy thinks. "Molly was the big-city girl, but she could be alarmingly dense."

Hey. Rewind. *I* always had to take care of *you*. Did you forget?

"Oh well, I'm talking out of my ass," she admits. "Probably wasting your time." Lucy turns the key in the ignition. "If you haven't figured it out already, I'm not the crown jewel of the Divine tiara," she says. "Molly is my mom's clone, and my dad idolizes my mother. End of story. But, God damn it, I did love my sister. I loved her." I wait for Lucy to cry. Not today. I may as well wait for the Pope to get married.

No one speaks for several blocks. As they turn into the drive, Hicks says, "I'll need the names of the friends you were going to meet that day to snowboard."

Lucy twitches ever so slightly. "Of course," she says. Ten minutes later, after goodbyes all around, she's on the road.

Hicks is not so lucky. His driver, once again, gets lost. By the time the man arrives, the wind is whipping snow into a tango and his return flight has been cancelled along with every other airplane flying east.

"I won't hear of a hotel," my mother says.

Which is how Detective Hiawatha Hicks came to spend the night under a faded lavender duvet in the twin bed that was mine, his head on my down pillow. Drifting into sleep, his last thought is of Lucy. He dreams of his first-grade teacher, who placed him in the slow group and was convinced he might never learn to read.

## Nineteen

# FUNNY BUNNY

Seven months after Annabel was born, I was four pounds over my pre-pregnancy weight, which had been only five pounds over my lifelong goal, a number I glimpsed once on the scale fifteen years ago after a camping trip where the nightly entrée was—I'm fairly certain—squirrels. When I looked in the mirror, I didn't mind what I saw. My hips were a tad wider, my belly even less flat than before, but my breasts appeared no worse for having nursed—I was glad I'd invested in two hundred dollars' worth of bras engineered by the likes of NASA.

"Guess who's paying me a visit?" I said to Brie one morning when she'd called en route to a trial.

I hated that on the first beat she answered, "Luke," and laughed. "Why?"

"Because he's an old friend," I said as I patted a mask over my face. It smelled of apricots and vanilla and promised to make each pore invisible.

"Right," she said, the way that means "I'm not buying it."

"Luke's sweet. He sent Annabel the most exquisite antique rocking chair." It was two feet tall, with original paint the pale yellow of sweet butter. It awaited my daughter like a throne. I could picture her when she was older, reading as she quietly rocked, identifying with Cinderella, lusting after glass slippers, and starting to plan her wedding.

"And I assume you wrote a lovely thank-you," Brie said. She knew I believed the ghost of Emily Post would stomp on my head if within a week of receiving a gift a sincere, original acknowledgment was not in the mail.

"Of course."

"You've fulfilled your social obligation. Why are you letting him come over?"

"He wants to see the baby, not me." Even I didn't believe me.

"You know how I feel. It's a mistake to let him near you."

"You're not giving me credit," I said, feigning indignation.

"Call me a realist," Brie said lightly. "Luke's always been crazy about you, and you're a little bit lonely and misunderstood." She hummed something that sounded like a dirge.

"Hey, everything's good here," I protested. Despite the fact that Barry was working exceptionally long hours, she knew I felt we were once again on terra firma. No missile launchings. No "promises" bouncing off walls.

"I'll shut up—you're a grown-up," she said, to my relief. "Give him a big, sloppy kiss for me."

"Highly unlikely," I said with my goodbye.

Luke was due in ten minutes. I washed my face. My pores stared back at me, still good-sized pixels. I dabbed on the tiniest bit of makeup and thanked God for inventing black boot-cut jeans. Annabel, all sixteen pounds of powdery innocence, was sleeping in her cool, darkened room. I'd put her down an hour earlier, and if I knew my daughter, she'd wake up merrily right after Luke and I ate lunch. On the kitchen counter, our meal waited—richly gold curried chicken salad, heirloom tomatoes layered with buffalo mozzarella and basil, a few small sourdough rolls, and one formidable fudge brownie, takeout artfully arranged on my second-best dishes. White wine was chilling along with a pitcher of iced green tea garnished with cucumber slices. I wanted Luke to think I'd made an effort, but not too much.

*There's no reason to be nervous,* I told myself. *Whatever you once felt for*

*Luke is an aberration, buried under layers of life.* Good, solid, fortunate life. I thought of my father's credo: *Make mistakes—just don't keep making the same goddamn ones.* There was no reason that philosophy couldn't apply now, except that a more cynical brain worm was wiggling for attention: *If you get to live your life over, make the same mistakes, only sooner.*

I fluffed the living room pillows and rearranged the roses. That still left a few minutes to mindlessly scan the arts section of the *Times* before the doorman called to announce that Mr. Delaney had arrived. On the way to the door I checked my reflection. The woman I saw was trying. I hoped only I noticed this.

"For you," Luke said, offering a large bouquet of deep purple anemones, an ear-to-ear grin, and the graze of lips on my cheek. I liked that he didn't wear cologne. He didn't need it. "And for the other lady . . ." From a large shopping bag he pulled out a package wrapped in pale pink paper, tied with a floppy orange silk bow.

I placed the gift on the coffee table. "The other lady needs to finish her nap or she will make a very bad impression," I said as I hung Luke's size forty-four long Burberry next to Barry's forty regular.

Luke's hair was shaggier than I remembered, and I had an impulse to brush it away from his eyes. Perhaps he'd lost weight—his cheekbones punctuated his face like parentheses. He was wearing a V-neck sweater the color of wisteria, which on most men would have been a questionable choice. On Luke it deepened the blue of his eyes.

"I'm glad to see your home hasn't become a toy showroom," he said in a sly, familiar tone. "My brother and sister-in-law apparently hold a major stake in Fisher-Price."

Since I'd stuffed the rest of her possessions in closets, only one basket of Annabel's most presentable playthings was in sight. "Come back in another year and then you can judge me," I said. Annabel had already acquired an obscene number of gaudy plastic contraptions that did everything but burp, and her drawers overflowed with clothes, half of which she'd outgrown before wearing. I was embarrassed by how the Marx family was single-handedly bolstering the gross national product, but was unable to say "Enough," especially to Kitty, my parents, Lucy, or Brie.

"She looks like you," Luke said, picking up a photograph of Barry and me in our Sunday-cozy robes. We were hugging a freshly scrubbed, two-month-old Annabel.

"Especially if you can picture me buck naked." The minute those words slipped out they seemed 200 percent too intimate.

Luke followed me into the kitchen, where I put the flowers in a vase. A few minutes later we sat down to lunch. He gave me an update on his recent shoots—Santa Fe, Prague, Sydney—and the studio he'd bought in Dumbo with a partner, Simon someone. I waxed proud about what a great sleeper Annabel was, how I'd discovered at least ten new cable television channels, and why I'd decided, after considerable debate, to stop making my own organic baby food.

"This stay-home-mommy stuff—do you love it?" he asked about twenty minutes into lunch. I did an instant replay to search for condescension. You never can predict on which side of the fence men your own age will stand regarding whether a mother belongs at home. Even ardent, high-toned, prochoice, antiwar, carbon-footprint-shrinking recyclers sometimes shock you silly with polemics about why a mother needs to make every peanut butter sandwich until kids become postdocs—especially when the mom in question is his wife. Whatever their own mother did was wrong, you invariably discover, and lots of these guys are the sons of fervent seventies feminists.

Nonetheless, my derision meter failed to buzz.

"You're the first person who's had the nerve to ask me that question," I answered, to stall. In fact, I'd originally planned to return to work, but a month after Annabel arrived, my boss was replaced by a new editor in chief whose reputation preceded her like a rogue tidal wave of entitlement. The two of us had one short meeting as my maternity leave was due to end. With an expression straddling shock and boredom, she quietly flipped through a portfolio featuring my last three years' worth of decorating stories. Two days later, the head of human resources called to say my boss was "going in another direction"—and I wasn't on her map.

Since I was twenty-two years old, I'd always had a job. Isolation terrified me. Even after all these months, I still couldn't picture life at home full-time. At a feverish pace, I'd put out feelers for a new position, but every job I heard about had such an insignificant decorating department that I'd be spending half my time ordering bubble wrap and the remainder packing and unpacking boxes the size of refrigerators. My ideal job would have been part-time, but when I raised that flag, interviewers all but shouted, "Next!" I suspected that each editor who interviewed me thought that, as a new mom, I'd be taking off every other day for this or that baby-related emergency.

"I love being with Annabel," I finally said with what I hoped was conviction, because it was gut-honest true.

"Something tells me there's more to the story," Luke said as he began to sip his second glass of wine. "My brother's wife tells me she can't figure out how one small body can manufacture so much poop."

"What gets me is the competition," I said tentatively. It wasn't just the running tab of which mommy had slimmed down to thinner than before she was pregnant or which child crawled faster, farther, and earlier. People kept score in ways I never would have imagined. Any mother who owned fewer than three strollers—an umbrella model for zipping in and out of taxis, a three-wheeled jogger for all the running she may or may not do, and, for everyday cruising, a heavy-duty Bugaboo Frog, which costs more than most people's first used car—was treated as if she were on food stamps. "I feel as if the rules for being a mother in this town are written in secret code and no one's given me the manual."

I read the expression on Luke's face as sympathetic and kept going. "All the other moms apparently got up at five one day and stood in line in a sleet storm to grab a spot in a *pre*-preschool swim class at the local Jewish community center. I tried to enroll Annabel the next week, but the class was sold out. When I expressed surprise to the woman at the desk, she looked as me as if I'd just wandered over the Mexican border."

"Ooh, nasty," he said, chuckling. "You don't get this in the e-mails. Let's hear more."

I rose to his challenge. "Okay. Nursery school. Really on-the-ball martyr-mommies are already discussing where to apply, and these are babies who can't even sit yet." Luke might have thought I was exaggerating for comic effect. I was not. "While they're mopping up drool, they're dissecting the schools' differences as if they were Harvard and Yale"—my voice sounded like I'd gulped helium—"which they may as well be, because I've been assured that if Annabel doesn't go to one of the 'right' schools, she can kiss her Ivy League dreams goodbye." As if fantasies of rowing crew on the Charles were what was making her sleeping eyelids flutter whenever I peered into her crib. "Not that I haven't started to get sucked into stuff myself," I admitted. In a few months, my daughter and I were slated to begin Magic Maestros, where we'd be entertained by live musicians who, for all I knew, might be off-duty violinists from the Philharmonic.

"So go back to work," Luke said after I ranted for ten minutes. "Or does Dr. Marx disapprove?" His tone had crossed into snide.

"Barry's okay with whatever I do," I told Luke, sounding as defensive as I felt. "But where, exactly, would I work?"

He idly ran his fingers around the rim of his wineglass. "How about with me?"

I imagined those fingers on my leg—and elsewhere—and shook my head to erase the image.

"Hey, why are you saying no without hearing more?" he said. I was fairly certain I detected disappointment.

"I'm not saying no. I'm not saying anything, because what exactly are you proposing?"

"Nothing full-time. But the jobs are really coming in now," he said, knocking the wood table twice, "and I could give you a lot of regular styling. I've been using lame freelancer after lame freelancer, and either these girls and boys won't get off their lazy rears or they have zero imagination. When they're good, they get booked up by my competitors or raise their rates to prices I can't afford."

Now it was my turn to offer the occasional "hmm."

"I can't pay you benefits or promise the arrangement will last forever—you know how work comes and goes," he continued. "Editors could get sick of me and not renew my contracts." Neither one of us mentioned that Luke owed part of his good fortune to editors' past fickleness: he'd come along when everyone was hungry for a new face and a new look. "Molly, all I can say is that you know how well we work together—you're the other half of my brain."

I couldn't disagree. I thought Luke's talent was astounding. Two-thirds of the glossy pages in my current portfolio came from our shoots.

"And you'd be doing me a favor—not that you owe me." He looked right into my eyes in a way that was both intimate and alarming.

Was this a come-on? *Don't flatter yourself, Molly,* I decided. *This is business. Nothing more. And not only is it the best offer you've gotten lately, it's the only offer, discounting a position that required commuting to a suburban location whose most attractive feature was the office's proximity to a Dairy Queen.*

"It could be fun," he added.

"Fun, huh?" A quaint concept.

I was trying to digest Luke's offer when I heard Annabel. Usually I didn't rush to grab my child from her crib—I liked to eavesdrop and try to translate her babble—but it was already close to two. I was eager to show off. "Do you hear her?" I said. "You'll have to excuse me for a few minutes."

I returned with my chubby, sweet-smelling daughter. At seven months, Annabel's hair had grown in blond and her skin felt as velvety as petunias. I'd dressed her in a lilac striped dress that matched Luke's sweater. My heart swelled with pride as I presented my baby.

Luke looked at her with his photographer's eyes. I knew him well enough to recognize appreciation. "So happy to meet you, Miss Annabel," he said, shaking one of her fat little fingers. She smiled, revealing three newly cut teeth, and kicked her legs like a baby ninja.

"Could you keep her company while I get her sippy cup?" I asked as I secured Annabel in her high chair. Learning to drink from a cup was a recent accomplishment, and I couldn't have been prouder had she mastered Italian verbs. When I got back to the dining room, Luke was playing peekaboo like a pro and Annabel was squealing with delight. He had that effect on women.

"Don't forget her present," he said, handing me the box. I opened it slowly and methodically, a habit that always drove Lucy—a born ripper—nuts. "It was this or the Brad Pitt action figure."

Inside was a large, squishy white rabbit with floppy ears. Annabel reached for it and promptly sucked its gumdrop-sized nose. "Thanks," I said, smiled, and reached over to kiss his cheek. "I'm glad the funny bunny won. What do you think we should call him?"

"Excuse me, but he already has a name. He's Alfred, just like my father—long legs, big ears, loved carrots."

"It's Alfred the bunny, Annabel," I said, rubbing the velvety plush against her arm. "He's from Uncle Luke."

Luke grimaced.

"Correction. He's from Mr. Delaney."

"Alfred is from *Luke,* Annabel," he said, checking his watch. "Luke, who has to leave now. Sorry. Meeting downtown."

I walked to the closet, pulled out his coat, and gave his cheek another hurried, virginal peck.

"Will you think about my offer?" he said.

"I will."

"Really?"

"Promise."

"Promise, then," he said as the elevator arrived. "I'll hold you to it."


When I checked on Annabel, she was curled around Alfred. She slept with him that night, and for every night thereafter, until love rendered him bald. Lack of fur never, however, diminished his appeal. Alfred the bunny became king among animals. He understood Annabel like no teddy bear or donkey ever could, and whenever I looked at them together, Annabel and Alfred, my mind invariably turned to Luke.

As for me, on Monday I interviewed nannies. Two weeks later, Delfina Adams entered our lives. The next week, I ordered business cards. And the week after that, I flew to Sonoma. Luke and I were scheduled for our first shoot.

# Twenty

# PICKUP LINE

*W*hy is this night different from all other nights? This night is different from all other nights because this night is Passover and this morning Kitty, as she does every year, is putting the finishing touches on a seder worthy of *Gourmet*. It's my tough luck that when I was alive I didn't tail her like I'm doing today, because I have finally learned how she makes her featherweight matzo balls. The recipe she guards as if it were the formula for Ecstasy is—the hubris!—square on the back of the Manischewitz matzo meal box, although she substitutes seltzer for water. That I can't bust that woman is driving me insane. Whom in the Duration can I report to who will care? Bob? I don't think so.

"Pinky, can you get the phone?" Kitty shouts to her maid, which is how she refers to Pinky Mae Springer, who has worked for Kitty these last thirty-eight years.

"It's Dr. Marx," Pinky yells back. She has known Barry since he wet his bed, but when he graduated from med school Kitty insisted that Pinky call him by this honorific.

"In a minute," Kitty says as she slips a large damask napkin into a sterling silver ring. Every napkin is fanned to exactly the same breadth.

I admire Kitty's perfectionism. Even her mind, I suspect, has hospital corners. She walks to the phone in the kitchen, her stiletto mules tapping on the tile floor like a snare drum. "Darling," she says to Barry in a voice she reserves only for him and which I believe she considers melodic and charming. "Did they arrive?"

*They* would be my parents, who were due in at eleven. Lucy is boycotting the seder and leaving tomorrow for St. Bart's to join a new boyfriend.

"They're in?" she says, having hoped my parents would cancel at the last minute. "Now I have to figure out where to seat them." Kitty always plots her table as if she were giving a state dinner for the crown prince of Saudi Arabia. With the phone still to her ear, she opens a drawer in the Sheraton buffet and retrieves two thick parchment place cards elegantly lettered in calligraphy. Kitty sets my father's card next to her own seat, while she puzzles over my mother's.

"The Girls are taking bets about what Claire will wear," she tells Barry. Linda, Suzette, Nancy, and Kitty have been steadfast friends for decades, with matching bracelets on their ankles. They're not just the original Mean Girls. They're resourceful. Before Google, there were the Girls. Whether you need a hot stock, a hot tamale, or a hot date, they always know the one. Had any of these ya-yas chosen to work, I have no doubt that they would have blasted the glass ceiling to Mars, but I never realized until now that my mother was of sufficient interest for them to critique her wardrobe, too label-deficient for their taste.

"I'm a *what*? Now don't call your mother that, darling," Kitty says, but she comes off playful, as if Barry has served up the most heartfelt term of endearment. "That isn't becoming." While she chats, she straightens the tall ivory tapers in their towering candlesticks and examines the kiddush cup that belonged to Barry's father. Its sterling silver, embossed with vines and grapes, is marred by a millimeter of tarnish. "Pinky," she shouts. "Can you come in here?"

In her crisp gray uniform, Pinky steps to it and removes the offending cup for a second round of polishing.

You can tell from one glance at this dining room that my mother-in-law is someone who takes herself seriously, and you'd better, too. She set the table yesterday, and I have to agree the woman has, as she herself might say, flair. I adore her china, which she had the foresight to select and receive—service for twenty-four, no less—when she married her second husband, Seymour Katz, who died three years ago. The dishes are an old Meissen pattern featuring a fierce dragon in a color she calls amethyst but which to me looks like regulation shocking pink, nearly the shade Annabel turned last year when she first laid eyes on them and asked why her grandmother uses "monster plates."

Nevertheless, I love the way these dishes set off spring flowers. For tonight's meal, Kitty has cornered the market on dogwood, freesia, and irises, which she's arranged in bouquets worthy of the entrance to the Metropolitan Museum. Her tablecloth is heavy French linen. I can picture it hidden in the bottom of a steamer trunk as an aristocratic family fled Paris when the Nazis came to call, although I believe the real story is that she inherited it from her mother, who won it playing cards at Lido Beach.

I love Passover. I miss Passover, my favorite holiday, although it wasn't always so. Christmas used to be way out in front until Lucy said, "Molly, can't you see through all the hype?" a word she learned when we were eleven.

Most Jews like me—who barely know Purim from Durham—agree that Passover is mostly about the singing. It's definitely not about the matzo, the bread of affliction that our forefathers ate in the land of Egypt, and which their descendants know as the direct route to constipation.

At Kitty's, Barry always chants the four questions—even though he is not the youngest at the table, as tradition demands. Off-key but with gusto, guests chime in on "Dayenu," "Eliyahu Hanavi," and "Had Gadya." The tunes aren't "Away in a Manger," "God Rest Ye Merry, Gentlemen," and "Deck the Halls," but they'll do.

Tonight, I plan to play the part of the Marx family's own personal stunt double for the prophet Elijah, said to drop in on seders worldwide. I'm hoping I'll run into Elijah in the Duration. Maybe the two of us could chat, spirit to spirit. Get his take on the Palestinian situation. But I've had enough seder prep for now. Kitty is moving on to gefilte fish, never my favorite.

I've been checking on Annabel all morning, but soon the teachers will be letting the children out early in honor of the holiday. Hauling my spectral ass to Central Park West takes, of course, no time. The first person I see in the lobby isn't Annabel—school hasn't let out yet—or even Delfina, waiting for her. It's Stephanie, who's hard to miss in low-rise jeans and an eye-popping bronze leather jacket. She appears to be talking to herself, though in fact she's carrying on a conversation through her headset. Judging by the volume, she's engaged in a full-contact sport with a travel agent, wrangling over the price of first-class tickets to Barcelona. I don't have to wonder who her seatmate will be.

So intently am I watching Stephanie that it almost fails to register that there's something off about this scene. It's not the security guard who peers halfheartedly into people's bags, the one you'd expect to miss a monogrammed set of assault weapons. It's not the nannies gossiping about their bosses in the corner, divided from the moms like the muggles from the wizards, and it's not the three handsome gay fathers who stand to the side in their own fraternity, where the price of admission is an adopted Chinese daughter or a son grown in a rented uterus. It's *her*.

As she stands still among at least a dozen women her own age, pretending to read *People*, I see her out of the corner of my eye, like the rat in the subway you sense before it scampers along the rails. Fading into the crowd, she's one more woman in a black coat and black boots with a black bag waiting for the elevator door to open and dislodge a group of giggly three- and four-year-olds.

Stephanie's son is in the first group that hits the lobby, and her curly-headed boy runs to her side, tugs her jacket, and shouts, "Mommy." She brings her index finger to her lips and mouths "Jordan, shhh." Part of me would like to Taser my sister and say, *"Her! That's who Barry's seeing!"* But that part of me would be the single once-living cell that isn't wondering what the hell Lucy Divine thinks she's doing here, casually pretending she has permission to pick up Annabel.

Two more groups of children run off the elevator. I am hoping that Delfina, usually prompt, will glide through the door. Then I remember that Barry gave her the day off because tonight she's going to help Pinky serve the seder meal. Annabel is supposed to go home with her buddy Ella and Narcissa, Ella's nanny and Delfina's best friend.

The elevator door opens one last time and both girls escape, waving goodbye to their teacher. Each bears a carefully crayoned matzo cover. Annabel's is decorated with rabbits and eggs in Easter colors. My girl, all right.

"Annie-belle," Lucy shouts. "Over here. Surprise!"

While her teacher chats up one of the mothers, Annabel spins like a dial and winds up pointed at Lucy. "Aunt Moosey!" she squeals. "Daddy said you weren't coming to New York!" She barrels into her aunt's open arms for a tight, lingering hug.

"What's this pretty thing you've made?" Lucy says, admiring Annabel's handiwork. "You know what? You can tell me about it later. Why don't you let me zip your jacket?" Lucy speaks quickly, releases Annabel, and gently pats her on the back.

Oy, *caramba!* Has Lucy lost every last marble? Where is my sister taking my daughter? It doesn't even matter if her motives are innocent—which I want to believe that they are. I have to. I must.

Annabel looks at her friend standing across the lobby and turns to Lucy. "But I was supposed to go home with Ella."

Hearing her name, Ella, who had been waiting near the door for Narcissa, trots over to Annabel and Lucy. There is no doubt in my mind that Ella will grow up to be a Supreme Court justice—that or a prison matron. She considers Lucy with deep suspicion. By the time this child is twenty, she will have a deep furrow requiring state-of-the-art facial filler. "And you would be?" Ella says, sounding flintier than I did, ever.

"I'm Annabel's aunt," Lucy replies. She glances around to look for Ella's mother or nanny and is relieved to see that the child is alone. "We have to run now, but you have a wonderful holiday. Bye!"

"But where's your yellow slip? Annabel needs permission to leave with you. Where *is* it?" I am expecting Ella to cuff Lucy while she arranges for an AMBER Alert. "It's the rule—you're breaking the rule," she adds loudly, which causes the few mothers left in the lobby to rubberneck toward Lucy. Stephanie is among them, still talking into her Bluetooth.

*You little four-foot troll,* I hear Lucy think. *I hope you grow up to get acne, cankles, and a nose even Barry can't fix.* She grasps Annabel's hand and tugs. Annabel won't budge.

"Ella's right, Aunt Moosey," my daughter says gravely. "It's the rule."

"Annie-belle," my sister says, crouching down and whispering, "I'm going to tell you a secret. One of the things they don't teach you in school is some rules are made to be broken. Got that? Come on. Trust me. I'm not just your aunt. I'm a nursery school teacher and I know stuff."

This time, when she tugs, Annabel looks at Lucy long and hard, hesitates for only a moment, then waves to Ella and follows her aunt. They are on the street when Narcissa ambles heavily through the door, a bakery box in hand. She bends down to kiss Ella, singing out, "Ready, my darling? Sorry I was late. Now where's your friend?"

Ella drags her nanny back to the door and points down the block. "She went with *her*," she bellows. "That lady. She says she's Annabel's aunt." Lucy and Annabel are still standing in the street, Lucy trying to hail a taxi as one after the next sails by filled with passengers. As Narcissa takes it in, her brow furrows, and I see where Ella has acquired her expression. "Annabel went with that bad lady. We need to do something."

"Stop that woman!" Narcissa belts out. Aretha Franklin has nothing on her. "Kidnapper! Pervert!" Ella echoes every word of the tirade, which Narcissa repeats in a loop, and like a sow and a piglet, the two of them begin to make their way down the block just as Stephanie and Jordan walk out of the building.

"What's going on?" Stephanie shouts.

"That woman," Narcissa turns around and yells. "She be stealing Annabel Marx."

"Annabel Marx? No!" Stephanie says, and thinks, *Un-fucking-believable.* "I'll get the security guard. Watch my son." She turns back into the building, leaving a bewildered Jordan standing alone, wondering whom he should chase after, Narcissa and Ella or his mother. Narcissa, weighing in at 210 pounds, is not fleet of foot, but she and Ella reach Lucy and Annabel just as the door of a taxi slams. Narcissa bangs on the car's side with her enormous vinyl tote. The driver presses down on the brakes so fast his turban tilts.

"You two get out this minute!" Narcissa yells as she continues to beat on the door. "Driver, she be stealing that little girl. Stop her! Kidnapper! Don't go!"

Lucy rolls down the window just enough to yell, "Mind your own business, you bitch. I am this child's next of kin. Driver, take off." But the driver stops the car and leans back, taking it all in. He pulls out his cell phone.

"You! Drop that phone!" Lucy orders. *I know what's best for this child,* I hear her think. *Molly would want me to look out for my own flesh and blood. Barry, that sorry excuse for a husband, he doesn't deserve this beautiful daughter, like he didn't deserve my beautiful pain-in-the-butt sister and made her life hell and—*

"You be stealing that child!" Narcissa says, flapping her arms as she pounds the window. Her bakery box falls, and black-and-white cookies spill into the gutter. Ella begins to whimper—those cookies are her favorite—and turns and points down the street, where Stephanie is running with the security guard at her side. She pokes Narcissa, who takes it in. "The cop, he's on the way," Narcissa shouts to Lucy. "Annabel, now don't you worry."

"Lady," the driver yells to Lucy, "you give that child back."

"Don't you dare talk to me that way."

Annabel's heart-shaped face darts back and forth between Lucy, Narcissa and Ella, and the driver, who has lost his turban. She starts to cry, quietly at first, but the noise builds to a wail. "Let me out, Aunt Lucy," she cries. "I'm scared. I want Delfina."

"Annabel, stop that!" Lucy snaps. The loudness of her voice makes Annabel cry harder. "Everything's okay. You're with me, Aunt Moosey. Driver, take off!"

The man won't budge.

"You ain't going nowhere," the guard, who has reached the taxi, shouts as he raps on the window. "Hell, woman, open that door."

"Or what?" my sister shouts. "You'll find a real cop?"

Stephanie is behind him. "I'm calling Dr. Marx now," she says, taking her phone from her right pocket and rapping the window with her left hand. "Whoever you are in there, you're insane. Let Annabel Marx go!"

"Fuck!" Lucy says. *I'm trapped,* she thinks. *Shit out of luck.* "God damn it."

She opens the door. Annabel tumbles into Narcissa's doughy, welcoming embrace. Lucy slams the door shut as the guard gives it a wallop. "Driver, take off," she says. This time he peels away as if he's leading the cavalry.

"Annabel, you poor baby, I'm here, I'm here," Narcissa says as she rocks my daughter's birdlike body. "Narcissa and Ella are here. Everything's okay."

But everything is not okay. My child is shaking. My lunatic sister should have known better than to duel with a tough Jamaican nanny. She should have known better, period.

I get inside Lucy's brain as she speeds away in the cab. I try to understand why she would behave like a crackpot, if I may use the technical term. But the inside of Lucy's mind roars with tumult. She is asking herself why she always makes the wrong choice. For now, at least, my sense of filial loyalty has been plucked away as if it were snatched by a big, black crow. All I can hear are my daughter's sobs. I have never felt more useless, more frustrated, or more dead.

*Twenty-one*

# BORDEAUX WISHES

D on't you love it?" Luke all but wagged a tail as he ran, arms out-
stretched, from corner to corner of the house and up an open
metal staircase.

"It's great if you've always dreamed of living in a giant sardine can,"
I said.

The house du jour was in Sonoma County, designed by a big-league
architect for a Silicon Valley boy genius who'd cashed out just in time. I
felt three feet tall standing under the terrifyingly high ceiling and
turned full circle to take in the mottled gray concrete floor with its art-
ful random cracks, the gunmetal walls, and the exposed circulatory
system of pipes. The front window, a glass waffle with six-foot-square
panes, had been manufactured for a car dealership. I squinted into the
sun and saw miles of vineyards, green and gold, gold and green, that
terraced the northern California hills.

"What's with the attitude?" Luke asked. "It's dazzling."

It was dazzling, all right. I'd read that at night you could see the
place from miles away, blazing like a UFO, and the instant the residence was finished, zoning ordinances were voted into place to bar
Erector Set knock-offs from pockmarking the countryside.

"C'mon," he said "This light—it's amazing. I would kill for a space like this."

"Mr. Delaney, you're not cool enough to live in a space like this," I shouted up to him. But I knew Luke and I would have no trouble taking jaw-dropping photographs here. I started to get excited, too.

"You're lucky I don't have a water balloon to drop on your head," he said, ripped a sheet out of the notebook he always carried, and sailed a paper airplane through the air from the balcony.

A few hours before, Luke had met me at the Oakland airport. He'd had a job in Big Sur and driven up from Los Angeles on the Pacific Coast Highway. As we made our way north, his voice-over described the view with childlike glee. "Seals playing tag in the water!" "Waves like *Moby Dick*!" We hadn't checked into our hotel yet. Luke was too eager to scope out the house where we'd be shooting, starting the next day. We went there first, slowly driving up a steep hill. The air here felt clean and dry. I forecasted three good hair days.

To say I had overprepared for my first job in more than a year was generous. For the past three weeks I'd noodled about the details day and night, putting in so much time that if I averaged it against the fee I'd be receiving, I might have earned more by cashing in bottles salvaged from the street. But I didn't want to disappoint Luke Delaney, my discriminating new boss. I fiddled and fussed, compensating for the fact that the house was not at all my style. I am, after all, the secret love child of Marie Antoinette and Charles Dickens.

"What did you think of the art?" Luke said after we'd cased the place and gotten into our rented convertible, unfurled the car's top, and started driving down the mountain. If Barry had been the driver, I would have bitched about how my hair was blowing into a Marge Simpson updo, but instead I acted as if I thrilled to the sensation of hot red dust grinding into my scalp. I was also aware of the fact that I might not smell all that clean. It was ninety-four degrees, and the minute you stepped outside you felt as if a Navajo blanket had fallen off a mule and onto your head.

The only contemporary art I knew beans about was hung on museum walls, and most of the last Whitney Biennial left me thinking that each artist had simply tattooed his neurosis onto a canvas. "That big blue one looked like Paul Bunyan's ox."

"You mean *the* Julian Schnabel?" Luke said.

Time to switch topics. From my straw tote I pulled out a pile of restaurant reviews. "Are you getting hungry? I've been reading up."

"I'm always hungry when it's on the client's dime," he said. "This is why I made a reservation for us two weeks ago." He mentioned wine pairings, foie gras, and basil ice cream.

"Terrific—I'm starving. In New York it's past dinner." Seven thirty-six, to be exact, and I was eager to get to my room and check on Annabel. I knew if I spoke to her in front of Luke, my coo would sound maddeningly precious. "Will Eric and Jasper be here in time to join us?" I asked. They were the assistants booked for the shoot.

Luke checked his watch. "They should've arrived by now." I was relieved. Chaperones, even if they were twenty-three, would set a tone of festive camaraderie.

We pulled into a village built around a leafy square. Healdsburg was a few blocks' worth of wine shops, pricey boutiques, restaurants, and hotels, and ours was supposed to be the hippest among them. While Luke disappeared to make sure every last piece of his equipment had arrived, I registered, and as soon as I got to my room, I phoned home.

"Delfina, it's me again," I said in my seventh call of the day. "How's Annabel?"

"She's fine, ma'am," she said. "Ate tofu for dinner." My baby was a little green dragon. "Loved her bath. Already sound asleep."

Aw. I'd wanted Delfina to put the baby's ear to the phone so we could have one of our one-sided heart-to-hearts and I could at least hear her squeak. "Well, that's good, Delfina," I sighed. "That's great. And don't forget, please call me Molly."

"Molly," she said. "I'll do that, Molly. Now, good night, Mrs. Marx. Speak to you tomorrow."

My room cost hundreds of dollars a night—the hotel was revered for its high-principled design, which meant that I had not one drawer or armoire in which to unpack and only a sliver of a closet half covered by a filmy curtain. Piles of clothes landed on every snazzy, pristine, uncluttered surface, until the place looked as if I were closing down a small boutique. I walked into the vast shower tiled with delicate mosaic in the greens of wasabi and edamame. As the warm water hit my head, sandy trickles rolled into the drain. I lathered my hair with grapefruit and aloe vera shampoo, conditioned with linden blossom balm, and stood comatose for minutes. Dripping and chilled, I dashed across the stone floor to retrieve the white terry robe hung on the bathroom's sole, ill-placed hook.

But first, I glimpsed myself in the full-length mirror—and froze. Who *was* that small but distinctly pear-shaped woman and what was she doing here? I was three thousand miles, three time zones, and one played-out flirtation away from where I belonged. All the scented body cream and caviar in the world, I suddenly realized, couldn't stop me from being homesick. I missed my child and, to my surprise, my husband. I must be out of my mind to have made this trip.

I should be in New York, snapping digital photographs of Annabel to send out to a list of fifty friends and relatives, some of whom, I was sure, would delete the e-mails without even opening them. I should be shopping for a new batch of children's books, looking into classes that would max out Annabel's potential, soaking up every moment of once-in-a-lifetime motherhood like French toast and maple syrup.

Much to the surprise of the woman who used to be me, back in the city Barry, Annabel, and I had settled into snug domesticity. Barry had become reasonably housebroken, and when the weather cooperated, we'd spend hours each weekend at the playground, steaming cups of coffee in hand, eager to meet others who tottered on this strange new precipice called parenthood. After his morning runs, Barry would often be the one to change Annabel's soggy nighttime diaper and give her breakfast. Sometimes I would catch him dancing around the room, Annabel in his arms, and my heart would be jelly.

Every night, after I put the baby to sleep, I'd fix my version of a low-fat homemade dinner, and while we ate, Barry and I would rattle on about Annabel, obviously the most precocious and charming baby on earth. Each Saturday, we paid Delfina an outrageous sum so she would sleep over, and we'd splurge on an evening out, even if all we did was eat pad thai at a local joint.

It wasn't a glamorous Manhattan life. It wasn't even a glamorous Sioux Falls life. But it was comfortable, which was the last word I'd have used to describe how it felt to be sitting in an over-air-conditioned, overdesigned hotel room, weary from travel, knowing that for the next four hours I'd be trapped in a flouncy four-star restaurant, trying to verbally joust with Luke and two recent graduates of Wesleyan and Yale.

I picked up the phone. "Hey, Luke," I said, trying to sound like one of the guys. "Please don't think I'm a thankless wretch, but room service is looking pretty sweet right now."

"I totally understand," he said, too quickly. "It was clear you were wiped."

Did I look that bad?

"Get some rest," he said, "and I'll see you tomorrow. Seven-thirty?"

I thanked him, hung up, and expected to feel relieved, but my vanity kicked in. Perhaps the real reason I hadn't wanted to have dinner with Luke was because I was afraid he'd put the moves on me, and I wouldn't know how to react. Since it was clear that wasn't going to happen, I felt like the hound at the pound that no one wants. I circled the room twice, flicked the television on and off, called Barry and discussed whether we should install a garbage disposal, devoured my artisanal vegetable salad in seven bites, and fell asleep while watching Johnny Depp on pay-per-view. I was in the wine capital of North America and hadn't even ordered a glass.

For the next three days, I labored like a migrant worker. Rise at six, quit thirteen hours later. Unpack. Pack up. Push away the ottoman. Move it back. Arrange a tray for imaginary guests. Pick a different tray and do it over, once with gherkins, once without. Lay down the hand-tufted wool rug. Decide it's better suited to an English boardinghouse. Roll it back. Run upstairs, forty-seven times. Make the bed. Sweep the floor. Remove stains from the marble counters. Resist the impulse to allow this loftlike aerie to metastasize into a Parisian flat crammed with flea market frippery.

"Beautiful, beautiful," the good-natured Eric would say after every setup. He was working as hard as I was, and not averse to pushing a sectional couch around the room until I decided where it should park.

"You go, girl," Jasper, the Yalie said to me, again and again. That expression should be banned, especially when repeated with an English accent via Nashville. I longed to stuff a linen pillow sham down his throat.

But the best praise came from Luke. "I think this one's going to be great," he'd say before he took a shot. Every time he finished, he'd turn to me with "Told ya so, Molly. Perfect. Just perfect."

As Jasper snapped Polaroids of each setup, he put them in a book, and by two o'clock on the third day, we could all see that our efforts had yielded a major success. There was nothing left to do. If the editor who'd sent us on this mission had any sense, the minute he saw Luke's film he'd put him under contract in perpetuity.

"How shall we celebrate?" Luke said after we'd packed up and gotten into Eric and Jasper's SUV to drive back to Healdsburg. The question was meant for all of us, but he was looking at me, sitting next to him in the backseat. Luke was wearing a black T-shirt and khaki cargo shorts, and his legs were stretched out, tanned and strong.

"My vote is to pull into that winery right there and drink Sonoma's finest until we're shit-faced," Eric said. "See the sign?"

"You go, girl," Jasper said to Eric. We all knew Eric was gay, but I loathed Jasper all the more for banging on it.

"The driver calls the shots," Luke ruled as he rolled his eyes at the back of Jasper's head. Since Eric was behind the wheel, he chose to turn off Dry Creek Road into the Ferrari-Carano Vineyards.

Some of the wineries we'd passed were little more than tumble-down shacks, but we could see we'd hit pay dirt. At the end of a drive, a vast pink stucco estate house with arched leaded-glass windows stood before us, fronted by classical gardens circling a fountain. The lawn was rolling and lush, the privets manicured. Thinking back to it, the place reminds me of the Duration, especially when Puccini wafts through the air.

"Holy cow," Eric said as he led us into the tasting room off the main lobby. It was all but devoid of other customers, but thousands of wine bottles glinted, there for the buying.

From behind a gleaming wood bar a white-aproned man greeted us. I have no idea if he knew a Barolo from a Chianti, but I liked the look of his shoulder-length salt-and-pepper hair, tied back in a pony-tail. "Would you care for a pour of our Syrah?" he wondered.

We would. And the zinfandel, the Tresor, the Eldorados—the Noir as well as the Gold—the fumé blanc, and, what the hell, the cabernet sauvignon. All four of us sipped and critiqued with flowing pretension.

We started with "fruity" and "earthy" and shamelessly worked our-selves up to "herbaceous with hints of anise, berry, and tobacco."

After nearly three hours, Eric and Jasper decided to drive back to town; they were heading to San Francisco. That I, a full-fledged mother, allowed these two to get into a moving vehicle now fills me with shame, but that's how drunk I was. "Don't worry," Luke said to them. "We'll find our way home." The proprietor was only too happy to give us a card for a taxi company: the longer our stay, the bigger his sale.

Eventually, Luke and I had sampled nearly every wine from the vineyard. I decided to ship home a case of the zinfandel. Luke picked the Syrah. I wandered around in a fog, lubricated as much by the past week's work as by that day's excellent vintages. Nor did the excellent company hurt. Whatever fear I'd had about living up to Luke's expecta-tions had been washed down the hatch, and we were laughing and showing off for each other.

"You go, girl," Luke said in Prince Charles' voice. In the moment, I thought he was hilarious.

Shaky on my feet, I was ready to call our cab when Luke motioned me out to the big white-tiled center hall and pointed to some steps. "Let's explore," he said, mischief in his eyes and voice.

"Are you sure it's okay to go down there?"

"The door's unlocked. I took a peek when I took a leak." Another line of his I'm now embarrassed to say that I felt deserved a hearty laugh.

We tiptoed down a short flight of creaky wooden stairs into a low-ceilinged windowless room the size of a basketball court. From wall to wall, heavy old oak barrels sat like monks, each presumably filled with wine. The cellar air felt refreshingly cool. Like Alice in her maze, I walked in one direction and Luke in the other, in and out of narrow aisles.

"Molly, come here," Luke stage-whispered from across the room.

"What is it?" I asked. Maybe he'd found a barrel with an open tap and we could polish off our afternoon with one last, secret swig.

"Come over here," he said. "You're going to love this."

I did.

He grabbed both of my hands and pushed me against the side of the tall wooden barrel. Then he kissed me, hard. His lips tasted better than any of Ferrari-Carano's premier selections, although I swear I detected a drop of the zin, with just a hint of boysenberry and licorice. He slid his cool tongue deep into my mouth and cupped my face in his hands while he tenderly and sensuously explored. "I've been dying to do that for days," he whispered.

I said nothing, but I let my hands roam to his back and my mouth stayed with his. "No" and "yes" both came to mind as he unzipped my jeans and slid his fingers inside me. I didn't stop him and answered his lust with my own, each sweet movement calibrated for maximum pleasure, his and mine, together, as my own hands found his flesh, hard and inviting.

By the time we heard footsteps, we were both on the floor, which in my bliss felt as comfortable as an inner-spring mattress. "I don't think I want to spend the night here," I said.

My hand in his, we walked up the steps and outside, into the twilight. The winery was closing and we were its last visitors to leave. I gave Luke the card for the taxi, which he called with his arm draped around my shoulder. He leaned heavily and deliciously against my side.

We walked, melted into one, toward the entrance, and stopped to kiss by a towering bronze statue. The figure was a wild boar said to roam the Sonoma Valley, where he stole away the grapes. A plaque announced him as Bordeaux: those who made a wish while they touched the giant snout were said to see their dream come true.

I looked up. The big boy's nose was rubbed to a coppery gleam. I stretched to reach it.

*Let me love the right man,* I said to myself. *Let me not ruin my life. Let me figure out what will make me happy.*

I knew I'd made three wishes, not one, and hoped that Bordeaux wouldn't fault me on a technicality.

# Twenty-two

# THREE GUYS GO INTO A BAR

B arry!" Stephanie says.

*It better be important,* Barry thinks. He's behind schedule, because surgery ran long today, which he's explained to me can happen when the patient is enormously fat.

As Stephanie begins to speak, his nurse steps into his office. "Sorry to interrupt, but Delfina's on line two," she tells him. "She says it's urgent."

"Later, Stephanie." Barry clicks off. He hopes Delfina isn't calling to make a sudden trip back home to take care of a sick relative. Or ask for a raise. Or resign. He worries about this every day. Delfina is the Swiss Army knife of his life, solving virtually every practical problem.

"Dr. Marx?" Delfina says to Barry. "Mrs. Marx's sister—"

"Lucy?" *What now?*

"Mrs. Marx's sister. She snatched Annabel," Delfina blurts out, her usual Zen-like restraint splintered. The way Narcissa, a Mary Higgins Clark devotee, relayed the incident a minute ago, Lucy had been ready to whisk Annabel away to, Narcissa speculates, a bunker under a chicken coop in some undisclosed location.

"Oh my God," Barry says, gulping air. "That bitch. Where's Annabel? Is she okay?"

"Annabel's fine—she's with Narcissa and Ella. I'm on my way over there. Mrs. Marx's sister"—Delfina no longer thinks it seems Christian to call her Lucy—"took off." After Barry reaches Annabel—"Hi, Daddy. Aunt Moosey came to my school! Yes, it was *very* exciting. No, she didn't say why. Daddy, Narcissa's going to make us milkshakes now. Bye"—he cancels four consultations: a sweet-sixteen chin job, a redo on one of those unfortunate noses from Kitty's generation that look as if they were pointed in a pencil sharpener, a postdivorce nose-jowls combo, and a fiftieth-birthday lift on a woman who loathed the neck rings she'd accumulated each year as if she were a redwood. He bolts from his office, hops in a taxi—Barry has the best cab karma of anyone I know—and rushes home, ignoring Stephanie's repeated calls.

When Barry is nervous, he paces. It is twenty minutes later now, and like a panther at a substandard zoo, he's traversed the long hall, the living room, the dining room, the kitchen, and back, again and again and again. Twice he has started to phone his mother and Detective Hicks—in that order—and thought better of it. Finally, he makes a call. "Stephanie. You aren't going to believe this."

"Jesus, finally! I've been trying to reach you everywhere." *God damn it,* she thinks, *who are you to duck my calls?* "Where are you?"

"Home."

"Then I'm on my way over," she says, seizing this unexpected gift. "I should be there in twenty minutes."

Barry continues his loop-de-loop, then suddenly goes into our bedroom and opens an embossed leather book. No BlackBerry for me. It had been my annual ritual to spend the better part of one Sunday in early January entering the stats of my nearest and dearest into a tasteful address book while I deliberated on who should make the cut. This year, I edited away three college friends and two former coworkers, and when four of these people showed at my funeral, I was shamed, deeply.

Barry reaches Brie at work. "Lucy's gone off the deep end," he says. I admire his restraint. "She made a grab for Annabel."

"Back up. That's impossible," Brie says. "Lucy Divine can be off, but she's not ready for an asylum."

"I assure you, she's both."

Brie's pause is a true seven-second delay, while she processes that Barry expects her to take action. Of what sort, she doesn't know, but she recognizes that only face time will do. "Shall I come over?"

"I would appreciate that."

Barry doesn't dislike Brie. He admires her brains and drive and thinks she's "drop-dead sexy." He's convinced that her current partner preference is temporary, contrived to show the world how progressive she is. But rapport between the two has been tamped down by Barry's intuitive, accurate awareness that his every fumble and flirtation has been deconstructed by Brie and me for years.

Thanks to a waiting company car, it takes exactly ten minutes for Brie to drive up Madison and cross the park. In my building, only two apartments' doors open on every floor. Brie and Stephanie enter the building at the same time, silently share an elevator, and, to their mutual surprise, exit together to walk to the Marx residence. Brie turns to Stephanie. Her first impulse is to extend her hand for a shake, but she checks herself. This stranger in tight jeans, spiky boots, and go-getter perfume could be one of my mommy-pals, Brie decides. The woman might take such a gesture as butch.

Brie fears being typecast and tends to overcorrect. Today she is wearing a snug white sheath and spectator oxfords as pointy as tweezers. Their gold metal heels could double as ice picks, and her quietly shimmering snake bracelet winds around one arm. She'd be pleased if you'd guess her occupation as a rock star's publicist, not corporate litigator.

Brie smiles warmly. Stephanie does not respond. "I'm Brie Lawson, Molly's friend," she says nonetheless.

"Stephanie Joseph," she answers coolly. "Annabel's therapist."

Liar, liar, pants on fire!

Barry opens the door. His thinning hair is tangled from running his hands through it and he's padding around barefoot, although he's still in his rumpled dress shirt and suit pants. "Stephanie, meet Brie. Brie, Stephanie." He leads both women to the living room and collapses on the edge of a suede ottoman. "I tried to call that bitch-maniac, but her cell is off."

"Same thing for me," Brie says. "We should get to Claire and Dan."

*Claire and Dan. Who might they be?* Stephanie wonders. She longs to be strategic and essential, but how? "What about calling the police?" she suggests in her gravelly, nasal voice.

"The police?" Brie says, looking at this therapist dressed for after-hours clubbing. *And when did Annabel start seeing a therapist? Barry never mentioned her.* "Please, let's not go there—at least not yet."

"I'm thinking restraining order," Stephanie says. "We're talking kidnapping, at the very least." But neither Barry nor Brie gives her the courtesy of a response. "Listen, we could all use a drink. Dr. Marx, is that New Zealand sauvignon blanc you served the other night still in the wine fridge?"

Barry turns to Stephanie. "Good idea," he says. "I finished it, but open another."

Stephanie walks toward the kitchen. *Not only does this therapist know what's in Barry's wine refrigerator, she has a damn good body,* Brie thinks, and I have to agree as I size up her endless legs and high, rounded butt.

"How are you thinking you want to approach this?" Brie asks.

"Hey, lawyer," he says. "I was hoping you'd have a plan."

"Dr. Marx?" Stephanie yells out from the kitchen. "Could you give me a hand in here?"

"Excuse me," Barry says, and disappears. After a minute, Brie looks at her watch. Two more minutes pass before they return, Stephanie minus her burgundy gloss, although artfully applied liner remains around her lips.

"None for me, thanks," Brie says when Stephanie offers her a glass of wine. "We shouldn't waste any more time before we call your in-laws," she says to Barry. "The call's got to be from you."

"I'm dialing them now," he says, and reaches my father, who has just finished unpacking at a small hotel in the East Sixties. My mother has walked to Bloomingdale's to scout for Kitty's hostess gift. Scented candle? Chocolate-covered pretzels? Whatever she buys, my mother feels it will be wrong, and on that point she is right.

"Barry," my dad says heartily, answering on the first ring. *"A ziesen pesach."*

"Same to you, Dan, but it's not such a sweet Passover, I'm afraid."

Dan braces himself for a bad joke. A Catholic priest, a Protestant minister, and a Hasidic rabbi walk into a bar. "Don't tell me. Your mother decided to serve sushi instead of gefilte fish?" he asks genially.

"Are you sitting down?" Barry says, wanting to handle this right. Like most people on earth, Barry genuinely likes my father.

My dad doesn't just sit. He stretches out his bulky body on the bed and looks at the ceiling, his phone pressed to his ear. "Sit down" is never a preamble to anything you want to hear.

"It's Lucy," Barry says, and I see my father exhale with relief.

"Oh, yeah. I am so sorry she's not joining us for the holiday, Barry. It was extremely generous of your mother to invite all three of us, and I hope she's not offended. But you have to understand, Lucy's not ready—"

"She tried to snatch Annabel this afternoon, Dan. She did. She showed up at the school and almost got away with it. Scared Annabel to death," he adds, which I doubt is true, although I certainly haven't forgiven my sister for her colossal insanity.

*These New Yorkers, bunch of drama queens,* my dad decides. "What? There must be some mistake." *The ceiling has a brown-ringed water stain as big as my head,* he thinks, *yet they charge almost five hundred bucks a night for this airless shithole.* My father hates virtually everything about New York—the industrial-strength coffee, the warp-speed tempo, and the noise to match, but especially the rip-offs. "Barry, kids that age make things up. Molly used to have this imaginary friend, Pogo." He realizes he is shooting off his mouth, too much and too fast.

"There were witnesses," Barry says. "I don't know what was in your daughter's head," he says, still kindly, and I feel admiration for my husband's self-control as he edits himself. "Lucy's head." Because once there were two daughters. "I'm wondering, do you?"

Did he ever? That my father adored us was enough, at least for me. I never expected to be understood.

My father is sitting up now, and his face has flushed to a fevered red. "No, Barry, I don't know what the hell my daughter could possibly have been thinking. But, damn, you have to give her a pass. Don't get me wrong—if she did this . . . thing, it's contemptible and, Christ, god-damn twisted, and we will get to the bottom of it." *How will I tell Claire? She will dissolve into the floor.* "Obviously, Lucy needs help." *We'll see to it that she's on some shrink's couch so fast her head will fall off,* he thinks. "We'll call her in St. Bart's and demand—"

"Whoa. St. Bart's?"

"That's where she's going."

"She was hoping to take Annabel to St. Bart's?" Barry says. Lucy is an even bigger wack job than he thought.

*Maybe St. Bart's was the cover,* my father realizes. Man, does he feel thick. "Barry, I haven't even spoken to my daughter"—*my only surviving daughter*—"since yesterday. I better try to call her now. Please, son." He is afraid he will cry. "You'll have to excuse me." He hangs up without saying goodbye.

Barry throws his arms up in an exaggerated shrug and looks at the two women facing him.

"Am I correct to assume that Dan and Claire didn't know a thing?" Brie asks, pushing her snake bracelet up and down her arm. She and I both catch Stephanie watching her. Correction: it.

Barry nods. He feels it's safe to say they may rule out Divine conspiracy theories.

"I still think the police should be notified," Stephanie says, not unreasonably. "Maybe she's going to try this again. Lucy could be— anywhere."

Lucy, however, is not *anywhere.* Her plane is getting ready to touch down at O'Hare, and she is debating whether she should call a twenty-four-hour lunatic hotline. She is sweating remorse, stinking with regret, lonelier than she's ever been. *I've really done it this time,* Lucy has the good grace to think. *Too damn impulsive, didn't think through my plan. Lost sight of the ball. Now I'm good as busted.*

Barry is weighing Stephanie's advice when Brie walks to the piano. At my husband's request, my solo photographs have been packed away—"I can't handle looking at them"—but several happy-family pictures remain. Brie's gaze settles on my face. I feel her missing me, remembering me, loving me, wanting to do the right thing on my behalf. *She's the only real friend I could ever trust,* Brie thinks. *Molly lives inside me now, and I owe her. This crazy thing with Lucy's going to suck up energy and divert from finding the pig that's responsible for Molly's murder. Yes, murder. Had to be a murder.*

*Am I in the room with a murderer?* The thought rattles inside Brie's mind. She turns to Barry and speaks slowly and softly, one of her canniest courtroom techniques. "Barry, let's think about Molly. You know she would never want you rushing to implicate her sister, no matter how unforgivable the offense. She'd want you to talk it through with Lucy—eventually—and then figure things out. Privately. Discreetly."

*Lucy should get what she deserves, and Molly was a wimp,* Barry thinks. I always suspected that he thought that, but it hurts to hear it. Stephanie downgrades me to moron and tacks on spoiled bitch. "Come on," she says. The wine has given her courage and a glow that isn't unattractive. "This is crap, people. The right thing is to call the police. Forgive me for saying this, but we shouldn't let sentimentality cloud good judgment."

Brie, Barry, and I all read the boldface subtext: *What does it matter what this Molly thinks? She's dead.*

"Stephanie," Brie says, her voice an icicle, "you're overreacting. Speaking as a lawyer now, I wouldn't rush to judgment. This is strictly an internal family problem."

*You, woman, are not part of the family* smacks Stephanie between her carefully made-up brown eyes, which she's narrowed to slits. *Neither are you,* her face volleys back. "Speaking as a friend of the family— and a therapist—calling the police seems to be the only responsible, objective, intelligent response." She lands on each adjective slow and hard. This is not a woman to underestimate.

Under other circumstances, Barry thinks, he might sit back and enjoy—even encourage—an old-fashioned catfight. But not today. He knows whom he should call, the person he should have phoned two hours ago. "Pardon me," he says, and disappears into the bedroom.

"Kitty, you're not going to believe this one." For the next few minutes he fills in his elite one-woman security force on the world news of the week. When he's finished, and effectively ten years old, he takes a deep breath. "So what's your call? Get the police on it?"

I see his face whiten as he listens to her directive, blunt and instinctive. He hangs up the phone and returns to the living room.

"So?" Stephanie says.

"Ladies, Kitty Katz has spoken, and as usual, she is right," he announces. "Police equal publicity, and sensational publicity will fuck my practice. No police." He laughs, but he is not amused. "I'll work something out with the Divines. At least for now."

"You're going to do squat?" As Stephanie stammers, she spits an *s* that lands on Brie, who flicks it off. Unfazed, Stephanie crosses her arms in front of her in a pose that I am certain she's practiced in order to make the most of her full, high breasts, which, Brie and I are both guessing, have benefited from enhancement, perhaps under the steady hand of Barry Marx, M.D.

"For now, yes," he says, and looks at his watch. "And if you will both excuse me, I'm going to pick up my daughter."

Stephanie's eyes bore into Barry's as she waits for him to ask her to join him in collecting Annabel. Maybe he will even ask her to accompany both of them to his mother's seder, about which he seems to have forgotten. He does neither. "Okay, well, see you later," she says.

Brie hugs Barry and squeezes his hand. "We'll talk," she says, and turns to leave.

A minute later, Brie and Stephanie stand silently side by side waiting for the elevator. When they enter and the door closes, they are still alone. Brie faces Stephanie and asks the question at the top of her mind for the last half hour. "Tell me, was it before or after when you two hooked up?"

Go, Brie, go! Departed minds want to know!

"My relationship with Dr. Marx is strictly professional." Stephanie's voice has bounced back to an almost musical timbre. "Although last time I looked, he was single. And now it's my turn." She smiles at Brie, but only with her mouth. "Does it hurt that your girlfriend Molly picked Barry over you?"

"I wouldn't get too attached to Dr. Marx if I were you," Brie says. "He's got the attention span of a jock strap."

"He seems interested enough."

"You'd never pass his mother's sniff test."

"You are so wrong," Stephanie says, and laughs. "It was Kitty who introduced us." She remembers how after a yoga class Barry swung by to pick up Kitty for one of their regular lunch dates. "The famous son," Stephanie had said as she stood on the sidewalk talking to her new pal Kitty, who'd spoken of him often and hadn't overestimated his appeal.

"If you want to be territorial about Barry, why don't you just pee on him?" Brie asks.

"Excuse me? I can't hear you up there on your cross."

The voices are getting louder, higher, and shriller. When Brie walks out to Central Park West and glides into a waiting town car, I want to cheer her, although I had always mocked her for that particular perk.

Stephanie turns the corner. I pray she steps in dog shit.

*I despise that woman,* Brie and Stephanie each think. *What a piece of work.*

# Twenty-three

# CLEOPATRA COMMANDS
# HER BARGE

I've got tomorrow all planned," Brie says as she wields her hairbrush in fluid strokes while blasting a blow-dryer in the opposite hand. Her arms are slim and defined, like a fourteen-year-old boy's. I always envied them. "I was hoping you'd join us this time."

Brie is bare-breasted, and the only woman I know who can pull off Brazilian-cut panties, which sit high on your hips to reveal a peek of cheek. Nothing droops, which she attributes to genetic roulette, but I know the elliptical machine gets part of the credit.

"Give me the rundown," Isadora says, and slowly sinks into the froth of a deep, free-standing tub. She rarely hurries, and starts each morning with a ritual bath no less than fifteen minutes long. When she designed the apartment, Isadora insisted on a white marble bathroom as big as the bedroom. It looks like a laboratory and is, a buzzing workshop where beauty is nourished and transformation begins.

Brie has plotted Saturday by internal MapQuest. "We'll start with brunch at Sarabeth's on Central Park South because I know Annabel will love the pumpkin waffles, then the carousel and a stroll up Madison, where I saw the most adorable dress—a pale blue gingham pinafore—then frozen hot chocolate at Serendipity. Oh, and a bookstore—she's ready for *Madeline*," she says. "In the late afternoon, a movie and pizza." She turns the mirrors to assess the back of her hair. It's as smooth as if it were painted. "I wish I could take her to the theater again, but I don't want to miss the shopping."

"That's way too much for a five-year-old," Isadora says as she lifts her left leg out of the bubbles, arches her foot, and gently pumices away nonexistent calluses. Her size fives are a point of pride. There is no dithering over polish shades. She gets a weekly pedicure, always Chanel Vamp. Isadora accepts no substitutes.

"Actually, Annabel's almost four," Brie says.

"Even worse. Are you mental?"

"Who made you queen mother?" Brie asks in a low voice. "Annabel's going to love it." She plans to will it so.

"But all this for a *niña*? We'll have one whiny little princess on our hands." Isadora laughs and thinks, *Just like her mother.* In the last three months I have learned that in Isadora's estimation I wasn't worth getting all lathered up about—its own insult. She didn't despise me, but when her mind floats in my direction, condescension is right there, too. "You, my darling Brie, are wrong," she says calmly. *Tía Sabrina es loca.*

"So, don't join us," Brie says, and shrugs. With that she puts on two coats of black mascara, stiffens her shoulders, and walks out of the room, Cleopatra commanding her barge.

When Brie and Isadora are pissed, it doesn't end in plates sailing across the room. They're alpha show dogs—an Irish wolfhound and a standard poodle. It's been almost a year now and there has never been a bite that drew blood: they express their animus through posture, attitude, and the occasional preemptive bark.

Since my death, this will be Brie and Annabel's third outing. It's possible that my daughter has aroused a latent maternal instinct in my dearest friend, who until now has failed to nurture so much as a pot of chives. But perhaps the time passed together, lovely as it is for both, is mostly Brie's way to stay close to me. Or—drilling down, because she's one of the most instinctively competitive women I ever met, which I say with deep respect—it's about one-upping Lucy and now Stephanie. Not that Stephanie's been all that interested in Annabel.

I would read Brie's mind, if only she herself knew it. But I have learned that despite substantial evidence to the contrary, her head is a lot cloudier inside than anyone would guess. That Brie is one slightly mixed-up babe makes me love her more.

A driver is waiting downstairs to deliver her to the office. When Brie arrives, she logs onto her computer and pulls up a new file. *Annabel.* She scrolls through case after sordid case of disputes where fathers, a surprising number of whom wear mullets and orange prison jumpsuits, have been denied custody of their daughters. Some dads were years delinquent with child support. Others are in the process of, say, switching genders. Nice to know ya, Duane. Y'all meet Dixie!

Brie bites her lip. She isn't finding the legal precedent of a widower who loses his child not to his wife's family but to his wife's friend. She isn't even coming close, and since she doesn't have time to continue the search, she switches to e-mail. A blitz of messages appears, mostly with headings in cryptic legalese. After she scans her inbox, the one she reads first is from hihicks@gmail.com. *Anything new at your end? Today, the mother-in-law.*

*I wish I had leads to feed you, Detective Hicks,* Brie's thinking. *I wish I could figure this out on my own, but I'm coming up with nothing. I'm counting on you. Why hasn't this case been solved already? What's taking so damn long? Are we forgetting that a woman died, a young, beautiful woman? My best friend. But I've got to keep my head in the game. Stay cool.*

*Hello Kitty—watch out—she hisses,* Brie writes back, and waits for a response from Hicks. There is none. This doesn't make her unhappy. It makes her thinks he's working hard. No nonsense. Good.

Brie answers a few more e-mails and is interrupted by a buzz from her assistant. Her first deposition waits.

I leave Brie to fight on behalf of liberty and justice for all and circle back to Kitty's building. Hicks enters. I half expect him to be carrying a bouquet: my mother-in-law attracts gifts the way other women do mosquitoes. She has one whole closet filled with tributes: tall reeds that slip into essential oils, Egyptian cotton dish towels in rainbow hues, pithy advice books she'll never read, Florentine notepaper, enemies' scalps.

"Detective," she says. "At last." Kitty Katz ushers Hicks into the living room.

I see an overdecorated Manhattan co-op, everything inert, just so.

But Hicks sees something else as his eyes sweep the room with the swift look-see he's perfected during his eight years on the force. Hicks sees money. His new condo, which is a big step up from his mother's place in a less cultivated section of uptown Manhattan, would fit into the foyer and living room. He never knew that beige came in so many varietals. Yet the room is far from dull, thanks to a mix of muted tapestry, mohair, silk, tweed, and velvet, especially the velvet, whose silken smoothness on a pillow he can't resist stroking when Kitty turns her back. Afternoon light boomerangs off a few well-chosen pieces of antique Murano in tutti-frutti colors. In another life, this taut, handsomely dressed woman was apparently the contessa of the Venice lagoon.

Hicks also can't help noticing that while he sees pictures of Annabel and many of Barry at different ages, there is only one of Barry, Annabel, and me, on a side table overshadowed by a pungent arrangement of tall peach roses and birds of paradise.

"Coffee? Tea?" Kitty says. Pinky is standing ready, unseen, in the kitchen.

"No, thank you," he says. "I'm aware that you're on a tight schedule, so if you agree, Mrs. Katz, let's dive in." Out comes the small black leather notebook, which isn't as pristine as the first time I saw it. He smiles. "Okay, let's take it from the top. Did your son and daughter-in-law have a happy marriage?"

*Has he had orthodontia?* is Kitty's first thought. Next she considers what the correct answer to the question might be. "Divinely happy." She laughs. "No pun intended." Although it was. "Devoted. Molly adored my son." *Who wouldn't,* her face says.

"No cracks in the surface, Mrs. Katz? Tensions, worries?"

"Of course. What young marriage doesn't have all that?"

"Just answers, Mrs. Katz. Just answers. And your own relationship with the deceased? With Molly?"

Kitty leans forward and extends her hand—age spots lasered away, sporting one hefty, square-cut diamond solitaire in a platinum setting. "You know, Detective," she says, "my own mother-in-law—that would be Barry's father's mother, may she rest in peace—interfered with my life no end." She has to stop herself from rolling her eyes at the memory of that particular hairy-chinned bat. "I made a point of never doing that." She pronounces "never" as if italicized. "I gave my son and Molly their space."

The truth: Kitty did give me a wide berth, but rarely a day passes when she and Barry don't speak. If she told Hicks this, he would understand, because in his family, interference equals love. The more meddling, the more love—two-thirds of a triangle completed by food.

*The Katz woman had no use for Molly,* Hicks jots in his notebook, using cop code only he would understand. "Was Molly the wife you pictured for your son?" he asks.

Ah, the answer? Please! Might Kitty have preferred a member of the right charity committees with, say, a golf handicap in the single digits? Too threatening, perhaps. A mini-Kitty? Yes, if the woman worshipped her as much as both of them worshipped Barry and was on board with advancing his practice, a woman who buried her own identify before the Barry throne.

"I never pictured a wife for my son," she says, in what might be her first honest answer of the day. Indeed, my bullshit meter has fallen silent.

A grin crosses Hicks' face. "Then you're a good sight different from my ma. She's had the girl picked out for me since I was twenty-three." Evian, who cornrows his mother's hair. Sweet kid, Evian. A shapely lady, all heart, just like Ma, who invites her to Sunday dinner at least once every two months. One of these days Ma will catch on to the fact that he is not Evian's type, a hot-shit detective who can't dance to save his life. But he and Ev play along and flirt away those Sunday afternoons. Every Christmas, he sends her the biggest box of chocolates Godiva sells. She gives him the thickest history book on the best-seller list. Once a summer, they take in a Yankee game and afterward, over beers and dogs, bemoan the unfortunate state of romance in America, their own lack thereof, in particular.

"Tell me about Molly, things only you know."

"Well," she says, savoring this tasty question as she lights up. "I don't think she had much confidence—"

This may be true, but I was working on it, and dammit, she didn't help.

"—or that many friends."

Heresy! A blatant lie! Kitty just didn't know many of my friends—

dozens of colleagues, current and former; five or six mommies; my book club; bicycle people; college buddies; even a few doctors' wives. Lucy, sort of. Brie!

"Let me amend that," she says, almost as if she heard me. "She has that lawyer from college who spoke at the funeral and, of course, male friends."

"And might you know their names?"

"Unfortunately, I don't, but I'm sure, with your sources . . ." She looks Hicks straight in the eye as she flicks her ash on a Baccarat plate. "And also, I must tell you she was envious of all the attention my son received. As you know, Dr. Marx has a thriving practice."

Envious of Barry? What a crock. I am outraged, but then I concede that Dr. Kitty might be on to something. Perhaps I was envious of how Barry always triple-lutzed through life, self-doubt as foreign to him as flying a helicopter, not that he wouldn't try to do that, given the chance.

"And her twin sister?" she continues. *Maniac,* Kitty thinks as she grinds her cigarette into extinction. "But I gather you're on to Lucy. My revelations will not be enlightening."

"She's a complicated one," he says. Hicks knows the woman wants to be brought up to speed. *Are we ready to throw her in the slammer?*

"*Complicated?*" Kitty lets loose with her signature cackle, half whinny, half caw.

"And interesting," he says. "Not to worry, we're on her. It's you I'd like to talk more about today, thanks." He looks again at his notebook and, while he's thinking, admires the portrait of a young dark-haired boy with a fox terrier. Barry, *le petit prince.* "Mrs. Katz, on the day of your daughter-in-law's death, where were you?"

"Now, finally, an easy question," Kitty says gaily as she lights a second cigarette. Or maybe it's her third. "In the afternoon I was shopping on Madison Avenue and afterwards played mah-jongg, like I always do on winter Fridays, with three of my oldest friends, Suzette, Linda, and Nancy." *Bam! Dot! Crack!* As if a confirmation from the mahj girls and boutique receipts corroborate innocence.

"So, getting down to business here," Hicks asks, leaning forward, using his most beseeching timbre—intimate, conspiratorial—"was Molly Marx the victim of some random crazy or was she intentionally murdered?" Slowly he pulls out a colored photo from the crime scene.

She gives a little gasp as she sees my face as filet mignon à la Sweeney Todd. "The latter, possibly," she says, rolling the word in her mouth like a sucking candy. "Yes, I think it's entirely possible that someone took her life on purpose."

"Why, Mrs. Katz?" His voice is rougher than before.

"That's what I can't fathom."

"Mrs. Katz, hazard a guess." It is an order.

"Someone would have had to hate Molly. Who, I can't say." Because she can't imagine me engendering that intense a response in another person.

"Could that person be your son?"

"No!" While Kitty is saying the word, her mind is racing. *Is this possible? Could Molly have done something so heinous the poor boy snapped like a bungee cord?*

"Another woman?" Hicks suggests. He lets the grisly photo of me stay face-up on the table.

"My son was a faithful husband." My bullshit meter reactivates with a loud bleep. *And if he wasn't,* she's thinking, *so what? Barry's father was no different, though he learned that diamonds cure suspicion and we both got on with our lives.* "And if he wasn't," Kitty adds, "how would I know? But I can safely say any woman—any other woman—my son would ally himself with would never be so vile as to commit murder. Frankly, Detective, I am deeply offended that you would even suggest this."

*It's my fucking job,* Hicks thinks, but tries to smile with deep sympathy.

"Which is why I'm thinking she . . ." Kitty pauses and takes a deep drag, which she would like to blow in Hicks' handsome face. "She most likely took her own life."

"Really? Suicide?" *That's a joke,* Hicks thinks. *Where's the motive? According to her internist and gynecologist, both of whom Molly saw at the first of the year, good girl that she was, she was healthy—no secret, gruesome disease, no pregnancy by some inconvenient man. The husband, well, he may be a player and a jerk, but folks say he spent plenty of time at home, and it's a pretty exceptional home at that.* "Your daughter-in-law rode her bike off the road, possibly right into the Hudson River? Did she intend to drown herself but didn't make it far enough? I don't quite get that. But let's not talk about how, tell me *why.*"

"She was one of those sad, unstable people who looked normal enough on the outside but was really the type no one could make happy." *Suicide, Kitty thinks, is going to get this detective with his wheedling ways sniffing elsewhere, away from Barry and away from me.*

This is why Bob has warned me not to trail Hicks in his investigations, because it will make *me* want to commit murder. I would like to crush and mash Kitty's most valuable piece of Murano and stir the shards into her tea, then force her to drink it slowly, to max out the poison and pain—even if Hicks ain't buying what she has to sell.

"No one could make her happy, not even your son?" he asks.

Kitty tilts her head down so Hicks can't see it. I can. She looks nervous, deeply agitated. "Some women just can't be content—the well of misery is that deep."

"Others have implied this." Hicks feels a sharp bang in his gut as he articulates this lie designed to draw out Kitty.

"Really?" Kitty asks. She'd like to believe this were true, but she smells a setup, even if this is the first time she's ever been questioned by a police officer.

"Yes, really, and what I'd like to know is, what could have made Molly Marx angry enough, and so deeply disappointed, that she would abandon her daughter and husband by taking her own life?"

As if she might discover the answer inside, Kitty picks up a green lacquered box that Pinky keeps filled with fresh cigarettes. "I'd like to know that, too, Detective Hicks."

He's being stonewalled, and Hicks feels his work here today is as finished as Kitty's last smoke. "Well, if anything comes to you . . ." He stands, stretches his legs, and shakes Kitty's hand formally. She steps back a step, almost as if she's frightened. *Did I overdo it?* she wonders.

Hicks leaves behind his card as Pinky materializes and hands him his raincoat. He does a double-take. *What the fuck. Does this other woman live in Ma's building? Nah, she just looks like that busybody next door.*

*Maybe Molly did kill herself,* he thinks as he stands in the richly carpeted hall, ringing for the elevator. Self-defense against big mean Kitty with her claws out.

Hicks has a craving for gravy and biscuits, for home. "Ma," he says on his cell phone as soon as he walks to Seventy-sixth Street, glad to get her on the first ring. "How do you feel about cooking on Sunday?" He shakes his head. "Sure, Ma, invite Ev."

*Twenty-four*

# NEED MEETS WANT

Y ou were brilliant," Luke said when the Sonoma pictures came back. "Get out your calendar, Molly Marx, because thanks to your good work, we have a job in Bridgehampton, and after that Nantucket, and then one right in town."

"*Our* good work," I said. I thanked him, put down the phone, and penciled in the dates, my hand trembling.

I'd been back from California for five endless days and four sleepless nights. Luke was taking up all the space in my head. I'd relived our vineyard romp so many times that I could have acted out both the male and female leads for the most discriminating of directors. This was our first post-Sonoma conversation. If there was a next move, I didn't know it, at least as long as I was stone-cold sober, which I fully intended to stay.

Luke downshifted to a low murmur. "Do you have any regrets?"

Did he? Because if so, I could no more imagine standing next to him at a shoot than I could see myself having Annabel's first-birthday party that weekend at Hooters. If Luke felt regretful, I'd simply cancel the jobs I'd written into my calendar. No looking back.

"Molly, are you there?"

"Regrets?" I said. What the hell. I'd tell the truth, and while I was at it impersonate an eighteenth-century courtesan. "None." I couldn't quite get a word like *darling* out of my mouth. "What about you?"

There was no hesitation, although I suspect Luke was waiting for me to elaborate. "I've never been less regretful in my whole life," he said. "Best day of my decade."

I said nothing.

"So how does lunch sound?"

"Great," I answered, trying to respond like a woman with no more at stake than a Cobb salad. "Thanks."

"At my place," he added, whipping out the E-ZPass to every illicit relationship. "What day can you make it?"

I didn't want to make decisions. I wished Luke could read my mind and know that. What I wanted to hear was *How about lunch tomorrow?* To that I would reply that I couldn't accept because Annabel had a play-date. One more day of longing from afar. Which was a lot simpler, and would absolve me of the guilt I was feeling along with the mightier wallops of sexual longing, full-tilt excitement, and plain old curiosity. But unfortunately, Luke was being entirely too flexible. This led to thinking that there was an *us*, which required me to stick around to see what would happen between the members of this attractive couple. I was not able to shout out, *Oops, I am terribly sorry, but it slipped my mind that I've taken a vow of fidelity in front of hundreds of people, a rabbi representing both thousands of years of Judaism and the sovereign state of Illinois, and the man who might be a cheater but just the same is my husband. No, sir. I can't have lunch. I shouldn't even have a Pepsi.*

So we made a date for the following week.

As I was on the way to Luke's apartment, my stomach lurched, and potholes weren't entirely to blame. The taxi driver stopped at his address, a four-story limestone building on a gritty street. There was a sprinkling of trash littering the sidewalk and no doorman. A woman walked out the front door and I breezed in. The lobby had a speckled terrazzo floor and black marble walls. I could see it in a decorating spread titled "Faded Glory." I stepped into the elevator, which rose in slow motion, a long, brass arrow pointing to each passing floor. I felt as if the arrow might leap off the wall and land in my heart.

A few months ago, Luke had decamped from the West Village for the East Village. To the remotely hip—a demographic to which I do not belong, now or ever—this hadn't been a pioneer neighborhood for more than a decade. *Rent*-style squatters had moved on. I'd heard about cunning boutiques sandwiched between locksmiths and filthy bodegas and knew the area was loaded with bistros serving fusion cuisine far beyond French/Vietnamese—Japanese/Guatemalan, Israeli/Palestinian? On account of this culinary creativity, four-star restaurants in sadly stuffy midtown and above were now empty night after night, especially on weekends. Yet despite all this, on my mental map of Manhattan, the East Village may as well have been the Balkans.

I stood outside 4B. Should I turn around? I'd gotten this far. I knocked.

"I didn't hear you buzz," Luke said a half minute later after he'd looked through the peephole. "Have you been waiting long?"

*Yes,* I thought, *I have been waiting thirty-five years to behave this way.* I suppose women do this all the time in Paris, in London, and right here in Manhattan. I, however, am a woman more comfortable deciding between wild- and farm-raised salmon than whether or not to sleep—again—with a man who is not my husband. I wished I'd stepped out of a forties movie where the wasp-waisted vamp wears a belted trench coat over a slinky satin dress with shoulder pads. At least then I could deliver some sparkling dialogue. Instead I said, "No, not long."

"C'mon in," he said, hanging my coat on a peg in an oak-paneled hallway that led to a big, square room. Burnished wainscoting ended above my head, beyond which the walls were an inky blue. The room had a twelve-foot-high ceiling; hanging from it, four dimly lit antique brass chandeliers cast a clinquant glow on this sunless day. There were two groupings of squashy brown couches, and a sensual dark red recamier next to a table piled with books. In the air I detected a faint scent. Green tea? Fresh pears? My nose traveled to a small pile of scented black rocks next to a photograph of a family that must be Luke's. In the far corner of the room a round table was set for two with rough beige linen placemats and sleek white dishes.

He really did mean lunch.

"Did you notice that over the outside door it says New York Free Circulating Library?" Luke said eagerly. Ah, he was nervous, too.

"I missed that," I said. "Should we have a do-over?"

"Shall we?" he said, and reached his arms around my shoulders as he melted against me. I closed my eyes and explored his mouth. There I was again, adrift, surrounded by a moat that kept reality at bay. I was circulating, all right. I felt as if I could feel my own blood rushing through my veins and every hair standing on end.

He took my hand. "Let me show you around." His arm encircling my waist, Luke led me to another hall, on which he'd hung dozens of his black-and-white photographs, not just pictures from work but bridges, many bridges. On one side of the corridor, a French door led to a study lined with bookshelves and covered with wallpaper on which peacocks strutted. "The birds are from the previous owner," he said. "I was planning to rip them out, but I'm beginning to think of them as pets."

"If you rip them out, I will kill you," I said, pointing. "The big fellow here just winked at me."

On the other side was the kitchen. Over an enameled sink—pristine and white—a stuffed deer's head stood watch, its graceful antlers the only curve in the room. The two bathrooms' walls were paneled, and in the larger one, a claw-foot tub faced a window overlooking a roof garden with iron furniture and a leafless tree growing in a large terra-cotta tub. Our tour proceeded slowly, Luke an eager guide. "I was able to salvage it from the original" or "Looks authentic, yes? Big fake" or "You've got to see this."

There was one last door at the end of the hall. As Luke placed his hand on the brass knob, I took a deep breath. To enter might be the most regrettable move of my life.

"I don't know what to do with this room," he said as he crossed the threshold. "Any ideas?"

I stepped inside. The walls were stark white. I turned my back on the black iron bed, plainly made with simple linens, and took in a baroquely carved mantel, also white, its hearth laid with birch logs. Hanging above was a blow-up of a nude couple entwined in sheets. I recognized the shot from Luke's portfolio and remembered the highly publicized story about the models, busted for snorting coke and hooking up on the job. In the center of the ceiling hung a trio of old ships' lanterns, tranquilly sparkling like magnums of vintage Champagne.

"Aside from the hockey stick in the corner, I'd say don't change one thing."

"Sorry, the stick stays—but one thing's missing," he said, emerging from the shadows.

I was wearing a cashmere V-neck, a pencil skirt, tights, and tall boots, but nonetheless I felt chilled. "I don't think I can do this, Luke," I said. My voice was a whisper.

"I want you," he said hoarsely. "And unless I'm crazy, you feel the same way."

"That's irrelevant." Painful, but irrelevant. "I'm sorry." I wasn't sure why I felt the need to apologize.

"Molly, I would never pressure you," he said, and hugged me close for at least a minute. I wanted both to continue and to stop. Luke steered me back to the hall, his hand on the small of my back. We walked into the kitchen and stared at each other without exchanging a word. The music—was it Diana Krall?—had stopped, or maybe I just couldn't hear it over the beat of my heart. He reached for two bowls on an open shelf and from a tall black stockpot ladled steaming carrot soup, redolent with ginger. Crusty bread and olive oil were already on the table, and a salad of soba noodles, sweetened with mango and spiced with chilies and mint, waited in the glass-fronted refrigerator. Our lunch had turned careful, controlled. As we ate and drank and finished with espresso, we spoke only of work.

I'd made the right decision to keep my skirt on and my guard up, I told myself. I felt church-lady solid, the ne plus ultra of virtue.

Shortly before three o'clock, when the last dish was dried, we kissed goodbye—chastely, sweetly. My pheromones behaving themselves, I walked out the door with a promise to e-mail him ideas for the next job.

The taxi hadn't traveled two blocks when I knew. I pulled my phone out of my bag. "Luke," I said, "I forgot something."

"Really?" he said.

"Yes," I answered. "Dessert."

I needed to feel the roughness of his cheek against mine and move my mouth down the length of his body until I found an even sweeter spot. I wanted to trace his profile with my fingertips and let them linger below. I needed and wanted more of what I'd tasted on that Caribbean island and while pressed against a floor beneath a cool vat of California chardonnay. Need and want were scrambled and I could no longer decipher, or even cared to decipher, my internal code.

I instructed the driver to return to the spot where he'd picked me up. When we got there, he asked if I wanted him to wait. "No," I said. "I may be a while." I twisted around the stone in my engagement ring so it wasn't glaring at me with reproach and dropped a twenty-dollar bill into his hand. The driver seemed happy, as did I.

This time when I walked into Luke's apartment, I headed straight into the bedroom, which is where I stayed until the afternoon ended, along with what remained of my innocence. In its place, I'd found something else.

# Twenty-five

# WHAT THE HEART WANTS

*I* know I was hasty," Lucy insists for the umpteenth time, "but I meant no harm."

"Lucy," Mom says wearily, "hasty hardly explains it."

"Okay, foolhardy, reckless, rash."

"Can you explain yourself, please?"

I thought my mother might end that sentence with "young lady."

"I still don't know what was in my head," Lucy says, "but you believe me, don't you, that I didn't mean to hurt Annabel or upset you and Dad?" Lucy's never been as gifted at talking to my parents as I was; she's never been able to charm them, ever. Every time she attempts to talk about the day she snatched Annabel, she sets her own trap.

All Claire Divine believes is that Lucy is certifiable. For exactly what, she's not sure. They are on the way home from the office of Dr. Solomon, the safety net Lucy now jumps into four times a week at five o'clock in the afternoon. My sister rejected the first four therapists Oxford coughed up. She'd have passed on this one, too, if she hadn't been afraid that if she didn't start treatment, she'd be exiled to Camp Wounded Soul to suffer through seminars on how self-destruction is for dummies. *At least,* Lucy thinks, as she and my mother pull into the driveway, *Daphne Solomon, M.D., has never once used the word* dysfunctional, *at least out loud.*

Lucy despises her current life, although she's come to realize this is as good as it's going to get. She'd had to negotiate with our parents, who acted as mediators with Barry, for permission to continue to teach. If it had been up to my husband, she'd have been exiled straight to Hazelden, a captive in a dungeon. To rehab what? she asked. For loving Annabel too much? Wanting a little quality time with her dead sister's kid? Worrying about a child's well-being? This is, of course, how she explained what has become known in my family as "the incident."

Barry has agreed to let Lucy stay under Divine house arrest. Lucy is an upper-middle-class parent's worst nightmare: a single, never-married, childless adult daughter returned to the nest, back in our old bedroom, as if she's been grounded for smoking a joint. If Target sold GPS ankle bracelets, my parents would buy one and solder it in place. Instead, they chauffeur Lucy to her appointments and to her job in the city as if she were fourteen.

Their life has become more embarrassing, suffocating, and uncomfortable than the most hideous reality TV show. When they all sit down to eat or watch a DVD, there is a firewall between my parents and sister, preventing even the most mundane chatter. Lucy can look neither parent in the eye. Today she helps haul in the seven bags of groceries bought at Sunset Market, puts everything away, and excuses herself to read upstairs. Lucy feels like the world's biggest loser as she stands in front of the bathroom mirror and searches for gray hairs. She plucked out her first one last month, and two more yesterday. By the time this nightmare is over, Lucy is sure, she will be silver-haired or bald.

"Fuck," she says aloud, and goes to her twin bed and pounds a pillow. "Fuck. Fuck. Fuck."

"Are you okay up there?" Mom shouts.

"Just dandy," she shouts back.

If Lucy wasn't cuckoo before—and she is convinced that she wasn't, just extremely "concerned"—living in this suburban petri dish will take her right there. I haven't worked myself up to sympathy, though I'm trying to travel the high road. I have chosen to pretend that Lucy is simply misunderstood. She doesn't have a screw loose, she loved me deeply, and her intentions are pure. I won't let myself believe that my sister's motives were those of a monster. I won't.

I also know that if Lucy realized I was thinking all of the above, she'd say, *Molly, you are such a goddamn dope.* Which takes me to my real bottom line: the incident makes me furious. It was and is a phenomenal time and energy suck, utterly unfair to my parents and to Annabel, who is now denied the company of her only aunt. It has only deepened the rift between the Divine and Marx clans, making it almost impossible for my parents to have even the simplest conversation with their only grandchild, not to mention resurrect the social life they have put on hiatus. Mostly, it's been a diversion that makes me worry that Hicks will go off on some tangent that moves him away from figuring out *why*, despite the fact that I know from observation that he's working 24/7, more or less, on the Molly Marx case.

But simmering at a slow boil—where will that get me? In the Duration we call people who do that Hornets. They buzz around, full of righteous indignation, and even other Hornets avoid them as if they have stinky feet. I've been talking about Lucy to Bob, my Dr. Solomon.

"Focus on the good memories," he said yesterday, as he always does, when we took our evening constitutional. This is his one-size-fits-all wisdom to calm the brain and soothe the soul, his downward-facing dog of celestial advice.

I thought it was a pile of caca. "How do you find a good memory when your anger's a riptide?" I asked.

"You're angry about a lot of things," he said. "You'll have plenty of time to sort it out. Tease out a warm memory with your sister and focus on it."

"Thank you, Angel of Death," I said. He hates when I call him that.

"Molly," he said, "do it. Dig deep. Find a happy Lucy thought."

For days, it was like looking for my pulse, and then I remembered. It was two years ago. For our thirty-third birthday my parents had been wildly generous and blew us to a week's stay at a posh Mexican fitness resort. They thought the adventure would help us bond.

For six days, we roomed together in a stucco hacienda that looked to be on loan from a miniature golf course. We rose at dawn, when the air was dewy and cool, and hiked the wildflower-covered hills, Lucy apace with the leader and I, naturally, at the tail end. After a breakfast fit for two longshoremen, we sampled every class. Lucy's favorite was Pilates, where she fell in love with a giant widget modeled after a medieval rack. In the afternoon, we played tennis. She won match after match, but I didn't mind, hypnotized as I became by the *thwank-thwank-thwank* of balls hitting the rusty-red clay court, the quintessential warm-weather percussion.

As each afternoon wound down, we treated ourselves to hot stone massages or had sturdy little Mexican ladies wrap our fried muscles in seaweed. Toxins banished, we napped in hammocks, spent the evenings enthusiastically beading bracelets we knew we'd never wear, and snoozed through lectures like What Does a Woman *Really* Need? Magnesium! By nine-thirty, we collapsed without even opening the beach books we'd lugged on the plane.

Somewhere between kick-boxing and Aerobics with Soul, the pampering and the meditating, we became confidantes. "I got dumped again," Lucy said on our last night. We'd turned off the light and the fragrance of jasmine and honeysuckle blew gently through opened shutters.

"Who was he?" I asked. I was aware she'd been seeing someone, but she hadn't mentioned a name and I knew that if I played *Meet the Press,* I'd be decapitated.

"You can call him dickhead."

"What happened?"

"Married."

"I thought you were too smart for that." She didn't say a word for a few minutes following that remark, and I thought maybe she'd fallen asleep, until she started speaking in a soft, unfamiliar voice.

"At first it was just hot, dirty sex and I got off on being part of a covert operation—when we'd finally get to see each other, we'd rip each other's clothes off. We'd meet at my place and every few months go away for the weekend. Remember my trip to South Beach?"

I did: the Delano Hotel, stone crabs, mojitos, underwater music, poolside bungalows. Lucy described it so vividly I thought I'd been there myself. "That was three years ago."

She sighed. "I'd see other guys, but gradually I let myself get totally into this sonofabitch, waiting by the phone, telling lies to my friends, acting unglued if he cancelled at the last minute, which usually he did."

She sat up in bed and wrapped her arms around her strong, tanned legs. "Christ, it's humiliating to tell you all this."

"Don't stop now."

"He kept saying he was going to leave his wife and move in with me. Can you believe I, Lucy Divine, bought that sack of shit?"

I was holding my breath. "What happened?"

"So two weeks ago, Jessica—she's another teacher—was at the hospital visiting her cousin who had a baby. And guess who was there looking through the glass into the nursery?"

"No!"

"She recognized his face from a picture she'd seen on my desk."

I heard Lucy sniffle. It was too dark to check for tears.

"Jessica took me aside the next day, saying she'd been up all night debating whether to tell me. I drove straight to the hospital." She paused. "David and his wife had had a boy. Looked just like him."

My stomach turned over. "Oh, I'm so, so sorry, Luce," I said. "What a jerk—"

"Molly, shut up," she snapped, back to the real Lucy. "I don't need your pity. Got that?"

In the shadows, I stared at my sister, whom I realized I hardly knew and might never know. "Fuck you, Moosey. I won't shut up," I said, and threw a pillow at her head. "You let yourself care for someone. What's so bad about that? If you did it over, do you honestly think you'd do anything differently? The heart wants what the heart wants."

"Who are you, Woody Allen?"

"I love you, that's all," I said. I don't think I'd ever told her that.

Lucy said nothing. Then I heard her voice, muted and fuzzy, a Xerox of a Xerox. "I always feel judged by you, Mrs. Marx with the perfect life."

"Perfect life?" I said incredulously, in a raspy squeak. I decided not to react to "judged" because she was right—I had judged her for more than thirty years.

"The darling toddler, the successful husband, the perfect part-time job, the huge apartment, the blond hair, the size six hips."

Of course she saw it that way. "I'll grant you Annabel, but Barry . . ."

"Trouble in paradise?" she said. Too quickly.

I'd walked into a Lucy ambush. I didn't want to betray Barry, but the sisterly thing would be to share. "Barry is a great dad, but sometimes he barely notices I'm around, and when he does, it's to criticize. He questions every decision I make. That is, when he hasn't ruled unilaterally and I get to decide on something."

"What did you expect? Do you actually believe all those drunken speeches grooms make at weddings about how flipped-out in love they are and how their wife is their ideal woman, an angel on earth?" I believe she followed this question with a snort.

"I think he sees other women," I said.

She had the decency to wait a moment before saying, "We all think that."

Mom and Dad, too? "But Lucy, there's more." I hesitated. "The thing is, there's this other guy." I didn't give one detail, certainly not Luke's name. "I never meant for it to happen." Even I realized I was speaking every cheater's native language, cliché. "But for a long time now, I've been meeting him at his apartment." I left out Nantucket, Amsterdam, Santa Fe, Yellowstone, and the Mall of America.

"*You* have a lover?"

"I guess you could call him that."

She laughed. "For midwesterners, we are a fucked-up pair."

I thought that was a fitting note on which to end the conversation. I didn't want to tell Lucy more; the details would, like an oil spill, pollute my real life. But as I had almost given in to sleep she said, "Molly, I think you should stop this thing with the other guy. The heart may want what the heart wants, but you could get hurt." She had flipped off the glib Lucy and become someone reflective and wise. "Like me." She sat on the side of her bed and tapped me on the shoulder. "I say this because I love you." The two of us started to cry—noisy, gulping sobs—and neither of us fell asleep for a good hour.

We slept late and missed not only the hike that morning but the van to the San Diego airport. And this, I told Bob, was the happiest memory I would ever have of my sister.

## Twenty-six

# LOVE ACTUALLY

"Are you and the ladies off to the land of very important paintings?" Luke asked.

Today I had planned to visit galleries with Brie and Isadora, as they were on the prowl for something large and sublime to hang on their naked living room wall and Brie wanted my advice. She'd called early this morning, however, to say that she needed to work. I couldn't picture an afternoon alone with Isadora, a woman as relaxing as gridlock, so Saturday loomed like an unlined page.

Barry was off to San Francisco, attending a pep rally for plastic surgeons. He'd spent weeks prepping—cruising Gucci for a suit that said wildly hip yet Park Avenue, the location of his office. He'd gotten his hair cut exactly ten days before, so it wouldn't look too freshly pruned. Barry wanted to be prime-time polished, ready to expound on his much-heralded weekend butt lift. ("A cheeky booty with zero squats!" *Vogue* had gushed.) He'd hesitated before accepting the speaking invitation, weighing glory against reality. Did he really want to share secrets with the rest of the profession? I believed the tiebreaker was a patient who'd offered to help him rehearse, numerous times, and curiously, always at night. I also believed she was an actress valued less for her talent than for her juicy body parts, many of which have been re-habbed by Dr. Marx.

"Brie cancelled," I said to Luke. "Something about a settlement meeting. How goes the drive to New Hampshire?" He was visiting his brother this weekend. I checked my watch. Eleven o'clock. "You must be in Massachusetts by now."

"The trip's not happening," he said. "My nephew is celebrating his fourth birthday with strep."

While I let the news wash over me, I said, "Poor kid," with what I hoped was appropriate concern. Maybe Luke and I could see each other. It had been twenty-two days. Clarification. We'd *seen* each other—at meetings, for coffee, and once for lunch at Le Pain Quotidien—but we hadn't been together in the way I'd grown to adore, more and more, for the past year or so. For the last three weeks, Luke had hosted Irish cousins who were enjoying Manhattan so much it appeared as if they were going to sleep on his couches until their green cards came through. On the second week of the Danny-and-Seamus show, Luke splurged on the St. Regis, a Manhattan convenience I recently learned that you can rent for an afternoon, not unlike a carpet shampooer. We wouldn't be returning there soon, though. Not only did the room cost as much as a small painting, but on the way out I spied one of Kitty's Girls, who may have been on a mission similar to my own. I vowed that never again, un-less I was in the vicinity of a grizzly bear, would I cower terrified behind a tree, indoors or out. Hotels were out.

A few hours earlier, Annabel had been spirited away by Kitty, who wouldn't be returning her until bedtime. They'd never spent a whole day alone together, and like many first dates, theirs began awkwardly when the name of the restaurant was revealed: Annabel had counted on Dunkin' Donuts, not Fred's at Barneys. But my daughter regained com-posure when she learned that her grandmother was also taking her to see the Alice in Wonderland statue in Central Park. As to the rest of the schedule, Kitty was sketchy, although I wouldn't have been surprised if she'd cram in an etiquette seminar for three-year-olds.

I'd already accomplished that day's first order of business, finding piles of Barry's credit card receipts and cell phone bills, which I in-tended to scrutinize later for evidence of philandering. Just then I was taking a break. I'd crawled back into bed, a *W* along with me, and had finished reading a passionate diatribe, "The Fatted Calf: When You Can't Fit into the Season's Boots," being thankful for a problem I didn't have, when Luke called.

"What are you doing right now?"

"I'm in bed." I did my best to purr.

"Really? What are you wearing?"

I looked at my XL T-shirt, left over from a breast cancer race-walk, hanging over saggy cotton boxers. "Not a thing. How about you?"

"Weekend grunge. I had coffee in Little Italy and I'm heading toward Chinatown."

"What do you say to dim sum?" I said, feeling an energy surge. "Meet at Golden Bridge in an hour?"

"I say I prefer your buns to theirs."

"Don't tell me the blarney brothers finally left?" Either way, I could scurry downtown in less than hour. "Did New York run out of beer?"

"No such luck—they're sleeping off last night," Luke said. "I was thinking of a certain elite uptown address on Central Park West."

Oh, really? I had gotten used to Luke's place. I had, in fact, gotten very used to Luke's place, where I knew the woodsy scent of his sandalwood soap, exactly how he folded and hung his thick gray towels, and where he kept his herbal tea, which I'd brew and take back into bed with us in tall pottery mugs, the steam curling my hair and warming my hands. Every time I stole an hour out of a workday to visit him, I'd play pretend, the R-rated edition. This was all too easy to do at Luke's, where there was no evidence of a husband and child or, for that matter, another woman. We'd simply love and laugh, love and talk, love and snap the occasional photograph, after which I'd grab his digital camera and delete the naked evidence. When the tea grew cold, it was a private mental signal to gather my things, kiss him goodbye, and shut the door on this erotic compartment in my lascivious little mind and return to what I used to refer to as normal life.

The home I shared with my family was, however, a vault within a vault, strictly off-limits. I'd never invited Luke here and didn't intend to start. I looked around. Barry's dry cleaning hung on the back of the bedroom door, ready to be divided by genus and species. The potentially incriminating stacks of receipts and phone bills that I'd set aside lay in a heap, awaiting review. On my dresser, in its simple sterling silver frame, Barry peered from our wedding photo. His dark brown eyes drilled into me.

"Molly, are you there?" Luke said. "I'd hate to think I'm boring you."

"Just musing," I said lightly.

"I worry when a woman muses. Are you thinking what I'm thinking?"

"And that would be?" I always liked when he'd recite the daily specials.

"Us. That bed you're in must be awfully lonely. And as I recall, the good doctor is in California and Annabel's gone for the day."

His voice was a challenge as much as a conscience-numbing anesthetic. I felt my resolve float away, revealing an emotion I could not name. Excitement? Happiness? Some sicko attraction to danger? I also briefly considered the state of my apartment, which would require a good twenty minutes of preening. Then there was the fact that I could use a shower, a shampoo, and, I dimly noted, a psychiatrist. But I said, "Be here in forty-five minutes."

"I'll pick up lunch," he said, almost like a considerate husband.

I was snipping the stems off apricot roses bought in a sprint to the corner deli when the doorman rang. "Alfred Stieglitz is here to see you," he said.

"Please send him up."

Luke filled my doorway. The smile on his face—bashful with a raunchy glint—replaced my anxiety with an intimacy certified by a cool, coffee-flavored kiss, the kind that requires no breathing. He'd barely piled his jacket and scarf by the door when I led him around the corner to the living room and pulled him down into a wide chair, avoiding the one where I snuggled and read with Annabel.

Normally, I liked to memorize every caress Luke offered, all the better to replay later when I biked or walked or showered. My rule was that I fantasized about him only when I was alone, but I'd already broken one rule that day and was on to demolishing a second commandment—number seven of God's top ten being long gone—as we moved to the rug and got down to basics.

Today, however, I couldn't enjoy myself. I kept glancing at the grandfather clock, half expecting to see Barry's face staring back at me. Exactly seventeen minutes later, I looked at Luke with relief. We could get dressed now.

"The bathroom is down the hall," I whispered as I pointed in the direction of Annabel's chaste, sunny chamber with its flotilla of rubber ducks and bubble bath marketed to calm overtired, cranky children. When he disappeared, I ran into my own bathroom, stuffed my hair under a shower cap, and blasted the shower water as hot as it ran.

I was happily wielding my loofah until my skin turned pink when over the rush of water, I heard a noise. The bathroom door, which I'd been careful to close securely behind me, flew open. I shrieked so loudly that the intruder let out a primal scream as well. The glass surrounding the shower was steamed—I couldn't see who'd entered. I did my *Psycho* bit again at an eardrum-shattering decibel.

"Calm down," Luke said as he slipped in beside me. "Jesus, Molly, everything's okay, it's okay." He held me to his chest as he deftly adjusted the water to a temperature below a rolling boil. "Are you trying to give yourself third-degree burns?"

*Sort of,* I thought.

"And what's that on your head?" Luke pulled off my protective purple plastic, gently pushed me under the nozzle, and started massaging shampoo onto my scalp. He ran his sudsy hands gently down my breasts, circling each nipple, and continued further south. I closed my eyes and tried to swim in the pleasure, but the clank of my colliding worlds was all I could feel. When the phone rang, dimly, in the bedroom, I was grateful.

"I better answer that," I said, squirming, shampoo stinging my eyes.

"Can't you let the machine take it?" he said as he held me close.

"It might be about Annabel." Or Barry.

"Ah," he said as he released his embrace. "Of course."

Leaving soapy footprints behind me, I flew into the bedroom, gently closed the door, and reached for the phone on the fifth ring.

"Good, you're there," Brie said. "I'm so sorry about today and was thinking. I could finish up here by two and we could still meet, at least for a movie. I feel like a bad friend standing you up."

"Gee," I said, "I already decided to meet Annabel and Kitty later."

*"Gee?"* Brie said. "You're spending your holy me-time with Kitty? And wasn't today all about her having Annabel alone for Kitty boot camp? Gee, pardon me, but I'm confused."

"Well, when you cancelled . . ."

"Never mind. I'll just stay here," Brie said, with her usual good nature. "And let me say, you are very weird."

When I returned to the bathroom, Luke was toweling off. The mood of merry seduction had vanished, and putting my arms around his waist did nothing to restore it.

"Listen, honey, do you want me to leave?" he asked as he pushed away my hands and began to walk toward the living room. "Be honest."

That might have been the best idea of the day. Yet as I followed Luke, who was skirted in a towel, the V of his torso trim and hard, I also considered how often I'd craved time with him in New York measured not in minutes but in hours. Perhaps that day was a grave miscalculation, but I wasn't ready to kiss Luke Delaney goodbye.

"What I'd honestly like now is lunch," I said, and tried to produce my most bewitching smile. "Together. Here." It had to be here, because who knew where Kitty might be lurking, Annabel in tow? "But first I'm going to wash out this shampoo and throw on some clothes. Why don't you look through the Netflix and see if there's anything you'd like to watch? They're near the TV in the living room."

He shot me a skeptical look. "Are you absolutely sure?"

"Please stay," I pleaded. "Please." Before he could answer, I left the room.

With each piece of clothing I put on, a bit of apprehension slipped away. When I walked out of my bedroom I wasn't sure if Luke would be there, but he was, barefoot, in jeans and a sweater.

"*Notting Hill, Love Actually,* and *Sabrina,* the 1954 and 1995 versions— I see a pattern here," he said, studying the movies.

"You were expecting *Smokey and the Bandit? Cannonball Run?* Maybe you'd prefer a cooking show? If we're lucky, a luscious babe will make osso bucco in her negligee."

He shuddered. "Just bring out lunch, woman."

Relieved to hear him laugh, I returned with the sandwiches he'd brought and basked in the mundane as we drank an eight-dollar Trader Joe's merlot and huddled under a moth-eaten afghan knit by my mother. When the movie rolled, I cried where I always cried. *Seems to me that love is everywhere,* I lip-synched. *If you look for it, I've got a sneaky feeling that love actually is all around.* This minute, for me, it was.

When the movie ended, I leaned against Luke's shoulder as we began to watch the Audrey Hepburn *Sabrina*. Ninety minutes later I opened my eyes. My head was in his lap.

"You snore," he said. That I also drooled was evident, but he was polite enough to ignore it.

"What time is it?"

"Time for me to go," Luke said. "I believe you said Annabel's due in the early evening."

"She won't be here for another hour at least." Kitty had said seven, but to be on the safe side, I'd want Luke out of the apartment by five-forty-five. We had twenty-five minutes. I began to kiss him.

Within minutes, our chemistry had kicked back into gear—we were taking pictures and enjoying the silk of each other's skin—when I heard a key in the lock. Bolting upright, I smoothed my hair, which had air-dried into a halo of frizz. I walked quickly to the foyer as Luke deftly disappeared in the direction of my bedroom and Kitty let herself in with a key Barry had apparently given her.

"Mommy!" Annabel said, running into my arms. "See! I got a manicure." She displayed her nails, each twinkling like a turquoise rhinestone.

"You're a princess," I said.

"Me too," Kitty said, and in an oddly girlish gesture presented her long, French-manicured gel tips.

"Mommy, Mommy." Annabel tugged at my sleeve. "Look what Kitty bought me!" She dumped a bag on the floor and pulled out a red feather boa, which she looped numerous times around her neck. It dragged to the floor. She resembled a very short Las Vegas showgirl.

"A lady needs accessories," Kitty said. "I wanted her to come back with me for dinner, but when I mentioned lamb chops, she said absolutely not. What do you and Delfina feed this child?"

I noticed that she left out Barry.

A civil daughter-in-law would take her mother-in-law's coat and insist that she settle in for coffee or wine and, in Kitty's case, a cigarette, although I hated when she smoked in my apartment. But my first action was a prayer that Kitty would think the beat-up brown leather jacket prominently piled on the chair, which I saw her eyeball, was Barry's. Fat chance. Not only could she recite a verbal inventory of his wardrobe, half of which she had purchased, but once a piece of clothing became the least bit worn she knew that Barry, like her, immediately abandoned it. By Marx standards, this jacket was ready for a thrift shop.

"Molly, do you have company?" She was a dog on a trail.

"Oh," I said. "Yes, I do. One of my colleagues is here. But she's in the bathroom—she's not feeling well or I'd introduce you. Brie and Isadora cancelled, so I scheduled an impromptu meeting."

As I rattled on, Kitty looked at me as if I was a bad liar, which I was. At least a minute of annotated, implausible explanation commenced.

"I wouldn't dream of interrupting—you go back to your *colleague*," she said, sweeping down in a cloud of Joy to kiss Annabel goodbye. Without so much as grazing my cheek with her lips, she turned and walked out the door. "Sorry to intrude" was all she said.

As I scooped my daughter into my arms, I could smell Kitty's smoke in her hair. "What do you say to a bath, Annie-belle, and then we'll have dinner, okay? But first, close your eyes tight. Very tight."

"A surprise?" she shrieked.

*Only if you don't cheat,* seemed like a poor choice of words. "Only if you keep your eyes closed," I said, and carried Annabel to her bedroom, glancing at Luke, who'd emerged from the master bedroom, padding quietly in stocking feet. He shrugged and blew me a kiss as he put on his shoes, grabbed his jacket, and tiptoed out the door, leaving it ajar so Annabel wouldn't hear a click. "Keep those eyes closed, Annabel," I warned twice.

A gift was already waiting on her bed, left there a few hours ago. While Annabel tore open the wrapping, I madly straightened the living room. That was when I discovered that in the rush, Luke had forgotten his digital camera. I ran to my bedroom and shoved it in my underwear drawer.

Only late that night—after Annabel's bath, chicken nuggets, reading her brand-new *Fancy Nancy* three times, and a five-minute chat with Barry—did I retrieve the camera to have a look before my normal deleting. There we were, shot after shot from today, each more compromising than the next. Guilty, guiltier, guiltiest.

# Twenty-seven

# WITNESS

$S$ometimes you need a witness to ratify that in fact you do see and feel what you think you see and feel. That's why I begged Bob to join me. We followed Hicks to a mom-and-pop coffee shop near his apartment. Over poached eggs, dry whole-wheat toast, and three cups of coffee (two sugars, plenty of milk—hold the hash browns) he's reviewing his thickening file, scrutinizing stacks of cell phone call lists and credit card receipts—mine (did I really spend all that on leg waxing?) as well as those from Barry, Lucy, Luke, Stephanie, Brie, Isadora, and even my parents. He hasn't labeled the file "suspects," but I gather that's who these other people are. Here and there, he circles a date or a phone number or carefully pens in a question mark.

"Thanks, Louise," Hicks says as he leaves a five-dollar tip.

"Solve that case, Detective," the waitress says. "Get them bad guys."

"I'm sure gonna try." *This may be my first case I'm handling as top dog, but I am not going to fuck it up like the Christina Rivera case. It's not just about respect in the NYPD and my future,* he thinks. *I'm getting to like this Molly. She reminds me of Franny, that white girl from college, the one I was afraid to ask out, the one who only now I realize was flirting with me full tilt, but I was too caught up in being one-down to notice. Franny, who got mowed by a truck while driving her decrepit Beetle. Franny, Molly, lovely, lonely . . .*

I beam at Bob.

Now Hicks is walking to his car, a Honda Civic so stripped it might as well wear DETECTIVE vanity plates. He drives downtown to the Sixties, curses the fact that when Mr. Trump and his cronies put up all those buildings they made it virtually impossible for visitors to park nearby, and finds a spot on West End Avenue. He begins to walk toward the cookie-cutter towers shadowing the Hudson.

"Your Hicks," Bob says, "gives good aura."

"You can see auras?" I wonder what one looks like. Cloud cover that stops rays that cause premature aging? A classic mist of blue ozone? Maybe Bob is using the term metaphorically and an aura is a Kierkegaard mind-twister, like "Life must be understood backward but lived forward."

"It's all around him," Bob says. "One of these days you may be able to pick up on auras yourself. It's an upgrade some of us get."

"If my powers continue?"

"Do you really have to ask?" *Nothing lasts forever,* Bob finds a way to say or imply every time we meet, as if anyone in the Duration needs to be reminded of this. Fond as I am of Bob, the guy could use irony supplements.

Since I first laid eyes on Hicks, he's grown at least two inches in confidence. He strides through Stephanie's lobby as if he's wearing a virtual tuxedo custom-tailored to his physique. What a pair of shoulders. Today Hicks looks ready to present an Oscar. The concierge treats him accordingly and sends him straight up to the thirty-first floor, where Stephanie Joseph stands in her doorway. Her eyeteeth are as lupine as I remember, although I now know that, unlike her sister wolves, she has more than one mating season per year. Stephanie is dressed in the sweet spot between accountant and trollop. Unbuttoned to create a plunging neckline, her snug cardigan is the peach of a blushing bride. A tweedy knee-length wool skirt shows off her narrow-arrow hips, and red peep-toe stilettos reveal a pedicure in a shade that recalls vampires. A silver and crystal pendant dangles between her breasts.

*The audition for* Law and Order *was yesterday,* I hear Hicks think as they shake hands.

"Detective," Stephanie says as she cocks her head to the side and motions him into the apartment. With the afternoon sun streaming through the floor-to-ceiling windows, you can squint all the way to New Jersey.

I'm tempted to try to pick out Serenity Haven, my final earthly resting place, but Bob pokes me. "You're a decorating specialist, Molly," he says, scanning the room. "What do you make of this place?"

My eyes do a quick 360. "Early model apartment," I bounce back. "Perfect as a snow globe."

Every piece of furniture is plug-and-play pristine, perhaps selected from a catalog for high-tax-bracket transients. There are stiff leather couches, the kind you see in a boutique hotel lobby people wander through on the way to the cigar bar. I pick up a whirl of glass, right angles, black, white, taupe, a tall vase filled with branches, and another with one lonely calla lily, but notice no magazines or piles of mail, no personal photographs, only the variety numbered in a series. I can't bring myself to venture into Stephanie's bedroom, where I might find a remnant of Barry's last moment in flagrante delicto, so instead, leaving Hicks behind, I check out Jordan's room. There is an orderly abundance of toys, stuffed animals, blocks, and books, to which I am always drawn first. Many appear to be well read. I would find this easier if she had the mothering skills of a mascara wand.

"A drink, Detective?" Stephanie says. "Fiji water? Espresso? Something stronger?"

Does she think this is a date? "I'm okay," he replies.

Stephanie points to a fawn suede couch across from a gas fireplace, which she flicks on. In an instant, flames hop and pop. Hicks sits and she faces him, crossing her excellent legs. "I'm going to ask you a few questions about your relationship with Dr. Marx," he says. "How would you describe it?"

"I'm his support team right now," she replies, glad she chose that response yesterday when this meeting was arranged. "He needs a friend." She answers the question with a practiced laugh that glissandos from high to low, and I imagine mermaids luring sailors to their death. One more reason to loathe this woman. I turn to Bob but see he's heading for the rocks.

"The Stephanies of the world intrigue me," he says.

"You too?" I sigh. I'd taken Bob for a guy who'd go more for a vet or a dental hygienist, like the fiancée he left behind.

"Please," he says. "Not my type. But I'm perennially fascinated by tenacity and nerve. Stephanie is out for Stephanie." He frowns. "But she's wasting this performance on Hicks."

Stephanie with her unearned air of superiority. "I hate her," I say.

"You should," he says, and his frown deepens.

I have never heard him fling one swear word. "Bob!" I say, delighted.

He shrugs. "I call it as it comes."

"When did your relationship with Dr. Marx begin?" Hicks asks, the slightest of smiles curving the corners of his lower lip. *I already know,* he thinks, *but it's more fun to hear it from you.*

"You mean our professional relationship?" This woman is bulletproof. Flinty. *Hicks is definitely into me,* she decides.

"Mrs. Joseph, let's not mess around."

"Ms.," she says in a practiced, sultry voice. "Mr. Joseph was my ex."

"*Ms.* Joseph, we're both busy people. Let's get on with this." Yesterday morning Hicks had another session with Barry, and last week round two in Chicago plus, one by one over the last month, interviews with two dozen coworkers—mine, Barry's, Lucy's. He doesn't need his chain yanked. He wants a break in the case, and his gut tells him Stephanie's got something he can use. What, he doesn't know. Each morning, his first thought is, *Intuition, call home.* "When did you and Barry Marx hook up?" Hicks takes out his black notebook and his pen.

When indeed? "It began after Dr. Marx's wife died."

My bullshit meter comes alive—*bleep, bleep, bleep!*—but I don't want to miss Hicks' reaction. *This broad is smiling too damn much,* he thinks. "You and Dr. Marx made regular calls beginning last fall," he says. A tickertape of calls. *Why would a smart woman like this think I wouldn't know about them?* he wonders.

"He's my doctor," Stephanie says, and in a practiced swish pushes away her shiny brown hair with its tortoiseshell streaks. "Those were professional conversations."

"Why did they generally take place at night or on the weekend?"

"I don't know about your physicians, Detective, but I'm happy to get a call back from mine anytime he feels like making one."

"What kind of condition required seven or nine phone calls a week?" Hicks says, allowing his impatience to show. "There's no record of his treating you."

"*Treating* her?" I say to Bob.

"Shhh," Bob says. "Listen."

"Okay, we started seeing each other last year," Stephanie admits.

A buzz saw slices through to the place where my heart used to be.

"Very casually," she adds, and sends Hicks a defiant look as she stretches out those words. "After his mother introduced us, I saw Barry in a restaurant, and one thing led to another. It took him months to admit he was married." *Faster than some,* I hear her think.

"Has he asked you to marry him?"

"Absurd." She laughs, although I hear her small prayer that someday he will.

"So at this point you'd call this primarily a physical relationship?" Hicks decides to switch to not-so-good cop.

"He's single and I'm single. Do you have any idea how hard it is to meet someone decent in New York?"

*Tell me about it,* Hicks thinks. *I haven't had a real relationship in two years.*

"I saw an opportunity and I took it," Stephanie says. "I'm not especially proud of it, but I'm not going to do a guilt trip, either. Barry and I were attracted to each other. I'm not the first woman to hook up with a married man and I won't be the last. The last time I checked, this was still legal. It started before Mrs. Marx died, but"—she regrets that she gave up smoking, because a cigarette would add a certain vodka-and-caviar drama now—"so what?"

"Now, was that so hard?" Hicks asks.

It was for me. Any woman who suspects her husband is cheating always hopes hubby really did have seven business trips to Longboat Key. The woman from high school he met for drinks *is* as big as an Aga stove. That copy of *Adultery for Beginners* belongs to his partner. Then the evidence plops on her head like pigeon poop. "I can't take this," I say to Bob.

"Buck up," he whispers. *Nothing pretty about self-pity,* he always says, along with *Coulda, shoulda, woulda—where does* that *get anyone?* In the Duration you learn that festering with regret changes not one thing. Had I reacted to Barry in life, I would have another story to tell, considering that the evidence of his infidelity was hiding in plain sight. I could go on and on with this line of reasoning, but Hicks has asked a question that's gotten my attention. "Tell me when you first met Mrs. Marx," he says.

"I can't—we never met."

BS!

"C'mon. Your children attend the same school."

"School's a big place," she answers, "where the nanny generally picks up Annabel Marx, who is not in the same class as my Jordan, and I'm not the room-mother type. No, we never met." *Molly Marx and I weren't technically introduced—I'm not lying,* Stephanie thinks while a memory flickers, an ember she stamps out in less time than it takes for her to blink. There was that shivery afternoon, murky as sludge. A day to forget.

"What did Dr. Marx say about his wife?" Hicks asks.

"Not much," she answers.

"Oh, come on, Ms. Joseph. Did he deny that he was married?"

"For a while he let me think he was single, but when I asked him point-blank, he practically boasted about his good marriage." *Which I took as a challenge,* she thinks.

"Did they have an understanding? Did she not get him?" *Poor complicated schmuck,* Hicks thinks.

"Actually," she says, "Dr. Marx said he was very, very attracted to me."

"Uh-huh," Hicks says coolly. "So now that your memory's returned, I'm wondering, where were you when Molly Marx was murdered?" The banter has turned as stiff as roadkill, and I believe his hushed tone is one of respect. Stephanie's holding back. Hicks knows it as well as he knows that she's not going to say any more. Not today. He can read it in the lightest twitch around her eye and the way she twists the silver ring that has replaced her wedding band.

"Who says she was murdered?" Stephanie asks.

"Ms. Joseph, the question," Hicks says. "Answer it."

"I must have been in town," she says, "because I remember hearing about it on the news that weekend."

"Dr. Marx says he saw you that night."

*Why would Barry admit that,* Stephanie wonders, *when we were both quite sure no one saw us and he paid for dinner in cash?* "We might have seen each other that night," she says.

"*Might have?* You don't remember dinner at Landmarc with Barry Marx the night his wife was left to bleed to death by the side of the road?"

I can't listen to this. But Bob gives me a look that says, *If you stay you might learn something.*

*Lock me up for shagging and throw away the key,* Stephanie thinks. "Okay, I had a bite with Dr. Marx. Very early in the evening. If we were trying to hide something, would we have gone to such a public place?" *There's a damn Whole Foods in the basement of the building, for God's sake.*

"Like I said, I'll ask the questions. Where did Dr. Marx think his wife was at that point?"

"I didn't ask." *I didn't care,* Stephanie thinks.

My bullshit detector, I've noticed, has stopped blaring.

"I think we're through here," Bob says kindly.

"I have to stay." My voice is barely audible.

"Are you sure that you hadn't met Mrs. Marx, ma'am?"

"Like I said, Detective, no." Stephanie is sounding tired, short-tempered, less sure.

"Where were you when Mrs. Marx was out biking the day of her death?" he asks.

"With my child," Stephanie answers. "At home."

Hicks lets the bad cop hammer away. Stephanie might be telling the truth. He can't prove otherwise.

"Please, Molly, can we leave?" Bob asks.

"Molly Marx has left the building." My mind is back in February, trying to put together the pieces.

*Twenty-eight*

# GIVING AS GOOD AS SHE GETS

"Is it possible that Barry and his mom had lunch this week at Berg-dorf's?" Brie asked when she called a few days after Barry had returned from San Francisco.

"He didn't mention it," I said. "But yes, probably." Every few weeks, Barry and Kitty met at the tiny café folded as neatly as a pocket square into the third floor of the men's store. In fact, he'd arrived home the other day with a navy duchesse satin tie with small red squares and another in plum and silver stripes. Both had Kitty written all over them. "Why do you ask?"

"You know our office manager, who went to Barry for a consultation?"

"The one who got burnt because he suggested she have not just her nose done but a full lift?"

"That one—and for the record, Barry was right."

"So?"

"Barry didn't seem to recognize her."

"A lot of women go in and out of that office. Anyway, he waits for patients to say hello first. Confidentiality and all that. Your point is?"

"I overheard this woman giving a play-by-play to one of the secretaries all about the conversation Barry and Kitty supposedly had at Bergdorf's."

A wave of nausea rose in my stomach.

"Do you want to hear it?" Brie asked. Her voice had dropped.

*No!* "Sure, spill."

"You won't shoot the messenger?"

"Talk."

I could hear Brie take a deep breath. "Kitty told Barry she thinks *you* are cheating—something about a man's jacket squatting in your foyer like a dirty dog."

"Go on," I said as my queasiness built. I was afraid I was going to puke.

"Barry said something like, 'News flash—we just had wild, animal sex six hours ago and everything's fine in that department.'" Then this woman started laughing so hard I could hardly understand her, but I think she said Kitty answered, 'Now, there's a snapshot for the family album,' and 'Barry Joshua, love, I'm afraid you're missing the point.'"

"Is that it?" I hoped it was.

"No, she scolded him like he was a little boy. That's what this fly-on-the-wall thought was funniest. Said it was time for him to 'grow up and be part of his marriage'—he had a wife and a child and if he didn't pay attention, he was going to lose them both."

"More?" I asked.

"Just that she said, 'Don't be a fool.' Or something like that."

Brie waited for me to respond. When I did not, she added, "Molly, this woman might have the wrong guy or made it all up. She's the twit who started that rumor that I was dating one of the senior partners."

Brie *had* been dating that senior partner. "You're right. It could be some other Barry Joshua's mom telling him off."

"Does any of this make sense?"

"I'm not saying." My synonym for *Guilty, as charged.*

"Okay," Brie said, drawing out the word as if she were taking a long toke on a thick joint. "If you ever want to talk, you know I'm here. But Barry Joshua's mother was right on one thing. Don't be a fool."

As soon as *The Daily Show* ended that night, I picked up *New York*. For two days, I'd been trying to finish an exposé on moms who anonymously rat out other families' babysitters on isawyournanny.blogspot.com. I'd visited the site. Last time, one item was about a caregiver feeding kids Ho Hos instead of organic crackers, and another was about a nanny burping in restaurants like a twelve-year-old boy and coughing insults at fellow diners. But once in a while the description of a nanny's behavior made me want to run to Annabel's room, scoop her up, and promise that nothing bad would happen to her, ever. No bored, mean, trash-talking, cell-phone-obsessed nanny was going to swat my little girl.

"I pinch myself every day that we found Delfina," I said, turning to Barry, but his eyes stayed married to Letterman. "She's amazing, don't you think?"

Barry ignored me. At midnight he flicked off his light without so much as a mumbled goodnight. I moved on to the magazine's culture pages. After I'd started the same review three times, I put out my light as well, stretched under the freshly ironed white sheets, and rubbed my icy feet against Barry's. He stayed as still as a corpse. Moving closer, I laid my arm around his shoulders. "Sweet dreams," I murmured as I felt him shift away.

That morning married life had seemed copasetic, at least on the surface—a location from which our relationship too rarely experienced liftoff. Barry had arrived home late Sunday from San Francisco, bearing gifts: a gold cable car to start a charm bracelet for Annabel, an Alcatraz mug for Delfina, and a small jade box for me. Late that evening, as we finished a pizza and emptied a bottle of Chianti, he'd admitted that he had been nervous about his speech. I found this endearing; I enjoyed my husband most when his guard was down, especially if his ardor was up. We made love that night, gently, and this morning, passionately. But whatever goodwill had existed between us had apparently washed away like a signature in the sand.

"Anything you want to tell me?" I said mildly, staring into the darkness.

"Or you tell me?" Barry answered a few moments later from the west coast of the bed, his voice low and controlled.

*That I'm in a chronic state of being crazy pissed at you and disappointed by you, but I've forfeited my right to bitch by being a complete harlot, and on that count I am oozing—no, make that exploding—with regret for my appalling lack of judgment.*

"You might want to know I am fully aware of the fact that you weren't alone in San Francisco" was all I said. I despised myself for having the hubris to accuse Barry, especially since I wasn't 100 percent certain about this.

"Come on! If you're talking about the patient who coached me, she's just a friend," he said, as if he'd been expecting an attack. "She was out on the coast visiting her brother. I thought I should say thank you. I took her to dinner." *Big deal,* his tone said.

I decided to drop my bomb. "One of many meals, I see, based on last year's Amex. I'm especially intrigued about the bar bills on those nights when you told me you were chaperoning at the temple's shelter. Was it Take a Homeless Guy to the Ritz-Carlton Month?"

"I can see where you'd want to steer the conversation away from yourself," he said, drily, "given what went down here this weekend."

"Excuse me?"

"You know what I'm talking about."

Did he have Alphonso the doorman on the payroll? Much as he revered his mother, based on Brie's recycled rumors I couldn't believe that he didn't have doubts.

"You said you wanted to talk," I said, "so let's. That is, unless you'd rather move on to your cell phone bills."

Outside, I heard dogs barking. But in our bedroom there was only silence, not counting the thrum of rage and guilt that pulsed through my brain. Barry. Luke. Luke. Barry. The compartments each tidily lived in had collapsed. After minutes—two or ten, I couldn't say—Barry turned on his lamp, walked to the closet, and from a sport coat hanging toward the back took out a pack of cigarettes. He returned to the bed, lit one, and inhaled, blowing blue smoke into the dim light.

"When did you start smoking again?"

"There are a lot of things you don't know," he said, and laughed. "Like that women throw themselves at me all the time. Patients, strangers, your friends."

"You poor, defenseless guy."

"Sometimes I respond, I admit it. But here's the thing—it means nothing. Less than nothing. Zilch."

"You're telling me that being with other women is just some sort of uncontrollable tic, like cracking your knuckles?" I let indignation flood the room, while I tried to ignore another version of myself that circled above, chanting "hypocrite" at the angry, self-righteous wife sitting up in bed, her nightgown falling off one shoulder. That Luke meant something to me, that I thought I loved him—did any of this make it better or different? Holier, perhaps? As I started to shake, tears fell on the blanket.

Barry put out his cigarette in the silver dish he kept on his night-stand. He got up, walked around to my side, pulled me to his chest, and cleared his throat. "Here's the only thing you need to know. You're everything to me," he said. "Correction. You and Annabel." He started to stroke my hair. "Maybe I haven't been the husband I should be. No, let me rephrase. I haven't been the husband I should be. I've been a schmuck. What I need to know is, will you forgive me?"

I felt as ready for this confession as I might be for a full body search at the dry cleaner. Were his words hollow or sincere, true or false, a stall tactic or a miracle breakthrough?

"I'm not sure what I'd be forgiving you for, exactly," I said, hiccup-ping.

"Don't ask me to elaborate," he said. "Tell me what you want from me, and I'll come through."

I thought I might be reading genuine anguish on Barry's face. "What I want you to do is talk to me," I pleaded. "To share a little of the real you"—whoever he is. Why didn't all men realize that, at least for every woman I knew, being listened to and revealing a secret truth or two is always the ultimate aphrodisiac? Luke got this. Why didn't my husband? Or did he share his dreams and hopes and fears and zany in-sights only with other women?

"We talk all the time," he said.

"But we don't," I answered wearily. "I don't know that we've ever had a real conversation that didn't relate to your work or Annabel or if the steak should be medium or medium rare."

"Oh, come on. Now you're being ridiculous. Throw me a bone here."

"It might take time," I said. It was definitely not anguish, I decided, that I was reading on Barry's face, at least not anymore. Could he be scared that I was going to blow his cover?

I'd suddenly become so tired I couldn't say or listen to another word. From a few blocks away, the bell of the church chimed once. I stood and grabbed my pillow. "I'm sleeping in the other room," I announced. Barry didn't stop me.

I woke to the smell of freshly brewed hazelnut coffee. Barry was standing next to the couch with two steaming mugs in hand. "Good morning," he said. He kissed me softly on the cheek. His hair was still wet from the shower, and in his face I could see the college senior I'd met almost seventeen years earlier.

"We need to get ourselves to a therapist." The words tumbled out of me, unexpected. "I heard of someone who's supposed to be good." I'd been carrying Felicia Stafford's name and number in my wallet for more than a year.

"If that's what you want, I'm in," Barry said. "Now get that adorable butt into the kitchen, or you're going to miss my pancakes."

# Twenty-nine

# KOI OR GIRL?

*I*'ve decided," Brie says. "I definitely want a baby."

Isadora's face, reflected in the glass of their kitchen cabinets, remains composed. As she reaches for the plates she keeps her back turned to Brie. "What makes you so sure you'll be a good mama?"

"Absolutely nothing," Brie admits.

I wish Brie knew, as I do, that she would be the finest of mothers. Before I died, Barry and I were still debating whom to pick to be Annabel's legal guardian, and Brie was my first choice. I'd have lobbied harder on her behalf if my decision wouldn't have insulted my parents and Lucy. I can't think of better guardians than my parents, but they live far away. And Lucy? Her advanced degree in early childhood development notwithstanding, after a year with my sister, Annabel might require after-school psychotherapy instead of ballet.

Barry wanted Kitty to be Annabel's guardian—"because Annabel's life could continue as it is." True, except that Kitty would send her to fat camp before she digested her first Oreo, and possibly destroy all proof that I was her mother. So the guardian issue remains unresolved. Like so much.

"What kind of mother do you think you'd be?" Brie asks.

Isadora takes two square black plates from the shelf and places them on the honed stone counter where Brie is sitting. From a metal basket she selects a large tangerine and starts to peel it with a sharp mother-of-pearl-handled knife. The rind, which perfumes the air with its fresh scent, snakes into a ribbon as she does the job with artistic precision. "Frightening," she says. "I'm exacting, self-involved, and impatient. Isn't that what you love about me?"

"Seriously, Isadora. You're not hearing me. I want a baby."

Isadora delicately dissects the denuded fruit and begins to slice segments into bite-sized pieces. An amused smile remains on her age-less, symmetrical face. "Do you plan to jet off to Malawi and claw one out of some impoverished woman's womb?"

"I want to get pregnant. That is, unless you'd rather carry our child."

"Have you totally lost your mind?" I do love Isadora's teeth—small, even, white as china. She laughed for so long I got an excellent view of them.

"You're not too old—you're only thirty-nine."

"That's the least of it. I'd rather have liposuction without anesthesia. The species will have to propagate without my help."

"Then I'll be the pregnant one—with your egg, if you want, implanted in my uterus. Done all the time." Brie never stints on research.

"*Mi amada*," Isadora says, and leans over to cup Brie's firm, pointed chin, the type that gets called "stubborn." "I love our life. Sleeping late, running away to Paris and Barcelona and Buenos Aires, me spoiling you, you spoiling me. Why give any of it up for a *bebé*? And what if that little egg and sperm grew a penis? Could you honestly see me as the mother of some midget jock? Go back to bed and wake up sane."

Brie stands and washes her plate and coffee cup. Even without my powers I know her well enough to realize she's going to table this topic—for now. "Maybe I'm just premenstrual," she says lightly. "You're right—I must be nuts to ever suggest bringing anything as messy as a third party into our life." The remarkable thing is that Brie is able to speak without a scintilla of sarcasm while the words *sybarite* and *indolent brat* flip through her brain. She knows how to bide her time, something I never learned to do.

So I'm surprised when only two nights later she raises the topic again. The two of them are eating at Koi, where the ceilings are as high as the prices. They're seated in a booth, taut thighs touching, ignoring the crowd. I find this hard to do, since obviously everyone here must pass a rigorous grooming and attractiveness test before they check their coats. At their banquette, Isadora selects a tiny rice block blanketed with very spicy, very fresh tuna—mercury levels be damned—and reaches to put the tiny orange delicacy into Brie's mouth.

Brie pushes it away. "Stop for a minute, please."

"Not hungry?"

"We need to continue our conversation."

"Need?"

"Okay, *want*—about the baby."

"What baby?"

"The one you don't want."

"That baby."

"We could adopt, but I'd rather be pregnant," Brie says. "I have to at least try to be a mother." *Molly wants me to have a baby,* I hear her think. It's crazy, the thoughts that we in the Duration hear attributed to us, but I am flattered and intrigued.

Isadora moves on to eggplant, whose glistening purple-black skin matches her inscrutable eyes. After the eggplant disappears, she lazily alternates between sesame-encrusted lobster tail, sautéed asparagus, and shiitake mushrooms, licking her full lips as she samples each one.

"Aren't you going to talk to me?" Brie asks. Apparently not. Isadora is Barry in drag.

"What is there to talk about?" Isadora finally says, defiant. "You know my position. I'm not going to debate or defend myself. I never deceived you. This is who I am. It's me or this mythical baby. Pick, my darling."

"Won't you even consider it?" Brie says, her voice silky smooth.

Isadora rests her chopsticks and meets Brie's gaze. "I had a baby," she says. "In my marriage to Pedro. Had the child lived, she would now be twenty. The *bebé* tore me apart in every way. I know this bloody experience, and now I have earned the right to be a hedonist. I want my decadent life where every day I wake up and think, *What would make me happy? What would make Sabrina happy?* I would like this life with you, love, but if not, not." Isadora clips every sentence as if she is pruning a rosebush.

I have always been immune to feeling anything toward Isadora except envy, but as I try to make room for empathy, my bullshit detector blares. What a crock. Not the part about Pedro—Isadora was married once, for fourteen months. But there was never a child, not even in Isadora's imagination or in the head of Pedro, which was filled with coke. I want to rattle Brie by the shoulders. I want to send her a harsh wake-up-toots-and-smell-the-bullshit psychogram, a ranting celestial e-mail.

"Honey," Brie says, all sympathy, "why didn't you ever say anything?"

Isadora casts down her eyes, as if she is exercising enormous self-control to maintain dignity.

"Why did you keep this a secret from me?" Brie asks again, taking Isadora's hand.

Isadora removes her hand.

They finish their meal without talking, without sipping a drop of warm, soothing sake. Brie pays the bill, which is steep. I follow them home. Isadora goes directly to bed, while Brie stays up until three, her mind racing. Why can't I be a dancing moonbeam who points her toward the truth? At the very least I long to haunt Brie's dreams, but Bob reminds me, time and again, that such behavior violates the Duration's bylaws, unwritten but transmitted on faith, and will terminate my powers. I can take no credit, then, for the conversation between Brie and Isadora the following week.

"I've made up my mind," Brie says at midnight on the fourth of a series of rainy days and nights. "I need to be in a relationship where having a baby is at least a possibility." She offers these words with tremendous tenderness, after many days of sleepwalking.

Isadora accepts the news without theatrics, but this time I feel compassion for a woman who has bargained and lost. I have searched her heart and believe she loves Brie. Now Isadora will have to search again for her matching sybarite.

When Brie returns from work the next day, Isadora is gone, along with her considerable library of books about twentieth-century art, early jazz, and contemporary architecture, her exquisite bags and hand-cobbled shoes, her Fendi furs and four-carat diamond studs, her elegant fruit knives and black bone china. Brie has twice as much storage space and an even larger vacancy in her heart, but she doesn't look back. "Molly," she says out loud now, because there is no one to hear her and tell her she is *loca*, "I can feel you guiding me."

She is wrong. The decision was entirely her own.

A few weeks later, Brie rescues Jones, a year-old chocolate Lab, and her apartment is overrun with squeaky toys, organic dog food, and sloppy kisses.

# Thirty

# THEIR STORIES AND THEY'RE STICKING TO THEM

"*L*et's go over this once more," Hicks says. "Your relationship to Molly Marx was—"

"Professional."

"And?"

"Okay, personal—for a while, off and on—but any . . ."—Luke fishes for a word—"intimacy between us was over well before she died."

Intimidation, intestines, indigestion, intifada, intimacy. Could Luke possibly make what went on between us sound colder and uglier?

"Mr. Delaney, the last call Mrs. Marx got was from you, and as I like to remind folks, half the truth is a big fat lie." *This guy's giving me nothing*, I hear Hicks think. *The husband, he's one more doctor who mistakes himself for God. But Delaney—something doesn't add up.* "What did you two talk about that day?"

"I don't recall."

This isn't a lawyer-coached response. It's true. Just as I can't tell you if I put 1 percent or 2 percent milk into my coffee the day I died, Luke has no recollection of cross-the-$t$-dot-the-$i$ specifics of what went on that day. "My guess is we discussed work."

Until today I've never mustered the courage to witness conversations between Hicks and Luke. I've been too raw, too confused, and entirely too chickenshit. As they face each other, Hicks towers over Luke, whom I'd always thought of as tall but who now looks not just shorter but older. He could use a posture lesson from my mother: *Shoulders back, chin up, darling.* The blue-gray shadows under his eyes may as well be tattoos, and he appears gaunt and more in need of a haircut than usual. His apartment is worse. Bathroom towels are funky and askew and his hockey equipment hides under a layer of dust in which I could easily scrawl my name if the Duration allowed such folly. Except for some Major Grey's mango chutney whose sell-by date most likely is older than the Colonial occupation, the refrigerator is empty. Luke's freezer, however, is stocked—with Stolichnaya, Absolut, and three vodkas labeled in Cyrillic, as well as Cherry Garcia and Dulce de Leche, unopened.

Since my body left this world in its lumpy radiance, Luke has accepted every job that's come his way, even the one in Sheboygan. Any escape has been better than New York City. But this explains only some of his home's disarray. He's not just backed up in his domesticity but deeply, profoundly sad—guilty and sad.

One of Hicks' more successful techniques is to say nothing and hope that whoever he's grilling will interrupt the discomfort with a shocking disclosure. He has a 62 percent success rate with this ploy, but not today. "There was a time when I loved Molly deeply and she loved me back," Luke says. "I will not deny that. I treasure the memories." Not that Luke lets himself take out those images, carefully archived deep in his mental hard drive. "But before that time, and after it—and during it—we were also colleagues. That's what we were when she died."

*Colleagues who wanted to be something more,* Hicks thinks. He focuses on how pitiful Luke sounds, but what I notice is that Luke's brain uses the present tense. *Molly and I love each other deeply.* As my ninth-grade English teacher said, there's power in grammar.

"I once thought, for a few weeks at least, that we should and would be together permanently." Two old people making sure the other takes their Lipitor and Avapro, loving the wrinkles in each other's faces, and finding lost reading glasses. "I hated that because of some cosmic snafu we didn't meet until after she was already married." *To that schmuck.*

*"If only we'd met sooner, everything would be different"*—the bumper sticker of every cheating man, Hicks thinks. *But I don't care what an asshole a husband is—only a weak, sniffling sonofabitch goes after another guy's wife. And I know this because I've been that weakling.*

This last musing of Hicks' interests me, almost as much as what Luke is thinking: *Molly was married to a man who didn't appreciate her, a man who never got her at all.*

"Did the two of you plan to be together?" Hicks asks.

"Never," Luke says emphatically, and too reflexively for my liking. "You and I have gone over this so many times. I was pure diversion. Molly would never have left her husband." *At least not for me.* "Although I'd be lying if I didn't admit I had the occasional fantasy about winding up together." *We'd have moved to a brownstone, maybe in Brooklyn, where I could see us cooking decadent pastas and me walking Annabel to the public school down the street, teaching her to take pictures and to sing Christmas carols when we'd visit my parents in New Hampshire. On the weekends when Annabel visited Barry, Molly and I would be all over each other, and barely crawl out of bed.*

Hicks' mind is roaming as well, to what happened to one lovely Lola. *Man, was I out of my league with her,* he remembers. He conjures this woman—more cultured, more educated, and infinitely more married than he. After his nonstarter Franny fantasies, Lola and he were a couple, sporadically and secretly, for four years. But Hicks never felt he had as much to offer her as he believed this goddess deserved, never begged for Lola to leave her chump husband. Then, *poof,* over—for Lola but not for him.

*Luke fuckin' Delaney's got Lola stamped all over him.* This Hicks knows.

Hicks can have his sashay down memory lane, but I don't want to stroll along with him. I'm weighing the knowledge he's convinced of— that Luke's still in love with me. It's an enormous ego stroke to believe this, but I've decided it's also revisionist history. Luke and I didn't make big plans, and a lot of that had to do with me, because I liked our togetherness with a dreamy patina, not the five o'clock shadow of reality. He never begged me to reinvent my life. Luke toyed with me, not the other way around. This is my story and I'm sticking to it, at least when I'm thinking that I'd be alive today had I not accepted that lethal pink flamingo drink from Luke, if we'd never danced, if we'd only been in Buffalo, not on Expense Account Island.

"Who ended things between you two?"

Luke clears his throat with a sound between a sigh and a groan. "The relationship ran its course. We both got tired of the lying and disappointment, the frustration and the subterfuge, the high drama. We moved on."

*Except you haven't,* Hicks decides. *Molly Marx is gnawing like a termite on that wooden heart of yours.* "And after that?"

"Detective, I spend every minute running away from my regrets. Every time the phone rings, I expect it to be Molly springing some brilliant idea on me for one of our shoots. I try to trick myself into thinking that she's just temporarily out of my life."

*How's that working for you?* Hicks wonders. He leans back on the leather couch and takes stock of the room, which could be comfortable were it clean. He can picture me here, taking a stemless wineglass from the tray on the sideboard, opening a decanter, and sharing a glass of decent Syrah with Luke Delaney, the kind of guy women think of as sensitive. *He's currently such a holy mess, it's not fair to judge him as a world-class lover. And as a killer? Could be. Every damn answer is vague and slippery and he has no good alibi. Zippo.*

Despite this, Hicks hasn't come on with a full frontal attack. With Luke, Hicks is Mr. Softie. Maybe it's a been-there-done-that guy thing.

"I don't believe she's gone," Luke continues. "Sometimes I go up to the park and sit and could swear that she's still there."

I am. A lot. I see him watching, waiting, wasting himself on emotions as useless as expired MetroCards.

"I think I'm going to see her walking or on her bike, that this is all a grotesque fuck-up."

Hicks decides on this point Luke might be speaking from the heart, because that's how it was for him until finally the big Lola boom faded to an echo. One day, Hicks realized that Lola was no longer the first thing he thought about each dawn and the last thing each night. He could listen to Marvin Gaye again, and other women started to look quite fine. But it took forever. He's only gotten there now, this year.

Then Hicks snaps back. "When did Dr. Marx find out about you two?"

"Barry Marx? He didn't." *Shit. Was he on to us?* Luke feels the same sickness in his belly that for the last few weeks has kept him from pouring his good or even his not-so-good vodka or breaking into the ice cream.

"You know that for a fact?" Hicks asks.

"No," Luke admits. *This detective is messing with me. Or maybe not. Could Barry have found out,* he's thinking. *Then what?*

"So how'd she die, Delaney?" Hicks' face is so close I wonder if Luke will turn away. He does not.

"I do a head trip about that day and night, Detective."

"Did she kill herself because she felt so damn guilty about you?"

Luke wonders, *Is this policeman mocking me?* "I doubt everything about what you just said—that she killed herself, to begin with." Luke makes this point with dignity, and I am proud he has found some.

"So it was an accident?"

Luke takes his time. "Not necessarily."

"Then say it," Hicks all but hisses. "Murder? Say it."

Luke can't. "That's my vision, and it haunts me."

"Is Barry Marx in this vision?" Hicks takes out his black notebook and his black pen. I hate to think the detective investigating my case can sit across from the big passion in my life and write only the skeptical, critical things I see him scribble about Luke. I miss Luke so much I feel almost physically capable of crying real tears.

"Oh yeah," Luke says. "He is."

*Thirty-one*

# SECOND OPINION

"I wish I'd known her," Brie whispered, as awed as the rest of the crowd in this garnet-walled gallery.

Brie and I were at the Met, headed now toward the curator's prize. There she hung, *Madame X.*

"What do you suppose she's thinking?" Brie asked.

" 'My boobs are better than yours'?" The woman's pearly skin shone against a black gown that would have been scandalous on any catwalk in any century. *Madame* wore a bemused smile, her profile turned away from contemporary admirers. I had rarely seen such an arrogant pose. In her day, this woman was considered to be quite the babe. Now, instead of having a sitting with John Singer Sargent, she'd see Barry about that nose.

"What I'd give to have her tutor me in the womanly arts," Brie said.

"Like you need help," I said.

"Do I have to remind you that the last man in my life was a lot more Norman Bates than Carl Jung?"

Brie's most recent suitor had, indeed, given new meaning to the profession of *psycho*analyst. I'd learned not to get Dr. Demented started on fat people who drove up American health care costs.

"Anyway, I've met someone new," Brie said as we moved to the next painting.

"Tell me," I answered, giving most of my attention to a moody rendering of four exquisitely dressed American girls whose fortunate genetic gene toss allowed them to be raised in Paris, not a midwestern suburb closer to Best Buy than a *boulangerie*. I knew this painting well. It had been covered in the art history course where I met Barry.

"He's a she," Brie said. "A gorgeous she." She brushed the hair off her face and tried to look blasé. I could tell she was anything but.

"Excuse me?" I said, spinning away from the portrait. "When did you switch teams? You haven't been without a man for, what, more than six months of the last sixteen years? I've always thought you should have a catch-and-release policy."

"I say it's high time for another gender."

I deposited myself on a bench. "Who is she?" *A venture capitalist? Titled Englishwoman? Cartoon princess? More importantly, will I like her?* When you're lucky enough to be a grown-up with a very best girlfriend, the idea of sharing her with another woman feels uncomfortably close to cuckoldry.

"She's my architect," she said. "Isadora Vega." The syllables rolled off Brie's tongue as if she were savoring a rich, decadent sauce. "Dark hair, big eyes that are almost purple, bigger brain, *muy Latina.*"

"The type Pedro Almodóvar would cast as the lead in a film?"

"A Velázquez Venus."

In silent agreement, the two of us stopped looking at portraits and began to search for one of the museum's cafés, not even stopping to browse among the minimalls of posters, umbrellas, and too-cute wine corks. We wove in and out of the building's familiar chambers as if led on a leash. "My treat," I said as we arrived at a small cafeteria overlooking Central Park, where in the late afternoon light I could see more leaves on the lawn than on the trees. Waving Brie away as I got out my wallet, I paid for two glasses of wine and followed Brie to a table by the window, thinking how she was always, literally, a step ahead of not just me but every other woman I knew.

"To . . . whatever," I said as we toasted.

"To happy surprises," Brie said, and offered up ten more minutes of juicy, girl-crush details. Lingerie shopping for the same bra size, double entendres, identical taste in Italian shoes.

As I listened, I debated whether to drop my own bomb. It was an afternoon for shocks, and Brie would be the last person to judge me for seeing a man who wasn't my husband. When my glass was almost empty, I said, "Since we're talking about relationships, I need your advice."

"What's Barry done now?" Brie's face was flushed with excitement and fair-to-middling chardonnay.

"Not Barry."

"Ah, Lucy, then?" Brie, who didn't have a sister, typically took the position that Lucy was guilty until proven innocent.

"Not Luce," I said in a low, conspiratorial voice.

"I give up, but for the record, I've suspected something's not right."

"How so?" For the last few months, I'd felt as if I could have won Best Actress for my convincing portrayal of a contented wife and mother.

"You forgot my birthday."

"No!" I said. But the next day was Thanksgiving, and Brie was born on November 17. Months earlier I'd bought her an antique magnifying glass hanging on a silver chain. I realized it remained stowed and wrapped, ready to present with a blank birthday card on which I had planned to copy a quote appropriate for a thirty-fifth birthday: "Life is really simple, but we insist on making it complicated."

"I had to celebrate with Isadora," Brie said, still playful. "Cocktail after cocktail. That's how things got rolling, so if you don't like it, blame yourself."

After I extravagantly apologized for the birthday gaffe, Brie moved on to a giddy account of the couple's first kiss and how Isadora slept over. And over. Now she was moving in.

"Enough about me—let's get back to you," Brie eventually said. "What's going on?"

I began regretting that I'd opened the door to talking about Luke. Brie was, I decided, too in the thrall of new romance, caught up with herself and herself alone. Not only did I doubt her current judgment, it also didn't seem fair to try to dim her bright light. Besides, continuing to keep our relationship all my own allowed me to believe that Luke and

I existed in an alternate universe with flattering light and an endless loop of mutual admiration. This was a place where I would prefer to stay.

"Molly, what's going on?" she repeated.

"Oh, nothing."

Brie tilted back her sleek head and laughed. "We've established that it's not nothing."

"Just forget it."

"Molly?"

"Okay, I'm seeing another man." As I blurted this out, my eyes fixed on an almost naked tree outside, I could swear that some other woman was speaking. "It started by accident." I was feeling like quite the fool.

Brie whistled softly. "Since when?"

"Since a while ago."

"I get it. You're not going to give me specifics. But play fair—tell me something."

I took a deep breath and exhaled words in a whoosh. "As long as it's lasted, he's made me feel like I am the most desirable woman on earth. When we're together I feel beautiful and impossibly clever, like I'm starring in my own movie."

"What does he look like?"

"An Irish poet." Brie nodded in appreciation. "He takes away all my anxiety, all my depression."

"Other women go shopping for that."

"And did I mention the sex?"

"But no, my friend has to get a little something on the side," Brie interrupted again to say, not unkindly, "Is he anyone I know?"

"No!" I lied. "Don't ask for details. Please. And stop smiling—this isn't as hilarious as you may think."

"Why are you offering up these crumbs now?"

Brie wasn't taking my confession nearly as seriously as I'd hoped and expected. I didn't want to admit that the impulse to blab about Luke must have come straight from some misguided desire to show that I, too, had a reckless anything-for-love stripe.

"You haven't decided to leave Barry?" Brie asked. The unspoken words in that sentence were *I hope.*

"Not at all," I said. "I've never imagined that this man"—the thought of calling Luke my lover seemed beyond pretentious, as if this movie I was starring in were Italian—"and I will wind up together, much as I care about him, which I do." Very much so, something Brie doesn't seem to understand. "He's not just a boy toy."

The afternoon sun was gone, and I could see myself, tense and trembling, reflected in the window glass.

"Please don't tell me this is the guy Kitty heard about," Brie said, wincing. "Please."

I stared at Brie. "Do you think I've completely lost it?" Now I really wanted this conversation to end, even if I'd started it. Talking out loud about what I had with Luke had cheapened it.

Brie didn't speak for what felt like minutes. "You're not asking me what I think, but I presume that's why you've brought this up, so I won't sugar-coat," she said finally. "I believe you care about . . . him . . . and I know that things at home aren't exactly in your target zone for perfection, but listen. An affair is never the answer. I say this from having been on the other side, numerous times."

I reached into my pocket and blotted my eyes with a tissue.

"End it—you've had your fun." Brie's tone was gentle, yet unyielding. "You'll kick yourself later if you make any other choice."

I'd counted on Brie for a warm, chummy response, maybe even a winking congratulation, not this. I felt as if she were adding two and two and insisting the answer was five. Didn't she understand that removing Luke from my life right now would be like switching from color to black and white?

"Get out," Brie said, grasping my hand.

Blinking with skepticism, I just looked outside.

"You've done harder," she said.

I had no idea what she was talking about. Nothing in my life had felt nearly as hard as the idea of never again being with Luke.

"We don't pick the people we fall in love with," Brie continued. "If this other man is the one you want to be with, I'm thrilled for you. Go ahead and blow up your life tomorrow to be with him. I'll be there for you. But if you're not willing to do that, your marriage can't get better if he's taking up all the space in your head."

No wonder Brie became a lawyer. She is painfully logical.

This conversation had ended. The two of us started to weave back through the maze of galleries, down the grand steps toward the coat check. Usually we made an obligatory stop to gasp at the ten-foot urns of two-thousand-dollar seasonal flowers. Not today.

I kissed Brie goodbye, hailed a taxi, and sleepwalked through Annabel's dinner, bath, and bedtime story. While Barry howled at YouTube clips, I set the table for the next day's parade-watching brunch, heaping branches and acorns into a centerpiece notches below my usual standard. The result all but screamed, *Paging Martha Stewart.* I gave thanks for the fact that the food for the brunch was being delivered, all the while trying to sell myself on cutting Luke loose. He would be arriving home that night, and in our last e-mails we'd made a date for Monday. I only had to pull the trigger.

But I needed fortification, and regretted, not for the first time, that I wasn't an alcoholic, a pillhead, or a follower of a calming New Age belief system. When I heard Barry start his shower, I decided to seek another opinion and picked up the phone.

"Free at last?" I said.

"Do you really have to ask that question of a teacher? Turkeys are gobbling in my dreams. Want to know what they're saying?"

"Save it—I only have two minutes and I need some instant advice." I heard water blast in the bathroom and Barry belting out "A Hard Day's Night," but I whispered nonetheless. "Remember that other guy I told you about?"

"The one I said you should stop seeing?"

"I didn't." I told Lucy my guilt had been exploding—I couldn't do this anymore.

"You're asking Lucy to open her psychiatric booth?" my sister said. "I'm honored."

Barry walked into the bedroom, a towel wrapped around his lean torso. "Who you talking to?" he mouthed.

"Lucy."

"Hello, Moosey," he shouted as he pulled on clean boxers and walked out of the room.

"Do you realize how much I despise that husband of yours?" she said.

"We don't have much time. What would you do? Quick."

"I'd call it off," she said. "Not worth it. At least, that's what I would do."

On Thanksgiving afternoon, Isadora left by two and Brie finished helping me clean up after forty-two guests, half of whom were under the age of five and had perched on my windowsills to get eyeball to eyeball with Snoopy. When they saw the monster-sized balloons, only three children had complete meltdowns. Fortunately, this year Annabel was not among them.

"I hope you don't hate me for being frank the other day," Brie said. "Was I a bitch?"

"An honest, sensible bitch." I surveyed my kitchen and tied the last gigantic bag of garbage, put my ceramic turkey-embossed platter on the highest shelf, and turned to hug Brie. "I just hate that you might be right."

# Thirty-two

# A FINE KETTLE OF FISH

During the past week, Brie started dialing the number four times. Today she lets it ring twice before she once again aborts her mission. The moment she puts down the receiver, the phone trills.

"What's on your mind?" Hicks says when she picks up.

"Detective?"

"I figure that you and your lady either want to ask me to dinner"—*or a threesome*—"or you have something to confess."

"On the first count, my partner moved out two weeks ago," Brie says as Jones stands before her, waiting for one more maniacal toss of his favorite chew toy. Brie flings the slimy hot dog across the room.

Hicks feels a twinge of guilt about the fleeting threesome fantasy. "Sorry to hear that," he says, shifting to strictly polite.

"I'm not," Brie says. She has empty spots in her cupboard and closet, but her heart is healing fast. "And on the second . . ." She looks at the picture of the two of us that she's restored to the bookshelf after its Isadora-enforced hiatus. We were twenty-one, prettier than we realized, clinking Champagne flutes on a *bateau-mouche*. Big hair, big dreams. "There's something that might be something. I was hoping we could meet. Please wait a second, and I'll get my BlackBerry."

"Whoa, you're going to squeeze me in between litigation and a manicure? I've got a case to solve, woman. What's wrong with now?"

Brie hadn't expected *now*. Now, she tells herself, is overbooked. Brie believes she's moved on from Isadora, and I can vouch for the fact that she's willed herself not to think about her, a decision reinforced by staying as busy as possible. Now is when Brie had planned to take Jones to the dog run and also when she hasn't yet washed her hair, since she's just returned from ninety minutes at the gym with the trainer she's booked, after which she visited three specialty grocers. All the ingredients for crawfish étouffée, starring a pound of startlingly pink crawfish she had FedExed from Louisiana, are waiting on the counter, since learning to cook is also on her agenda for now, along with calling her mother and reading last month's issue of the *Economist*.

"I'm waiting, Ms. Lawson," Hicks says.

Jones returns, panting for yet another toss. To make sure she gets the message, he barks, loudly and continuously.

"Dog-sitting?"

"No," Brie says. "Jones is all mine. He's the new love of my life, and he desperately needs to burn some energy."

"Same here," Hicks answers. "I'll meet you."

*Hicks must be getting nowhere on Molly's case if he's this eager to see me*, I hear Brie think. She almost feels sorry for the guy. Then her eye lands on our picture. Her mind switches to me and it makes her both happy and sad to think of meeting Hicks. "Can you be in Union Square at one?" she says.

Hicks smiles; maybe he'll get a break. He sees the pieces of my case spinning in midair, UFOs smacking him in the head. By default, it's looking more and more to him as if my death was random rotten, an accident of dumb luck or the handiwork of a long-gone lunatic who ran me off the road. He's ruled out suicide, which he doesn't think I had the skill set, or sufficient torment, to implement.

For the last week, at eight or nine o'clock, when Hicks turns off the light in his bare-bones office, he's entertained cutting bait, thinking he'll just have to move on and hope to be anointed supersleuth for some other case in the future. I have heard him apologize to me: "Sorry, Molly, no breakthroughs today."

Then all night I'm in his dreams, begging him to figure out how I wound up dead. *Go*, Hicks, I plead. Please! I'm counting on the Hiawatha Express. I'm praying for it. Someone has to figure out the whys and how-comes to explain why I now reside in the Duration. Down there, I can only hope that you and perhaps you alone are feeling my anger, which roils inside me along with guilt and pain and longing.

During the night, Hicks wakes several times to read his latest library book—this week's is by Cormac McCarthy—or to simply stare at the ceiling or out the window, toward the bodega where his friend Marco sells lottery tickets. The next day while Hicks shaves, he glances in the mirror and decides he looks like hell. Then he usually talks to me. "Molly Marx, tell me what happened, girl. There's got to be an answer." He'll stop to buy his newspapers from Marco, takes the train to his office, and thinks the same thing while he tries to concentrate on the *Post* and the *Daily News*. When he walks into the precinct, he makes a fresh pot of coffee, chews through his files a few times, picks the brains of Detective Gonzalez and the other big and little kahunas nearby, and makes more calls, more appointments. Every few days he walks again down by the river, hoping to find some crumbs that will lead him to the answer.

Hicks has been investigating my case for five months. He needs a break.

"Deal," he says to Brie. "I'll meet you by Charlie, that cheese dealer from Rensselaer County." Charlie's a redneck who knows his Emmental from his Gruyère.

"See you in forty-five minutes," Brie says.

On Saturday, as you stroll the Greenmarket, you can practically smell the succulent meals that will be prepared that night. I had forgotten how much I loved it here. The Marx family always ate well the day I pedaled to the Greenmarket. I'd fill my basket with round, crusty breads; sugar-sweet baby vegetables; buttery lettuces, good black earth still clinging to their leaves; tomatoes exploding with juice; oatmeal-raisin cookies the size of my hand; and always, a huge bouquet of whatever flowers sang out, *Buy me, baby, buy me*.

Hicks gets there early, as I do. He is off duty, looking even more princely in cords and boots than in his finely tailored workaday clothes, the ones that are more expensive than the other guys on the force realize. He heads to one of the biggest stands, deliberates over seven kinds of potatoes, and finally buys fingerlings, selecting each slender, pale gold jewel one by one.

"How are you going to cook those?" Brie asks, walking up beside him. Despite her firm hand on Jones' leash, the pup jumps up and leaves a dirty paw print on Hicks' heavy gray zippered sweater. "Oh, I am so sorry," she says, yanking away Jones as she brushes the mud off his sweater.

Hicks feels a spark of . . . something. *My luck that she prefers women,* he says to himself. *Don't think about her that way, fool.*

"This guy definitely needs a crash course at obedience school," Brie says.

Hicks laughs. "Don't most men?" He strokes Jones' warm, smooth back. "You like potatoes, huh, boy?"

"He likes everything. He's going to be a hippo when he grows up."

*I doubt that,* Hicks thinks. He considers how people choose animals that resemble them. This dog's going to be long and leggy, like Brie Lawson, who he has decided looks a lot less brittle in a pair of faded Levi's and a down vest than she does in her uptown attorney togs. "C'mon," Hicks says. "I need some fresh herbs to roast these."

"Show me," she says. "I know nothing."

"That I can't believe, smart lawyer like you."

"Hey, if it wasn't on the bar exam . . ."

"So, you have something to tell me?" he says, leading Brie and Jones to a small booth for dainty, string-tied bunches of rosemary, oregano, and thyme. He lifts some rosemary to Brie's nose and she breathes in its earthy fragrance.

"I doubt it's anything," she says tentatively, her eyes fixed on the herbs. It's hard for Brie to go on, because she has convinced herself that to share this information violates *my precious memory and flawless reputation,* especially because she's not even sure if she's right. "But Molly," Brie says, turning to look Hicks in the eye, "had a boyfriend." She, of all people, speaks the word as if *I had gonorrhea. Shame on you, Brie, but I know it's your worry talking.*

That's the big breakthrough? "Who was he?" he asks. Hicks already knows all about Luke, and hopes Brie will be talking about another guy.

"Molly would never say, and I'm fairly sure she broke things off before she died. At least I told her to." *Okay, I'm arrogant,* she thinks, *but*

*Molly usually followed my advice.* "When I asked her about him, she'd always give me that don't-go-there look. I'm thinking the person who might know more is Lucy. Have you asked her?"

"Done," Hicks says.

"What does she know?"

"Not much," he says. What she had to say filled less than a page. As he leads Brie to the cheese seller, Hicks does exactly what Brie does as a lawyer—says little and hopes his prey will fill in the blanks. This time it works.

"The only thought I have is that the guy might be the one she works with, Luke Delaney, who I'm sure you've talked to," Brie says. "I've been with them together a few times, and you know how you can feel something about a couple?"

He nods. *I certainly do,* Hicks think. *I might be feeling it now.*

"I know Luke from years ago and thought I sensed it," Brie says, "but when I asked Molly, she flat out denied it." Twice.

"Why didn't you say anything sooner about this?"

"I wasn't sure. I'm still not. If Luke and Molly were involved, I couldn't see why he'd deny it, and also, he's a decent guy who I don't want to get in trouble." As soon as she finishes her sentences, she realizes it sounds ridiculous, as if she cared more about Luke than me, but she knows she'll make it worse if she backtracks and tries to correct what she just said.

Hicks turns his head to look at Brie for a full minute, which makes her extremely uncomfortable. *Does he think I'm lying?* she wonders. But that's not what's in Hicks' head. She is relieved when he turns his attention to the guy behind the table.

"What you got today, Charlie?" he asks. Hicks tells himself that if this job doesn't work out, he's going to move upstate, buy a herd of goats, and learn to make cheese. He's already ordered two used books on the subject from Amazon. Every few weeks he logs on to real estate websites and pictures himself with forty acres, a shiny green John Deere, a manure spreader, a brush hog, and a compost heap. Even one of New York's finest can dream.

"Try this ricotta," the vendor says, offering Brie and Hicks tiny wooden spoons filled with opalescent white cheese. "Heaven?"

That's another thing I miss: really sharp, tangy tastes. Also anything salty, crunchy, or spicy. Dammit—and every other word in the vocabulary of your average Tourette's sufferer—I miss food. Fresh, home-cooked, fancy, not fancy. I especially miss Italian—even the Olive Garden—Indian, French, Thai, Vietnamese, Peruvian, everything but midwestern-bland. I miss McDonald's fries, pastrami on rye, dim sum, dark chocolate bars studded with almonds, the hamburgers at Gramercy Tavern, my own spaghetti and meat sauce, my mother's hokey Thanksgiving sweet potatoes with marshmallows, hamentaschen, butterscotch sundaes, and Kitty's cheesecake. I think especially about the fudge cake covered with shaved chocolate I'd planned to buy that last afternoon. *Life is short—eat dessert first* should have been my religion.

"I'm going to have to bring home some of that, Charlie," Hicks says, pulling out his wallet. I've noticed that he actually weeds out its receipts every night so its fine leather doesn't bend and bulge. "And two of those." He points to the chèvre wrapped in green grape leaves. As they walk away, he gives one to Brie.

"Detective, is this bribery?" she says, lifting the cheese high as Jones sniffs it curiously.

"There'll be more where that's coming from if you know anything else about your friend's case," Hicks says.

"I wish I did," Brie says. "You have no idea."

Every day since Brie got Jones, she's been talking to him about me. "You'd have loved Molly, Jonesy. She was silly, like you. There was the time when we didn't have dates on New Year's Eve and at eleven-thirty we got all dressed up to have martinis at a hotel bar in town. And Molly couldn't sing on-key, but she was always the first to volunteer for karaoke, so no one else would feel like an idiot. Her song was 'Night and Day.' "

Brie carries on like that until I have to leave. I can't take it.

When Brie turns to inspect a row of beribboned pound cakes, each loaf no bigger than a good-sized tropical fish, I see Hicks look at her in admiration and outright surprise. *I feel comfortable with this woman,* I hear him think.

The thought flashes through his mind just as Brie is thinking the same thing. *This Hicks, he's easy. I could use a little easy right now.*

I am wondering if my powers have anything to do with this connection. Could I be willing it to happen? I'm going to have to talk this over with Bob, who has never mentioned the spontaneous combustion of matchmaker capabilities.

I'm getting very excited.

"Detective, what's your opinion on crawfish étouffée?" she asks.

"In my top ten," he says. "Providing it's swimming in garlic and cayenne like my Grandma Hattie cooks it down in New Orleans."

I have never known my friend Brie not to act fast. Do it, Brie, do it, because there's no way Hicks will. Don't fail me now. Don't fail yourself.

"I'm inviting you to dinner then, that is, if you're available," she says before she remembers that she can't cook. "If you promise not to expect too much."

Why can't I hug her? I truly can't recall if I have ever seen my best friend blush.

"I accept," Hicks says. *Maybe I am getting my break,* he thinks, and then he douses the thought. *No expectations, boy,* he says to himself. *No expectations.*

"Seven?" She has shocked herself but doesn't regret it, and since she's on a roll, hoping tonight is a beginning and not another ending, she continues. "I have another question."

He nods.

"May I please call you Hiawatha?"

Once again, Hicks doesn't hesitate. "Absolutely not," he says, and strolls away. Brie can't see the smile on his face, but I can.

# Thirty-three

# WRAP PARTY

*H*ow about we meet at the Morgan?"

"We haven't seen each for three weeks and you want to meet at a library?" Luke said.

"I was thinking of the dining room," I said, the spot where I could least imagine a fur-flying scene. Decorum bonded the hush-hush Morgan's brown, shoebox-sized bricks, and its restaurant flew so far under the radar I couldn't imagine anyone younger than eighty lunching there. This safely excluded Kitty and every friend she or I had except my neighbors Sophie and Alf, who I happened to know were in the Galápagos.

"Hey," Luke said, "I admire an original Mozart manuscript as much as the next guy, but I've been dreaming about you." While I was searching for a response he elaborated. "Your lips, your skin on my skin, the way you smell like sunlight and happiness—"

"Stop," I said. Through endless motivational self-lectures—during my shower, my sleep, and my commutes—I'd promised myself that after that day Luke and I would be a wrap. But I wanted to terminate everything in person, to see him one last time and dive Lucy-style to the bottom of our relationship's murky pool. I told myself that whatever we thought we had between us deserved as much. "I don't have a lot of time today."

"So let's reschedule," Luke said, breathing deeply, clearly puzzled that I had brushed off his poetry. "How's Thursday?"

I'd trained for that day as if it were the bad-girls' marathon. Postponing was not an option. I pulled the phone away from my ear and stared at it as if it might offer an answer. "Molly?" I could hear Luke saying. "Are you there?"

*What's one more abbreviated apartment visit?* the phone asked. *See him. You'll take a mental picture and carry it with you for the rest of your life. Then it will be over. Skedaddled. Monogamy forever forward.*

"Okay," I said. "I'll be at your place at one."

When I arrived, Luke stood in the doorway wearing his usual welcome-mat grin, shy but sly. He enveloped me in a tender, tight embrace, which as my automatic pilot ignited I found I could not resist. Not that I tried. I circled my arms around his shoulders, leaning into him. *God damn you, Luke,* I thought. *I am going to miss everything about you. Every decadent molecule.*

As the kiss continued, a remote, still-functioning part of my brain noted that there I was again, whizzing down the double-black diamond that always led us to the same place. My thumbs slipped into the back of Luke's jeans, where his warm skin invited me to come closer. No underwear. No self-assurance shortage. He easily led me by the hand to the bedroom.

"Would you like your gift before or after?" Luke asked as he lit the remains of a candle I'd given him early in the fall. A faint scent of ginger enveloped the room as the flame burst and sputtered, casting shadows that pirouetted on the walls.

"After," I said. "After."

"Does that mean you want me as much as I want you?" he said as he pulled my sweater and then my lacy camisole over my head.

I would never know the answer to that question. But what I said was "Allow me," unbuttoning his shirt as if he were the promised present. I knew this much: whoever believed that couples should hurry to become stark naked is missing half the point. I lazily moved my fingers along Luke's bare chest, tracing his dark, curly hair until I reached his belt, which I unbuckled in one deft, practiced move, and continued on to his jeans. I pushed them to the floor as he did the same with mine.

*Stop now, Molly,* I told myself. *There's still time. All bets off.*

My flesh ignored my brain. As we went on, I was a photojournalist, out of body, circling and shooting away. Who is this wife—not old, but surely old enough to know better—recklessly playing in sheets that aren't hers, running her hands along a man's well-muscled back, tasting his sweet mouth with her tongue and lips? Who is this man who knows exactly how to love her and acts as if he does?

"Molly, where are you?" Luke said, stopping and finding my eyes, which had not closed. "You're in orbit."

I answered with numerous thoroughly animated body parts. Soon enough the journalist left the room and I alone remained, giving myself to Luke with the urgency of a woman shipping her soldier off to war. I memorized every stroke and sigh, every small scream and low, satisfied groan. They would have to last for a lifetime.

Then it was over. The two of us lay side by side, wordless. I closed my eyes and tried to think of . . . nothing.

Luke stepped out of the bed and disappeared into the hall. Cool air touched my shoulders and back, which were beaded with sweat, his with mine, mingled, Luke-and-Molly No. 5, the now and forever fragrance. I wanted to yank the downy comforter to my forehead and burrow beneath it, to postpone what was to come, but when Luke returned I was sitting up, half dressed, if a chartreuse lace hipster thong counts as clothing.

"It's the last of the Syrah," he said, handing me a glass of wine as he sat on the rumpled linen. "To us," he said, clinking my glass. "I told you I missed you. Tell me how much you missed me. This time in words."

*He's playing you an overture, Molly girl,* I told myself, twice. *Don't miss your cue.* But I was preempted.

"Wait," Luke said. "Your gift." He put down his glass and walked to the armoire. My inner Annie Leibovitz came to life and captured the small scar on his back from when he was a Cub Scout and fell from a tree and needed seven stitches. When Luke returned, he carried a small box. I eyed the white package with curiosity spiked by guilt.

"Open it," he ordered, a smile lifting his face.

I quickly untied its bow and peeked. Catching the candlelight were lilac-blue gemstones, small and round, framed in warm matte gold and dangling from delicate gold threads. The earrings suited me. I might have chosen them myself.

"With your blue eyes," he said, looking for a sign that he'd picked well. "They're Victorian. I bought them at auction."

*Luke, you're making this too hard,* I thought. "They're perfect," I said. This was true. "But such an extravagance . . ."

"You deserve them." He pulled me to him and we kissed, once for each earring, and I slowly replaced my prim pearl studs with the antique treasures, which Barry surely would not notice. "Thank you. You shouldn't have." *I wish you hadn't.*

"They're for Christmas," he said. "But you know me—zero impulse control."

*Which goes for both of us,* I thought. *And do I know you?* I didn't even know myself. *Don't be a wuss. Don't waste time. Whatever the protocol might be for what you plan to do, this isn't it. Start talking.* But first I dressed, taking time to wash carefully, including the streaks of mascara that had migrated beyond my lashes, making me look as if I'd lost a fight. By the time I left the bathroom, Luke was back in his jeans, still shirtless, and had moved into the living room.

"What'll it be?" he asked, combing through CDs. "Django Reinhardt? Josephine Baker?"

"You pick," I said. I wondered if a country and western star had written a twangy ballad about a cosmetic surgeon's wife breaking up with her lovable photographer boyfriend. If nobody has, somebody should. But moments later, Edith Piaf's voice began "Les Amants de Paris."

Luke sank into one of his couches and motioned me toward the space beside him. The opened bottle of wine was on the table next to our glasses, which he'd refilled. "Wouldn't it be great to go to Paris?" he said. "Maybe I can cook up a trip. It's corny, but what do you say to April? I know this place near Montparnasse, twice as romantic and half the price of Shutters." Shutters was the exceedingly charming hotel where we'd stayed in Santa Monica. We'd gotten up early each morning to take long windy walks by the Pacific.

"I think we're getting a little ahead of ourselves," I said as I pulled out the camera.

"Oh, man," he said. "There it is. Thanks—I've been missing that sucker. Want to take some shots now?" he said. "Hand her over and give me a big Molly smile. Too bad you have all your clothes on." I believe he winked.

"Luke, I don't think so."

"Not in the mood?" he said. "You look so good right now I'd like to go right back into the bedroom."

"Luke, I can't."

He put the camera on the table, brushed away a lock of hair from my forehead, and cradled my face in his hands. "What's wrong?" he asked.

I closed my eyes to stanch the tears I knew would come. My effort didn't work.

"Please don't tell me we have a problem. Did Barry find out about us?"

I was sorry I was wearing the new earrings—I never should have opened the box, never should have let myself do a lot of things. But I refused to be one orgasm short of rational thought. I was glad I'd prepared a speech.

"Luke," I started. "I can't do this anymore, and it's not because Barry knows about us, because I don't think he does. It's that every minute of every day I feel as if I'm in an opera that keeps getting louder and louder. I can't hear my own voice anymore. I can't think. This feels wrong. I love you, but—"

He put a finger on my lips. " 'I love you, *but.* ' " Luke stood, crossed his arms, and walked a few steps away from me. Tension ironed horizontal lines in his forehead. "But you're going to break my heart?"

"But I do love you. That's not it."

He started talking as if he were slicing off each sentence with a knife. "Excuse me, Mrs. Marx, but weren't you more than happy to be all over me fifteen minutes ago? When did you make up your mind about this? Have you spent the last few weeks planning how to break things off or did the idea just occur to you?"

I was despising myself for being the sort of spineless, duplicitous woman who had chosen to have this conversation after I went to bed with him. I looked at Luke miserably, hopelessly. I wished I could go into the bathroom and start banging my head against the tile floor.

"I thought our feelings were based on love and kindness and re-spect," he said. "I guess I'm the fool here."

He looked angry but he sounded sad, and that made it worse. I'd come here to unload everything I'd been thinking for the last few weeks, to take each particle of doubt and build it into the Great Wall of China, to separate us, and now it was coming out wrong. "We're not to-gether all the time," I added, as if that needed to be pointed out. "We've never discussed that this would last forever, that you wouldn't—couldn't—be with other people."

"I don't want to 'be with other people.' Don't you get that? You're making me feel like a fool, used and deceived."

"How have I deceived you?" I heard my voice rising. "I've no more deceived you than you've deceived me."

"Look who's on her high horse," Luke said quietly. "The doctor's wife." He stared at me. "And by the way, I don't buy that your marriage is one coast-to-coast crap storm. You're never going to leave him, never, not in my lifetime."

I'd hoped for poignant eloquence and gotten a cheesy daytime drama. *But you and I have never even talked about being together,* I thought, and hissed, "Well, I certainly won't leave Barry now." I snatched my bag and walked toward the front hall. I took the time to remove the ear-rings and place them on a table, then grabbed my jacket and slammed the door behind me, breathing heavily as I ran down the stairs, not bothering to wait for the elevator.

As I reached the second-floor landing, Luke shouted at me, run-ning down two steps at a time, "Molly, come back. I don't want to fight. You've blown everything out of proportion. This is idiotic."

When I shot out the front door, one of his neighbors was exiting a taxi, which I took as a sign. I mumbled apologies as I bumped the woman and catapulted myself into the cab. It tore away as Luke reached the sidewalk. In the rearview mirror, I saw him, still shirtless, growing smaller and smaller.

"Where to, lady?" the driver said.

*Good question,* I thought.

*Thirty-four*

# DR. STAFFORD AND DR. SCHTUP

*S*o?"

When did marriage counselors convene and decide this was the word to kick off deep introspection? What did Felicia Stafford, M.D., expect me to say, that Barry and I were here to discover, on a scale of 1 to 10, if our conjugal discord was off the charts or merely and pitifully average?

Never had I felt more cynical. I hadn't entered into matrimony a skeptic, but my own behavior and seventy-two questionable charges to Dr. Barry Schtup's credit cards had turned me into one. If I, Molly Divine Marx, could have morphed into a cheater and believed that my husband was unfailingly unfaithful for—basically—always, then couldn't every other wife be in the same stinking, sinking lifeboat?

*Snap out of it, Molly,* I told myself. *Grow up. You can make this right. Isn't that the reason we're sitting in this tastefully furnished Fifth Avenue office at three o'clock on a glum Tuesday?* I had parked myself across from Dr. Stafford in the middle of a couch upholstered in the orange of a deer hunter's jacket. I wondered if she'd chosen the fabric for its happiness quotient or to remind patients not to pull out a shotgun. There was ample room next to me, but Barry had chosen a stiff Windsor armchair at a right angle to both of us. On the end table separating us was a large box of tissues.

"So, we hoped you could help us," I said, shifting in place, trying to get comfortable. I'd obsessed about what to wear. My version of a mini? Well-worn three-inch ankle boots? Even a hint of cleavage? Bimbo, bimbo, bimbo. Jeans, a cotton T-shirt, or cargo pants? Juvenile. I settled on flat leather boots, a black cashmere turtleneck, and a long black skirt, although God only knows what Dr. Stafford would read into its schitzy diagonal hem.

"And you, Dr. Marx?" Dr. Stafford said.

Barry's voice was even and soothing, waves at the beach. "Things haven't been right for a while."

*Or ever,* I thought. I glanced at the doctor's hands. Wedding ring. Check. I looked at my own. Yup, still there. As married as yesterday.

"Why do you think that is?" Dr. Stafford asked.

She wasn't the sturdy Margaret Thatcher I'd expected. I asked myself if I could stand to have a psychiatrist this attractive. The doctor was tall and slim as a bread knife, no more than forty-five, and wore a crisp Katharine Hepburn—esque white shirt and trousers of driftwood gray, which sat on the hips she barely had.

Barry gave the doctor his patient-seducing grin and it brought me back to Fifth Avenue. I knew this smile well. Its subliminal message was, *You can rely on me—I reek of integrity. I'm a heck of a plastic surgeon, and an even nicer guy. I would never screw up—at golf, at work, at anything.*

Dr. Stafford, I decided, was going to like him best.

"We haven't taken our vows seriously enough," Barry said in the earnest tone of the Rhodes Scholar he'd missed becoming, he claimed, by *this* much.

*Our vows?* Could my husband have heard them at all when his mind was on a mission to meet up with another woman during our wedding reception? Dr. Stafford said . . . nothing, her silence an ellipsis that beckoned Barry or me to jump right in and spout whole paragraphs of well-constructed prose explaining why our marriage stopped short of bliss.

"Molly, do you want to weigh in?" she asked.

The session cost two hundred dollars an hour. I thought I'd better speak. "Barry's right. We probably haven't approached our relationship with enough . . ." I fished. Gusto? Sincerity? "Gravitas." *Gravitas*? What kind of an op-ed word was that? I never remembered saying it, ever.

"Do you want to continue to be married to—may I call you Barry?" Dr. Stafford said, looking quickly at Barry and then again at me. "That's one of the initial questions I like to ask in a first session."

*But why did you have to start with me?* I wondered, although lately I'd asked myself the identical question at least once a week. "Yes, I do, definitely," I said.

I did not want a divorce. Was my impulse due to the lack of an exit strategy—with or without Luke—or actual, albeit conflicted, love in which Annabel played no small part? More the latter. I did not want my daughter to suffer. That sentence sounded meager, but I hated to think that Annabel might ever be in pain, especially if I was the cause of it, and there was something we—Barry and I, together, her parents—could do to give her the childhood she deserved.

"And?" Dr. Stafford asked.

I assumed "and" meant "why." Two pairs of arched eyebrows faced me.

"Barry's essentially a good person," I began. "He adores Annabel— she's our daughter. Three and a half. He's smart. He's funny. We have a history." As Nana Phyllis would say, he's also a great provider, which I both took for granted and thought it was crass to point out. There were also, of course, Barry's looks, which I'd stopped noticing, but were high in the plus column. "He makes me laugh." Sometimes. "Oh, I already said that."

I decided not to add, *I haven't been the best wife. I've screwed things up grandly all on my own, whether Barry knows it or not.*

"Molly," she said, "you could be describing a friend."

"Actually, Dr. Stafford," I said, focusing on a silky cord around her neck—which was easier than looking into her eyes—"that's the thing Barry isn't. I don't think he even likes me much, and he definitely doesn't get me, and so . . ." I felt I might have to live or die by these words; how to say it? "I don't really trust him. I don't think I ever could or have. In the most basic way, I don't feel protected by him." Which has nothing to do with the handsome income he generates, I realized.

"I don't feel safe around Barry, and that's a bigger problem than any-thing."

The room grew as quiet as Manhattan after a heavy snowfall. Dr. Stafford swiveled her chair to the left. Was she delighted that it hadn't taken us even ten minutes to hit nasty?

"Barry?" she asked. As we both waited, my eyes wandered to an ab-stract oil painting hanging over my husband's head. The scrambled rainbow colors could be a diagram of my emotions.

"I see where Molly would think that," he said at last. "I can get very caught up in my work, with my hobbies."

I tried not to roll my eyes. Hobbies? *"I live for visits to small, out-of-the-way hotels and to explore the city's finer cigar bars. You: available on nights when I'm 'working,' and for long walks on white-sand beaches near conferences in sunny locales."*

"And Barry, do you want to be married to Molly?" Dr. Stafford asked.

Barry leaned forward. "Unequivocally," he said, looking only at her. "My wife's beautiful, sensual, talented, a great mom, but none of that's as important as the simple fact that"—he leaned to reach for my hand, a foot away from him—"I love her." I jolted slightly at his touch.

"And only her?" the doctor asked.

Dr. Stafford was smarter than I thought.

"Only her."

*Do I know you?* I wondered.

"Molly says she can't trust you," the doctor said. Her tone was purely reportorial.

"Yes, I heard her."

"We'll get into why not later, I hope, but for now, Barry, I want to know—can you trust her?"

Is this where I break down in tears, wipe away my snot, and inter-rupt? *Hold on—let me tell you why you shouldn't. Because I'm coloring out-side the lines, too! On the bad-wife scale, I'm an eleven.*

"Yes, I think I can," Barry said. "But Dr. Stafford, if she'd seen the need to . . . have another relationship . . . I could understand where Molly might be coming from."

He was still looking only at our shrink. I could have been in Sri

Lanka. His handsome-doctor grin had been replaced by the serious-ness of a Senate candidate apologizing for the hooker in his hotel room.

"Doctor," Barry continued, his fingers clasped and flexed, almost as if he were praying, "I haven't always been faithful."

*Oh, really?*

"But that's going to change," he said, without a scintilla of visible shame. "Or I wouldn't be here."

"Barry, go a little deeper with this. That is, if you agree, Molly?"

I nodded. *Sure. Drill deep. Right through my heart. Spit out all the gore. If it helps, refer to notes.* This counseling had been my idea, but I'd begun to feel that everything Barry might get off his chest would sink into mine like darts.

"I'm already trying to change," he said. "Only yesterday this ex-tremely attractive patient invited me to lunch, ostensibly to talk about becoming my publicist, but I've already told my receptionist to cancel her."

Would that be Stephanie, or Sherry, or Shelley someone whose card Delfina had found in Barry's pocket before she brought his coat to the dry cleaner? On the back, he'd scrawled an address and apartment number. Riverside Drive. Now I wished I hadn't told Delfina to throw away the evidence. I also wished I could believe Barry.

Dr. Stafford looked in my direction. The half smile she'd used with Barry had collapsed into a horizontal line. She'd definitely taken his side. "If there were one thing you could change about your husband, what would it be?" she asked.

*I'd like him not to stare at my thighs as if he thought they should be Photoshopped to 70 percent of their size. No, I can do better than that. I want Barry to like me as much as he does his mother and give me half as much at-tention.* Maybe Dr. Stafford would let me ask for two changes. *In that case, I'd like him to think that one in ten of my idiosyncrasies is endearing, not worthy of the kind of reform you plan every New Year's.* But she did ask for one change. I had to pick.

"During dinner, I'd like him to ask me how my day was," I began, "and listen, actually listen, to my answer."

"Uh-huh," she said. "Barry, how about you?" I thought Dr. Staf-ford's tone implied, *That wouldn't be so hard, would it, man?* I hoped she'd goose him in that direction, but instead she asked, "What would you change about Molly?"

As if he were spiking a volleyball, Barry bounced back. "I want her not to be so dubious. To believe I want a fresh start."

"Okay," Dr. Stafford said like a pleased parent. "Where do we go from here?"

*At these rates, why is she asking us?* The three of us sucked in air and waited for something to happen. I turned to glance outside, but the shades were drawn. I felt like a bug who'd walked into a roach motel. Then I decided that dishonesty was a luxury I could not afford.

"Doctor," I said, "can we dial back? Because I haven't been entirely honest. I'm probably being naive about marriage and maybe entirely unrealistic," I began, wishing I could ditch the habit of apologizing. Barry never did, nor Kitty nor Brie nor Lucy. Especially not Lucy. "But I think I just set my expectations a little too low."

Dr. Stafford tilted her chin in my direction. Her skin was the kind of flawless that comes from a power higher than Bobbi Brown. I couldn't find a sunspot or a squiggly red vein, and yet she appeared radiantly Botox-free.

"I want more from my marriage than for Barry to pretend to listen to me yak about my day. I want to come first. We can count off my flaws from here to the Fourth of July, but I want him to find at least some of them endearing." I swallowed a big bubble of air. "I want Barry to look at my face and melt." Like my dad does with my mom, even when she's just come out of the shower. That, especially. "I want him to feel that the happiest accident he ever had was meeting Molly Divine, that I'm in every breath he takes." Was I sounding like a bad greeting card? I didn't care. I had the undivided attention of the other two people in the room and was determined to continue.

"I need to feel my husband is absolutely bonkers about me—that our home isn't the Twilight Zone." *Good job, Molly,* I thought, liking that phrase. "And"—I turned toward Barry—"if I can't have this, then maybe we shouldn't be married, because I think I'm at least as deserving of love as the next wife, and I've obviously sold myself short."

I felt as if I'd delivered a commencement address.

"Is there anything else?" Dr. Stafford asked.

"One more thing," I said, watching Barry size me up with the undisguised curiosity he usually reserves for comely females at other people's dinner parties. "I want to feel exactly the same way about my husband. About you, Barry." I touched him with my eyes.

What could Dr. Stafford possibly say that would change my mind now that I finally knew it? But she began talking. I saw Barry's mouth move, and then the doctor's. Him, her, him, her, him for a long time. My mind had switched off the sound.

As my phone audibly vibrated, both of them looked at me. I felt their eyeballs, but checked the caller's number nonetheless. It was the fourth time Luke had tried me over the last few days.

"Do you have to take that?" Dr. Stafford said.

"No, it's just a work call. Sorry." Deeply sorry. Luke had already left two messages pleading with me to reconsider the previous week's conversation, to make a date to meet him or at the very least to call back. I hadn't responded, not even when he described a trip to Paris for late January. He couldn't wait for April. We'd be staying in a hotel hidden away in a seventeenth-century building on the Left Bank. Visits to the Musée de l'Orangerie and the Cinémathèque Française. Dinner at a candlelit, Michelin three-star restaurant in the shadow of the Eiffel Tower. Nutella crêpes morning, noon, and night if that's what my wounded heart desired.

"Molly," Dr. Stafford said, "is there more you want to add to our conversation?"

"That I'll try," I said, "if Barry will." I meant it.

"So," Dr. Stafford said, "it's time to stop." She looked first at me, then at Barry. "I'd like to see you after Christmas. Then we can dig in with some real work."

I bet Dr. Stafford couldn't wait for her next appointment of the day, where the couple actually had worries they didn't manufacture—serious, sympathy-worthy anguish brought on by losing a child, a breast, a job, or a Pomeranian. She'd probably already classified our problem in the subbasement of hair and waistline loss.

We all did a dance with our calendars and picked weekly slots. Couples counseling would be the gift that kept on giving twice a week, Tuesday and Thursday, at three. I shook the doctor's hand, which felt smooth and small.

We walked out to Fifth Avenue and began to head south. Barry put his arm around my waist and pulled me close, leaning in. It was a gesture that I like as well as a kiss, although I don't recall ever having mentioned that to my husband. I could feel the warmth of his compact physique. Neither of us spoke.

Across the street, workers at the Met were hanging a blue banner. All I could see was the flourish of a name. Cézanne. I repeated it to myself, and it buzzed in my ear like catchy French music. This caused my mind to make an unfortunate involuntary leap to strolling hand in hand with Luke along the Seine, stopping at the stalls of several *bouquinistes.* I tried to cancel the image and concentrate on Barry, who I saw glance toward the Met as well.

As we got to Seventy-ninth Street, where he would turn left to return to his office on Park, we stopped. "I have an idea," he said. "What do you say to a second honeymoon? I've always wanted to stay at the George V. April in Paris? I'll call the travel agent tomorrow. Why don't you sign up at Berlitz?"

"I'll get right on it," I said.

# Thirty-five

# COSMIC LAVENDER

Delfina Adams treats my Annabel as if she were her own blood. She detangles curls, dries tears, sells her on asparagus because of its double wallop of vitamins and fiber. Delfina can make the junk mail disappear, set a table to the standard of the First Lady, and never let the shrunken Marx family run low on apple juice, Fig Newtons, or peanut butter, but cleaning is not her métier, nor is it expected of her. Miracle Maids, a battalion of earth-friendly elves, arrive twice a week with dancing mops and lime green noncarcinogenic potions.

The germs, streaks, and smudges in this apartment are gone. I, however, am still here, surprised to see Delfina tenderly polishing my desk. As if she were massaging its creaky two-hundred-year-old bones, she rotates a supple linen dinner napkin retired from active duty. I inhale the lemon scent, an aphrodisiac designed to seduce women into performing homely household tasks. After ten minutes, Delfina stands back, squares her tall, competent frame, and smiles in appreciation of the result. In the burnished mahogany, I see her oval face reflected with its high cheekbones and eyes as warm as brown sugar.

Delfina opens the double doors on the desk's hutch top. "Oh, Lord," she says out loud. "That missus sure could make a mess."

Tidy on the outside, tumult inside, me to a T. Shelves sag under a pile of unpaid bills and envelopes, many envelopes. Roller ball pens—black and only black—discarded pocket calendars, an expired passport, friends' Christmas photo greetings ("Happy everything! Love and kisses, the Cohens and Mugsy"), and dog-eared business cards crowd the cubbyholes along with thirty-nine-cent stamps, a tape measure (*that's* where it is), and, inexplicably, a plumy purple feather.

Delfina whistles. "Okay, Dr. Barry said to empty the desk." She looks at the clock on the nightstand. Ten-fifteen. "Shouldn't take too long," she says, to offer herself encouragement. She sets aside an overdue library book and begins to pluck out the obvious trash. Into a carton saved from the last Fresh Direct delivery go magazine subscription notices, bunches of faded receipts, and an ad for twenty-dollar opera seats. Damn, why hadn't I bought one? For years I lived twenty-five blocks from Lincoln Center, but I never once saw *Madame Butterfly*.

I am recalling other items on my lengthy to-do list—learn to tango, bake sourdough bread, build a house with Habitat for Humanity, plan a trip to the beaches of Croatia, take pole-dancing lessons—when I spot it, a pale lilac envelope carefully sealed with wax, as if the sender were nineteenth-century European aristocracy. Delfina's slim hand, tastefully manicured, reaches for the envelope and, with efficient dispatch, drops it on the heap. It lands right side up.

*To my darling Annabel,* the envelope says in my loopy penmanship. Based only on the *p*'s and *b*'s, a graphologist once sized up my self-esteem as alarmingly low, but I took care with this document. Every letter is precise and, I hope, pulsing with ego.

Delfina does a double take. "Lord, what is this?" she says, wrinkling her brow. She lifts the fat, square envelope to the light, as if a seventy-five-watt bulb could reveal its secrets. The heavy paper ain't talking.

Delfina stands utterly still, breaks a sweat, and looks around the room to make sure she is alone. She removes a cell phone from her pocket and calls Narcissa. "Can you talk?" she whispers.

"Of course," Narcissa says. In the background, Delfina and I both hear the Food Network. I, a charter member of the Rachael Ray Sucks Community, am forced to hear that loudmouth reel off fifteen ingredients, ending with truffle mousse pâté, that her ravenous disciples need for her thirty-minute hamburgers. I hope that anyone who believes that life is fair will be disabused of that notion when they consider that I'm in the Duration and Rachael rules the world. Narcissa snaps off the television mid-"yum-o!"

"There's a letter here, hidden, from the missus."

"My, my, my, my, my," Narcissa says. "Imagine that. After all this time."

"What should I do?" Delfina continues to whisper.

"Mail it?"

"It's the kind of letter you just hand to someone."

"Open it, woman! Read it out loud!"

"I can't do that—it's not right." Delfina lives by her church's principles. I was reminded of this on a regular basis, when she would hit me up to buy raffle tickets. Once I won a free meal at a Caribbean restaurant in Brooklyn. Excellent jerk chicken. Her pastor's son owned the place, and as I recall from his family photo on the wall, Delfina's Reverend Moneybags visited the same barber who coifs the Reverend Al Sharpton.

"Who's the letter for? Dr. Barry? A secret boyfriend?"

Did everyone think I had a boyfriend?

"No, Annabel."

"But that little child, she can't even read. You'd need to read it to her." Ella reads not just letters but whole books, as Narcissa never fails to mention. "So technically—"

Like most West Indian housekeepers in our neighborhood, thanks to her powers of persuasion, Narcissa is paid better than not only every editorial assistant in Manhattan but also 20 percent of the attorneys who've recently been sworn into the New York Bar. But Delfina is unconvinced. "I don't think it's my place to open this letter," she says. *God will punish me,* I hear her think.

"Then what are you going to do about it?"

Delfina peers again at the clock—it's almost eleven—as she moves to plan B. "I'll let you know," she says, and hangs up. She places the envelope next to the Bible she keeps next to her bed. With Baby Moses now safely in the bulrushes, she returns to sort through the rest of the stuff in the desk very carefully. Who knows what else she might find? A winning lottery ticket, perhaps? She checks the Bible every few minutes.

I stare at the envelope and remember everything.

I'm proud to say there were times in my life when I had a sense of occasion. This was one of them. First, I visited a stationery store, since I didn't want to write this letter on my MacBook and simply hit print. As soon as the saleswoman told me a particular shade of paper was called Cosmic Lavender, I decided it was my destiny and ordered a hundred sheets with a swirling white monogram. I sat at this very desk, opened the lid of the navy blue box, lifted a sheet, and slowly copied the text I'd rewritten endlessly over the course of a week. I only earned B's in English, but I felt I made my point.

*Darling Annabel,* I'd begun. *When you read this letter, there are things I want to make sure you understand. . . .*

Delfina tries to drift through the day as if it were ordinary. She and Annabel visit the butterflies at the Museum of Natural History and cook colorful wagon-wheel pasta for dinner. During Annabel's bath, she reads her *Madeline* and tucks her into bed. At eight-fifteen, Delfina retreats to her bedroom next to the kitchen, where she moved in after my work with Luke started taking me across the globe. We painted it together in a shade Delfina chose after considerable deliberation, a smoky plum called—inexplicably—Lazy Afternoon. Perhaps Delfina picked it because her life has offered so few of those.

"Did the painter fall into grape jelly?" Kitty asked when she saw the walls. But I always admired Delfina's conviction on the matter of this paint and much more. When Annabel pokes her head into this hidden domain with its white organdy curtains, floaty as bridesmaids' dresses, she thinks she's entered an enchanted kingdom.

A few hours later, Barry walks through the door with *her.* Delfina is still up, watching Lifetime, although usually she's asleep by now. She hears Barry leave Stephanie to hang up her own coat while he heads straight to Annabel's room, where he brushes away her blond hair for a soundless kiss on a plump, damp cheek.

"Good night, angel," he whispers. Annabel opens one eyelid, says, "Your whiskers scratch, Daddy," turns over, and tries to reboot her dream.

In the kitchen, Stephanie pulls a bottle of water out of the refrigerator. Another woman is at home in my home. She knows where to find the coffee beans and my favorite café au lait bowls, as well as my thickest, newest bath towels and the Dr. Hauschka lemon body oil I hoarded because it cost thirty dollars for only 3.4 fluid ounces. I want to pour the bottle of water on Stephanie's fluffy, salon-blow-dried head. Let her dehydrate, with lips so scaly Barry will refuse to kiss them. See if I care.

Barry and Stephanie walk, arms wound around each other's waist, toward the bedroom. As she sits on my side of the bed and unzips her tall, spiky boots, Stephanie sees the letter. "Hey, Bear," she shouts to him in the bathroom. "There's an envelope here for Annabel."

Stephanie pulls open the drawer on my bedside table, finds an emery board, and begins to file a ragged edge on one of her long nails. The casual intimacy of the gesture makes me as enraged as the fact that Barry shouts back, "Be there in a minute, baby." I despise that he calls her that as much as I loathe the way she carelessly pushes back my ivory matelassé coverlet. My ritual was to carefully fold it in thirds and lay it on the mohair chaise in the corner. I suddenly feel as attached to this bedcover as if it were from my grandmother's trousseau, not casually ordered on sale from a website I can't remember.

Barry walks into the room as Stephanie lights a candle. It gives off a musky scent. My husband is only two steps from the bed when his eyes fall on the envelope. He freezes. "Where'd that come from?" His tone is accusing, as if Stephanie is playing a practical joke. He scowls, which makes her scowl back.

"What's wrong? You look like it's going to explode." She hands him the letter. "Here."

He doesn't want to touch it. "It's for Annabel," he says.

"Okay," Stephanie says. She stretches out the word and gets up to take her turn in the bathroom. *What's gotten into him?* she wonders. *Why's he gone all serious on me?* When Stephanie emerges, doing justice to an abbreviated black camisole, the letter is out of sight, although Barry has read it. He slumps against the pillows, his muscular legs stretched in front of him. Stephanie walks to his side and waits for him to move over. When he fails to budge, she begins to knead his shoulders.

"Not now," he says, and removes her hands.

"Want to go to sleep?" I admire her seductive tone.

"Actually, I'm wide awake," he says, although in the taxi riding home from the theater, he'd dozed.

"Well, that's good," she says, "very good," and waits for his embrace. It doesn't happen, not even when she circles her tongue in his ear. "What's going on?"

In the same situation I might have cried, but Stephaniewoman, made of razor blades and gumption, feels anger, which is exactly what I myself am feeling now. My wrath is a bottomless well, an echo of a larger, unnameable emotion. When Barry fails to answer Stephanie, she quickly dresses. *This guy is heavy weather,* she thinks. *Or maybe he just needs more time. I can wait,* she thinks. *The good body, the medical practice, the money. I can learn to be patient.* Before my husband's lover leaves the bedroom, she kisses Barry lightly, hoping her touch will be the rabbit's foot that reverses the evening's direction.

He pulls away. "I'm sorry," he says. "This has nothing to do with you."

"Want me to stay?" *Say yes,* she hopes. *I'm your answer.* When he stares ahead, Stephanie says, "I'll speak to you tomorrow." She walks out of the room as confidently as she entered it. As soon as Barry hears the front door shut, he snuffs the candle and takes the letter from the nightstand drawer to reread its three pages. By the end of the first page, he dabs his eyes with the hem of the sheet, deeply exhales, and reaches for the phone.

"What time is it?" Kitty mumbles after the fourth ring.

"Just past eleven."

When my mother-in-law's sleeping pill begins to wear off enough for her to register that her only child is on the phone, her panic registers. "What now? Is something wrong with Annabel?"

"Kitty, we're fine," he says, although he doesn't believe it. "But I've found a letter. From Molly."

"So?" Kitty says. *Why is this an occasion for waking me?* she wonders. *Has Barry gotten weepy over some old love note? Maybe he drank too much tonight, or isn't coping nearly as well as he appears to be. He's working and he's dating, for God's sake, and Stephanie's the kind of woman men like. He's moving on with his life, as he should.*

"So? Do you want to hear this letter or not?"

"Okay, read the thing," Kitty says as firmly as she can through a pharmaceutical haze, but all she hears is a low snuffle that sounds as if Barry might be crying. She repeats the words, this time with the kindness of a mother. "Read it, darling."

" 'To my darling Annabel,' " he begins as I lip-synch " *'When a mother loves a child for eternity, every time that daughter breathes the mother is breathing along with her, hoping that every one of her child's dreams come true. My love for you never stops and never will. It goes around and around like a carousel, a hula hoop of hugs.' "*

Barry stops. He squeezes shut his eyes, hoping to stem his tears.

"Is there more?" Kitty whispers hoarsely over the white-noise machine tuned to "country eve." *Falling asleep to crickets wouldn't do it for me, but it works for her.*

"Yes, a lot. Molly even gets around to me."

"And me?" Kitty is now awake.

"You, Mother, didn't make the cut."

"Just as well." *No love lost there,* she thinks. "Who else knows about this?"

"No one," Barry says, having decided that Stephanie doesn't count. "Absolutely no one." *I'm glad Delfina can't hear this. Who does Barry think found the letter?*

"First thing in the morning, you've got to call that detective and show this to him," Kitty says as the wires connect. *The letter is the ticket for the Marx family to get its life back. No more sideways stares from the manicurist or the bitch at the dry cleaner who pretends she can't speak English. No more sudden hushes when I walk into the locker room at my club. Of course, everyone will dish the dirt about Molly's having taken her own life, and maybe I'll have to remind them, with Jackie Kennedy dignity, that my daughter-in-law was a bit—how shall I put it?—on the high-strung side. People will shake their heads, feel sad for Barry, and sadly debate the best way to explain the tragedy to poor little Annabel. People will be full of advice on what Barry should say.*

"I'm not going to Hicks before I call Molly's parents."

*Right. The Divines,* she thinks. "Darling," Kitty says, "that won't be easy. I'm so sorry for you." *My son shouldn't have to be going through this. But this is the end of the road that has taken me on the worst ride of my life,* she thinks, *worse than when Stan*—that would be Barry's father—*gambled away his business and my brother had to bail him out.* "At least we'll have closure."

" 'Closure'? What are you talking about, Mother?" Barry's voice rises despite his fatigue. "I don't see how this letter proves a thing. Molly could have written it anytime after Annabel was born."

"Come on. Sweetie, you don't want to connect the dots. You're too upset. Totally understandable."

"Suicide? Really, I doubt it," he says, but maybe his mother is right. He needs to sleep on the possibility. He repeats this sour-milk word—*suicide*—several times to himself. "Good night, Kitty. And don't tell anyone about the letter, promise?"

"Would I lie?" she says.

*Aren't you the mother who promised my life would always be happy?* he remembers as he hangs up the phone.

In two minutes Barry is as dead asleep as he always was as a resident. He wakes at his normal hour, doesn't remember a dream about a vacation when we went to Prague and I got lost, and goes for his run as the sun rises over the park. With every tread, his brain considers what to say to my parents. I am warmed by the thought that he wants to cushion the blow. When he returns home, Annabel is eating breakfast.

"Don't forget to leave those muddy shoes in the hall, Daddy," she says, in little-wife mode.

"Don't forget to give your father a big hug," he calls back as he brings in the *Times* and the *Wall Street Journal.* Barry has cancelled the *Post,* since I'm the only one who read it except Delfina, who misses it. I was never able to start my day without Page Six and a glance at my horoscope. He swoops down to snuggle Annabel, who wiggles in her seat as she kisses her father's cheek.

"Ick, you're sweaty," she says.

"Coffee, Doctor?" Delfina asks.

"Good morning, Delfina," Barry says.

If he would actually look at Delfina, standing at the counter, he'd see her biting her lip and twisting her ring. She can't bring herself to ask about the envelope.

"No coffee just yet, but thanks," he adds, depositing the newspapers on the kitchen table and padding to the bedroom in his stocking feet. He rushes through a scalding shower and dresses in a shirt and trousers before he picks up the phone. I am glad it is my father who answers.

"Dan," Barry says, his hearty effort falling short.

My father reads voices like Gypsies do palms. "Everything okay in New York?"

"Annabel's great," he says, but struggles to support this thesis. "Growing like a weed, starting to recognize letters."

"Well, that's good." In Chicago it's not even seven. "What's up that you're calling so early?"

Barry drums his fingers on the nightstand. "Dan, I came across a letter," he says. "From Molly."

Since I died, my father's gained twelve pounds, mostly in his face. He strokes his brand-new jowls. "That so?"

"I'd like you to hear it," he says.

*Do I want to endure this alone?* my father thinks. Last night my mother, who's developed insomnia, read a mystery from two until four in the morning, and she's still sleeping. The woman is practically a saint, but when he wakes her she nips like a Jack Russell terrier and doesn't mellow until after she's anesthetized by her second jolt of java.

"Dan, are you there?" Barry says.

"I'll call you back in ten minutes, Barry. Claire should be on the line."

Ten minutes, ten hours. It feels the same to Barry. After thirty-five minutes, the phone rings. "Barry dear," my mother says, "good morning. Read us this letter you've found."

She doesn't disintegrate until he gets to the part about her.

No one teaches you how to be a mother, Annabel. I was lucky, because I had Grammy Claire, the best mother in the whole world, who didn't realize that every day she was showing me how to be a parent someday myself. She has special powers. When I

was little, she could just look at me and know if I had a temperature or wanted a graham cracker or had fibbed to Lucy.

My parents, who are sitting side by side, each with a phone to an
ear, grab each other's hand as the letter continues to extol my father's
fourteen-carat-gold virtues and moves on to what to me passed for
wisdom.

1. Don't marry a man who thinks you talk too much, doesn't make
   you laugh at least twice a day, or farts in front of you and isn't
   embarrassed. (Feel free to disregard the last part after six months
   of dating.)
2. Never wear ankle strap shoes, unless your legs turn out to be a lot
   longer than mine.
3. Learn to roast a chicken.
4. Even though Mandarin Chinese would be more practical, make
   French your second language. You'll be at home in Paris, where I
   hope you will take a junior year abroad. When you do, order the
   hot chocolate at Angelina's.
5. Print out your pictures and put them in an album. Label! Date!
6. Don't waste time balancing your checkbook.
7. When you're crabby, fake a good mood.
8. Never ask a two-year-old a question to which she can answer,
   "No!"
9. Make at least one new friend every year.
10. Don't judge people by where they went to college.
11. When in doubt, paint your walls the color of vanilla ice cream.
12. Remember that Big Macs have 24 fat grams.
13. Keep your perfume in the refrigerator.

And so on. The list covers every area of banal daily life—hair,
friendship, diet, skin care, and, of course, home decoration—until it
finally ends.

50. Most important, Annie-belle: toughen up. God gives everyone
    her own special bag of breaks, but what makes the difference
    between happy and sad is whether you waste time being jealous
    and small. Don't. Learn to recognize good luck when it's waving at
    you, hoping to get your attention. Sometimes the universe tries

very hard to send you a message. No matter what life hands you,
angel-girl, bounce back. Be resilient. Self-pity is a waste, and life
is short enough without it. Do not feel sorry for yourself and don't
expect everything to be perfect. Work on getting a sense of
proportion—you'll know what that means when you're older—so
you can handle the disappointments that march along every day
like ants. When nothing good happens, stand up straight and
think of all the better things ahead. . . .

But there is no ahead for Molly Divine Marx, and my parents are
shutting down. "Stop, Barry," my father says. "We've heard enough."

"The thing is," Barry asks impatiently, "this is what's spooking me.
Do you think Molly . . . knew she was going to die?"

"Like when you're thinking about someone and then the phone
rings," my mother says, "that funny feeling in your bones?"

"Not exactly. I'm looking at this letter, which Molly clearly put a lot
of thought into, and wondering about . . . something else."

The silence between Highland Park and Manhattan drops like a
shroud. "Do you honestly think our daughter might have taken her own
life?" my father says, barely choking out the words, as outraged as if
Barry has accused me of molesting a child. I love how my parents rise to
my defense. They have never made me prouder.

"That's preposterous," my mother says, trying not to bellow at her
son-in-law, who she knows is upset. She can't even think suicide. "You
lived with our daughter and she was sunshine, pure gold. Is there
something you want to tell us?"

There isn't.

*Did you make our daughter miserable?* they are both thinking, and
Barry gets that as the message oozes through the phone lines.

"Have you called Lucy yet?" my mother asks.

"Maybe you want to tell her yourself?" Barry asks, hoping they'll
bite.

"We'll call to warn her, but you're the one with the letter," my father
points out. "She should hear it."

Even if she'll laugh at my quotidian wisdom.

Barry says goodbye and puts the letter in the inside left pocket of
his sport jacket. The envelope is as alive to him as I am not, throbbing

for attention. Five minutes later he's in a taxi, debating whom to call first, Lucy or Hicks, when his cell phone rings.

"Let's get one thing straight—my sister would never kill herself," Lucy says. She has traded her usual voice for the cool, low tone of a corporate president ready to eat another company alive. "I don't know how you can suggest it, even as a boneheaded theory. She'd never commit suicide. Absolute idiocy."

*Please make Barry understand this,* Lucy, I think as I watch her drive to work and talk on speakerphone.

"Who's saying she did?" Barry asks.

"Whatever you found I need to see. Immediately." *Molly was a sentimental fool,* Lucy thinks. *This is probably one of those earnest letters a mother writes when a child is born and whips out when the kid graduates from high school. She probably got the idea from a women's magazine.*

Lucy is almost right. I wrote the letter when Annabel turned three and was planning to give it to her at her bat mitzvah or when she got her period, whichever rite of passage arrived first.

"You know, Lucy, this letter doesn't seem like the sort of thing to fax." Is that what she wants, to prove that he hasn't faked it? He tries to stop short of sarcasm, but in any conversation he's ever had with his sister-in-law, it's the rhythm he knows best. "But let me read this one part now. *'I have always hoped that someday you'd have a brother, but I'm going to share a secret. Before you were born, I asked God for a little girl, and that's exactly what I would pray for again, because I've had a sister, and there is nothing more wonderful in the whole wide world.'"*

"Barry!" Lucy screams as she skids to avoid an oncoming car. "Stop! I'm going to get into an accident. That's all my parents need, two dead daughters."

"I'll overnight you and your parents copies of the letter—you'll have them by tomorrow," he says, bordering on kind. "And I should alert Hicks. Agree?" He doesn't care what she thinks, because he's already made up his mind.

Lucy likes being asked. "You should," she says. Tears drip on the front of her jacket. She wishes her eyes had windshield wipers. "So I guess we'll talk later, after the letter arrives?"

"We will," Barry says. His taxi passes a flower shop selling big tubs of blue hydrangeas. I filled our home with these flowers the moment they were sold each spring. *It's a sign,* he tells himself. *Go ahead. Ask.* He flashes to the incident with Lucy at Annabel's school, about which he's still fuming, no matter that my sister has written her own letter to him, of deep apology. Barry considers that he may be losing all reason and that his mother will be ready to commit him to an institution. "Lucy?" he says. "I need a favor. . . ."

She braces herself for a nasty hit. *No, I will not fuck myself,* she thinks. *Why am I being civil to Barry? This guy is vermin.*

"After the High Holidays, could you please come to New York? It's time that someone goes through Molly's stuff. I can't bear to do it my-self." *And Molly would hate it if I asked my mother.* "I was going to ask Delfina or Brie or . . ." *But now that you've been on house arrest for all these months at your parents', you've done your time, and I can ask you,* Barry thinks.

*You need me,* Lucy thinks. *But more importantly, my sister needs me.* The moment for a smart-ass retort disappears. "I'll be there."

*Thirty-six*

# TRUE CONFESSIONS

*I* watch Barry slip into a maroon velvet pew. "What do you think of all this?" I ask Bob, who's never attended a Yom Kippur service. He likes bagels, Billy Crystal, and Sandra Bullock (Jew—not a Jew? Discuss) and says *mazel tov,* but that's as Jewish as he's ever gotten.

"Why isn't the place packed? What's with the empty seats? Those of us raised with Confession couldn't get by baring our souls one measly time a year. We'd be hanging from the rafters and snaking a line around the block, banging to get in, begging to upload our sins."

Why didn't I bring Bob last night, when the confessions were in freefall and eleven people tried to squeeze into rows meant for eight? Almost every soul had stripped to emotional underwear, with varied degrees of contrition and honesty. When the collective sob of the Kol Nidre bounced off the vaulted Moorish ceiling, there was a collective swaying and moaning, well-dressed willows in the wind.

"You'll see—the place will fill up as the day goes by." I turn my attention to Barry, standing bull's-eye in a circle of loneliness, trying to pray. I'd love to know for what, exactly.

"For the sin which we have committed before You under duress or willingly," Rabbi Strauss Sherman says in his express-from-heaven boom. Worshippers listen carefully to the spiritual boilerplate. "For the sin which we have committed before You by hard-heartedness . . . inadvertently . . . with an utterance of the lips . . . with immorality . . . openly or secretly . . . with knowledge and with deceit . . . for all these, God of pardon, pardon us, forgive us, atone for us." After Rabbi S.S. says this, the invisible but exuberant choir repeats it, should anyone have missed the point.

*Pardon me,* Barry is praying. *Forgive me.* Like my Papa Louie and every male ancestor before him, he's wrapped inside a silky blue-striped *tallit,* determined to make God, today's star, hear him.

Yesterday, after Kitty's dinner—matzo balls floating in golden chicken soup, tangy gefilte fish, prime rib, baked potatoes the size of Annabel's shoes, and mile-high apple tart—Barry started fasting. For him this is new. Already, his stomach is saying, *Feed me,* and because he didn't wean himself off caffeine a few weeks in advance—my secret weapon—his head throbs. I'm not sure why our forefathers felt this particular physical hardship put a person in the mood for prayer. Maybe there's someone in the Duration who can clue me in on that.

I've never thought of either Barry or myself as religious. Even though he'd recently been appointed a trustee of the congregation and once in a while we'd attend a service, on most Friday nights we'd go to a movie, miles from a sweetly braided challah. Since I died, however, Barry—along with other mourners—has ushered in the Sabbath at temple and made a sizable donation to Annabel's school. As a result, on the fifth floor of this very building there's a well-stocked Molly Divine Marx Art Room whose centerpiece is an aquarium filled with hundreds of mollies in cocktail-hour hues—Gold Dust, Creamsicle, and other shimmers, plus the occasional active-wear Molly in neon green or orange.

"Want to see Big Molly?" I ask Bob, eager to get away from Barry's obvious discomfort—and to lose my own. "She's a Ghost Pearl." I often get lost watching her and like to believe a speck of my soul circulates within this plump female and her hundreds of babies.

"Later," Bob says as he settles in.

"For the sin which we have committed before You by false denial and lying," the rabbi continues.

Bob gives me that look of his that telegraphs, *Get serious.* Maybe he has some atoning to do—I can't get into his head and he rarely talks about himself—but my better guess is that he feels I could do with some of my own confessing. There's plenty of transgression, wickedness, and moral trespassing to go around. I need to be accountable.

Rabbi S.S. has moved along to the sin of scoffing. I consider it. Nope. Scoffing, not my thing.

"For the sin which we have committed before You by a haughty demeanor." On this count, my mind free-associates to Kitty. Where is that woman? Does she feel she needs no atonement? And what about the also absent Stephanie, who must be a member of this synagogue, since her son attends their nursery school? Does she honestly feel she's sailed through the year sin-free? Come on. Let me count the ways. But I'm running up my own tab thinking about both of them, especially now that Rabbi S.S. is shifting into Molly territory.

My own sins are manifold, bacteria on a sponge. My essence curls inside Barry, so that we might beseech God as a team, as together as we've ever been. He is praying intensely, with the strain on his face I see when he does a pull-up, trying his best to make the Big Guy hear him. *I blew it,* he's saying. *Molly is gone and I'm to blame. To blame. To blame, to blame.*

"And for the sin we have committed before you by a confused heart."

A confused heart? Hey, God, over here. Was this always in the service, or did You slip it in expressly for me? I'm still waiting to meet You in the Duration, but I have not given up. You bet my heart was, and is, confused. It's unhinged, in a spin. Do I have regrets? Does Yankee Stadium sell peanuts? Maybe I shouldn't have married Barry or should have gotten out early, after the wedding or even before. But then Annabel wouldn't be here, and how can I regret my child? I know You wanted Annabel to be. Which leads me to think that Barry and I could have learned to live happily ever after, Your five-year plan. Okay, God, maybe we got a running start in the wrong direction, but thanks to Dr. Stafford we'd reversed course. Some people grow up at twenty, the rest of us by forty if we're lucky. But yes, God, in short, my heart was confused.

Should I have stayed away from Luke? Not my finest hour. But God, You know better than anyone that I never intended to hurt Barry. Can we both at least agree that while he wasn't the best husband, my point wasn't to be cruel? I know You know that what I felt for Luke was authentic. My passion for him was the most glittering emotion You ever let me experience, second only to the love I felt for my child and my parents. It was the rarest rainbow of sentiment: capital-*L* love. Can that be bad?

God, let's talk. What was I supposed to do when You threw us together? Luke drew me to Luke. I didn't run in his direction because he was the Other Guy. Why did You do that? Not that I'm blaming anyone but myself. You knew I could never resist a man who listened to me the way Luke did, who manipulated my body as if it were a PlayStation 3, and who happened to look and smell and smile like, well, Luke. Did You put him on earth and let him trip me up just to tease?

Ah, but the moment for silent meditation is over. Rabbi S.S. is at it again.

"On Rosh Hashanah it will be inscribed and on Yom Kippur it will be sealed . . . how many will pass from the earth and how many will be created. Who will live and who will die at his predestined time and who before his time?"

My heart's more than confused—it's riddled with questions that I have the rest of eternity to sort out. Top of the list is why I, Molly Divine Marx, stood in this very synagogue twelve months ago, prayed as ardently as the women next to me and behind me to be inscribed and sealed in the Book of Life for one more year, but wasn't among the chosen. Yes, I'm as hideously culpable as any other commandment violator in this room. I am an emotional felon. But I can't believe that Your thinking is so simplistic in the cause-and-effect department that infidelity is what has landed me in the Duration, especially when Barry and Luke got to stick around. You can't possibly have a double standard, that cheating is worse for women than for men.

"Who by water . . . fire . . . sword . . . beast . . . famine . . . thirst . . . storm . . . plague . . . strangulation . . . stoning. Who will rest and who will wander, who will live in harmony and who will be harried . . . who will enjoy tranquillity and who will suffer . . . who will be impoverished and who will be enriched . . . who will be degraded and who will be exalted?"

That elegant, mustached gentleman with the ebony cane who always sits in front of us—he looks as delicate as the white lilies on the altar. Will he be here next year, or six feet under? That enormous mom from Annabel's school—will it make a rat's ass of difference if she deep-sixes the Häagen-Dazs, joins Curves, and hitches her star to Jenny Craig? Will Kitty make the cut? My mother? Does being sealed in the Book of Life truly depend on how many merits and demerits a person has in her account and whether her atonement is heartfelt, or do You have a short list created by celestial lottery?

Barry is counting on the former. I know this much from listening to him. He's fretting more about the future than the past.

"Do you think he's really sorry?" I ask.

"I do," Bob says. I would like to believe him. I'm working on it. Bob's not a cynic. I am.

"He wishes everything were different," Bob says. "Listen to him."

Diffuse early afternoon light floods through stained glass, highlighting congregants in gilded pools of sun as they offer up silent entreaties. I tune back in to Barry, waiting for him to make a wish on Stephanie's behalf, but his head is wrapped around Annabel, his mother, and "poor sweet Molly." It's a pitiful appeal, and I am relieved when he moves on to a lengthy entreaty on his own behalf. He augments his case with anecdotes. *God, remember the time I waived my surgery fee because a child had a cleft palate and the parents couldn't pay? See what a good father I am to Annabel? Take note of all my charitable contributions—thousands and thousands of dollars. Please recall the unsolicited raise I gave Delfina and the way I forgave Lucy. Don't forget I'm a good son. The best. I call my mother every day.*

"In the blowing of the wind and in the chill of winter, we remember them," the rabbi says.

*Do* they remember me, really? Can they hear my giggle and picture my eyes? Know which eyebrow was higher than the other? Remember the taste of my chocolate chip cookies? Listen to Chris Botti or Chris Rock and recall, *Molly thought those guys rocked.*

I've had enough. All this remembering can bring a girl down when there's no promise of blintzes smothered in sour cream, stuffed with cottage cheese or syrupy blueberries, to reward her at the end of the day's fast, especially when the whole point is bargaining with God for one more year of blood, sweat, and tears of joy, for one more dizzying year of life. "In the blueness of the skies and in the warmth of summer, we remember them," Rabbi S.S. intones as Bob and I take off. Before I leave, I glance back once more.

Barry's been here all day long, prayer oozing from every pore, but damn, he still looks guilty.

# Thirty-seven

# WARDROBE MALFUNCTION

*L*ucy lays a trio of my most beloved garments on the bed. "Did my sister think she was a prima ballerina?" she says out loud to herself. "Why would anyone ever need three lace skirts?"

The answer is obvious, if only to me. One skirt is layers of tulle that looked fetching with flats and a boatneck top whenever I tried to channel Audrey Hepburn. Another grazed my ankles. It's the color of iced cappuccino, matches a filmy camisole that Lucy has yet to discover, and makes me feel tall, like an Italian heiress. The third is a gold pouf that barely hits my knees. I wore it once, to an Academy Awards party where I, Oscar the cross-dresser, won for Best Costume.

I don't expect Lucy to appreciate my finery. To Lucy, clothes are a necessity, end of story.

I watch Lucy and not only do I miss my critical, irascible sister, but I'll admit it, I also miss clothes—buying them, fondling them, and pretending that I'm someone else when I wear them. I miss my clothes, strangers', and even mistakes-in-the-making I scoffed at in magazines. Maybe I am a scoffer after all.

Every few hours, Lucy phones my mother. "What should I do with the outfit Molly wore to Annabel's naming?" Another nursing mommy might have chosen a flowing tunic and stretchy-waist pants that coordinated with projectile vomit, but I'd honored the occasion in a winter-white bouclé sheath and coat.

"I'd like it," my mother says. "Ship it here." She'll hang it next to my wedding gown and hope it still smells of my perfume. Which makes me wonder, would my fortunes have been different if my scent had been, say, Paris by Yves Saint-Laurent and not Eternity by Calvin Klein?

"The sheared beaver coat you gave her senior year? It's molting."

"Maybe a charity wants it."

"Her cheerleading uniform?"

"Home."

Not the Smithsonian? I'm crushed.

"A boatload of black pants?" Lucy asks, wondering why ten pairs were necessary. I wore them all, cheap, expensive, gabardines, silk, wools, low-rise, cropped, cords, and especially the ones designed by Karl Lagerfeld for H&M. Fifty-nine dollars' worth of unadulterated pleasure.

"Honestly," my mother says, moving along to cranky. "Use your own judgment." She catches herself for snapping.

This is the second day of the purge. Lucy already showered Delfina with piles of handbags and sweaters. Today she came to work with a gaily branded satchel—Coach! Coach! Coach!—instead of her reliable vinyl tote. I hope she looks inside the hidden zippered compartment, where she'll find a twenty-dollar bill.

For Lucy this is a triathlon that requires focus and stamina. She doesn't want Annabel to see her mother's worldly possessions exhibited as if a yard sale were in progress, so she's limiting her efforts to when my daughter's away. My sister hasn't even laid eyes on Barry. She's checked into a small hotel on Madison, where she passed last night watching an American League playoff game along with a Kirin beer and a chaser of unagi rolls. This morning she charged through Central Park, timing her power walk to arrive after Annabel left for school.

But now, even though Annabel won't be home for hours, Lucy's heading out, shifting a duffel from hand to hand. The subway pulls into the station as she races down the steps. Good sign. Whenever the mass transit gods smiled on me, I considered the event to have profound cosmic significance. Unfortunately, I also read meaning into reverse karma, such as picking the seat next to the guy who'd forsworn deodorant or the teenage girl who shrieked "Motherfucka!" because my leg brushed hers.

Lucy gets off at Columbus Circle. Brie suggested lunch spots all over town—the Little Owl, Pastis, Le Cirque—but Lucy vetoed every one: too far, too French, too phony. She is not impressed by forty-dollar entrées, steaks with a resumé, gawking taxidermy, pickle juice cocktails, or snowy white truffles. The last food trend Lucy got on board with was frozen yogurt. What's really going on is, of course, pride and prejudice. Lucy wants to be on an equal footing with Brie, not faced with her air-kissing a maître d' or whipping out a black Amex card, insisting that Lucy be her guest. She'd rather eat toads than let Brie pay.

Brie and Lucy finally agreed to meet in a small café within a vertical mall that overlooks the park. Lucy arrives early and waits. And waits. She's standing at the café's entrance. Bouchon Bakery is first come, first served, not a place where she'd be graciously seated and offered a drink. I wish I could tell her that she may as well read the first two chapters of a book at the Borders on the floor below: it's going to be a while.

Predictably, Brie is twenty minutes late. By the time she waves from the escalator, my sister's face has crimped into a grimace.

"Sorry," Brie says, airy and smiley. "Couldn't get a taxi." Liar. She found one instantly, eight minutes ago, after she left her office on Madison and Sixty-first. I learned to work around Brie time, but Lucy considers tardiness an offense right up there with coveting your neighbor's ox. Brie hesitates about whether to kiss Lucy's cheek. The opportunity passes. "Good to see you!" Brie says, grinning too brightly.

"You too," Lucy answers as they walk to a long communal table. They hop on the tall chairs, facing each other. Brie and Lucy are nearly the same height, although Brie is a champagne flute, Lucy a sturdy highball. Aside from my funeral and shiva, I can't recall them being alone together. Certainly, they've never shared a meal without me as referee.

Lucy decides to get to the point. "I thought you'd like these things," she says, and slides the bag to Brie's side.

Brie eyes the duffel uncomfortably, as if it might contain my head.

"C'mon, Brie," Lucy says. "Look inside."

Brie opens the bag and carefully unfolds the gold skirt; a pair of kiwi-green silk pajamas; a hand-crocheted gray sweater, delicate as

Charlotte's web; and a scarlet jacket elaborately embroidered with silver flowers and butterflies. I'll say this for Lucy—our tastes may have harmonized like olives and ice cream, but in picking these treasures, she's aced it.

Brie keeps her tears locked up inside. After she wordlessly refolds every piece of clothing, remembering how I looked in each one and adored these particular things, she wonders, should she put her hand on Lucy's arm? Get up, walk around, and hug her? My sister exists in a sentimental no-fly zone that Brie knows better than to try to invade. Instead she says simply, "Lucy, thank you. I'm touched—beyond words—and very grateful for all these ways to remember Molly." The formality of the statement does nothing to mitigate the tension that fortifies the air like humidity.

"You're welcome," Lucy says.

"Are you sure you don't want all of this?"

"Could you honestly see me in a gold skirt that wouldn't cover my ass?" Lucy says. *Doesn't Brie know me at all?* she wonders. "I'm sure Molly would've wanted you to have them. In fact, if there's anything else you'd like, let me know."

There is. Brie would like to get Lucy talking—about Barry, about Annabel, and mostly about why exactly she thinks I am not able to be at the table right now, making sure that the two of them don't end in a hammerlock. But Brie doesn't have the combination to Lucy. While she thinks about what to say next, Lucy selects a new topic. "What's good here?" she asks as she glances at the menu. "I'm thinking about tomato soup with the grilled cheese."

"Never had it," says Brie, who, despite her name, isn't the sort to gobble an inch of cheese oozing between thick slabs of white bread. "I always order the endive and watercress salad."

*Which is why you have no thighs,* Lucy realizes. *What the fuck am I going to talk to this woman about?* Lucy is losing sight not only of the most obvious theme—how I died, ladies—but also of how smart Brie is, how kind, and how much I got out of having a friend twice as resolute as I would ever be. As if I ever would have gone hang-gliding on my own.

"How does Annabel seem to you?" Brie asks. Letting Lucy clean out closets is one thing, but has Barry actually allowed Lucy to be alone with Annabel, given the kidnapping that almost was?

"I haven't spent enough time with her to tell," Lucy says. "We hung out a little yesterday afternoon"—chaperoned by Delfina, who rode shotgun—"but then I had to head out." *To avoid Barry.*

"Saturday after next I'm taking her to MoMA," Brie said.

*Exactly what every kid her age needs,* Lucy thinks. *She'll take one look at the Van Goghs and have nightmares for weeks. Enough with this small talk,* she decides. "So, what do you hear from that detective? Anything new?" Hicks hasn't returned her call from a few days ago.

"He's evaluating the suicide theory," Brie says. "Given the letter . . ."

"The letter? What a crock," Lucy says. "I don't know when my sister wrote that sop, but I'm positive it wasn't to announce that she was going to off herself."

"Can you prove this?" What Lucy saw as mawkish, Brie found sweet. Then again, she is now the devoted surrogate mother to a leaping canine who sleeps at the foot of her bed. Every day, maternal muscles she never knew she had begin to twitch.

"Of course I can't *prove* it," Lucy says. The look on her face might be defiant—or defensive. "It's a gut feeling."

"Well, for what it's worth, I agree."

"Really?" Brie's stock has spiked on Lucy's Nasdaq. She is enormously pleased. "And how recently did you speak to the good detective?" *The guy who should have unraveled this mystery by now. How could any other case vie for his precious time?*

"Last night," Brie says as the food arrives.

"Really?" She's already on the warpath about Hicks being more responsive to a mere friend than to flesh and blood. "What does New York's finest have to say?"

Nothing that Brie wants to repeat. She takes a small bite of watercress, holding her knife and fork aloft as if she were raised by the Von Somebodies of Vienna, not outside of Portland, born to Sunshine and Herb, stringy, Birkenstock-wearing potters. Brie's table manners annoy Lucy. "I feel like there's something you're keeping from me," Lucy says, using the voice that always works with her students. *Jackson, get out of the block corner this minute—it's snack time! Emily! Look at me. Now.*

Brie tilts her face and tries to stay composed, but she breaks out in a small grin. "Lucy," she whispers after a moment, "the most amazing thing happened last night. Hicks and I slept together."

Lucy doesn't want for friends—fellow teachers, running buddies, college classmates, neighbors of every stripe, dogs, cats, hamsters, old people at the center where she volunteers, friends' toddlers. But she has no friends like Brie, who bill almost a thousand dollars an hour and take up with a spoiled South American heiress who speaks lisping Castilian Spanish.

"What about Isabella?" she blurts out. *Isn't one lover enough?*

"Isadora?" Brie says. "It didn't work out. We want different things."

*I'll say,* Lucy thinks. *Can't this woman pick a gender and stick with it? It's fucking unfair. I haven't had a date in eight months, and it's not as if I didn't notice Hicks. I have eyes.*

Brie feels the rumble of Lucy's rage and sees that she'll have to float this conversation. "Detective Hicks"—she hasn't yet been able to call him Hiawatha or even Hi—"is different from every other man I've been with, in a remarkably good way." The kissing was longer and sweeter, until she wanted to moan in boldface type, and he caressed her as if she were close to holy, which Brie has no desire to be in this man's presence and plans to make clear. When she looks in Hicks' eyes, every filthy-fabulous thought she's ever imagined suddenly seems like lyrics to a song her body knew by heart.

Brie looks up from her salad at Lucy, thinking, *Give me something here. Act like a girl! Your sister would have been all over me.* Were I there, I'd say, *How did it happen? Were you both drunk? Who said what first? His best move? I've never been with a black man—is it better? Way better? Okay, forgive me for asking, but is he, I don't know how to put this, huge? Does he make you laugh? Listen to you? Are you in love? And, for extra credit, do you think Hicks is?*

Brie is right. I would be rattling on like one of those regrettable squawking parrots you order on QVC after midnight. I want to reach out and hug Brie. I've been rooting for her and Hicks, the kind of standup guy every woman needs if she decides to give men another shot. I predict that she's finally found her equal. And yes, I'm not being entirely unselfish—maybe the relationship will be the kick in the butt Hicks needs to solve my case.

"So you and the detective," Lucy finally says. "I'm curious. How did it happen?" *What do other women do that I don't?* This is what my sister wants to know. Lucy feels as if every female but her has received annotated, illustrated directions on how to attract and keep a man. Were such instructions the secret prize in their first Tampax box?

"It just happened," Brie answers. Like it always does. One minute you're having an ordinary conversation, complaining about presidential campaigns that last as long as getting a master's; the next, all the atoms around you have realigned. Suddenly there's no one else in the bowling alley or on the plane or at the hardware store. You notice that his eyes are undressing you, and you wonder what it would feel like if your hands were under his shirt.

Brie senses an openness she's never noticed before in Lucy's face and for a few seconds feels as if it's me sitting across from her. There's a connection. Brie wonders, *Could I make this woman my friend? I could use a friend.* There's a canyon in her heart that I used to fill. She turns over the question as she takes her last bite of salad.

"It's going to happen for you, Lucy," Brie says. "I know it." The minute the words tumble out she's sure my sister will take them as condescending. She's forded a river and found a grizzly bear on the other bank.

"Yeah, well, whatever," Lucy grunts.

"Do you have time for coffee?" Brie asks.

"No can do," Lucy answers, and waves to the server. "There's a lot I haven't gone through yet, and I don't have much time before Annabel gets back."

"Could you use some help?" Brie asks. "I could cancel my afternoon appointments."

"I've got it covered." Lucy's face has closed down. You can practically hear the grinding grate.

Brie takes out her wallet. "You're my guest."

"Absolutely not," Lucy says as she lays down five crisp tens, gets up, and slips into her jacket. "This one's on me. But I have a favor to ask."

"Shoot," Brie says.

"Your boyfriend. Tell him to find my sister's killer."

The next day—after dragging seven bags of Molly-abilia to the thrift shop—my sister finally gets down to my drawers. Yesterday, knowing Aunt Lucy was visiting, Annabel refused to go to ballet. Delfina reluctantly watches Oprah in her room, popping out every ten minutes to check on my sister and daughter bonding over Nemo. Lucy gives Annabel her bath, reads her a story, and just as our daughter nods off, Barry arrives.

"You're good to take care of all this for me," he says as he pours them each a glass of amaretto. "How's it going?"

"By tomorrow the dig will be complete," Lucy says.

"Any rare finds?" Barry pokes the fire, and the flames salute him.

"Not really, unless you count a green reptile belt—I assume that means I've reached the Paleozoic era, or at least the eighties." Lucy has decided to keep my Swatch, which matches the one she lost years ago.

She glances at Barry, who seems to be studying the fire. She knows she owes him. "About that crazy thing I did at Annabel's school—I was wacko. I wrote you, but I need to say it out loud. I'm so sorry. But it was done out of love, misguided but—"

"Forget it," he says as he refills his glass. "I have." *Almost.*

He certainly doesn't want to talk about it. All day he's been marinating in estrogen. This afternoon was nonstop consultations, culminating with a fifteen-year-old who fought with her mother over the rhinoplasty Madame Pixie Nose was insisting on so the two of them would look related. Then Stephanie lambasted him for forgetting some dinner date she swore they'd made for tonight. Even his nurse eyed him as if he were Dr. Mengele. Barry wishes he could mainline the liqueur. He offers Lucy another pour, but she declines. He looks hard at his sister-in-law, whose straight-arrow posture accentuates her bountiful chest.

Lucy feels his stare. "Time to go," she says abruptly. "I'll see you tomorrow night." But she won't. She's booked an afternoon flight, and she's not in the mood for a weepy goodbye.

The following morning Lucy faces my highboy, whose drawers are carefully lined with pale purple paper that long ago lost its lilac scent. If you were a Victorian woman who owned a chemise, two pair of drawers, a corset, five ribbons, and a bonnet, this narrow chest would have been practical. In my case it's jammed with black tights, bras, thongs, socks, nightgowns, camisoles, and random sex toys. I loved the highboy's walnut sheen, its deeply carved flowers, and especially its wavy mirror, which allowed me the luxury of merely estimating my hair on off days.

Lucy starts at the top—bras—and works her way down. She sorts quickly to avoid feeling anything, since wandering through another woman's lingerie is like being in the same bed with her when she's having sex. It takes her less than an hour to get to the bottom drawer, where she spots the flannel nightgown she sent me when I was pregnant. Whenever I wore it, I was Maria in *The Sound of Music*. No whiskers-on-kittens gal herself, Lucy nonetheless gently fingers the dainty eyelet around its yoke. This, she suddenly decides, she will save for herself.

She shakes out the nightgown and holds it up. From its voluminous folds, a black-and-white photograph falls on the rug, facedown.

One day Luke set up a tripod and we posed, again and again. This shot was the one I saved. My eyes are closed and I'm laughing. Not an especially flattering pose. What I loved about the photo was the way Luke is looking at me with a pour of pure honeyed tenderness. Only I might know how blue those eyes are, but any casual observer can see they're filled with love. On the back of the photograph, I've written *November*. Lucy can tell from my haircut that the captured moment happened within the last few years.

She feels chilled. Her breath comes in short bursts. Lucy stares at the picture and with her index finger touches my face as if she is stroking my cheek. "Jesus, Molly," she whispers. "How dumb could a woman be? If you loved this guy, whoever this lug nut is, why didn't you leave your husband? And if it's Barry you love, why would you keep this red flag in your drawer?"

She does have a point.

Lucy tries to read the face of the man in the picture. *This guy loves you,* she thinks. *And you probably felt the same way.*

Lucy wipes away a tear. She quickly slips the picture into her pocket, ties together the last bag, and walks out of the room.

*Thirty-eight*

# KLUTZ, CUTS, GUTS

*H*icks' office is nothing special—twitchy fluorescents, a wooden floor that's never flirted with polyurethane, and a metal desk so dented you wonder if it's been kicked. It has. He sits in an oak swivel chair that, to the irritation of Detective Gonzalez, who shares the cubicle, he mindlessly spins—and squeaks—as he studies his bulletin board. On it is what I like to think of as a growing shrine to me, with photos of Barry, Lucy, Kitty, my parents, Brie, Isadora, and Barry's nurses (including the fawning witch who always sniveled, "Dr. Barry will have to return your call"). I also see a cattle call of interchangeable women who I assume are patients. One is Stephanie; others I recognize from the funeral and shiva, the rest are high-maintenance strangers. The centerpiece of this sacred masterpiece is a map Hicks has drawn—rather well—of the path from my home to my next-to-final resting place. X marks the spot where my life ended, the spot that's got Hicks thinking out loud.

"Did someone off you or did you do it to yourself? Tell me, pretty lady."

I wish I could. So does Gonzalez. She's sick of Hicks tossing questions into the office air, which smells of day-old coffee, mustard, and air freshener working overtime. "Hi, you talkin' to me?" she mutters. Georgia Gonzalez may demonstrate the subtlety of a hockey player, but she has instincts Hicks trusts as much as—maybe more than—his own.

"Sorry there, G.G. I didn't mean to interrupt your solving a Very Important Crime," he says. "Put any drug lords in the slammer today?"

"You don't honestly think that woman killed herself, do you?" They chew over my case every day. Gonzalez read my letter, which almost made her cry—she's a mother, after all—and announced to Hicks immediately that it was too prim to be a suicide note.

It's taken a few days for him to come to the same conclusion. "Nah, I don't think it was a DIY," he admits. "That'd make my life too easy, and it's also too damn hard to kill yourself by running your bike off the road. Unless she screwed up when she was heading for the river to drown. Nope, today I'm leaning back toward damn nasty accident."

He conjures it. Klutz, cuts, guts. Mud, thud, blood.

"I keep thinking the mother-in-law hired 1-800-Kill-Her." Gonzalez says this with a half smile that makes her tough, round face look almost pretty. "When I taught kindergarten I used to tell kids' parents that learning to share's a lifelong job. Wants her boy all to herself."

"Ya think?" Hicks gets up, coffee cup in hand, to face Detective Gonzalez. "And when were you a nursery school teacher? Scares the nuts off me to think that you were entrusted with impressionable young minds."

Gonzalez looks away. "A lot you don't know. I am a woman of deep mystery."

"How do I prove that Kitty Katz did it?"

"Not my case."

"G.G., did you not just tell me about learning to share?"

Gonzalez finishes her coffee and takes out a lipstick in her signature shade of iridescent tangerine. She applies it without looking in a mirror.

"Don't go all cliché there, G.G. Does *your* daughter-in-law hate you?" Hicks went to the wedding last year of Gonzalez's son, eighteen and a father. The kid was a standup guy when his girlfriend got knocked up.

"Maria worships me."

"Kitty Katz more or less said the same thing about Molly."

I didn't overhear that particular conversation, but I love that we're on a first-name basis, Hicks and I.

"What about the demented sister?" Gonzalez looks Hicks in the eye.

"*Crazy*'s not the word for Lucy Divine," Hicks says, even if Lucy can't prove where she was the day Molly died. "You're jerking me around, G.G., my friend." The notes in Hicks' file on Lucy run along the course of *intense, envious, high-strung, bitter.* "But no, I haven't ruled her out," though as Hicks is getting to know Lucy, he likes her more and more. She's no killer, his gut tells him.

"And the bad boy himself?"

"Dr. Strangelove?" Hicks perches on Gonzalez's desk, tosses his coffee cup into the trash, folds his arms, and leans against the wall.

"I was thinking of the other guy," Gonzalez says as she mimics his posture. When Hicks isn't around, I've seen her stare long and hard at Luke's picture. We have that in common.

"I'm leaning more in the doc's direction myself, but no, he hasn't dropped off my list." As predictable as spam, every day Barry hits Hicks with "What's new, Detective?" But my husband's tenacity hasn't convinced Hicks that he's innocent. He can't account without a doubt for where he was at the time of my death. Neither can Luke. Then again, no random runners or bikers have emerged from the ether to pin a crime on either one.

"Where do you stand with the harem?"

"Ah, the ladies. So many women, so little time. Always someone new to meet." Every day, Hicks' trail leads him to yet another current or former patient who he suspects might provide a clue.

"The friend and her Latin babe?"

*Ping.* Brie's mention turns Hicks to mush. His stern NYPD shell is screeching, *Unprofessional,* but every other constituency within his body is doing a tap dance to celebrate last Saturday. Brie is going to be his little secret. He doesn't want this newly sowed romance—dare he call it that—trampled by the verbal assaults of his dear but cynical friend G.G., although in the past they've shared details of romantic entanglements. There's been no reason for such discussion, however, in longer than Hicks would care to recall. Still, he's not ready to introduce and beat to death the baffling case of Sabrina Lawson, Esq., and Detective Hiawatha Hicks.

"The friend has been duly interrogated, I assure you. She can account for being in São Paulo the night of the event, and Molly Marx didn't seem to matter much to Ms. Vega one way or another. I can't see her getting herself in a lather over her."

"You don't know Latin women very well, do you, Hi?"

"No," he says. "I don't. I don't claim to know any kind of women very well, G.G." *Molly, especially.* Hicks looks at the bulletin board. *Maybe I should get myself some darts and wherever one hits, that's who did it,* he thinks.

*Thirty-nine*

# A SMALL WORLD, AFTER ALL

*I*'ll take it." I didn't need the dress, but I wanted it—and not just because it made my hips look narrow. I coveted this wisp of wine-red
velvet because it was new, which was the way I wanted Barry to see me.

"Will you be taking the package with you?" the waif at the cash register asked as she twirled a coil of wiry copper hair sprung from her
bun.

It hadn't occurred to me to have the dress delivered, but the
weather forecast was for rain and, what the hell, I was feeling what—for
me—amounted to devil-may-care. "You know what?" I said. "Please
send it." I gave the girl my credit card, feeling virtuous that the price
was 40 percent off. Was this because Barneys' truly haute shoppers had
caucused and agreed to snub this garment? No matter. I could picture
the spaghetti straps showing off my shoulders and the skirt swirling
around my knees as Barry and I took the floor to swing-dance. The
other night, after we tucked Annabel into bed, we'd actually popped in
a CD and practiced in the kitchen.

We'd been invited to a Valentine's Day party. For the last few years,
I'd felt almost like Lucy, inclined to boycott the love-drug holiday even
in her classroom, to the relief of most four-year-old boys and the dis-

may of all the girls, who generally threatened to stage their own St. Valentine's Day Massacre when they learned of this outrage. At the very least, I never knew what kind of cards to buy Barry and thus avoided the primary categories—sex addict and snooky-wookums—in favor of those in the neighborhood of funny (*I'm not interested in a normal relationship. I like ours better*). Three cards were tucked away, waiting for my flourishy inscription, along with a pair of silk boxer briefs.

Last February 14 had presented the additional challenge of the Luke factor. But this year I didn't want to think about him, the fondue we'd fed each other at Artisanal, my favorite next-best-to-Paris bistro, or his persistent calls—at least once a week—which I'd been dodging. Every time Luke's face flashed in my brain I tried to activate my denial button. Once in a while, it functioned, blinking *Luke who?* If I visualized him as an alien life force infecting my heart and soul, I could banish his image and voice for hours at a time. I was determined to make room for Barry and Barry alone, whom I reminded myself to think of as "my husband."

I floated out of the store. So did my umbrella, which in a burst of independence reversed and landed in the gutter. I wasn't going to let my favorable mood be washed away by this annoyance or the fact that I appeared to be invisible to every cruising cab. I walked to the bus shelter. When I opened my wallet I discovered I was a quarter short of exact change. With birthday party manners, I begged twenty-five cents from a senior citizen, boarded the bus, and held tightly to the overhead bar as the vehicle belched up Madison Avenue. On the corner of Seventy-ninth Street I waited patiently for a second bus to carry me through the park. On Amsterdam Avenue, I got out, stepped directly into water, and soaked my suede flats.

"I hate when that happens," said a stranger who, in exiting the bus, had leaped over the puddle with a leggy *brisé*. I took in the raincoat, matching hat, and knee-high boots—one Chanel too many, even if the getup was bona fide. The woman was about my age, maybe younger, the type who appeared to have acquired a water-repellent finish.

"No biggie," I said as dirty slush oozed into my tights. I was determined not to let something this inconsequential ruin my afternoon, not after this morning.

Earlier that day, Barry and I had finished our seventh fifty-minute hour of Dr. Stafford's psychic sorcery. Through the doctor's judicious questioning, fortified by the odd epiphany, half-remembered dreams, and my unmitigated optimism, I'd become positive that this counseling was steering us toward closeness or even—should I let myself think the word?—intimacy. And the day before, while putting away Barry's shirts, I came across legitimate evidence in the form of a package from Kitty's favorite jeweler. I carefully untied the red silk ribbon to snoop, and was rewarded by the wink of a multifaceted pale pink stone heart pendant glittering within a setting of pavé stones the color of plum jelly. It wasn't what I might have chosen for myself—way more Kitty than Molly—but when I carefully lifted the necklace out of the velvet box, it nestled perfectly in the hollow of my neck. I stared at my reflection and felt the thump of my achy-breaky heart.

My husband was making amends, trying to give us another running start toward happiness. I wouldn't let myself think otherwise. I seriously doubted that it was a gift for Kitty, and not even Barry Marx could be brazen enough to buy a tender—okay, rather gaudy but still notably sweet—gift for another woman and store it in our very own bedroom, a mere six feet from our marriage bed. This meant the things he'd been saying in Dr. Stafford's office must be true. As I sloshed along, thinking about the next weekend's Valentine's Day party, my actual heart beat wildly, a sensation I hadn't felt toward Barry since, well, ever.

Halfway down the block I noticed Madame Chanel keeping pace with me, maybe six feet to my right. "Want to get under here?" she said to me, nodding toward her umbrella, apparently escaped from a golf course. "There's plenty of room."

My feet were cold, slipping inside my ruined shoes, and the rain was landing on my head. "Yes!" I said, and scurried toward my savior, thinking this was exactly the sort of fortuitous, munificent gesture I should attempt to write up, speckled with wit, and send to the "Metropolitan Diary" column of the *New York Times*. "Thanks. I'm heading downtown a few blocks to register my daughter for swimming lessons."

Annabel refused to put so much as a toe in the water, and Barry and I had decided that the situation had to be faced. Still, even if it was true, why do I always blather?

"That's where I'm headed, too," the woman said. Her voice was slightly nasal, not up to Chanel standard.

"No kidding?"

"Really," the woman said. "Apparently, my son's amphibious."

"How old is he?"

"Three and a half."

"My daughter is about that age. She's Annabel. And I'm Molly, by the way."

She turned toward me. "Nice to meet you, Molly." She gave me a lingering, sideways smile and pronounced my utilitarian name slowly, as if she'd never heard it before. I waited for her to volunteer her name and perhaps her son's, but she offered nothing. I tried to take a discreet but closer peek at this stranger, but the rain and the difference in our heights—she was tall—made that difficult. Even under the umbrella and in the downpour, however, her teeth were hard to miss. Were they capped or was she just overzealous with a bleaching kit?

The two of us continued to walk silently for several blocks until we reached our destination and stopped under its awning. Coco Chanel snapped shut her umbrella and easily pushed open the heavy glass door for both of us. We entered the building's lobby, which was thick with mothers, nannies, strollers, and toddlers. The smell of damp wool and chaos was in the air.

"Mrs. Marx?" someone shouted as an elevator discharged an additional supply of noisy women and children.

I turned in the crush. "Narcissa?"

"Yes, ma'am," she said, waddling toward me. "You here for the swimming? I just signed up Ella. Better hurry—it's nearly full up."

"Rats," I said, and thought a stronger word. Once again, had every other mother mastered this drill and arrived hours ago? Why had I wasted time shopping or not sent Delfina to take care of this chore? Because I always underestimated the ballsy competition of New York moms and because I wanted that dress and because Delfina was back at the apartment, supervising Annabel and, for that matter, Ella, which was why Narcissa was here. "Well, good to see you, Narcissa. I'll give it a go." At least if Ella was in the swim class, it would be easier to sell Annabel on the idea that practicing the dead man's float in pee-warmed water was something she should look forward to doing every Wednesday at three.

The next elevator was too full to enter. And the one after that. I finally mashed myself into the fourth car that came along, and when the door opened on the fifth floor, I saw that my umbrella-toting buddy was there, too, and had already reached the front of the line, with only one woman ahead of her. She must have run up the stairs. *Note to self,* I thought. *Next time, haul ass.*

"I saved you a spot," Coco shouted to me, causing the other mothers and nannies to glare.

"Hey, no way," one of them said. "I got here first. Fair's fair."

The complainer was right. "Thanks, anyway," I said. I walked to the back of the small room and started to search in my bag for the Home section of the *Times* when I heard my phone blare "When the Saints Go Marching In." By the time I found the phone—in my coat pocket, under the crumpled Barneys receipt—I'd missed the call. Luke. His third that day, not that I'd answered any of them.

I put away the phone and opened my newspaper. I found it hard to concentrate. Luke was not just back in my head, whispering, taunting, and warmly blowing into my ear—he was coursing through my body like Wi-Fi.

The phone rang again. Once again I ignored his ring. *I've known saints,* I thought, *and you, my friend, are no saint.* The phone sounded again.

"If you're not going to take your calls, at least turn off your damn phone," the woman ahead of me snarled, attracting the attention of everyone in the small room.

Why hadn't I grabbed that bitch's place in line when I had the chance? "I'm sorry if I'm bothering you," I replied, "but I have to keep my phone on." Delfina might call, or Barry.

"You know, you're not only annoying, you're rude," Squawk Box hissed.

The phone rang again. The room grew silent as the woman's stare dared me to answer it. The phone blared and the saints marched.

I felt trapped and intimidated. "Hello," I said. "No, I really can't talk now." Luke's voice was casting its usual spell. "I'm not kidding, I can't . . ." He went on for a bit, his rhetoric less pleading than calmly, appealingly persuasive. "I disagree—that's a terrible idea." Damn, he was persistent.

I felt a force push me toward him, gentle, invisible like a breeze.

"Okay, okay, You should have been a lawyer. Okay, we'll meet . . . we'll talk. But not today, because . . ." I looked outside. The rain had suddenly stopped. The sun had come out. "Because I'm going . . . biking." As I clicked off, my resolve began to crumble.

I sensed that every eye and ear in the room had been trained on me and my call. They were Argentina, I was Evita. I tried to set my cell to vibrate, but the saints blared again. I did my best to lower my head and whisper. "Of course I have feelings for you." As if that were ever the real problem.

"Molly, I love you," Luke said, to me and the whole room. Apparently I'd hit the mechanism for speakerphone.

"I'm going biking now," I said. "We'll work this out some other time." I couldn't listen. "I'm getting off now." I snapped the lid of my phone shut and shoved it in my pocket, trying to avoid glances and snickers.

Fortunately, the registrar motioned me to step forward. The woman's fingers tap-danced on her computer keyboard. There would be room for Annabel, the last slot. *Keep breathing,* I told myself. *It's still a good day.*

As I began to complete the form, the woman in the Chanel raincoat, who I noticed had been standing off to the side, swished past me without saying so much as goodbye. *She certainly runs hot and cold,* I thought just as this woman also got a call.

"Barry," I was almost positive I heard her say. Her volume wasn't pianissimo, and unless I was being utterly paranoid, I had the feeling that she wanted to be overheard. "Well, that's very interesting, but I can top that. You didn't tell me your wife was attractive. Anyway, news flash. You were right. She is definitely seeing someone."

I looked up. The woman was gone.

# Forty

# EVERYBODY MUST GET STONED

Run this by me again—*why* do we need an unveiling?" Barry and Kitty are finishing their second cup of triple-filtered coffee one Sunday. My husband sees himself reflected in the new double-wide, glass-doored stainless-steel refrigerator and thinks what I think: what was wrong with the kitchen his mother put in nine years ago—Shaker cabinetry, granite countertops, and a fridge that kept food as cold as required? When you have enough money, however, as well as an architect on speed dial, you can amuse yourself by selecting warming drawers and six-burner professional ranges and still eat out five nights a week.

For someone who spends more time each year in a one-legged king pigeon pose than in prayer, my mother-in-law is, nonetheless, the Wikipedia of Judaic heritage. "That's what's done," she says. "The ceremony has to take place before the one-year anniversary of a death."

"Or else?" Barry says.

"Tradition," Kitty says. She discards the fleeting notion of exhibiting self-control. "Besides, let's say you and Stephanie get engaged. You'd want the unveiling to be out of the way, wouldn't you?"

Barry chokes on a thick slab of Bermuda onion, which crowns his poppy-seed bagel.

"I'm talking hypothetically, of course," Kitty says. "Although that girl's just what you need."

What qualifications is my mother-in-law referring to? A big mouth? I'm going with the big ambition. Kitty sees women as the hard drive behind male success. While I believe she's of the opinion that any daughter-in-law is largely just a biological requirement necessary to produce grandchildren, her pragmatic half dictates that as long as a male offspring has to marry, he'd best trade up to someone a lot like her.

"You're way ahead of yourself," Barry says after he stops coughing.

"Am I?" Kitty turns her back to refill her black-and-white-striped porcelain mugs—hers is lined in shocking pink, his in pistachio green—and predicts an engagement before the summer. Maybe a destination wedding. She's always wanted to see the Seychelles. Dubai, Bhutan, and Bali are also on Kitty's wish list, but certainly Stephanie will have her own ideas. One thing Kitty knows is that there's nothing subtle about a thirty-four-year-old woman who invited her to lunch at Saks and then suggested a stroll to her uncle's teensy-weensy jewelry store on Forty-seventh Street, where she casually pointed out a 1920s Art Deco diamond solitaire almost as big as the shop. Asscher cut, significant baguettes. Another mother might have been appalled, but Kitty admires Stephanie's self-assurance. She believes a woman needs focus as much as state-of-the-art bedroom expertise. "Leave the unveiling to me," she says to Barry. "Order the stone."

Barry did—which is why Rabbi S.S. is warming up his vocal cords to once again be in service to my family tomorrow, why I can practically smell the cinnamon-raisin babkas, yeasty and plump, rising in their silvery loaf pans, and why a marble monument waits under wraps at Serenity Haven. It's pinkish gray, not unlike Kitty's recently installed tinted concrete countertops.

I take a gander under the drape, hoping Barry might have exhibited a trace of originality with the stone's inscription. While I haven't decided if I'm more Bette Davis ("She did it the hard way"), Karen Carpenter ("A star on earth, a star in heaven"), or Dean Martin ("Everybody loves somebody sometime"), surely Barry could have done better than *Molly Divine Marx, beloved daughter, wife, and mother.* Simple and dignified, yes, but where's my mystery? My élan? My cheeky, noir-ish humor? I might have liked *Molly, biker chick.* Or even something in shockingly bad taste: *My grandparents went through the Holocaust and all I got was this?* I did, after all, die at only thirty-five.

My Divines arrived last night, two days ahead of Sunday's noon service. Annabel will be joining Grammy and Grandpa at the Children's Museum later this morning, but Lucy's begged off. I trail her as she leaves a coffee shop on Broadway and begins to walk north. She appears immune to the December air as she tramps briskly past colossal produce markets, Barnes & Noble, and a bank whose unique selling feature seems to be its handy branches in Auckland and Kuala Lumpur. Never looking up, she trudges by glassy condos piercing the gray sky. She all but race-walks, staring ahead.

Not even the somber majesty of Columbia University makes Lucy blink, but on 120th Street she hangs a left and pauses to admire the Gothic splendor of Riverside Church, which makes Temple Emanuel-El, the snazziest synagogue in North America, look as drab as a drugstore. Lucy doesn't, however, linger. She heads over to Grant's Tomb.

Now *there's* a final resting place. Ever since the Parks Department was shamed into spiffing it up—this happened at the moment when Times Square did a 180 from working girls, porn, and peep shows to tourists, Oreo Overload sundaes, and Disney blockbusters—I used to drop in on my friends Ulysses and Julia, parking my bike at the rack outside. "Who's buried in Grant's Tomb?" was Papa Louie's idea of a riddle, which he delivered with his Groucho brows wiggling. By kindergarten Lucy and I could spit back, "No one!" The general and the missus are *entombed* in twin Beaux Arts sarcophagi.

Lucy skips the inside of the monument, although she glances at the engraving above its entrance: *Let us have peace,* which I always thought was an ironic epitaph for one of American history's most hell-bent hawks. Lucy stuffs her hands deep in the pockets of her purple down coat and turns toward the woods skirting one of the designated nature preserves. FOREVER WILD, the sign says.

When Manhattan people think *park* it's Central, with its showy lakes and gondolas, the kelly green Sheep Meadow, and a zoo that's home to neurotic polar bears. Even if they live nearby, few locals venture into Riverside, the anorexic four-mile stepchild also designed by the grand master, Frederick Law Olmsted. Despite the fact that Meg Ryan and Tom Hanks met cute by its flowerbeds in *You've Got Mail*, Riverside is low-key, as befits this side of the city. Bikers, runners, and dog walkers take care of business here, but it remains a park for a quick hit, not a holiday.

Lucy winds down an overgrown path to the level above the lonesome Hudson, where the wind whips off the water, chilling her face and reddening her cheeks. It feels fifteen degrees colder than on Broadway. Whoever is around at this hour moves at a quick clip, whether on two feet or four. As she strides forward, the tassels of her knit hat bob like Heidi's braids.

Two golden retrievers zoom past. Their master soon follows and stops to check his watch. It's past nine, the witching hour when dogs must return to the leash, lest their owners get slapped with a fine big enough to buy a decent dinner for two. "Sigmund," the owner shouts, "Hamlet, come here." But the dogs ignore him, perhaps embarrassed by their names. They run to Lucy, who bends down to stroke their furry heads and give them a welcome behind-the-ears scratch.

"There you boys are," the man says, reaching them as the larger of the dogs jumps up to lick Lucy's face and the other tries to bite one of her tassels.

She decides that a pet lover is safe for conversation. "Can you tell me how to get down to the river, please?" She points in the direction of the George Washington Bridge, which dangles in the distance like a strand of gray Majorca pearls.

"Sure," the man says with an open smile. He looks like the kind of guy Lucy might like—shaggy-haired and broad-shouldered, not a label in sight, discounting the Yankees cap. He carries the *Times* sports section under his arm. Columbia professor or shrink, I guess. This neighborhood is well stocked with both. "Let's see. There are a few twists and turns." He strokes his beard as he looks into Lucy's eyes. His eyes are green, his accent Australian, and his tone cheery. "I could lead the way."

I decide that he's divorced. His kids are with Mommy this weekend and he has a day stretching ahead of him in which he's going to braise short ribs with blood-orange juice and *herbes de Provence* while he drinks a Châteauneuf-du-Pape, listens to the Saturday afternoon opera, and reads a sturdy biography of Winston Churchill. Lucy, buy this lottery ticket. I worry about you being alone, and this dog owner has good guy written all over him.

*I wish I knew how to flirt,* runs through Lucy's head. *Other women meet men everywhere. Me? Never. And I could do worse. This man's eyes are intelligent. I like his taste in animals and reading material.*

But does my sister let him lead the way? "Oh, that won't be necessary" is her knee-jerk response.

"Chicago," the stranger says, and smiles again, wider this time. There is a small, dear space between his front teeth. He knows he's crazy, but what if this woman would join him for a cup of coffee? He likes her face, devoid of makeup or a visible attitude. They'd get to talk, maybe do a movie, browse a bookstore and then, who knows?

"Chi-caw-go, yes. How can you tell?" Lucy, like every midwesterner, believes everyone has an accent but her.

"Actually, I got my degree at the university there," he says, and waits for Lucy to banter. A man would have to sky-write "I am trying to pick you up" before she might notice that someone found her appealing.

"Great school," she says finally. *Should I tell him I live two miles from Hyde Park?* she thinks. *Nah. Why would he care?* "So, if you could point the way for me?"

He does, and curses himself—why didn't he ask for her number?—as he watches Lucy walk north until she is the size of his fingernail, her purple coat small as a berry.

Finally, my sister reaches the water. She stares at New Jersey as if it will reveal the answer: how did Molly die? Barry, she's convinced, has pushed for tomorrow's unveiling to put a lid on the wrack and ruin of was-she-pushed-or-did-she-jump? The unspoken, preposterous assumption wafting toward Chicago seems to be that I must have engineered my own death. "Molly would never do something so idiotic," she screams at the river. Her eyes follow a barge that makes its sluggish way on the choppy water. "Molly's been goddamn Swift-boated." Lucy shakes her head and makes a sound, a laugh mated with a moan.

Lucy spoke to Hicks yesterday. What does *he* know? Nothing, it seems, at least nothing he's going to tell Lucy. She's been fishing for weeks, debating. Should she show him the photo? She wishes like hell she'd never found my adulterous ephemera, evidence—but of what?

If Mystery Man was involved in my death, Lucy keeps wondering, wouldn't an NYPD detective have sniffed him out on his own by now and hung him by his thumbs until he confessed? She speculates that Hicks has gotten to this guy and that Hicks doesn't think he did it. In that case, why sully my reputation? The person she wants most to protect is Annabel. Why should her niece ever have to think of her parents as anything less than deliriously happy? Why not keep that fiction going?

From her pocket, Lucy withdraws the photograph of Luke and me. *At least you look happy, sister,* she thinks. *I hope you adored this man—and he adored you back. Wherever and whoever this fool is, I hope he still does.*

Lucy turns back to the park and gazes in both directions. *Molly, this is where you took your last breath—I wish I knew where, exactly.* She walks to the water's edge, presses her lips to the image of my smiling face. She thinks about tearing the picture in two and keeping the half with me. "No, you two should be together," she concludes, and tosses the photograph into the Hudson.

"Let there be peace," she murmurs. "Let there be peace." She bends over, puts her crossed arms on her knees, and hangs her head, weeping.

The picture bobs in the waves and floats rapidly downstream in the murky water. Lucy turns away from the Hudson, but I watch the photo as if it were flesh and blood—Luke terrified, running for his life, a man escaping.

## Forty-one

# SAM I AM

As the photo sinks in the Hudson, I ring with emptiness that falls short of an emotion, because a feeling would be alive, even if—especially if—it smolders with heartbreak and anger. I am a shadow, a dried leaf, a shriveled stalk, a hollow gourd. I am a lost hope, a broken promise, a memory, an unspoken phrase. Mother Nature has cleared her throat and I am . . . gone.

I can't stay and watch Lucy as she walks away from the river. Why didn't she show some good sense, abort today's mission, and have coffee with Sigmund and Hamlet's owner, then go home with him for sex, short ribs, and the rest of her life? They'd join a food co-op, pop out twins—little brown-haired boys, one named Louie for our grandfather and the other Jake, because it's Lucy's favorite name—and live happily ever after, going off to Australia each winter and Italy in August. Lucy would coach Louie and Jake's soccer team, start her own nursery school, and be a very good and beloved wife and mother.

I turn. Bob is in my face. I gasp, scream, and pound his chest. "Dammit, people are imbeciles, aren't they? Life makes no sense."

"It's time," he says quietly, grabbing my wrists to restrain me.

"Time for what?" Was there an obligation I'd missed?

"Time to move on," Bob whispers.

"What are you talking about?" I plead. Just yesterday I watched Annabel learn to write her first shaky *A*, tilting like a crooked chalet. I was there when Brie and Hicks rented a car to drive to a country inn. They plan to snowshoe—that is, if they get out of bed. I checked on my father after his physical—he has to go on Lipitor, but his blood pressure's fine. Oh, and the doctor wants him to drop twenty pounds. I watched my mother plant a quince branch in potting soil covered with velvety moss—she's coaxing spring into arriving early this year, and hopes to be rewarded soon with delicate white buds. I even sat next to Barry and Stephanie and a thousand other screaming sports maniacs at a Knicks game, until I decided that if I was in the mood for torture, there's C-SPAN.

"You have to ask what good your powers are doing you, Molly," Bob says. "Longing for a life that's over, seeing other people making love and chocolate chip cookies and mistakes . . . Do I have to spell it out for you?"

"But I'm not ready to end this. You told me my powers would last until—until they're terminated. Why should I be the terminator?"

I hear my own fear. My plan was to wait it out and pray that my abilities would continue—not forever (who'd want that?), but at least until the mystery of my death is solved and, far more importantly, until Annabel grows up. But when does that happen these days? After she gets into college or turns twenty-one or graduates or starts to work or lives in her own apartment or is married or has a child? I don't want to go AWOL now.

"Having powers doesn't mean you need to use them," Bob says in the voice of the pediatrician he'd hoped to become.

Perhaps we can negotiate. "Okay, let's say I take a break." Not giving up completely, a hiatus. "Then what?"

"I'd say it's a deal, and that it's time for you to meet someone," he says. "I've been watching you—"

No kidding. Does he think he's invisible? Bob's on every corner, Brother Starbucks of the wild blue yonder. "Who's this someone?"

"Don't be so suspicious. You'll see soon enough." Bob, always preaching patience.

As I wait, the days unroll into a long ribbon of nothing. I skip the trip to Serenity Haven. Thou shalt unveil without me. Mostly I obsess about Annabel. How did the school carnival go? Has she progressed to *B*? Did Delfina take her for a haircut? Not bangs, I'm hoping. Not with her curls.

My mind drifts. Will Stephanie convince Barry to go to Venice, hoping he'll propose? Will Brie like Hicks' mother's Sunday dinner? Will Mama Hicks like Brie or be appalled that her son is with a white woman? Will Isadora try to get Brie back? The trip to Japan my parents cancelled—will they reschedule? Might Lucy replace her futon with a grown-up couch? Adopt a cat? Will Kitty switch dermatologists?

Who's Luke with now—the blonde he met who resembles me more than my own twin or the skinny, surprisingly smart model with the curly black hair and breathy lisp? Will Hicks solve my case, with or without Detective Gonzalez's intuition? My old life is the world's best soap opera, viewing audience of one.

I try to manufacture some willpower that would prevent me from dropping in below. A deeply embedded vein of superstition helps me not to cheat, and as interesting as Down There is, Bob has not just tantalized my imagination, he's gotten me worried. What if the person he says I'll be meeting is from within my own circle? Let's say Kitty topples during a headstand in yoga class, breaks her neck, and we have to be roommates. Or even worse, what if Lucy or Brie or my parents or—don't go there, Molly—Annabel arrives? I freeze-dry myself so I do not have to consider any of these unspeakable options.

On the fourth day, Bob reappears. He is not alone. A tall man is at his side.

"Sam, this is Molly," he says. "Molly, Sam."

"But—but—but what are you doing here?" I'm jabbering. I'm also being rude.

"I'm asking myself the same question," this Sam says. "Who *are* you people?"

"Molly's going to be your guide," Bob says. He gives Sam the same rigmarole he once spoke to me. Relocation, the Duration, powers, up, down, don't cheat, blah, blah.

"What happened to you, Sam?" I say, because I shouldn't be thinking about myself now. This poor guy is in that first posttraumatic stage

I remember well: shock, disbelief, and trying to figure out why he can't find his pulse. "Try to remember."

Eventually he speaks. "I was thinking about this woman I'd just seen, lost in a long riff about what it would be like if we have coffee and I talked her into spending the day with me. There was something about her—the openness of her face, the kindness of her eyes . . . Then one of my dogs broke off his leash—we'd been walking in the park—and ran across Riverside Drive, and I started to chase him. Next I was under an SUV whose driver was on his cell phone." It spills out in a rush. "That's as much as I know."

"What was your dog's name?"

"Sigmund."

"Are you a professor?" I ask.

"No," he says, looking at me as if I forgot to switch on my brain.

"A shrink?"

*Please don't tell me I treated this woman,* Sam thinks. *Is there some special hell for Freudians where you have to listen to patients drone on for all of eternity, my mother this, my mother that?* "I'm an analyst," he says. He mentions the New York Psychoanalytic Society and Institute.

I can tell I'm supposed to be impressed.

"Why do you ask?" he adds.

"You look like a shrink, that's all, which might come in handy here."

"Where the hell is *here*?" Sam runs his hand through his full head of chestnut hair, which for a dead guy looks remarkably healthy.

"Oh, I'll explain everything, but first I have a few questions." I check to see if Bob is lurking. He's not, but to be safe I lower my voice. "Sam, the woman you were thinking about when your accident happened—what was she like?"

His smile turns him handsome, gap between his front teeth and all. "Gorgeous," he says, looking away, as if he's seeing her this very minute. "And one thing that struck me was I'd guess she's the kind of female who'd never think of herself that way. Almost my height, brown eyes that drill into you, right past the lies. Magnificent eyes. The minute I looked into them I had this tingly sensation that we were supposed to be together. Fuck, I was dying to follow her." He shifts his gaze to me and doesn't speak for a few minutes. "You know, if a patient were telling me this story, I'd have told him he should have gone after the woman. When you meet someone and know she's it, don't stand there like a tree. All your happiness can depend on how you react to one fucking impulse. You have to pay attention."

Why did Bob think I'd be the right match for Sam? I have no idea of what to say next. I'd like to ask if his dogs survived, but he probably doesn't know, and the image of Sigmund—or was it Hamlet?—writhing in the street is more than I can bear. "Relax, Sam," is all I can think to say. "You'll have plenty of time to sort this out. As we like to say in the Duration, keep breathing."

He laughs, and I know we'll get along.

"Love your accent, by the way. Australian?"

"South African."

Damn.

"You sound like her," he adds. His voice is dreamy, like he's just woken up, which in a way he has. "Are you from Chicago?"

"We have to talk."

# Forty-two

# CRAZY IN LOVE

Lucy was the athletic one. She left me in the Illinois dust as she kicked and served and swung like a boy, and she wasn't just chosen first for every team but invariably anointed captain. Best all-around camper, Lucy Divine. Below a sad-eyed elk head, a plaque still hangs in the rec hall at Big Beaver Lake Girls' Camp, which I permanently boycotted once I learned the boys' camp's anthem about the girl Beavers across the lake. The end of camp was no big loss, because while I liked the lanyards and weenie roasts well enough, team sports skinned my knees almost as much as my ego. Riding a bike, though, was different— a ticket to freedom that required swatting fewer mosquitoes, memorizing fewer rules. From the time my father liberated my red-hot Huffy from its training wheels, I made that sucker fly.

"Moosey, wanna ride today?" I'd say every summer morning.

Biking never got old, but my bikes did, and every three years, my parents bought me a shiny replacement, a tradition I kept going. My current model was a yellow hybrid worthy of Hermès, recently purchased in honor of turning thirty-five. I was eager to take it out and see if the bike lived up to the salesman's hyperbole. Annabel was out with

Delfina and Ella, and riding would give me a chance to think through the corner I'd backed myself into with Luke. I brooded best on wheels.

I switched into cotton big-girl panties, because a bike and a thong went together, as Barry liked to say, like a dyke and a schlong, and layered on a jersey and the padded pants that gave me an even bigger bustle-butt. As I found my backpack and gloves, the phone rang.

"Barry?" I said.

"Yes, your irresistible husband. Why so surprised?"

"Because I usually have to leave three messages before you call back," I answered with immediate regret; I could hear Dr. Stafford, in her patrician tone, reminding both of us that few relationships improved with sarcasm, which she—given to food metaphors—likened to a heavy hand with cayenne pepper.

"What's for dinner?" Barry asked.

*This dear new Barry, who cares if we'll be eating fish or chicken, home-cooked or takeout, couldn't possibly be connected to Chanel Mommy,* I told myself.

"Salmon in parchment paper, with sugar snap peas and those fake french fries I bake with kosher salt." I'd already set the table with orange tulips and candles, and I decided that on the way back from my ride I'd swing over to the Silver Moon Bakery and pick up something decadent for dessert. Maybe I could manage Barry's favorite, the fudge cake with a thatched roof of chocolate shavings.

"Did you get Annabel into swimming?" he asked.

He remembered that was on my day's to-do list. The man was trying. "Yes," I said. "Last spot."

"Score one for supermom. And what are you up to, Molls?"

*He's awfully chatty,* I noted. I loved it. "I'm going to take out my new bike."

"Now?"

"It's almost spring," I said.

"It's February," he said with a top note of criticism. "Where are you going at this hour?"

Central Park functioned as my front yard, but if I went further west I'd be near the bakery. I decided I wanted dessert to be a sweet surprise. "I haven't decided."

"Be careful."

"When am I not?" I said. "See you later."

Did Barry actually think I'd be reckless? Me? I slipped into a wind-breaker with garish reflective stripes augmented by numerous glow-in-the-dark stickers, courtesy of Annabel. In this getup, a blind person could see me.

As I walked toward the kitchen, my cell phone rang. Luke and the Saints again. I hadn't taken him for a guy who'd work this hard for the last word.

"Yes?"

"Can you talk?" he said.

"Only for a second."

"I really need to see you." He sounded like a man recently arrived in triage. "Now, baby."

*Baby?* Corny as that word may be, when it fell out of Luke's mouth, I was his hostage. His voice began to seep into my skin like a rich, soothing balm. Still, I said, "When I told you before that I'd see you, I didn't mean today."

"But I'm nearby."

Coincidence? I thought not.

"Name the spot," he said. "The diner? Le Pain Q? Anywhere."

*Idiot,* I thought, applying that label to myself. *You need to be inoculated against Luke as if he were a deadly protozoon.* The other half of my brain ragged back, *Except, dammit, you love that he's interested. Admit it. You're there.*

"Molly, say something."

"I shouldn't, Luke," I answered slowly. *I am a degenerate alcoholic and you are a kegger. I. Will. Not. Take. A. Sip. There should be a twelve-step program for women like me, and I need to attend a daily meeting.*

"I'm off for a bike ride," I said.

"Where to?"

"Riverside, probably. What does it matter? It's too late. But I'll call you tomorrow. I promise. We'll talk."

"You'll call me on Saturday? Really? You've never called me once on Saturday."

That's how rattled he got me. "Monday, then."

"I cannot wait three days, Molly. We have to get this cleared up now."

"Luke, what we have to do is stop"—stop whatever *this* is.

"Give me one good reason."

"Seeing you is making me crazy," I shouted. "I can't handle the deception. It makes me despise myself. I hate women like me. I've always been highly judgmental about cheaters and—"

"Love trumps cheating. I'm crazy in love with you. Don't you get that?"

My eyes landed on a framed snapshot taken at my wedding. Barry and I were having our first dance. Was that the last sane moment in my life, when the band's sultry soloist sang "It Might Be You," which was a good three hours before I saw Barry walk out of my parents' powder room followed by Ms. Toffee Frost?

I could hear Luke breathing, expecting a response. *I'm crazy in love with you, too,* would not be inaccurate, but I only got to crazy. "Luke, I don't know what to say." Except that I had to get out of here.

"How about 'I love you'? Because I think you do."

At the front door, keys were jangling. I didn't want Delfina and Annabel to see me unhinged, tears falling as though I'd turned on the faucet. "I promise you we'll talk—after the weekend. Hold on. But right now, no."

"Molly—please. See me for ten minutes. Today."

"Luke, goodbye," I said. I clicked off and grabbed a paper towel to mop my face, took my helmet from its hook, and slammed the back door as the front door opened. I wheeled my bike through the basement corridors and around to the front.

"You just missed Dr. Marx," Alphonso, the doorman, said. I registered how odd it was that Barry, whom I was in no shape or mood to see, hadn't mentioned coming home early. We'd spoken less than fifteen minutes before. I couldn't think about that now.

I clipped my bike shoes into the pedals and took off, pushing hard.

Only when I was on the street, two blocks away, did I realize I'd left my phone on the kitchen counter.

Forty-three

# PERSONS OF INTEREST

*I* watch Hicks open his mail. Bill, bill, the *Economist*, postcard from the ophthalmologist ("Any way you see it, it's time for a checkup"), *Cook's Illustrated*, and an invitation to his cousin's wedding, about which he knows to expect an earful from his mother, given that Willy is eleven years younger. But the most interesting piece of mail is a flimsy white envelope with no return address and a computer-generated label. The red stamp features a large Hershey kiss and a heart inscribed with the word *love*. He carefully opens the envelope. Why had someone sent him a clipping featuring a suit from Ascot Chang, an ego-tripping Shanghai custom shop he'd poked his head into once and only once? A polo shirt would set him back a hundred bucks.

"Brie, babes, I sure hope you aren't buying me a present," he says when she walks into the kitchen, wearing one of his Macy's shirts and, he hopes, nothing else. That she outearns him five to one is the hot potato in their relationship. She says it doesn't bother her, so why should it bother him? It's a question Hicks contemplates at least twice a day.

"I thought your birthday wasn't for four months," she says, popping a grape into her mouth and another into his before she hugs him. "Is this a hint?"

"Is *this*?" Only when he waves the clipping in Brie's face does he see its flip side. On a page titled "In This Issue" is a photograph featuring, among others, Luke Delaney and Molly Marx. With a yellow marker, the sender has circled their hands, which may or may not be touching. Hard to tell. A label has been attached to the picture, with a caption: *Killer?*

Person of interest L. Delaney. He isn't an official suspect, though he phoned Molly, Hicks has noted, numerous times on the day she died, including the last call she received. Hicks knows Luke's hiding something. What he's hiding is the question, for Hicks and for me.

Luke's broken up during the interrogations, but his story's been consistent. As recently as two weeks ago, he called to see how the case was progressing. "Nowhere" would be the appropriate answer.

"What magazine do you think this is from?" Hicks asks.

Brie looks at it closely. *"Town and Country."* Actually, it's *Departures.* The photo was taken on a beach in Santo Domingo, my last location trip with Luke. "But what does this picture prove? Molly and Luke Delaney worked together and possibly slept together. Occupational hazard. Happens all the time." Brie should know, since she did the same thing with the same guy, which she's decided she'll never share with Hicks.

"The more important point is who sent this," he says.

"Is that a statement or a question?"

"It's whatever you want it to be."

Brie sits on the aluminum bar stool next to the granite counter that separates Hicks' compact, immaculate kitchen from his small living room with its black leather love seats and circular steel dining table. He won a real estate lottery to buy this condo, which is less than a mile and yet a giant step away from his ma. *Could I live with this man?* Brie is starting to ask herself. If the only thing that matters is how deeply she cares for him and how anal-retentive they both are, the answer is a resounding yes.

"Who sent it?" she says. "My money's on Barry, good old guilty Barry."

"Guilty of what?"

"Of something, I'm sure."

"That'll get you far in a court of law," he laughs. "You don't suppose it's from big bad Lucy?"

"Lucy wouldn't play games. She'd call and say, 'My moron sister was having an affair and the guy whacked her. Nail him.' " Brie's Lucy impersonation used to make both of us convulse with laughter.

"What about Kitty, trying to point the finger away from the good son?" Hicks asks.

"Or herself," Brie said, although in her heart, Brie doesn't see Kitty as a killer. Brie can't read Hicks' look. "You know I'm kidding, right?" she says.

"How about this?" Hicks says as he draws Brie to him and pulls her hair out of its clip so that it hangs loosely down her back. "Molly's in love with Delaney, but Delaney loves someone else. But Molly won't leave him alone. She goes all *Fatal Attraction,* acting like a bitter, vengeful she-devil. So he suggests they take a bike ride together. At a scenic spot they stop and she thinks he's going to kiss her, but instead he pushes her off her bike into the water and leaves her to drown."

"Never," Brie says. "But what about this? Barry and Molly go for a ride together and get in a fight. He pushes Molly—accidentally or on purpose is the piece I haven't worked out yet—and she falls in the river. He panics, pulls her out, and gives her artificial respiration like the good doctor he is. When he realizes she's massively injured and will most likely die, and he's absolutely 200 percent positive no one's seen what happened, he leaves the scene of the crime."

"What's his motive?"

"She knew he was cheating for the nth time, and she was going to sue for divorce and take him for everything."

"Very interesting, Detective Lawson," Hicks says. "Or maybe they fought and then the putz rode off and never looked back, so he never knew Molly lost control of her bike. Reckless endangerment."

"Oh, so you like Barry. Well, maybe Luke really was at the movie he said he went to but left early and caught up with Molly in time to get rid of her because he's a textbook psycho and if she wouldn't leave her husband for him, then he didn't want Barry to have her. Or—"

"No, I've got it," Hicks says. "What about this?" He slips his hands under the shirt Brie's wearing, quickly establishes what's underneath—nothing—and ends the discussion. Only after Brie leaves, two hours later, does he look again at the clipping.

Hicks makes four phone calls, to Luke, Barry, Kitty, and Stephanie, and tells them to expect a visit from him tomorrow.

*Forty-four*

# KILLJOY

I rode north on Central Park West, slowing or stopping at almost every corner, turned left on Eighty-sixth Street, and passed the apartment building where Marion Davies was kept by William Randolph Hearst. Hats off to Marion. There's a woman who knew how to handle a lover.

Turning right, I ducked into Riverside Park, where an American flag snapped in the breeze. Damn, it was windier than I'd thought. I continued on past the Hippo Playground. If the fair weather held, I'd surprise Annabel with a visit there tomorrow. I traveled for only a bit on the promenade before I rode through the dank fieldstone tunnel that ran under the parkway and took me to the Hudson.

GO SLOWLY, a sign commanded. RESPECT OTHERS. *Exactly. Luke, don't tempt me. Enough. Respect that I'm trying to turn the page.*

I dismounted to take in the view. To the south, the Hudson widened. I could pick out Jersey City, a place I knew only from weather reports. In the northern distance the George Washington Bridge half hid under the mesh of fine gray mist. Even at this time of year, when dusk came before dinner, it was too early in the afternoon for its lights to cast their glow. Closer by, high on a hill, Riverside Church lorded over the tomb of Ulysses S. Grant.

I climbed back onto my bike and picked up speed. A few yards to my right, separated only by a fence better suited to a prison, cars hurried by in the opposite direction, the drivers' eyes straight ahead, on their mission. *Go, go, go. Beat the other guy.* Man, it was loud. The din of traffic never failed to amaze me, but I could tune it out. I always had. Suburban Illinois might have been my birthplace, but I was a New Yorker and I could activate my inner iPod. I sang out off-key, doing my throatiest Janis Joplin. " 'You know, feeling good was good enough for me, good enough for me and my Bobby McGee."

I sped past a small stand of scrubby pines guarding the empty tennis courts, winding left to Cherry Walk, a scraggly string of bike path bordered on the left by low stone embankments. The rocks sloped straight down to the lapping edge of the gloomy river barely a foot or two below.

In lyrics, life is always distilled to quaint, deceptive clarity. But women I knew wouldn't drown their woes in Southern Comfort, nor were they willing to trade all their tomorrows for a single yesterday. Before bed, they did fifty sit-ups, popped a Lexapro, contemplated having a baby or a consultation with a top divorce lawyer, and counted the months until their vacation, when they could liquefy into a beach under a broad-brimmed hat and a creamy slather of SPF 45. Until then, they soldiered on and kept their shoes and optimism shined, responsible, cut, and colored, inside and out.

I was determined to do better than that. I couldn't lead a halfway life in a halfway home.

The intermittent sun had called it a day and rain was starting to fall again. It felt refreshing, washing away the old Molly, cleansing my attitude. I planned to cycle all the way to the bridge, make sure that the little red lighthouse Annabel and I loved had withstood the winter, then turn back and zip over to the bakery. If the sprinkle got worse, I'd shift to plan B and exit by Fairway, where I could buy Barry one of those tiny cherry pies he polished off in two servings—a peace offering, even if he thought it was just dessert.

As adrenaline kicked in, my brain began to drain—comfortably, pleasantly, and reliably. That was as much the point of cycling as any benefit to my hip measurement or cardiovascular system. I took scant note of the skate park, the basketball courts, or even the path's painted dividing line, blue and steady as a vein, separating north-traveling bikers like me from those heading south. With each revolution, I could feel my tension release, my resolve grow.

On Monday I would call Luke. To avoid him was cruel; the sweetness of our history deserved more than jagged conversations. In plain, sans serif language I'd tell him this would be our last conversation. It would be over.

Except—I squinted—there he was, Bobby McGee Delaney himself, a tall streak in a navy windbreaker and jeans, standing by the side of the road. "Stop so we can talk," he shouted.

I was touched that Luke had gone to this length to find me, but I wasn't prepared, and I felt trapped. "Oh, Luke, not now," I shouted back. "It's too late." I meant that in every way, but I tried to keep it kind and casual. "I don't have the time."

"Molly, I'm here and we need to speak," he yelled.

I begged to differ; my face said as much.

"You don't get how much I love you."

Perhaps, but I didn't want to listen. I wanted to keep it clean and manageable.

"I love you, Molly. I do."

Maybe he did. Maybe I owed him. Maybe this was my *Casablanca*. A whole lot of maybe.

"Okay," I said. "Grant's Tomb is up the road. Walk there and wait for me. I'll see you inside."

He shot me a skeptical look. Did he honestly think I'd ditch him?

"I will," I said. "In ten minutes, fifteen at the most."

"Grant's Tomb," he said. "I'll be there." And he was off.

I'd ride to the bridge as I'd planned, check out the lighthouse, circle back, meet Luke, and we'd talk now instead of Monday. I didn't want to pose, to pretend. I wanted to make right in my life what wasn't. I wanted to change. I *would* change, starting that very day. Even if the wrong man loved me, I told myself, I refused to be one more woman who smiled meekly and tried to make the best of her 5-on-a-scale-of-10 life.

I wouldn't get out my knife sharpener. I'd break things off gently but irrevocably, like snapping a brittle twig, and Luke and I would go our separate ways. I'd face my husband with the first layer of guilt scrubbed away. I knew I was doing the right thing, which gave me a blast of speed.

Yes, I had feelings for Luke.

No, I wasn't prepared to act on them.

Yes, I might always love him.

No, nothing he could do would change my mind.

With each rotation of my wheels, I became more convinced. I, Molly Divine Marx, could do this. I began rehearsing.

*Luke, I will love you forever but* . . . Nope. Nobody likes a *but*.

*Luke, from the beginning we both always knew* . . . Except we didn't.

*Luke, you are deeply precious to me and because of that* . . .

I got busy editing away clichés, picking them off like lint. I barely noticed that the late afternoon sky had darkened as efficiently as if someone had dimmed the lights. The raindrops had become a steady march, pelting my helmet. I heard a clap of thunder. Bass drums.

As I was deciding whether I should skip the lighthouse and go straight to Grant's Tomb, there was suddenly a second, larger thunderclap. Cymbals.

The sky started exploding. Which is why at first I didn't hear the other sound, which began growing louder. And then it was unmistakable: the grinding of another biker's gears behind me. Closer.

Too close.

I thought I heard someone call my name. Had Barry followed me? I twisted back to look over my shoulder. This tailgater apparently had prepared for the weather by cashing in a hefty gift certificate at L.L.Bean. I'm talking serious, textbook gear, rubbery black from toe to head, ending in a hood that slid over a helmet. I was looking at a Garanimal in mourning, a biker so sleek but loosely tailored that the he within might be a she; I could not see the outlines of the person's body, but I did see sunglasses—large, dark, and heavy.

*Excuse me, did I miss the paparazzi or the forecast for the hurricane?* I wanted to shout. But the rider shouted first.

What was the voice saying? "On your left"? "Be careful"? Or was this person screaming my name? The words were swallowed by thunder. Platinum lightning ripped the heavens and rain began pounding even harder, unmercifully, horizontally. I was trapped in the monsoon cycle of a car wash, but I kept pedaling, trying to ignore the grand vizier of foul weather chic behind me, concentrating on keeping my line. Yet as my wheels skidded through runoff from the sudden squall, I could sense the presence hovering close. Way too fucking close. Didn't he realize how dangerous this was, or was he right up my ass because he thought I could shepherd him through the tempest? Darth Vader had picked the wrong Girl Scout.

When he failed to pass, I considered cursing him out in my reliable crazy-lady howl, the one that had worked when a thief with an extra dose of hubris had tried to steal my wallet. In a courthouse. At jury duty. But what if this dick-brain was, say, a deranged bike messenger, out to rob me—or worse? This was, after all, a city with a fairly imaginative crime blotter.

I needed to get away. I decided to edge as far as I could toward the fence that separated the bike path from the traffic, even though puddles there were already deep. Water splashed my pants and, for the second time that day, oozed into my shoes. I could feel the slosh under my socks. Whether that was Barry or not, he was right. Who rides a bicycle in February? Had I, a responsible mother with biking skills that didn't surpass average, mistaken myself for a Tour de France contender? I was officially a moron.

I craned my head. The person was yelling. ". . . talk to you." At closer range the voice sounded shrill, nasal, of a higher pitch. Not Barry. And now there was no mistake. He—or she—knew who I was.

"Molly Marx! Slow down!"

"What are you doing?" I screamed. But it actually looked as if this wheeled deviant was coming at me. Pissed off and scared shitless, I tried to yell, "Back off! Stay the fuck away." The sound refused to leave my throat. I started to gasp and wheeze.

"Pull the fuck over!" the biker screeched while skidding into a puddle, flying at me on the right like a missile.

I had to pedal away from this banshee freak. I could do it.

"Face it, Molly. You and Barry are done! He thinks you're a joke. Ignoring me's not going to change that! He doesn't love you anymore."

"Who *are* you?" I shrieked.

"C'mon, you know exactly who I am!"

Suddenly I did. I understood everything and was fortified with an emotion both strong and pure. I believe it was white-hot hatred. I twisted to try to get another look—to be completely sure. That's when we collided and I lost my grip. My arms flew above my head like a demented cheerleader, any control surrendered. One foot broke loose. But the other refused to budge from its clip as my bike zigzagged in a dizzying swerve to the left. I watched this as I might a horror movie, until I had to close my eyes. Finally, the bike started to slow.

I thanked God. As Papa Louie liked to say, if a Jew doesn't expect miracles, she isn't a realist.

Then I saw my destination, the sharp, serrated edge of a rock. In slow motion, it met the soft plain of my forehead and gashed my skin, dripping blood into my mouth. My bike landed on top of me in a deafening clatter of entwined spokes and jeering, hideously cheerful yellow metal.

"Christ!" someone said. "Don't you dare do this." I was fairly sure the disembodied voice was not my own.

I heard my bike splash and the spray of the Hudson iced my face, my neck, my shoulders. Then I felt . . . nothing.

The bike-bitch towered above me and freed my foot. Or perhaps I disengaged myself, like a hero-mom who'd hoisted four tons of minivan that had pinned her toddler. I was at the water's edge. All I could see and smell was the brackish river. How demon-fast was that current? When was the last time I'd had a tetanus shot? Would I even remember how to swim?

As the Hudson threatened to suck me into its maw, I snaked myself forward—bouncing and sliding in a desperate break-dance—and stretched to reach for the spike of a protruding green-slimed rock. I forced up my arm, the pain virtually unbearable. In the sudden movement my eye caught a glint stuck to the Velcro that fastened the wrist of my windbreaker. I'd snared a treasure, a glittering pink heart pendant encircled by plum-colored pavé stones, the same heart that had dangled from the necklace Barry was going to give me, that or its evil twin. *Happy Valentine's Day, Molly. Here's another knife in your heart.*

With a frozen hand—my glove shredded—I reached for the taunting bauble. I snatched it, cool, hard, and glossy to the touch. As if I were grasping God, I wrapped my fingers tightly around the heart.

My leg seared. My shoulder pulsed with savage pain. I was soaked, yet sweating profusely. From what I remembered of anatomy, I guessed

I'd cracked my clavicle as easily as if it were a wishbone on a rotisserie chicken, yet my leg and shoulder were half the agony of my insides.

I wanted to shut my eyes again.

Gather my breath.

Take a time-out.

I thought I heard a voice imploring me to stay awake, to not surrender to the slicing ache, to the rush of frigid water. It cried, "Molly," a distant soundtrack coming from the middle of a bell. It was a voice that I'm not sure even existed, a voice both filled and filling me with fear.

"Sorry," it said.

Someone bent low. Was the person going to help me or kill me? But all that happened was that the heart was pried from my hand. I heard a small splash. Footsteps. And then I heard . . . nothing.

I was alone now, drowning in my own silence.


I could see the sky. While I couldn't move my neck or raise my head, I could faintly make out a billboard on the parkway. *Getting home late?* it said. *Tell your TiVo to start without you.*

I tried to laugh, and when I couldn't, I cried out, yelling, "Help . . . help me . . . help me, someone," but the traffic was deafening. Could anyone even hear me where I lay, discarded like a piece of garbage, hid amid the brambles? I screamed, flinched, and screamed once more. Each time I yelled out, it felt as if razor blades were digging into my ribs, yet I would catch my breath and scream again and again and again . . . continuing until all that came out were feeble animal mews and gurgling moans.

Someone would find me. Someone had to find me. Soon.

I told myself, out loud, in a whisper, to stay calm and awake. I counted to one thousand and recited the alphabet—in English, then in French—and played the rhyme game, as Lucy and I had done in grade school, taking turns calling out the first word that came to mind.

*Lucy, Moosey, juicy, Gary Busey, Watusi, Cousin Brucie, goosey, Debussy.*

*Molly, trolley, volley, Bengali, dolly, Ollie, holly, Norma Kamali, collie, Salvador Dalí, jolly, Polly, golly, Mexicali, "Zum Gali Gali," folly.*

Pure folly.

Was that Luke I was seeing, standing above me—telling me to hang on, that he was going to get help? Was that him, or just a hope, a prayer, love dressed in blue jeans?

*Luke, duke, Dubuque, Baruch, fluke, Herman Wouk, puke, spook.*

Had I actually been run off the road by a marauding hag dressed in black, Coco Chanel's worst nightmare, or was this a hallucination, a vision fucking with my mind? Had a woman claimed she loved Barry? Was it that Barry loved her and not me?

What did it matter? The only thing that counted was staying alive.

I tried to concentrate on the top spire of Riverside Church, Annabel's Burger King crown pinned against the charcoal sky. I began to run through Annabel's life, starting with that night that I was fairly sure the sperm had gotten the egg and all the cells were busy growing a new person. Almost nine months of astonishing pregnancy, every flutter kick a promise. William Alexander. Alexander William. Would I ever get to meet him? I skipped to Annabel's delivery. Bringing home my pink, bald, beautiful baby. Nursing in the wee hours, a milky team, the two of us alone together rocking in the green velvet chair. Annabel's first tooth, first laugh, first ice cream cone, first lollipop, first doll, first tantrum, first haircut. Learning to crawl like a crab along the shiny wood floor, to walk, to say "mommy." Starting nursery school, ballet, starting everything.

I tried to remember each birthday party, each party dress, each cake, especially the chocolate teddy bear I'd baked myself for her third birthday, showering it with coconut to hide frosting I'd heaved on in slabs to cover my sloppy work. Blowing out candles. *Are you one? Are you two? Are you three? Are you four?* Not four. Not yet. I had to stay alive for four. I needed to get to four. One, two, three . . .

*I will always be Annabel's mother. I will always be Annabel's mother,* I repeated over and over again. My last thought before I closed my eyes.

## Forty-five

# HERE'S TAE US

*E*ternity is an endless comfort, settling like a baby's breath or a sweet dusting of confectioner's sugar. In the Duration, I fly through time like a jet does clouds. Time piles up in snowdrifts, pristine and endless. We do not measure in days or decades. We do not measure time at all.

"Back then"—such bad form to say *alive*—"did you think much about death?" Bob asked once. "Did you have nightmares? Premonitions?"

Sam did. As a shrink, he lived in people's heads, one of the world's most consistently terrifying places, tangled by twisted relationships and moth-eaten regrets. Patients would depart his office and, as surely as they exhaled with the relief he afforded, Sam would repeat the captured anxieties in his sleep, working through the puzzles of their hearts.

Worries? Certainly I had them. Worry was my ring tone; I heard it all day long. But authentic nightmares? Rarely. I ruminated about worst-case scenarios, mostly. Yes, too many of them did come true. Yet when I try to recall these problems burning holes in my happiness, my memory feels thick and lumpy as oatmeal.

Sam and Bob are still part of my expanding circle, which gives new meaning to "it takes a village." Jordan, Stephanie's son, is here now, the fatal victim of a heli-ski accident in the Bugaboos. He was gazing at grand granite spires, and *kaboom*. Gone.

Afterward, Stephanie was never the same, the only good that came from that tragedy. She's become tortured by thoughts of divine retribution, which has made Barry's life tricky. A daughter of Great Neck, Stephanie Lipschitz Joseph Marx has taken a turn toward freakishly *frum*. She now keeps glatt kosher, covers her short gray hair with a wig, and believes this headgear looks like the real McCoy. Stephanie refuses to get in the car on the Sabbath. This makes it hard for Dr. and Mrs. Marx to get to his honeymoon gift to her, a soaring glass and steel weekend retreat on a beach on Long Island. Whenever Stephanie's not looking, Barry smuggles spareribs into the cathedral-sized kitchen.

Still, the two of them are almost 100 percent monogamous. If Barry has schtupped anyone else these past twenty-some years, his wife doesn't know or doesn't care. It helps to have so much money she could use it to wipe her tears. That and the anger management classes, which Dr. Stafford insisted Barry take: he and Stephanie were having a joint session in Dr. Stafford's office and Barry threw a book at Stephanie and shouted, "Shee-it, I wouldn't piss in your mouth if your teeth were on fire."

Barry blames Stephanie for . . . something. He doesn't know the half of it, nor does anyone else.

Narcissa arrived soon after Jordan. Diabetes. Delfina badgered her about how big she'd gotten—for her son's wedding she had to sew two emerald green bugle-beaded dresses together—but Narcissa never listened. I love how Narcissa and Jordan have grown to love each other. She took that loose-limbed, frizzy-haired teenager to her ample bosom, and I often see the two of them laughing and singing, he spanning octaves in his Roy Orbison imitation, Narcissa in a sweet soprano that belies her size. Jordan has followed Narcissa to the Born-Agains. What a friend he has in Jesus!

My father's here now. Choked on a thick, juicy steak, medium rare, the day after he ran a marathon with Lucy. Not the worst way to go, although he was only seventy-four, with silver hair curling over his neck like a movie director. "Daddy," I repeated about a hundred times when he and I were reunited, holding on to each other for what we used to call dear life. "Daddy, Daddy . . ."

"Molly, sweetheart," he responded. "You were robbed, honey." But I shushed him. In the Duration, we don't question when people fall short of their Biblical three-score and ten. We leave the judging for the living. What was, was.

My father couldn't wait to tell me about the Molly Marx trial, hung jury and all. The hideous mess, I learned, was dissected to the point where anyone with an IQ beyond 95 would happily commit corporate reports to memory rather than be tortured with another nanosecond of breathless tabloid coverage. But because the players were photogenic, worldly, and white, producers and editors ran with the story instead of, say, reports of limbless, brain-injured soldiers returning home from Iraq.

"The trial became a Rorschach," my father said. "One day I logged onto AOL and could have voted for who I believed was guilty. By the way, sixty-eight percent of women polled found your friend Luke innocent."

He always calls Luke my "friend," as if the two of us never shared more than a strawberry soda and a taxi.

"I was offered a cameo in the made-for-television movie," he adds. "To play a crusty old detective. Can you believe the bad taste?"

I can. It's been a long time since I was an invisible looky-loo sticking my nose into life below, but I hear things. I hear a lot. What I wanted my dad to talk about, though, was Annabel. Did she really grow up to be brilliant and beautiful and almost five-nine?

"Oh, yeah. She got Kitty's figure, your mother's face, and Lucy's height."

"Too tall to dance Clara in *The Nutcracker*?"

"Well, that, and she gave up ballet for basketball."

"Didn't she get anything of mine?"

"Yes, darling. Your wonderful hair."

Did he not know that I owed my blondness to chemistry? Then I saw a twinkle.

"Annabel got your smile, that way you lit up every room. You can't not love that girl. She's you all over again."

"Why did she go to college in Scotland?" I had it on good authority that she'd been accepted to Princeton—the director of admissions arrived here after she was gunned down by an alum whose child she'd rejected.

"To get away," my father said, "from strangers pointing fingers, from the squabbling between Barry and Stephanie. And she took Jordan's death hard. Those two kids would always be standing together off to the side, heads together, like ducks on their own private ice floe." He stopped talking and simply gazed into my eyes. For a moment, I could feel what it was like to be whole and alive.

"But life is funny," he said.

Isn't it?

"If Annabel hadn't gone to Scotland, she'd never have met Ewan. At first your mom and I were upset. We thought your little Annie-belle was searching for some kind of father figure. But Lucy came to her defense. She was right."

She often was.

"When she got married, Annabel might have been a child herself—nineteen, a baby—but Ewan is exactly what she needs."

"Tell me about her wedding. Did you and Mom go?"

"Of course! Your mother found Ewan very dashing in his kilt. There were so many candles I thought that old pile of a castle might melt, but your daughter said she wanted it to look like *The Age of Innocence* because Lucy swore it was your favorite movie."

My first thought is that my sister keeps my flame alive as if I'm Princess Diana. My second: is Martin Scorsese still directing?

"Each toast was better than the next," my father said, and broke into a pretty fair Scots accent. "Here's tae us; who's like us?" he said, answering his question with "Damn few—and they're a' deid." Then he looked around and the two of us roared in laughter as only those in the Duration can.

# Forty-six

# UNENDING LOVE

I'd stopped going below when I recognized my visits as cruel and unusual punishment, self-flagellation making me sadder, angrier, and lonelier. I learned to simply float within the Duration, and allowed my memory to wash away. If I ever knew exactly how I died, I gradually forgot more than I had ever learned or remembered. I stopped searching for answers and started searching for peace.

I'd fallen into what Sam has diagnosed as a hyperthermia of the soul; I'd crawled into a snow cave of amnesia. "It happens to people whose lives end the way yours did"—violently, recklessly, unforgivably. Young. "Feeling your father's love, though, may unlock some memories." Sam's theory sounded like a mountain of psychocrap, but I began to see the truth in it. This made me want to return one last time, though my powers were like muscles hanging loose after a long illness.

Then it wasn't a choice, really. I begged my father to travel with me, but he said he wasn't ready, that he may never be ready. Dan Divine can't stand to see his Claire with another man.

Two years after he died, my mother married her next-door neighbor, a widower who'd confessed that he'd always been nuts about her, which Lucy and I had guessed years ago from the way his admiring eyes hung on her like Christmas lights. Claire Divine is one for the books, a woman who's twice found true love, with its purple passion, peachy tenderness, and bright white understanding. I don't think my father begrudges my mother her play-it-again happiness, but he doesn't care to hear it sigh and call her "Clairey babe."

Up until now, my complete British Isles experience has consisted only of London—antiquing, eating too many crumpets, and noting that people seem strangely attached to the word *rubbish*. Now here I am. A greenish sea by this coastal Scottish town is calm as ancient porcelain, and the first crocuses are pushing through rocky soil. If a flock of tiny, black-faced sheep wandered down the lane, herded by Little Bo Peep herself, I would not be surprised. In the distance, for some other occasion, bagpipes wail as if they themselves are grieving. Yet in this plain stone chapel, the mood is pumped with joy. I enter and feel at home here, as if I've taken a beloved book from the shelf and stepped inside an earmarked page. The source of this intimacy I cannot explain, but I have learned that just as life is a long, rolling sum of mysteries, death is no different.

I turn and there she is, Annabel, a nasturtium encircled by hummingbirds, standing radiant and straight as she walks to her seat, turning right and left to acknowledge well-wishers. By her side is Ewan, sheltering a very young boy and girl with ruddy cheeks and hair the color of pralines. "The spitting image of their father," someone whispers of the children. Annabel is their fairy stepmother. She is carrying a bundle wearing the Campbell family's christening gown and bonnet, creamy old lace the color of eggnog, its fabric soft as feathers. The sweetly sleeping newborn, unaware of this dignified hoopla, has the other half of my attention.

The chapel fills, its heavy wooden doors thrown open, the air catching a fresh sea breeze. Love flows round, Annabel gazing with warm disbelief at her child as I once looked at her. I drink in everyone, everything, and my emptiness begins to fill.

A clergyman, bent and kindly, starts the service, giving thanks for this moment of gladness, the birth of a child. "Our God, we turn to Thee with full hearts for these thy children, Ewan and Annabel Campbell." His r's roll gently, water flowing over polished old rocks. "Help them, that they be wise and patient parents, understanding the care required of a young one's growing body and mind. Give them courage in times of difficulty."

I begin to pray involuntarily, to a God with whom I've had my share of differences. *Spare them from grief,* I ask of God. *Protect Annabel, protect her husband and his children. Protect this baby, this grandchild.* I use that word in true wonder. It is grand that my child has a child, a child whom I do not know but who, too, is grand indeed.

The minister goes on, his voice a melody, and I gaze around the room. There's my mother, her face—to my eyes—young. She is leaning on her brand-new rock, a man not half as handsome as my father, but with a round, sympathetic face. He understands that even today's happiness brings it all back. He strokes my mother's hand, arthritic but soft to the touch. She can blink and it could be the February of my death, the future a shadow blocking her view. But she is wise enough to blink again and return to today, where fulfillment rules.

Hicks and Brie whisper and laugh. Around her neck hangs the silver magnifying glass that I gave her long ago. Faint lines etch the decades. She is a queen, with dark hair twisted into a chignon. Hicks has retired his earring, started wearing glasses, and grown thicker, as befits an attorney of his stature. After my unresolved trial, which he took as a personal failure, he studied the law at night. Brie and he practice together, Lawson and Hicks, the go-to firm if you're crawling with guilt. They are doing well, more together than many couples who have married. Yesterday, after golf, they decided that Scotland is so magnificent perhaps they should buy a home here. But how could they give up the hilly green of Columbia County, and where would Hicks keep his goats? Rich people's problems, good to have.

A late arrival, a tall, well-upholstered woman with a plump, unlined face and one white streak in her dark hair, slides into the row behind Annabel. She leans forward to kiss her cheeks and hold her close. Annabel surrenders herself to the embrace and snuggles next to this mother bear. "Aunt Moosey, you got here," she says.

"We're all here now," Lucy answers. We are.

That includes a young, smiling rabbi who's traveled in a red convertible from Edinburgh. A sunbeam bounces off the brocade of his silky square black yarmulke as he offers a *shalom* and calls Barry to pray over sacramental wine. Barry, who has traveled here without

Stephanie, walks a bit stiffly—last month he had his knees replaced, the price for all that running on unforgiving pavement—but he smiles broadly and is the image of his father's pictures. He is one of those rare men improved by his shaved head. Barry raises the family kiddush cup brought from New York, his surgeon's hands still steady around the silvery stem, entwined with grapevines and memories. I hear the Hebrew words, chanted in his strong, sure voice, and wonder what he is thinking.

I realize I no longer care or need to know. He belongs to another woman now.

The minister calls Annabel and Ewan, who places his hand on his wife's slender back and they walk slowly and carefully, she cradling their sleeping child. The two of them reach the front and kiss. Ewan flicks away a tear from Annabel's eyes. I have nestled within her, and this touch returns my powers with a jolt. The emotion Annabel feels is crazy glee dusted with the slight despair she always tries to chase away when she wishes I were present. Today, I am. *God, if you're in this room, make her know that.*

"Will the godmother please come forward?" the minister asks.

*Salagadoola, mechicka boola, bibbidi-bobbidi-boo.* We have a godmother. She walks to the front. For this occasion, the proud great-aunt is wearing sensible shoes and flowing sapphire blue clothing. With her white streak and her husband's ring on her finger, she is, finally, Lucy in the sky with diamonds. She stands next to Barry and yes, there is an embrace—nothing showy, but a real, albeit short, connection.

"This child," the minister asks, "does she have a name?"

"She does," Ewan answers. He smiles at Annabel. "Her name will be Molly," he says. "Molly Divine."

Perhaps God *is* in the building.

"Molly Divine Campbell," the rabbi says to the sleeping baby. "For whom are you named, my wee *bubbelah*?"

"For my mother," Annabel says. *Long gone,* she thinks, *but in my heart, never forgotten.*

"For my sister," Lucy says. "And if my sister is in this room, I hope she won't mind if I read a poem she wrote when she was a girl."

Will Lucy never cease to embarrass me? We'll see about that.

" 'Strip from me the dove velvet mantle,' " Lucy begins.

*Let the bay-pale corn silk glaze my shoulders*
*As I sing a duet with God.*

Before it all, I did believe in God.

*The rivers echo choruses*
*The stars, a silver descant,*
*Pebbles garnish the sanctified mud*
*The shells, the snails, the shadows of the starfish.*
*Amid the crescendo, a plant grows*
*Chanting the liturgy of roots veining the loam*
*Beginning to learn of toadstools and Russian olive trees.*

Where did Lucy find this? Was I ever really a moony sixteen, waiting for my life to happen? Lucy's eyes pierce me and press me to the stone wall.

*My last dream lingers*
*Now I wait only for spring's kiss*
*Go now. Let me fall in love.*

My sister removes her reading glasses, puts down the poem, and looks at Annabel and then her grandniece. "That's what I wish for little Molly," she says. "That she will fall in love."

Amen. Let her fall in love, young and for forever, the way it seems that her mother has.

In deference to the mingling of two faiths, there will be no sprinkling of water on the baby's head, though if Jesus were present, I'm sure he would be welcomed. He and I still have yet to meet, but others in the Duration, believers, have sightings all the time.

"The godfather? Will he come forward?" the minister asks.

He does, tall as ever, his eyes more deeply sunken than when they looked into mine. He has watched over Annabel all her life, cultivating the role of the witty, wandering uncle with the good stories and the good presents. He is a man who reveals little, a man nobody knows.

I'd always hoped Lucy and Luke might wind up together, but that was my naiveté on overdrive. Once, when both of them drank far too much, they had an evening of unabridged, ill-considered passion, but afterward each admitted they felt my presence in the bed—even though I absolutely was not. Lucy and Luke sprang back to friendship before its statute of limitations expired. They stay in touch, largely through postcards annotated with cryptic messages. Lucy married many years ago. Her husband is a sculptor of some note and secretly jealous of the mystery his wife and Luke Delaney share, but this husband is not so envious that he would stop transforming Lucy into breathtaking art. My sister was born to be molded in clay, chiseled in marble, cast in bronze. Every piece he crafts shows her enduring strength and determination.

And Luke? Is he happy? I look at him and know. Not yet.

"Annabel has asked me to read a poem she has always recited on the anniversary of her mother's death. Molly Marx," he says, "was my dearest friend." *There's no way Annabel could read this poem herself and keep a dry eye,* he thinks, and wonders if he can. Annabel smiles, urges him to begin, and Luke and I both see my smile in hers.

"We are loved by an unending love." I know this poem, written by a rabbi.

> *We are embraced by arms that find us.*
> *Even when we are hidden from ourselves*
> *We are touched by fingers that soothe us.*

Luke breathes these words in a half whisper. As if he himself is hiding, he wears a soft, trimmed beard, a charcoal smudge on his craggy face, which is beginning to settle into the softness of sixty, which will be his next birthday. He speaks the poem from memory.

> *Even when we are too proud for soothing.*
> *We are counseled by voices that guide us.*
> *Even when we are too embittered to hear.*
> *We are loved by an unending love.*

Little Molly begins to stir. My daughter pushes back the bonnet to admire her baby's face. She lifts the child so that Ewan can stroke her strands of pale blond hair. There are quiet words between them on which I do not want to intrude, and I have no need to, because seeing Molly and Annabel is all I want.

Annabel, Ewan, and Molly walk down the middle aisle and through the opened doors, outside, where moss connects the old stones the way we connect with one another, our histories mingled. They chat with my mother and her husband, their friends, with Barry, with Hicks and Brie, with Lucy, with Luke, these people I have loved, brought together once again by, as Nana Phyllis would say, such a *simcha*.

Suddenly, Annabel puts her hand on Ewan's arm and stops. She and Molly turn toward where my essence lingers, alone, back by the chapel, peeking out from beside an ancient oak. She is struggling to see someone. She smiles my smile. Molly opens her sleepy eyelids, delicate as butterflies. All our eyes meet, and love joins us as surely as if it were a live current. I know Annabel knows, and it is enough. It is everything.

Then Annabel blinks and returns to her life.

I, the late, lamented Molly Marx, take one last, long look. I am done. Complete. I am rested now. I can return to the Duration, for whatever is to come.

Can they feel it? I do not know.

## Acknowledgments

Lucky me. I have had the privilege of working with a superb editor, Laura Ford, publishing's rising star. I thank her along with Ballantine's outstanding team, especially Susan Corcoran, Libby McGuire, Gina Centrello, Kim Hovey, Christine Cabello, Katie O'Callaghan, Alexandra Rudd, Rachel Kind, Rachel Bernstein, and Brian McLendon. Steve Messina, I am grateful to you and your colleague Sue Warga for the careful copyedit. Mary Wirth, Robbin Schiff, Susan Turner, and Victoria Allen, I applaud your choices for design.

Much gratitude to Christy Fletcher and Melissa Chinchillo of Fletcher & Parry for their energy and enthusiasm, as well as Howard Saunders and Shana Eddy of United Talent Agency, whose confidence and creativity I value tremendously. A loud shout-out, too, to fellow novelist Elizabeth Ziemska, whose early, rousing reaction kept me going.

Our Monday night writing workshop has been my steady pulse these last few years. Thank you, Charles Salzberg, for your leadership, structural brilliance, and deadlines, a writer's most essential tool. Without them I'd still be staring at my computer in pajamas. I am indebted to Vivian Conan, Patricia Crevits, Sharon Gurwitz, Sally Hoskins, Paul Hundt, Marilyn Goldstein, Judy Gorfein, Erica Keirstadt, Margaret Kennedy, Patty Nasey, Leslie Nipkow, and Betty Wald. Your laughter and generous ideas are the Super Glue that keeps me together. Rabbi Rami Shapiro, thank you as well for your inspiring poetry.

My family is my loving infrastructure. Robert, Jed, and Rory, I adore you and am immensely grateful for your sharp wit and tender support. Betsy and Vicki, sisters both, thanks for taking the time to read rough drafts. Last of all, I am beholden to my parents, Fritzie and Sam Platkin. I'd like to think they are in the Duration, smiling.

The Late, Lamented Molly Marx

Sally Koslow

A Reader's Guide

## A Conversation Between Molly Marx and Sally Koslow

**Molly Marx:** Since you're the author of *The Late, Lamented Molly Marx*, I thought it was high time for a conversation. Greetings, Sally Koslow, book-lady.

**Sally Koslow:** Molly, it's lovely to meet. Please allow me to say I'm sorry for your loss. I hope you don't mind that instead of a condolence note, I wrote you a novel.

**MM:** I'm flattered, but puzzled. Most authors write about the living. Where did you get the idea for my book? If you don't mind me saying so, the concept's kind of creepy.

**SK:** I was attending the funeral of a neighbor and from what I knew of her, her eulogies didn't add up. I began to wonder what the woman in the coffin might be thinking about these tributes. Would she be happy? Sad? Cynical? Shocked that hundreds of people turned out to say adios, given that she was a recluse? Whoops—I meant "very private person." This led to my ruminating on how it's a fundamental fantasy to be curious about who might attend our funeral and what would be said, both publicly and privately. I meant no disrespect to the deceased, but before I walked out of the service I knew I wanted to write a novel that flowered from this conceit.

**MM:** Readers say this book is funny. "Witty" gets tossed about in reviews from bloggers and on Amazon.com, and *Publishers Weekly* notes the novel's "hearty dose of hilarity." But let's face it, Sally, you are not a funny person.

**SK:** Fair enough, though I'd like to point out that the epitaph my fellow high school creative writing students wrote for me was "slit her throat with her own tongue." Or was it "pen?" Still, Polite Sally doesn't feel she should repeat every rogue observation that flits across her brain.

Fiction is different. Even your snarkiest thoughts—*especially* your snarkiest thoughts—have a chance of being pinned onto the page. Between us, I love that the book makes some people chuckle.

**MM:** Why a mystery, when your first novel, *Little Pink Slips*, wasn't in that genre?

**SK:** Your story had to be a mystery because when I started writing it I didn't know how you died. As the novel unfolded you and I discovered the truth together. I like to create characters who slowly reveal themselves.

**MM:** No anal-retentive plot outline? No stickies wallpapering your office? I'm disappointed.

**SK:** Sorry, but I simply try to tune in to my imagination and let it lead the way. It helps to take myself for a run and wait for ideas to bubble up.

**MM:** You mean you're not a bike rider, like me?

**SK:** You're much braver than I am. City traffic scares the sunscreen right off me. I rode my bike once on that path by the Hudson River where you lost your life and I was terrified—it was so close to the water! No barriers! Someone could drown there!

**MM:** You're telling me the two of us are quite different.

**SK:** Not at all. I put a lot of me in you, Molly.

**MM:** Those flaws of mine you listed at the beginning—they're your flaws, too?

**SK:** Yes, except that I'd rather cook than buy takeout, and I subscribe to *The New Yorker*, not celebrity magazines—those I read at the manicurists'. I'm also diligent about removing my makeup before bed and always laugh at my husband's jokes. He cracks me up.

**MM:** Here's another way that we're different. You don't have a daughter, and my Annabel is—*was* (the hardest part of no longer being alive is remembering to use the past tense)—the closest thing to my heart. How could you possibly know what being the mother of a daughter feels like?

**SK:** It's true that I have two sons, Jed and Rory, and no daughters, but I was inspired by my six young, adorable nieces: Amaya, Ella, Ivy-Reese, Lily, Siena, and Zoe.

**MM:** That letter I left for Annabel, where I listed my rules for life—are they your rules, too?

**SK:** Many are rules I wish I adhered to, like printing out my pictures and putting them in an album, which, sad to say, I never do.

**MM:** Given what we have in common, I gather it wasn't hard for you to write me. Which character was the hardest to write?

**SK:** Barry. He's complicated and I wanted to do him justice. Despite his philandering, narcissism, and insensitivity, he could be charming and he tried to atone for his sins. He's also a devoted son and a good father, even before he rose to the challenge of being a single parent. And while he didn't do well by you, Molly, I believe he loved you. Marriage—never easy, right?

**MM:** No kidding. Neither was having a sister like Lucy. Do you have a sister and was she the model for Lucy?

**SK:** I have a sister, but she's not much like Lucy. She got married when she was in college, has two kids, is of average height, and hates to run, although, like Lucy, she prefers practical clothes.

**MM:** That reminds me. I wouldn't call *The Late, Lamented Molly Marx,* chick-lit—parts of it were sad, heartfelt, and almost philosophical—but what's with all the clothes?

**SK:** I love clothes. I used to be an editor at a magazine, and got dressed up every day for work. Yes, Molly, one used to dress up for work, especially when he or she was an editor-in-chief, which I was for more than a decade. Now most of the time my stilettos and leopard-print coat hibernate while I'm working at home in running shorts, yoga pants, jeans, or pajama bottoms. I brought clothes into your story not only because you can tell a lot about a person by their clothes, but because I miss getting dressed up.

**MM:** The German translation of my book, *Ich, Molly Marx, Kurlich Verstorben,* was a bestseller. Why do you think that German readers like my story?

**SK:** A friend of a friend, a German professor, thought it might have to do with curiosity about contemporary Jewish culture, especially the customs of somewhat assimilated Jews in New York City, which play a role in the book.

**MM:** Kitty would love to hear that. She'd take all the credit. Now, why all the poetry?

**SK:** I assume you mean the poetry at the funeral in Scotland, as well as the lines from "Hiawatha," when Hicks visits Chicago? When I was starting to write your book, I heard the poem "An Unending Love" and found it exquisite. Its author, Rabbi Rami Shapiro, gave me permission to include it in the book. The other poem at the Scottish funeral was something I wrote in high school. Good thing I saved our literary magazine, *Of Toadstools and Russian Olive Trees.* Its name was selected by our teacher from one of my own poems. I've been writing since I was a teenager.

**MM:** Whoa—you had me at Hicks. Love that name. How did you think it up?

**SK:** I didn't. It's real. I was visiting the Vietnam War Memorial in Washington, D.C., and this extraordinary name leaped out at me. To honor Hiawatha Hicks, SP4, who died in 1968, I decided to borrow his name. I'd like to think you'll meet him in the Duration.

**MM:** Me, too. And speaking of the Duration, those of us here thought it was our big secret. Who told you about it?

**SK:** Sorry, but if I tell you I'm dead. No offense.

**MM:** What do you want your readers to take away from this book?

**SK:** If readers are simply entertained, I will be delighted. But I also hope that *The Late, Lamented Molly Marx,* will cause readers to reflect on the brevity and inscrutability of life and the complexity of human relationships. Perhaps it will foster a carpe diem attitude. I do think we all should try to pack in as much as we can, and never take life for granted.

**MM:** What's your next book about?

**SK:** I'm fascinated by women's friendships, especially when they don't run a smooth course. *With Friends Like These* explores four women whose friendships get messy. Think of it as *Divine Secrets of the Ya-Ya Sisterhood* meets the *Avenue Q* song "Schadenfreude," which means happiness taken from the misfortune of others. Readers may see themselves and their friends in one or more characters.

**MM:** My epitaph was plain vanilla—Barry picked it. What would you like yours to say?

**SK:** "Just let me read one more page."

**MM:** We've got to stop now, or I'll be late for the master class on the Moonwalk that I'm taking with Michael Jackson. The Duration has its perks! Thanks for the chat, Sally. I hope we'll meet again.

**SK:** Me, too, Molly. But not for a long, long time.

## Questions and Topics for Discussion

1. *The Late, Lamented Molly Marx,* grapples with the theme of loss. Molly's major challenge throughout the book is learning how to let go and come to terms with her death. In what ways has she accomplished this by the end of the novel? In your own life, have you ever had to grapple with loss and letting something go? What helped you?

2. The novel is prefaced by an Oscar Wilde quote: "The true mystery of the world is the visible, not the invisible." How do you interpret it? How does it apply to the book?

3. The novel presents a version of an afterlife. Do you believe in an afterlife? If so, what is your vision? How did you arrive at your view?

4. If you could be present at your own funeral, what would you be most curious to see?

5. The character of Bob functions as a moral compass and a spiritual sherpa for Molly. What do you think Molly gets out of this relationship? Has there ever been a "Bob" in your life and if so, who is it and what role did he or she play?

6. After she arrives in the Duration, Molly discovers that she has what she refers to as "a built-in bullshit detector." To this Bob responds, "You always had that ability. You just never bothered to activate it" (page 30). Do you believe that most people "know" more than they choose to acknowledge?

7. Is Molly mature or immature for her age? Does your opinion of her change as the novel progresses? How do you define maturity? How has your definition evolved as you yourself have gotten older? Do

you think adults used to be more mature at an earlier age in the past?

8. Why did Molly marry Barry? Do you know women who have married men who you think aren't their equals? And the reverse: Do you know men who've married women who you think aren't their equals?

9. Molly suspects that Barry is a philanderer. Why do women like Molly stay with men like Barry under similar circumstances? Should they have split up? Is he a good father?

10. Throughout the novel, Molly wonders if she's made mistakes in her marriage. Do you think she has and if so, what are they?

11. Molly and Barry sought the help of a marriage counselor. Do you think that counseling helped them? In general, do you support the idea of therapy and counseling?

12. How do the women in Molly's life—Lucy, Brie, Kitty, her mother, Claire, and Delfina—affect her over the course of the novel? What does each woman offer her? In what ways do they ultimately help or hurt her, knowingly or unknowingly? Which women have had the most profound effect on your life?

13. Did becoming a mom help Molly grow up? Do you think that she s a good mother? If you have kids, how did you arrive at your notion of what makes a good mother? How does motherhood enrich a woman's life? Make women's lives harder?

14. The anthropologist Margaret Mead has observed that the relationship between sisters is often the most troubled one in the family. Mead also says that eventually, the sister relationship becomes the strongest one in the family. Do you agree with Dr. Mead on either of these points? Why do you think that so many sisters can't get along?

15. How would you describe the friendship between Molly and Brie? What qualities do you think need to be present for women to main-

tain enduring friendships? Have you ever lost a friendship because of a monumental change in one of your lives?

16. Molly does not enjoy a smooth relationship with her mother-in-law. Why is this relationship often difficult?

17. Who is your favorite character? Your least favorite character? Why?

18. How would you categorize this book—as humor? A mystery? Contemporary women's fiction? Why?

Don't miss Sally Koslow's next novel

*With Friends Like These*

Read on for an exclusive peek at the first chapter

# CHAPTER 1

*Quincy*

"A fax hit my desk for an apartment that isn't officially listed yet—you must see it immediately." Horton's voice was broadcasting an urgency reserved for hurricane evacuation. But in 2007, anyone who'd ever beaten the real estate bushes would be suspicious of a broker displaying even an atom of passivity. Shoppers of condos and co-ops in Manhattan and the leafier regions of Brooklyn knew they had to learn the art of the pounce: see, gulp, bid. Save the litany of pros and cons for picking a couch.

Several times a week Horton e-mailed me listings, but rarely did he call. This had to be big. "Where is it?" I asked while I finished my lukewarm coffee.

"Central Park West." Horton identified a stone pile known by its name, the Eldorado, referring to a mythical kingdom where the tribal chief had the habit of dusting himself with gold, a commodity familiar to most of the apartment building's inhabitants—marquee actors, eminent psychotherapists, and large numbers of frumps who were simply lucky. With twin towers topped by Flash Gordon finials, the edifice lorded it over a gray-blue reservoir, the park's largest body of water, and cast a gimlet eye toward Fifth Avenue.

"I couldn't afford that building," I said. If Horton was trying to game me into spending more than our budget allowed, he'd fail. While the amount of money Jake and I had scraped together for a new home seemed huge to us—representing the sale of our one-bedroom in Park Slope, an inheritance from my mom, and the proceeds from seeing one of my books linger on the bestseller list—other brokers had none too politely terminated the conversation as soon as I quoted our allotted sum. What I liked about Horton was that he was dogged, he was hungry, and he was the only real estate agent returning my calls.

"That's the beautiful part," he said, practically singing. "You, Quincy Blue, can afford this apartment." He named a figure.

We could, just. "What's the catch?" In my experience, deals that sounded too good to be true were—like the brownstone I'd seen last week that lacked not only architectural integrity but functional plumbing.

"It's a fixer-upper," Horton admitted. "Listen, I can go to the second name on my list."

"I'll see you in twenty minutes," I said, hitting "save" on my manuscript. I was currently the ghostwriter for Maizie May, one of Hollywood's interchangeable blow-dried blondes with breasts larger than their brain. While she happened to be inconveniently incarcerated in Idaho rehab, allowed only one sound bite of conversation with me per week, my publisher's deadline, three months away, continued to growl. I hid my hair under a baseball cap and laced my sneakers. Had Jake seen me, he would have observed that I looked "very West Side"; my husband was fond of pointing out our neighborhood's inverse relationship between apartment price and snappy dress. As I walked east I called him, but his cell phone was off. Jake's flight to Chicago must be late.

Racing down Broadway, I allowed myself a discreet ripple of anticipation. Forget the Yankees. Real estate would always be New York City's truest spectator sport, and I was no longer content to cheer from the bleachers. Two years ago, my nesting hormones had kicked in and begun to fiercely multiply, with me along for the ride. We were eager to escape from our current sublet near Columbia University. I longed to be dithering over paint colors—Yellow Lotus or Pale Straw; flat, satin, or eggshell—and awash in fabric swatches. I coveted an office that was bigger than a coffee table book and a dining table that could accommodate all ten settings of my wedding china. I wanted a real home. I'd know it when I saw it.

Horton, green-eyed, cleft-chinned—handsome if you could overlook his devotion to argyle—stood inside the building's revolving door. "The listing broker isn't here yet," he said, "but you can get a sense of the lobby." A doorman tipped his capped head and motioned us toward armchairs upholstered in a tapestry of tasteful, earthy tones. Horton unfurled a floor plan.

I'd become a quick study of such documents. "It's only a two-bedroom," I said, feeling the familiar disappointment that had doused the glow of previous apartment visits. Was the fantasy of three bedrooms asking too much for a pair of industrious adults more than twelve years past grad school? Jake was a lawyer. I had a master's in English literature. Yet after we'd been outbid nine times, Jake and I had accepted the fact that in this part of town, two bedrooms might be as good as it would get.

"This isn't *any* two-bedroom," Horton insisted. "Look how grand the living room and dining room are." Big enough for a party where Jake and I could reciprocate every invitation we'd received since getting married five years ago. "See?" he said, pulling out a hasty sketch and pointing. "Put a wall up to divide the dining room, which has windows on both sides, and create an entrance here. Third bedroom." He was getting to how cheap the renovation would be when a tall wand of a woman tapped him on the shoulder.

"Fran!" Horton said as warmly as if she were his favorite grandmother, which she was old enough to be. "You're looking well."

The woman smiled and a feathering of wrinkles fanned her large blue eyes. The effect made me think that a face without this pattern was too dull. "Did you explain?" she said. Her voice was reedy, a piccolo that saw little use. She'd pulled her silver hair into a chignon and was enveloped in winter white, from a cape covering a high turtleneck to slim trousers that managed to be spotless, although they nearly covered her toes.

"We were getting to that, but first, please meet my client, Quincy Blue. Quincy, Frances Shelbourne of Shelbourne and Stone."

I knew the firm. Frances and her sister Rose had tied up all the best West Side listings. I shook Fran Shelbourne's hand, which felt not just creamy but delicately boned. She stared at my sneakers and jeans long enough for me to regret them, then turned her back and padded so soundlessly that I checked to see if she might be wearing slippers. No, ballerina flats. Across the lobby, elaborately filigreed elevator doors opened. Fran turned toward Horton and me and with the briefest arch of one perfectly plucked eyebrow implored us to hurry. When the doors shut, she spoke softly, although we were alone. "The owner's a dear friend," she said. "Eloise Walter, the anthropologist." She waited for me to respond. "From the Museum of Natural History?"

I wondered if I was supposed to know the woman's body of work and bemoaned the deficiency of my Big Ten education.

"Dr. Walter is in failing health," she continued, shaking her head. "This is why we won't schedule an open house."

Every Sunday from September through May, hopeful buyers, like well-trained infantry, traveled the open-house circuit. Jake and I had done our sweaty time, scurrying downtown, uptown, across, and down again, with as many as a dozen visits in a day. Soon enough, we began seeing the same hopeful buyers—the Filipino couple, the three-hundred-pound guy who had the face of a baby, a pair of six-foot-tall redheaded teenage twins who spoke a middle European tongue. By my fifth Sunday, in minutes I could privately scoff at telltale evidence of dry rot. Silk curtains draped as cunningly as a sari could not distract me from a sunless air shaft a few feet away, nor could lights of megawatt intensity seduce me into forgetting that in most of these apartments I would instantly suffer from seasonal affective disorder.

"You'll be the first person to see this one," Horton added by way of a bonus. I could feel the checkbook in my bag coming alive like Mickey's broom in *Fantasia*.

When we stepped out of the elevator on the fourteenth floor, Mrs. Shelbourne gently knocked on a metal door that would look at home in any financial institution. From the other side, a floor creaked. A nurse in thick-soled shoes answered and raised an index finger to her lips, casting her eyes toward a shadowy room beyond. The scent of urine—human, feline, or both—crept into my nostrils, followed by a top note of mango air freshener. "Doctor's sleeping."

My eyes strained to scan a wide room where old-fashioned blinds were drawn against the noon sun. An elderly woman, her hair scant and tufted, was folded into a wheelchair like a rag doll, despite pillows bolstering her skeletal frame. Dr. Walter looked barely alive. Mrs. Shelbourne placed her hand on my arm. "We shouldn't stay long in this room. I'm sure you understand. Alzheimer's."

"I do—too well," I said, rapidly beholding the high ceiling and dentil moldings, while memories of my mother, scrupulously archived yet too fresh to examine, begged for consideration. I pushed them away even as my mind catalogued herringbone floors with an intricate walnut border and the merest wink of a crystal chandelier. Mrs. Shelbourne grasped my arm and we hurried into a small, dark kitchen with wallpaper on which hummingbirds had enjoyed a sixty-year siesta. In front of the sink, which faced a covered window, linoleum had worn bare. There were scratched metal cabinets and no dishwasher, and I suspected the stove's birth date preceded my own. I thought of my unfinished chapter, and cursed my wasted time.

Halfheartedly I lifted a tattered shade. "Holy cow," I said, though only to myself. Sun reflected off the park's vast reservoir, which appeared so close I thought I could stand on the ledge and swan-dive into its depth. Far below, I could see treetops, lush as giant broccoli. The traffic was a distant buzz. I felt a tremor. The subway, stories below? No, my heart.

Picking up my pace, I followed the brokers through the spacious dining room and down a hall where I counted off six closets. I peeked into a bathroom tiled in a vintage mosaic of the sort decorators encourage clients to re-create at vast expense. We passed through a starlet-worthy dressing room and entered a bedroom into which I could easily tuck my current, rented apartment, with enough space to spare for a study. As Mrs. Shelbourne pulled the hardware on draperies bleached of color, I could swear that a strobe had begun to pulse. From the corner of my eye I saw a black cat slink away while Horton kicked a dust bunny under the bed, but I took little note of either. As I stood by the window, I was gooey with the feeling I'd experienced when I first laid eyes on the Grand Canyon.

The silvery vista spread casually before me might be the most enchanted in the entire city. I closed my eyes, traveling through time. Women were skating figure eights in red velvet cloaks, their hands warmed by ermine muffs. Bells jingled in the evergreen-scented air as horses waited patiently by sleighs. I blinked again and the maidens wore organdy, their porcelain skin dewy under the parasols shielding their intricate curls. I fast-forwarded to my girlhood and could imagine the large, glassy pond below was the crystal stream beside my grandparents' log-hewn cabin in Wisconsin's northern woods, the bone-chilling waters of Scout camp, perhaps Lake Como of my honeymoon scrapbook.

Beside this champagne view, the fifty-four other apartments I'd considered seemed like cheap house wine, including the possibilities that cost far more—almost every one. I pulled myself away from the window and looked back. Walls were no longer hung with faded diplomas, nor was the carpet worn thin. Mirroring the reservoir, the room had turned gray-blue. I saw myself writing at a desk by the window, lit by sunbeams, words spilling out so fast my fingers danced on the keyboard like Rockettes. This time my manuscript wasn't a twenty-year-old singer-actress' whiny rant. It was a novel, lauded by the critics and Costco customers alike.

I could see myself in this room. My face wore deep contentment. The bed was luxuriously rumpled, since a half hour earlier Jake and I had made love, and now he was brewing coffee in our brand-new kitchen, as sleekly designed as a sperm. Perhaps he'd already gone out to bike around the park or was walking our shelter-rescued puppy. Tallulah, the little rascal, loved to chase her ball down our twenty-foot hall.

In every way, I was home.

SALLY KOSLOW is the author of the novel *Little Pink Slips* and the forthcoming *With Friends Like These*. Her essays have been published in *More, O: The Oprah Magazine,* and *The New York Observer,* among other publications. She was the editor in chief of both *McCall's* and *Lifetime,* was an editor at *Mademoiselle* and *Woman's Day,* and teaches creative writing at the Writing Institute of Sarah Lawrence College. The mother of two sons, she lives in New York City with her husband.

# Join the Random House Reader's Circle to enhance your book club or personal reading experience.

## Our FREE monthly e-newsletter gives you:

- Sneak-peek excerpts from our newest titles

- Exclusive interviews with your favorite authors

- Special offers and promotions giving you access to advance copies of books, our free "Book Club Companion" quarterly magazine, and much more

- Fun ideas to spice up your book club meetings: creative activities, outings, and discussion topics

- Opportunities to invite an author to your next book club meeting

- Anecdotes and pearls of wisdom from other book group members . . . and the opportunity to share your own!

To sign up, visit our website at
**www.randomhousereaderscircle.com**

 **When you see this seal on the outside, there's a great book club read inside.**